Praise for Joan D. Vinge's C

Dreamfall

"Vinge displays her potent imagination in the creation of a world that remains fascinating. She also displays virtuoso quality in her delving into the emotional torments of her characters, so that one emerges at the end feeling very satisfied."

—*Analog*

"A powerful book . . . Cat (of *Catspaw* and *Psion*) is back, and he's as tough and streetwise as ever."

—*VOYA*

"Another well-written SF novel from the Hugo Award–winning author of *The Snow Queen*. Enjoyable and engaging."
—*The Washington Post Book World*

"A tense, lyrical human drama in a complex future setting. Vinge has created a world that is exotic and, more important, believable. Her characters come alive through masterly writing."

—*Ontario Whig-Standard*

Catspaw

"A rich tale of palace intrigue that is both crisp and captivating. *Catspaw* also comes with enough plot twists to keep you on edge."

—*Providence Journal*

Psion

"Ambitious, effective science fiction adventure."

—*Booklist*

Books by Joan D. Vinge

The Snow Queen Cycle
The Snow Queen
World's End
*The Summer Queen
*Tangled Up in Blue

The Cat Novels
*+Psion
*Catspaw
*Dreamfall

*+Heaven Chronicles
Phoenix in the Ashes (story collection)
Eyes of Amber (story collection)

The Random House Book of Greek Myths

*denotes a Tor book
+forthcoming

DREAMFALL

JOAN D. VINGE

TOR®

A Tom Doherty Associates Book
New York

DREAMFALL

This edition of *Dreamfall* has been revised by the author.

Copyright © 1996, 2004 by Joan D. Vinge

This book is printed on acid-free paper.

Edited by James Frenkel

A Tor Book
Published by Tom Doherty Associates, LLC
175 Fifth Avenue
New York, NY 10010

www.tor.com

Tor® is a registered trademark of Tom Doherty Associates, LLC.

Library of Congress Cataloging-in-Publication Data

Vinge, Joan D.
    Dreamfall / Joan D. Vinge.—1st ed.
        p. cm.
    "A Tom Doherty Associates book."
    ISBN 0-765-30342-6
    EAN 978-0-765-30342-4
    1. Life on other planets—Fiction. 2. Telepathy—Fiction. I. Title.

    PS3572.I53D74 2004
    813'.54—dc22   2003071151

First Edition: May 2004

Printed in the United States of America

0 9 8 7 6 5 4 3 2 1

To
Dr. Frederick Brodsky
Dr. Anna Marie Windsor
Dr. Richard Reindollar

"We arrive at truth, not by reason only, but also by the heart."
—Pascal

ACKNOWLEDGMENTS

I would like to acknowledge the invaluable input and support of the following people, without whom neither this book nor my life in general would be in such good shape right now—Jim Frenkel, Barbara Luedtke, Carroll Martin, Betsy Mitchell, the Peach-Poznik clan, Mary and Nick Pendergrass, and Vernor Vinge. Thanks, guys—you're the best.

"What's th' goal of th' game, Mr. Toad? A *monster* slain? A *maiden* saved? A *wrong* righted?"
"A standoff achieved."

—Bill Griffin

I have spread my dreams under your feet; Tread softly, for you tread on my dreams.

—W. B. Yeats

The road to Hell is paved with good intentions.

—Karl Marx

DREAMFALL

ONE

FIVE OR SIX centuries ago, the Prespace philosopher Karl Marx said the road to Hell is paved with good intentions. Marx understood what it meant to be human . . . to be flawed.

Marx thought he also understood how to end an eternity of human suffering and injustice: *Share whatever you could, keep only what you needed.* He never understood why the rest of humanity couldn't see the answer, when it was so obvious to him.

The truth was that they couldn't even see the problem.

Marx also said that the only antidote to mental suffering is physical pain.

But he never said that time flies when you're having fun.

I glanced at my databand, checking for the hundredth time to see whether an hour had passed yet. It hadn't. This was the fifth time in less than an hour that I'd found myself standing at the Aerie's high parabolic windows, looking out at a world called Refuge; escaping from the noise and pressure of the Tau reception going on behind me. *Refuge from what? For who?* The background data the team had been given access to didn't say.

Not from Tau's bureaucracy. Not for us. The research team I was a part of had arrived at Firstfall less than a day ago. We hadn't even been onworld long enough to adjust to local planetary time. But almost before we'd dropped our bags here in Riverton, Tau Biotech's liaison had arrived at our hotel and forced us to attend this reception, which seemed to be taking place in stasis.

I dug another camph out of the silk-smooth pocket of my bought-on-the-fly formal shirt, and stuck it into my mouth. It began to dissolve, numbing my tongue as I looked out again through the Aerie's heartstopping arc of window toward the distant cloud-reefs. The sun was setting now behind the reefs, limning their karst topography of ragged peaks and steep-walled valleys. A strand of river cut a fiery path through the maze of canyons, the way it must have done for centuries, transforming the landscape into something as surreal as a dream.

Below me, the same river that had turned the distant reefs into fantastic sculpture fell silently, endlessly over a cliff. Protz, Tau's liaison, had called this the Great Falls. Watching the sluggish, silt-heavy waterflow, I wondered whether that was a joke.

"Cat!"

Someone called my name. I turned, glancing down as I did because some part of me was always afraid that the next time I looked down at myself I'd be naked.

I wasn't naked. I was still wearing the neat, conservatively cut clothes I'd overpaid for in a hotel shop, so that I could pass for Human this evening. Human with a capital H. That was how they said it around here, not to confuse it with Hydran: *Alien.*

An entire city full of Hydrans lived just across the river. There were three of them here at this reception tonight. I'd watched them come in only minutes ago. They hadn't teleported, materializing unnervingly in the middle of the crowd. They'd walked into the room, like any other guest. I wondered if they'd had any choice about that.

Their arrival had crashed every coherent thought in my mind. I'd been watching them without seeming to ever since, making sure they weren't watching me or moving toward me. I'd watched them until I had to turn away to the windows just so that I could breathe.

Passing for human. That was what they were trying to do at this party, even though they'd always be aliens, their psionic Gift marking them as freaks. This had been their world, once, until humans had come and taken it away from them. Now they were the strangers, the outsiders; hated by the people who'd destroyed them, because it was human to hate the ones you'd injured.

The butt end of the camph I'd been sucking on dissolved into bitter pulp in my mouth without doing anything to ease my nerves. I swallowed it and took another one out of my pocket. I was already wearing trank patches; I'd already drunk too many of the drinks that seemed to appear every time I turned around. I couldn't afford to keep doing that. Not while I was trying to pass for human, when my face would never really pass, any more than those alien faces across the room would.

"Cat!" Protz called my name again, giving it the querulous twist it always seemed to get from someone who didn't believe they'd heard all there was to it.

I could tell by the look on his face that he was coming to herd me back into the action. I could see by the way he moved that he was beginning to resent how I kept sliding out of it. I took the camph out of my mouth and dropped it on the floor.

As he forced me back into the crowd's eye I looked for somebody I knew, any member of the research team I'd arrived with. I thought I saw Pedrotty, our bitmapper, on the far side of the room; didn't see anyone else I recognized. I moved on, muttering polite stupidities to one stranger after another.

Protz, my keeper, was a midlevel bureaucrat of Tau Biotech. His name could have been anything, he could have been any of the other combine vips I'd met. They came in both sexes and any color you wanted, but they all seemed to be the same person. Protz wore his regulation night-blue suit and silver drape, Tau's colors, like he'd been born to them.

Probably he had. In this universe you didn't just work for a combine, you lived for it. *Keiretsu,* they called it: the corporate family. It was a Prespace term that had followed the multinationals as they became multiplanetary and finally interstellar. It would survive as long as the combines did, because it so perfectly described how they stole your soul.

The combine that employed you wasn't just your career, it was your heritage, your motherland, existing through both space and time. When you were born into a combine you became a cell in the nervous system of a megabeing. If you were lucky and kept your nose clean, you stayed a part of it until you died. Maybe longer.

I looked down. The fingers of my right hand were covering the databand I wore on my left wrist—proving my reality, again.

Without a databand you didn't exist, in this universe. Until a few years ago, I hadn't had one.

For seventeen years the only ID I'd worn had been scars. Scars from beatings, scars from blades. I'd had a crooked, half-useless thumb for years, because it had healed untreated after I'd picked the wrong mark's pocket one night. The databand I wore now covered the scar on my wrist where a contract laborer's bond tag had been fused to my flesh. I had a lot of scars. The worst ones didn't show.

After a lifetime on the streets of a human refuse dump called Oldcity, my luck had finally changed. And one of the hard truths I'd learned since then was that not being invisible anymore meant that everybody got to see you naked.

"You've met Gentleman Kensoe, who heads our Board. . . ." Protz nodded at Kensoe, the ultimate boss of Tau, the top of its food chain. He looked like he'd never missed a meal, or a chance to spit into an outstretched hand. "And this is Lady Gyotis Binta, representing the Ruling Board of Draco." Protz pushed me into someone else's personal space. "She's interested in your work—"

I felt my mind go blank again. Draco existed on a whole separate level of influence and power. They *owned* Tau. They controlled the resource rights to this entire planet and parts of a hundred others. They were the ultimate keiretsu: Tau Biotech was just one more client state of the Draco cartel, one of a hundred exploiting fingers Draco had stuck into a hundred separate profit pies. The Draco Family, they liked to call it. Cartel members traded goods and services with each other, provided support against hostile takeover attempts, looked out for each other's interests—like family. Keiretsu also meant "trust". . . . And right now Draco didn't trust Tau.

Tau's Ruling Board had drawn the unwanted attention of the Federation Trade Authority. Cartels were autonomous entities, but most of them used indentured workers from the FTA's Contract Labor pool to do the scut work their own citizens wouldn't touch.

Technically, the Feds only interceded when they had evidence that the universal rights of their laborers were being violated. The FTA controlled interstellar shipping, and no combine really wanted to face FTA sanctions. But I knew from personal experience that the way bondies were treated wasn't the real issue for the Feds. The real issue was power.

The FTA was always looking for new leverage in its endless balance-game with the combines. Politics was war; the weapons were just better concealed.

I didn't know who had reported Tau to the Feds; maybe some corporate rival. I did know the xenoarchaeology research team that I'd joined was one of Tau's reform showpieces, intended to demonstrate Tau's enlightened governmental process. We'd come here at Tau's expense to study a living artifact called the cloud-whales and the reefs of bizarre detritus they had deposited planetwide. The Tau Board was sparing no expense to show the Feds they weren't dirty, or at least were cleaning up their act. Which was a joke, from what I knew about combine politics, but not a funny one.

It was just as obvious that Protz wanted—expected—everyone on the team to help Tau prove its point. *Say something,* his eyes begged me, the way I knew his mind would have been begging me if I could have read his thoughts.

I looked away, searching the crowd for Hydrans. I didn't find any. I looked back. "Good to meet you," I muttered, and forced myself to remember that I'd met Board members before. I'd been bodyguard to a Lady; knew, if I knew anything, that the only real difference between a combine vip and an Oldcity street punk was what kind of people believed the lies they told.

Lady Gyotis was small and dark, with hair that had gone silver-white. I wondered how old she really was. Most vips on her level had the money to get their genetic clocks set back more than once. She wore a long, flower-brocaded robe that covered her from neck to foot. Nothing about her said *combine vip* except the subtle, expensive design of her necklace. Its scrolls were the logos of corporations; I recognized Tau's somewhere midway up her shoulder.

I also recognized the pendant at the center, a stylized dragon wearing a collar of holographic fire. I had the same design tattooed on my butt. I must have been gorked when I'd done it, because I couldn't even remember how it got there. I didn't tell her that wearing Draco's logo as body art was something we had in common.

Lady Gyotis smiled at me, meeting my stare as if she didn't notice anything strange about my face, not even the cat-green eyes with their long slit pupils: Hydran eyes, in a face that was too human, and not human enough. "A pleasure," she said. "We are so pleased to have you as a part of the study team. I'm sure your unique perceptions will add greatly to whatever discoveries are made."

"Thank you," I said, and swallowed the obedient "ma'am" that almost followed it out of my mouth, reminding myself that I didn't work for her, any more than I belonged to Tau. This time I was part of an independent research group.

"We feel his being a part of the team will demonstrate our goodwill toward the"—Kensoe glanced at me—"local Hydran community." He smiled.

I didn't.

"Let us hope so," Lady Gyotis murmured. "You know, the inspection team from the FTA is here tonight." I'd met the Feds; I didn't envy Kensoe. But then, I didn't feel sorry for him either.

"Yes, ma'am," Kensoe said, glancing away like he expected assassins. "We'll be ready for them. I think they'll find the, uh, problems here have been grossly misrepresented."

"Let us hope so," Lady Gyotis said again. "Toshiro!" she called suddenly, lifting her hand.

Someone came through the crowd toward us. Kensoe stiffened; so did I. The stranger coming toward us wore the uniform of a combine's Chief of Security. I checked the logo on the helmet he hadn't taken off, even here. It was Draco's. His business-cut uniform was deep green and copper, Draco's combine colors. A lot of meaningless flash paraded across the drape he wore over it. His ID read SAND.

There was no way in hell a Corporate Security Chief would cross half the galaxy from the home office just to attend this party. I wondered exactly how much trouble Tau was in.

"Lady Gyotis." Sand bowed slightly in her direction, smiling. He was still smiling as he followed her glance toward me.

I couldn't tell what the smile meant. *Couldn't read him. . . . Stop it*—I couldn't force my own face into an expression that even resembled a smile. I'd met a lot of Corpses in my life. I'd never met one I liked.

Sand's skin was smooth and golden; his cybered eyes, under epicanthic folds, were opaque and silver, like ball bearings. One glance from eyes like that could scan you right down to your entrails. The last CorpSec Chief I'd known had had eyes like that; they came with the job. The more power a combine vip had, the more augmentation came with it. Usually the most elaborate wire jobs didn't show; most humans were too xenophobic to want the truth visible, about themselves, about each other. There was nothing I could see about Lady Gyotis that looked abnormal, even though she had to be hiding a lot of bioware. Draco's subsidiaries made some of the best.

But in some occupations, looking strange was power. Sand's was one of them.

"Mez Cat," Lady Gyotis was saying, "may I introduce you to Toshiro Sand, Draco's Chief of Security"—as if the evidence wasn't obvious enough by itself. She didn't introduce him to Protz or Kensoe. Protz and Kensoe looked like they wished they were anywhere else; maybe they'd already met him. "He was also most impressed by your interpretive work on the Monument."

I grimaced and hoped he took it for a smile. He held out his hand. I looked at it for a few heartbeats before I realized what it meant. Finally I put out my own hand and let him shake it.

"Where are you from, Mez Cat?" Lady Gyotis asked me.

I glanced back. "Ardattee," I said. "Quarro."

She looked surprised. "The Hub?" she said. Quarro was the main city on Ardattee, and Ardattee had taken Earth's place as the center of everything important. "But wherever did you get that charming accent? I've spent much time there, but yours is unfamiliar to me."

"Oldcity," Sand murmured. "It's an Oldcity accent."

I looked up to see her glance at him, surprised again. She'd probably never even seen Quarro's Oldcity—the slums, the Contract Labor feeder tank. I'd tried to get the sound of it out of my voice, but I couldn't, any more than I could get the place itself out of my memories.

Sand looked back at me. "Then I'm even more impressed by your accomplishments," he said, to my frown.

I didn't say anything.

"I expected you to be older, frankly. The concepts in your monograph suggested a real maturity of thought."

"I don't think I was ever young," I said, and Lady Gyotis laughed, a little oddly.

"Mez Perrymeade told me the original interpretation was yours," Sand went on, as if he hadn't heard me. "That remarkable image about 'the death of Death.' What was it that gave you the key to your approach?"

I opened my mouth, shut it, swallowing words that tasted like bile. I didn't believe that he meant anything he was saying, that they were really looking at me as if I was their equal. I wished I knew what they really wanted—

"Cat," a voice said, behind me; one I recognized, this time. Kissindre Perrymeade was there at my back like the Rescue Service, ready to pick up the conversational ball I'd dropped. She'd been cleaning up my social messes ever since we arrived; her sense of timing was so good that she could have been the mind reader I wasn't.

I nodded at her, grateful, not for the first time. And went on looking at her. I'd never seen her dressed like this, for a combine showplace instead of fieldwork. She'd never seen me dressed like this, either. I wondered how she liked it; if it made her feel the way I felt when I looked at her.

We'd been friends for most of the time I'd been getting through my university studies. Friends and nothing more. As long as I'd known her she'd had a habit named Ezra Ditreksen. He was a systems analyst, and from what everyone said, he was damn good at it. He was also a real prick. They argued more than most people talked; I never understood why she didn't jettison him. But then, I was hardly an expert on long-term relationships.

Kissindre was the one who'd badgered me until I put into coherent form the ideas I'd had about an artifact called the Monument. Its vanished creators had left their distinctive bio-engineering signature scattered throughout this arm of the galactic spiral, encrypted in the DNA of a handful of other uncanny constructs, including Refuge's cloud-whales.

Kissindre was with her uncle, Janos Perrymeade. He was a vip for Tau, like most of the warm bodies at this party. It had been his idea to bring a research team here; he'd gotten the permission and the funding for us to study the cloud-whales and the reefs. I looked at Kissindre and her uncle standing side by side, seeing the same clearwater blue eyes, the same shining brown hair. It made me want to like him, want to trust him, because they looked so much alike. So far he hadn't done anything to make me change my mind.

Ezra Ditreksen materialized on the other side of her, at ease inside his formal clothes, the way everyone here seemed to be except me. His specialty wasn't xenoarch; but the team needed a systems analyst, and the fact that he was sleeping with the crew leader made him the logical choice. When he saw me he frowned, something he did like breathing. Not seeing him frown would have worried me.

I let him claim my place in the conversation, not minding, for once. It didn't matter to me that he'd never liked me, didn't bother me that I didn't know why. For a rich processing-patent heir from Ardattee, there must be more reasons than he had brain cells. Maybe it was enough that he'd seen Kissindre sketch my face once in the corner of her lightbox instead of making her usual painstaking hand drawing of some artifact. I took another drink off a passing tray. This time Protz frowned at me.

I looked away from him, reorienting on the conversation. Ditreksen was standing next to me, asking Perrymeade how he'd come to be Tau's Alien Affairs Commissioner. It seemed to be an innocent question, but there was something in the way he asked it that made me look twice at him. I wasn't certain until I saw a muscle twitch in Perrymeade's cheek. *Not my imagination.*

Perrymeade smiled an empty social smile, one that stopped at his eyes, and said, "I fell into it, really . . . An interest in xenology runs in the family." He glanced at Kissindre; his smile was real as he looked at her. "I had some background in the field. The time came when Tau needed to fill the Alien Affairs position, and so they tapped me."

"You're the only agent?" I asked, wondering if there could actually be that few Hydrans left on Refuge.

He looked surprised. "No, certainly not. I am the one who has direct contact with the Hydran Council, however. The Council communicates with our agency on behalf of their people."

I looked away, made restless by a feeling I couldn't name. I searched the crowd for the three Hydrans; spotted them across the room, barely visible inside a forest of human bodies.

"I suppose the job must pay awfully well," Ezra murmured, drawing out the words as if they were supposed to mean something more. "To make the . . . challenges of the work worthwhile."

I turned back.

Perrymeade's smile strained. "Well, yes, the job has its challenges—and its compensations. Although my family still won't let me admit what I do for a living." His mouth quirked, and Ditreksen laughed.

Perrymeade caught me looking at him; caught Kissindre looking at him too. His face flushed, the pale skin reddening the way I'd seen hers redden. "Of course, money isn't the only compensation I get from my work—" He gave Ditreksen the kind of look you'd give to someone who'd intentionally tripped you in public. "The conflicts that arise when the needs of the Hydran population and Tau's interests don't intersect make my work . . . challenging, as you say. But getting to know more about the Hydran community has taught me a great deal . . . the unique differences between our two cultures, and the striking similarities. . . . They are a remarkable, resilient people." He looked back at me, as if he wanted to see the expression on my face change. Or maybe he didn't want to see it change on Ezra's. His gaze glanced off my stare like water off hot metal; he was looking at Kissindre again.

Her expression hung between emotions for a long second, before her lips formed something that only looked like a smile. She turned back to Sand, her silence saying it all.

I listened to her finish telling Sand how we'd reached the conclusions we had about the artifact/world called the Monument and about the ones who'd left it for us to find—the vanished race humans had named the Creators, because they couldn't come up with something more creative.

The Creators had visited Refuge too, millennia ago, before they'd abandoned our universe entirely for some other plane of existence. The cloud-whales and their by-product, the reefs, were one more cosmic riddle the Creators had left for us to solve, or simply to wonder at. The reefs were also, not coincidentally, the main reason for Tau's existence and Draco's controlling interest in this world.

"But how did you come to such an insight about the Monument's symbolism?" Sand asked—asking me again, I realized, because Kissindre had given me all the credit.

"I . . . it just came to me." I looked down, seeing the Monument in my memory: an entire artificial world, created by a technology so far beyond ours that it still seemed like magic; a work of art constructed out of bits and pieces, the bones of dead planets.

At first I'd thought of it as a monument to death, to the failure of lost civilizations—a reminder to the ones who came after that the Creators had gone where we never could. But then I'd seen it again, and seen it differently—not as a cemetery marker, but as a road sign pointing the way toward the unimaginable future; a memorial to the death of Death . . .

". . . because he has an unusual sensitivity to the subliminals embedded in the matrix of the Monument." Kissindre was finishing my explanation again when I looked up.

"Yes, well, that is what he's best at, that sort of instinctive, intuitive thing," Ezra said, shrugging. "Considering his background . . . Kissindre and I put in long hours of search work and statistical analysis to come up with the data that supports his hypothesis. We constructed the actual study—"

I frowned, and Kissindre said, "Ezra . . ."

"I'm not saying he doesn't deserve the credit—" Ditreksen said, catching her look. "Without him, we wouldn't have had a starting point. It's almost enough to make me wish I were half Hydran. . . ." He glanced at me, with a small twist of his mouth. He looked back at Sand, at the others, measuring their reactions.

There was a long silence. Still looking at Ditreksen, I said, "Sometimes I wish you were half human."

"Let me introduce you to our Hydran guests," Perrymeade said, catching me by the arm, trying to pull me away without seeming to. I remembered that he was responsible for overseeing Tau's uncertain race relations. "They want to meet you."

I realized suddenly that I was more than just another interchangeable team member, a node in an artificial construct created to impress the FTA. I was some kind of token, living proof that they weren't genocidal exploiters—at least, not anymore.

Everyone and everything around me slipped out of focus, except for the three Hydrans looking at us expectantly from across the room. Suddenly I felt as if the drinks and the tranks and the camphs had all kicked in at once.

The Hydrans stood together, looking toward us. They'd stood

that way the entire time, close to each other, as if there was strength in numbers. But I was alone; there was no one like me in this crowd, or in any other crowd I'd ever been a part of. Perrymeade led me to them, stopped me in front of them, as if I was a drone circulating with a platter of mind-benders.

The Hydrans wore clothing that would have looked perfectly appropriate on anyone else in the room—just as well cut, just as expensive, although they didn't show any combine colors. But my eyes registered something missing, the thing I always checked for on another human: *Databands*. None of them had a databand. They were nonpersons. Hydrans didn't exist to the Federation Net that affected every detail of a human citizen's existence from birth to death.

Perrymeade made introductions. The part of my brain that I'd trained to remember any input recorded their names, but I didn't hear a word he said.

There were two men and one woman. One of the men was older than the others, his face weathered by exposure, like he'd spent a lot of time outdoors. The younger man looked soft, as if he'd never made much of an effort at anything, or ever had to. The woman had a sharpness about her; I couldn't tell if it was intelligence or hostility.

I stood studying them, the angles and planes of their faces. Everything was where it should be in a human face. The differences were subtle, more subtle than the differences between random faces plucked out of the human genepool. But they weren't human differences.

These faces were still alien—the colors, the forms, the almost fragile bone structure. The eyes were entirely green, the color of emeralds, of grass . . . of mine. The Hydrans looked into my eyes—seeing only the irises as green as grass, but pupils that were long and slitted like a cat's, like theirs. My face was too human to belong to one of them, but still subtly alien. . . .

I felt myself starting to sweat, knowing that they were passing judgment on me with more than just their eyes. There was a sixth sense they'd all been born with—that I'd been born with too. Only I'd lost it. It was gone, and any second now their eyes would turn cold; any second they'd turn away—

I was actually starting to tremble, standing there in my formal clothes; shaking like I was back on some Oldcity street corner, needing a fix. Perrymeade went on speaking as if he hadn't noticed. I watched the Hydrans' faces turn quizzical. They traded half frowns and curious looks, along with a silent mind-to-mind exchange that once I could have shared in. I thought I felt a whisper of mental contact touch my thoughts as softly as a kiss . . . felt the psionic Gift I'd been born with cower down in a darkness so complete that I couldn't be sure I'd felt anything.

"Are you—?" the woman broke off, as if she was searching for a word. She touched her head with a nutmeg-colored hand. Disbelief filled her face, and I could guess what word she was looking for. I watched the expressions on the faces of the two men change, the younger one's to what looked like disgust, the older one's to something I didn't even recognize.

Perrymeade broke off, went on speaking again, like someone refusing to acknowledge that we were all sinking into quicksand. He droned on about how my presence on the research team meant there would be someone "more sensitive to Hydran cultural interests—"

"And are you?" The older man looked directly at me. My eidetic memory coughed up his name: Hanjen. A member of the Hydran Council. Perrymeade had called him an "ombudsman," which seemed to mean some kind of negotiator. Hanjen cocked his head, as if he was listening for the answer I couldn't give—or for something else that I hadn't given, could never give him.

"Then I suggest," he murmured, as if I'd shaken my head—or maybe I had, "that you come and . . . talk to us about it."

I turned away before anyone could say anything more or do anything to stop me. I pushed my way through the crowd and headed for the door.

TWO

I STOOD IN the cold wind and the deepening twilight on the riverside promenade, wondering again why they'd called this world Refuge. The city lay behind me, its distant sounds of life reminding me that sooner or later I'd have to turn back and acknowledge its presence: Tau Riverton, the orderly, soulless grid of a combine 'clave, a glorified barracks for Tau's citizen/shareholders, whose leaders were still eating and drinking and lying to each other at the party I'd just bolted from.

Ahead of me a single bridge arced across the sheer-walled canyon that separated Tau Riverton from the city on the other side. The canyon was deep and wide, carved out by what must once have been a multikiloton waterflow. Now there was only one thin strand of brass-colored river snaking along the canyon floor, a hundred meters below.

I looked up again at the bridge span, its length brightening with unnatural light as the dusk deepened. At its far end lay not just another town but another world, or what was left of it. *Hydran. Alien.* This was as close as the preprogrammed systems of the aircab I'd hired would take me—or anyone—to what lay across the river: *Freaktown.*

From here I couldn't tell anything about the town on the other side, half a kilometer away through the violet dusk. I stole glances at it as I drifted along the light-echoed, nearly empty concourse toward the end of the plateau. Ghost voices murmured in my ears as my databand triggered every tight-beam broadcast I passed through. They whispered to me that there was a fifty-credit fine for spitting on the sidewalk, a hundred-credit fine for littering, fines up to a thousand credits and including a jail term if I defaced any property. There were subliminal visuals to go with the messages, flickering across my vision like heat lightning.

I'd never spent time in a combine 'clave before. I wondered how its citizens kept from going insane, when everywhere they turned they got feedback like this. Maybe they simply learned to stop seeing, stop listening. I was pretty damn sure they learned to stop spitting on the sidewalk.

What was left of the river poured like dregs from a spilled bottle over the barely visible precipice up ahead. Up on the heights, poised like some bird of prey, was the Aerie. I could see its streamlined gargoyle form, the fluid composite and transparent ceralloy of its body straining out over the edge of the world like a death wish, silhouetted against the bruised mauves and golds of the sunset sky.

I remembered how I'd left it; thought about the drinks I'd had up there tonight, that maybe I'd had too many, too close together. I thought about the trank patches I'd put on even before I got to the party.

I reached up and peeled the used, useless patches off my neck. I dug in my pockets for a camph; stuck the last one I had into my mouth and bit down, because it didn't matter now if having another one was a bad idea. As the camph numbed my tongue I sighed, waiting for it to take out all my nerve endings the same way, one by one. *Waiting.* . . . It didn't help. Tonight nothing did. Nothing could.

There was only one thing that could give me what I needed tonight, and I wasn't going to find that in Tau Riverton. And with every heartbeat I spent not looking across the river, my need grew stronger.

Damn you. I shook my head, not even certain who I meant. I leaned against an advertising kiosk, letting the shifting colors of its display holos bleed on me. The voices murmuring in my ears changed as I changed position, urging me to *go here, buy this,* reminding me that there was a fine for loitering, a fine for defacing a display unit. The colors turned the clothing I'd bought this afternoon into something as surreal as my memories of tonight's reception.

I looked back across the river again, pushing my hands into my pockets. The season was supposed to be spring, but Riverton was located far south, near Refuge's forty-fifth parallel, in the middle of what seemed to be high desert. The night air was cold, and getting colder. The cold made my hands ache. They'd been frostbitten more than once, back in Oldcity. Quarro's spring had been cold too. I watched my breath steam as I exhaled; condensation touched my face with dank cloud-fingers.

I began to walk again, back the way I'd come, telling myself I was only moving to keep warm. But I was moving toward the bridge, the only point of intersection that existed for two peoples living on the same planet but in separate worlds.

This time I got close enough to see the access clearly: The arched gateway, the details of the structure. The guards. Two armed men, wearing Corporate Security uniforms, Tau's colors showing all over them.

I stopped as their heads turned toward me. Suddenly I was angry, not even sure why . . . whether it was what those uniformed bodies said about the access between their world and the one on the other side, or just the fact that they were Corpses, and it would be a long time before the sight of a CorpSec uniform didn't make my guts knot up.

I made myself move toward them with my empty hands at my sides, wearing neat, respectable clothes and a databand.

They watched me come, their faces expressionless, until I was only a few steps from them under the gateway arch. It was warm under the arch.

My databand triggered the pillars on either side of me; they came alive with mindnumbing displays of data: maps, diagrams, warnings, lists of regulations. I saw my own image centered in one of the displays, a scan of my entire body showing that I was unarmed, solvent . . . and not quite sober.

I stared at the double image of my face, the file-match side by side with the realtime image, looking at them the way I knew the guards would look at them. Seeing my hair, so pale in the artificial light that it was almost blue. I'd let it grow until it reached my shoulders, pinned it back with a clip at the base of my neck, the way most students of the Floating University had worn theirs. The gold stud through the hole in my ear tonight was about as conservative as I could make it, like my clothes. The light turned my skin an odd shadow-color, but it was no odder than the colors the guards' skins had turned in the light. I glanced down, away, hoping they wouldn't look at my eyes.

One of the Corpses studied the display while the other one studied me. The first one nodded to the second and shrugged. "In order," he said.

"Evening, sir," the second Corpse said to me with a tight, polite nod. Their faces looked hard and disinterested; their faces didn't match their manners. I wondered what subliminal messages their helmet monitors were feeding them, reminding them always to be courteous, to say "please" and "thank you" when they rousted a citizen, or they'd see another black mark on their record, a debit from their pay. "You have business over on the Hydran side?"

"No," I muttered. "Just . . . sightseeing."

He frowned, as though I'd said something embarrassing or something that didn't make sense. The other guard laughed, a soft snort, as if he was trying not to. "Not from around here," the first one muttered. It wasn't really a question.

The second one sighed. "It's my duty, sir, to point out to you that your blood alcohol level is high, indicating possible impaired judgment. No offense, sir." His voice was as flat as a recording. Flatter. "Also, sir, I'm required to show you this information." He pointed at the displays. "Please read the disclaimer. It states that you accept full responsibility for anything that happens to you on the other side of the river. That's the Homeland over there. It's not Tau's jurisdiction; it's not Tau's responsibility. We don't guarantee your safety." He looked hard at me, to see if I was tracking what he'd said . . . looked harder at me as he suddenly got a good look at my eyes: the grass-green irises, with the long slit pupils like a cat's.

He looked at my whole face, then, and started to frown. He glanced at the information display from my databand on the wall behind him—undeniable proof, to both of us, that I was a full citizen of the Human Federation. He looked back at my face again; his frown didn't go away. But he only said, "Curfew is at ten. Crossing closes for the night . . . if you want to come back." He was already turning his back on me as he finished it. He muttered something to the other guard as I went on my way. I didn't hear what it was.

There were only a few people moving across the bridge on foot. I tried not to look at the ones I passed, the ones who passed me. They kept their eyes to themselves. One or two small private ground vehicles went by, so unexpected that I had to dodge out of their way. The canyon below the bridge's span was full of shadows; far below, light danced on the hidden water surface.

By the time I'd reached the far end of the bridge I only had eyes for what lay ahead. All I could make out were vague shapes and random patterns of light, but every step seemed harder to take than the last.

I let my concentration fall inward, trying to force something to happen in my mind; trying to focus, to listen, to reach out and speak in the secret language that a thousand other minds must be speaking, must be hearing, just beyond the bridge's end.

But it was no use. They were psions, telepaths—and I wasn't. *Trying* only proved again what I already knew: That what was gone was gone. That what was past help should have been past grief by now; long past this sick hunger—

I was trembling, the way I'd trembled at the reception under the stares of the three Hydrans. I told myself that I was cold, standing here with the night coming on, at the end of winter on an alien world where I was a total stranger. That my body's reaction wasn't because I felt so terrified that I wanted to puke, wanted to do anything but go on.

Because I couldn't do anything but go on. I started forward again—knowing I wouldn't sleep nights, wouldn't eat, would never be able to concentrate on the work I'd come here to do, unless I let myself do this.

I stepped off the far end of the bridge, on Hydran ground at last. Once this entire planet had been Hydran ground; until we'd come and taken it away from them. This was their homeworld, their Earth; they'd made this world the center of a civilization that had spanned light-years the way the Human Federation did now.

Their civilization had already passed its peak and been in decline when the Federation made first contact. We'd been glad enough then to finally have proof that we weren't alone in the galaxy, more than glad that the first "aliens" we encountered looked more like humans than some humans looked like to each other.

Genemapping studies had proved that the resemblance wasn't just a coincidence of cosmic proportions: humans and Hydrans seemed to be the two halves of a long-divided whole, who might both owe our very existence to an incomprehensible bioengineering experiment. That we might be just one more of the Creators' enigmatic calling cards. Hydrans and humans . . . the haves and the have-nots, separated by one thing: psionic ability.

Hydrans were born able to access the quantum field, the bizarre subatomic universe of quarks and neutrinos hidden at the heart of the deceptive order we called Reality. The quantum-mechanical spectrum could have been turtles all the way down, for all the sense it made to ordinary human beings; even though human brains only seemed to make sense if they functioned by quantum rules. The average person could barely take quantum electrodynamics seriously, let alone imagine a way of collapsing the probability wave to manipulate the QM field.

But a psion could tap the QM field instinctively, manipulate improbabilities to the point where using the Gift directly affected the tangible, visible world that they shared with "normal" psi-blind humans. The macrocosmic entrainment of quantum effects allowed a psion to do things humans had believed were impossible before we met the Hydrans. That one crucial difference had been the Hydrans' strength. And it had been their fatal weakness when they finally encountered us.

In the beginning, the Human Federation and the Hydrans had coexisted in peace. It had seemed only natural, when two "alien" races meeting in the depths of space discovered they were similar down to the level of their DNA. It had seemed only natural that there would be cooperation, friendship . . . intermarriage. Mixed-race marriages began to produce mixed-blood children, spilling Hydran psi genes into the sterile waters of the human genepool like droplets of dye, staining it a new color.

But the peaceful coexistence of first contact hadn't lasted. The more often the Human Federation encountered Hydrans living on exactly the kind of worlds that interstellar combines wanted for exploitation, the less they wanted to acknowledge that Hydrans had a prior claim to them.

Relations went downhill from there, went downhill faster as the combines discovered that when they tried to push the Hydrans off their worlds, the Hydrans wouldn't push back.

Because of what they were, the things they could have done

with unchecked psi powers, the Hydrans had evolved in ways that made them virtually nonviolent. If you could kill with a thought—reach into a chest and stop a heart, cause an embolism in the brain, break bones without touching them—there had to be some way to prevent it.

There was. If a Hydran killed someone, the backlash took out all the defenses in the killer's own mind. Any murder became a murder-suicide. Natural selection had done them a favor . . . until they met the Federation.

Because humans had virtually no psi ability, they'd never had any real problem with killing. They swept the Hydrans up like birds in a net, killing them fast in hostile takeovers; killing them slowly by pushing the survivors onto "homelands" that made them outcasts on their own world, or "relocating" them to places like Oldcity, where I'd been born. There were still humans born with mixed blood, but most of the blood had been mixed long ago, before humans and Hydrans had begun to hate the sight of each other.

Those humans who still carried a few Hydran genes in their DNA pool were treated as less than human, especially if they showed any psi ability, which most of them did. Without support, without training in how to use their Gift, psions were "freaks" to pureblood humans, who made sure they sank to the bottom of the labor pool and stayed there, ignored when they weren't actively persecuted.

If you looked very Hydran, if your mother happened to have been Hydran—if you were a halfbreed, a product of miscegenation so fresh that most people you met had been alive when it happened—it was worse. I knew, because I was one.

I'd spent most of my life in Oldcity, Quarro's buried slum, doing things that never got into most people's nightmares just to stay alive. And I couldn't even use the Gift I'd been born with, the telepathy that would have let me know who to trust, how to protect myself, maybe even let me understand why the things that always seemed to be happening to me kept happening.

In time, with a lot of luck and a lot of pain, I'd gotten out of Oldcity. I'd learned to read, and then to access; I'd learned about the heritage I'd lost with my mother's death, so long ago that I couldn't even remember her face.

And now, after too many years, too many light-years, I was finally standing on Hydran ground.

There was nothing, no one guarding this end of the bridge. I looked back over my shoulder at the lighted span. It seemed impossibly long and fragile, surreally bright. I saw the guard-post at the other end. And I wondered suddenly what the hell made them think they could keep a people who could teleport— send themselves through a spacetime blip to somewhere else in the blink of an eye—from going anywhere they wanted to. But then I remembered that you couldn't teleport to a place you'd never been.

Or maybe the guards were intended to keep the humans where they belonged.

A pair of humans passed me, wearing Tau business dress. The way they moved said that they were in a hurry to get onto the bridge and away. Ahead of me the street was darker than the bridge had been; there was no artificial lighting. It was probably getting hard for Tau citizens, with their human eyes, to find their way.

It surprised me that the Hydrans hadn't made things easier for night-blind humans. But then, maybe that was what the guard had been trying to tell me—maybe no human in his right mind visited Freaktown after dark.

I started down the nearest street. Even in the darkness I could make out every detail of the buildings that fronted on it. None were more than three or four stories tall, but they merged like segments of a hive, with no clear sign of where one ended and the next began. The architecture was all organic curves; the walls were made of a material I couldn't identify, that felt like ceralloy. Almost everywhere the smooth, impervious surfaces had been covered with murals of colored tile, which must have been set into the matrix before it had hardened.

I couldn't have pictured anything less like the isolated geometry of the human city across the river if I'd tried. I wondered whether the Hydrans had built their city intentionally to answer Tau Riverton. But then I remembered that the Hydran city, like the Hydrans, had been here first. It was the human city that was the insult, the act of defiance.

I went on, following the winding course of the streets deeper into Freaktown, trying to lose my sense of alienation in the growing darkness. A few more ground vehicles passed me. Their passage through the ancient streets echoed from every exposed surface; their windows were always dark. There didn't seem to be any mods at all in the air above this side of the river.

The more my eyes adjusted to the night and the strangeness of everything I saw, the more I began to notice places where the patterns on the walls were damaged or crumbling. I saw the fallen tiles that lay in talus slopes of dust and rubbish; barricades of abandoned junk; bodies slumped against walls or stretched out in the shadows, sleeping it off.

The dirt, the derelicts, the way the buildings fronted on the street, began to make me think of Oldcity, Quarro's hidden underbelly, where the roof of the world was only ten meters high, and walls closed you in wherever you turned. I wondered why the resemblance hadn't hit me right away. Maybe because I'd lived too long in Oldcity; because it was what I was used to. Maybe that was all.

Or maybe I hadn't wanted to see Hydrans as anything less than perfect, to discover anything that forced me to admit they were flawed, embarrassing, too human . . . too much like I was.

I tried to stop looking at the broken walls. The people passing me were all Hydran now. Almost all of them wore human-style clothes that must have come from across the river. Most of the clothing looked like it had been worn for years before it had ever touched Hydran skin.

It surprised me that there were so few people on the streets, so few buildings showing lights or signs of life. I didn't see any children. I wondered if they all went to bed with the sun, or whether there was something I was missing. Most of the adults had hair as pale as mine; most of them had skin that was the color of spice: ginger-gold, nutmeg-brown, cinnamon. The colors were as varied as the colors of human skin, but not really any color I'd ever seen on human flesh, even mine. They all seemed to move with a kind of uncanny grace that I almost never saw in humans.

Refuge was supposed to be their homeworld: their Earth, the place their civilization had started out from. According to Tau's data, the Hydrans living in Freaktown and on the surrounding reservation were Refuge's entire surviving population. The remnants of cultures and races from all parts of the planet had been swept up and dumped, like so much dust, here on this "Homeland"— the one piece of ground left to them by Tau/Draco . . . the piece that must have had the least exploitable resources.

It made me uneasy even to think that the handful of people I'd seen on the street tonight might actually be a representative sample of their numbers.

People looked back at me, half curious if they noticed I was looking at them. Some of them went on staring after I'd passed. I could feel their eyes on me, but I couldn't feel their minds. I couldn't tell why they were staring, whether it was the way I moved or my face or the fact that when they touched my mind they met a wall.

No one spoke to me, asked me the obvious questions, muttered behind my back. They didn't make any sound at all. You walked down a street in a human city and you heard conversation, arguments, laughter. Here I felt like a deaf-mute; here there was only silence, broken by an occasional shapeless far-off sound that seemed to echo forever, like there was no distance.

I'd heard once that when Hydrans were with their own kind they didn't talk much; they didn't need to. They had their telepathy: They could reach out to each other with their minds, prove each other's reality, know each other's moods, know that all around them were living, breathing people just like them. They knew all that without speaking, without needing to look at each other constantly.

Humans didn't. Humans had to bridge that unbridgeable gap with speech, and so they were always talking, proving that they weren't as alone in the universe as they were inside their own minds.

Most of the buildings along the street had doors or windows at street level. Most of those were shuttered, private; a few were wide open, like they were inviting everybody inside. Occasionally I saw the phantom outline of an opening that had been walled up. In other places the access was only a rough hole knocked in the wall, shattering a perfect line, the wholeness of a mosaic pattern. I wondered why anyone would do that.

I thought about the humans coming across the river, who

couldn't mind their own business or walk through walls. I wondered whether the sealed-up walls, the crude doorways, were a kind of subtle message to their visitors or whether they were just another sign of social disintegration.

Most of the doorways looked like they opened on shops of one sort or another. There were occasional signs, some in Standard, some in a language I didn't know, some of them lit up. I even saw one that was holographic, shimmering in the violet gloom like a hallucination. I began to think that the signs were like the holes in the wall: Freaktown spelling it out for the humans, the psionic have-nots, the deadheads. . . .

I wandered the streets for nearly an hour, without anyone challenging me or even acknowledging me. At last, numb with cold but more or less sober, I stopped in front of what looked like an eatery. No one had harassed me so far. I told myself that it would be all right to go inside, to sit down with them and eat what they ate, to pretend for an hour that I actually belonged somewhere.

I stepped inside, ducking my head because the ragged doorway was low by human standards. I was only medium height, but not many of the Hydrans I'd passed in the street were as tall as I was. I felt a breath of forced air kiss my face as I moved through it, keeping the warmth and the cooking smells inside, the cold evening out. I wondered whether it was human tech from across the river or a telekinetic field generated by someone inside.

I stopped just inside the doorway, glad to feel warm again as I inhaled the smells. They were strange and strong, making me realize how hungry I was. A dozen people were scattered around the room at low tables; singly, in couples, even a family with a child. The parents and child looked up together, suddenly wary. I stood there a little longer, my eyes moving from face to face, not able to stop looking at the strange beauty of their features. Finally I crossed the room and sat down at an empty table, as far from anyone else as possible.

I searched for a menu, suddenly wondering whether you couldn't even get something to eat here if you couldn't read minds.

"Can I help you?"

I jumped. Someone was standing at my elbow, looking down at

me. I wasn't sure whether he'd come up behind me without my knowing it or whether he'd teleported here to my side. My Gift wouldn't tell me, any more than it would tell me who he was or what he wanted from me. I took a long look at him and decided he must be the owner.

"Can I help you?" he asked again, in Standard, and the soft, lilting way he formed the words hardened just a little.

I realized that everyone in the room was looking at me now. The looks weren't friendly. "Some food—?" The words sounded flat and foreign as they came out of my mouth.

His face closed as if I'd insulted him, as if he was controlling himself with an effort. "I don't know who you are," he said very quietly. "I don't care what you are. But I'm telling you now, either stop what you're doing or get out."

"I'm not doing anything—" I said.

Something caught me by the back of my jacket and hauled me up. "Get out," he said, "you damned pervert." Something shoved me from behind. It didn't feel like his hand.

He didn't have to use his psi on me again. My own panic drove me out the door and into the darkness. *God, they knew. . . . They knew what I was.*

Out in the street someone caught my arm. I turned, my hand fisting. My eyes registered the slack face, the vacant stare of a burnout. The Hydran mouthed words so slurred I couldn't tell whether they were even in a language I knew.

Swearing, I jerked free and moved on, not caring where I went, as long as it was away from there.

By the time my head had cleared enough so I realized what I'd done, I was lost. There had been signs, some way of backtracking, when I'd left the eatery. There were no signs of any kind that I recognized, now. There was no street lighting either, and Refuge's single moon hadn't risen yet. If there were any shops they were closed and unmarked. The only lights I could see were high up, unreachable, probably the lights of private homes. The building here were just tall enough to keep me from using the bridge to guide me back where I'd come from.

No one else seemed to be on the street now. I felt more relief

than frustration as I realized how alone I was, because I couldn't
have asked for help now if I'd been bleeding to death.

I swore under my breath. I'd lived most of my life in a place
where knowing the streets meant survival; and now I was lost.
There weren't even any maps of Freaktown in Tau's public
access; even my databand couldn't tell me where I was, or how to
get out of here. Why the hell had I even come to this place, just to
prove what I'd always known . . . that no one had ever wanted me,
that there was nowhere I'd ever belonged?

I started back the way I'd come, head down and shoulders
hunched, shivering with cold and praying I'd make the right
combination of turns to get my miserable ass out of there before
curfew.

At last I saw the bridge lights, somewhere in the distance up
ahead; heard the sound of human voices moving toward me. I
turned another corner, breaking into a jog—slammed into someone running, so hard that we almost went down together.

A woman's voice cried out as my hands caught her falling
body. I felt something drive into my brain like a knife of thought.
My mind blocked her instinctively at the same moment that I
realized she was holding a child in her arms.

She cried out again—*shock, fury*—as my mind turned back
her attack. She gasped out words in a language I didn't know, and
all the while I kept shouting, "It's all right, I won't hurt you, it's
all right!" trying to make her listen and understand. "What's
wrong? Do you need help—?"

She stopped struggling, as if my words had finally penetrated.
Suddenly her body went limp in my grasp. The child trapped
between us didn't make a sound as the woman collapsed against
me, panting. I felt her body's fever heat even through my clothing.

She looked up at me then, and I finally saw her face: A fey,
green-eyed Hydran face, golden-skinned, framed by a wild tangle
of pale hair. . . . A face out of a dream, every alien, haunted line
of it; and yet every curve and plane was somehow as familiar as
the face of a lost lover.

"I . . . I know you?" I whispered, frozen in the glare of impossible prescience. "How—?" A trapdoor opened under my
thoughts, and I fell through—

The woman made a small sound, almost a whimper, of disbelief. One hand rose, tentatively, to touch my face. *(Nasheirtah . . . ?)* she breathed. (You. You—) Her expression became equal parts wonder and terror, mirroring my own, as I slowly raised my hands to touch her face.

(Anything . . .) I murmured as my entire life telescoped into that single moment's contact. (Anything at all.)

(Always. Forever . . .) Her eyes filled with tears, her hand dropped away. (Nasheirtah—)

"What—?" I whispered, uncomprehending.

She looked down suddenly, as if my eyes were a searchlight. "Help me," she said, in perfect Standard, but with her voice just barely under control. "Please help me—they want to take my child!" She looked over her shoulder. Light-echoes danced across building fronts in the distance down the street.

"Who does?" I asked.

"They do!" she cried, shaking her head at me, with a look that was half desperation and half incomprehension. "The Humans—"

And in the depths of her green eyes, their black slit pupils wide open to the faintest hope of light, I saw another midnight: *Another Hydran woman and her child . . . light-years away, a lifetime ago—with no one they could turn to, no one to save them from that Oldcity alley where their world was ending in blood and pain. . . .*

"Please—" she said, and pressed something into my open hand.

My fingers spasmed shut. I nodded, not looking at it, and let her go. She disappeared down a side street I hadn't even noticed.

I stood frozen a few heartbeats longer, with my stupefied mind trying to follow her into the night and my body begging me to get it out of there. And then suddenly the ones who'd been after her were in front of me, shouting; I saw lights, I saw weapons— I ran like hell.

Behind me I heard someone bellow, "Corporate Security!"

Shit— I ran faster.

Lights appeared ahead of me, dropping out of the sky, as a CorpSec cruiser landed in the street.

Before I could even slow down something invisible slammed into me like a tidal wave, and I drowned. . . .

THREE

I OPENED MY eyes again to the blinding glare of an interrogation room. I squinted them shut. "Shit," I said. But that wasn't what came out of my mouth. The sound that came out of my mouth was completely unintelligible.

My face hurt, because I must have fallen on it. My hair had come loose from its clip; it was full of dirt and getting into my eyes. Every nerve ending in my body was sparking like a live wire as the stunshock wore off.

But that wasn't what was wrong with my mouth: They'd drugged me with nephase—flypaper for freaks. I knew without feeling for one that there was a drugderm on my neck, put there by the Corpses to short-circuit my psi, if I'd still had any psi ability that I could use. I remembered the nausea, the slurred speech: the simulated brain damage. I tried to reach up, to make sure there really was a patch on my throat—

I couldn't move my arms. Either one. I looked down, saw my body held prisoner in a hard metal seat, my arms strapped to the chair arms. I stared at my hands, feeling panic abscess inside me.

Don't lose control. . . . Don't. I took a long, slow breath and made myself look up.

Half a dozen Corpses were waiting there, as if they had all the time, and patience, in the world.

"Where is he?"

I looked at the one who'd spoken. BOROSAGE, his data-patches read. He was a District Administrator, from the flash that showed on his helmet and uniform sleeve. He looked like a real bottom-feeder. These were the Corpses I knew, not the kind who wore dress uniforms to corporate receptions. These Corpses were wearing riot gear: dressed for business, their real business, which had always been making the existence of street rats like me even more impossible than it already was.

Borosage was massive and heavy; his body was starting to go to fat, as if he'd been promoted to a level where he didn't have to give a damn anymore. But there was nothing soft in his eyes. They were bleak and treacherous, like rotten ice. A gleaming artificial dome covered the left half of his skull; blunt fingers of alloy circled his eye socket and disappeared into his skull, as if some alien parasite had sunk neural taps into his brain.

I couldn't imagine what kind of injury would leave him alive and leave him looking like that. Maybe he'd had it done on purpose, to scare the living shit out of his prisoners. I looked down as he caught me staring; looked at his hands. His knuckles had more scar tissue on them than mine did. I knew how they'd gotten that way. They scared me a lot more than his face did.

I looked away from his hands with an effort, down at the databand on my wrist, the undeniable proof that I was a citizen of the Human Federation, and not some nameless piece of meat. "I want a legal advisory link," I said.

What came out of my mouth was more unintelligible sludge. The Corpses laughed. I took another slow breath, my hands clenching. "Want. A. Legal."

The laughter got louder. Borosage closed the space between us in one step. He held his fist in front of my face. "You want advice, you Hydran fuck? My advice to you is, answer the questions, because it's going to get harder to talk every time you don't."

"Not Hydran! Regishurred . . . ci'zen," I said; spit splattered his fist. "I. Got. Rights."

"You can inscribe your rights on the head of a pin this side of the river, freak."

"Databan'—!" My arm jerked against the restraint. Cold sweat was soaking through my shirt.

He took a step back; his hand dropped to his side. I let out the breath I was holding as he looked down. His face twisted. He poked my databand, and it beeped; pulled on it until I swore. "This is yours—?" he said finally, looking hard at my face, at my eyes. "Are you trying to tell me you're human?"

I nodded, my jaw muscles aching as I waited for his expression to change.

He looked at the others. His grin split open. "What do you think, Fahd?" He jerked his head at the lieutenant leaning against the door. "This prisoner claims he's a registered citizen. Got the databand to prove it."

Fahd peered at me. "You know, in this light he almost looks human." He moved closer. "The eyes could be a cosmo job, if he's one of those perverts." He smirked. "Except I've never seen anyone but a freak talk that way after we put the patch on him."

"Exactly my point." Borosage looked back at me again, and his grin soured. "So what is it, boy? Are you mixed blood? A 'breed?" He ran a thick finger along my jaw. "You do look like a 'breed. . . ."

I tried not to listen to what they said after that, about my mother, my father, about whores and gang rapes and how no decent person would let a thing like me live. . . . I sat motionless, breathing the stagnant overheated air, until they ran out of ideas.

And then Borosage freed my wrist—the one that wore the databand. Disbelief leaped like a fish inside me.

He didn't free the other hand. "Look at you," he said, picking at my sleeve. "Dressed up like a Gentleman of the Board. Wearing a databand. Trying to pass. Who did you think would believe it? Did you think we would? . . . You know what I think, freak?" he said to me, holding my hand. "I think you stole that databand." He jerked my arm forward, and one of the other Corpses handed him a descrambler.

I swore silently. I'd had one of those, once. A descrambler could access the personal code of a databand in less time than it took the owner to remember it. It was about as illegal as everything else that was happening to me right now. I watched a run of data flow across the digital display, and then suddenly the datafeed stopped. It flashed NO ACCESS, the symbols so clear that even I could see them.

Borosage swore, this time. I started to breathe again; glad, not for the first time, that I wore a thumb-lock on my deebee. Unless I thumbed it in the right spot, the only way it would come off my wrist was if somebody cut off my hand. I'd bought myself some extra security, because I knew how easy the regular locks were to descramble.

"What did you do to jam this?" Borosage shoved my hand into my face.

"*Mine—!*" I said, and then, looking down, "Phone fun'shun!" The function light didn't go on—the processors didn't recognize my voice. Borosage made a disgusted noise, as if I'd just proved that the band was stolen. I tried to see what time it was. I didn't get the chance, as he strapped my hand down again.

I told myself that someone had to be wondering where I was. They could trace me as long as I still had the databand on. Someone would come after me. I just had to hold everything together long enough so that these bastards didn't maim me before it happened.

Borosage's scarred hand caught me by the jaw. "You know you're in real trouble now, freak. The sooner you tell us everything you know, the sooner I'll think about letting you make a call, or even take a piss." He let go of me, with a twist of his hand that made me grunt as it hurt my bruised face. "Where's the boy?"

"What. Boy?" I mumbled. I braced myself as his open palm came at me, but that didn't make it hurt less when it hit my face. My head slammed against the seatback. I tasted blood; felt it leak from the corner of my mouth.

"Kidnapping," he said, through the ringing in my ears, "is a serious offense. I am talking about the human boy whose databand we found in your possession. Joby Natasa, age three standard years, son of Ling and Burnell Natasa. He was kidnapped by the Hydran woman employed to care for him. We almost caught her tonight—but we caught you instead." He leaned into my face again. "Now, you know what I think? I think this whole thing was politically motivated. I think you might be some kind of terrorist." He took a step back, peeling off his uniform jacket. "Do you still want to tell me you don't know what I mean—?"

Jeezu— I shut my eyes, remembering the look in the eyes of the woman carrying the child. *Her child; I'd thought it was her own child.* She hadn't looked like a terrorist—she'd looked terrified. Looked like my mother, on the night she was butchered by strangers because no one had been there to save her. . . .

But she wasn't my mother. It wasn't even her child. I'd been nothing but a fucking mark, letting her slip me that databand. I wondered suddenly why she'd done it to me; why she hadn't just teleported herself and the boy away, and left the Corpses behind.

But I couldn't answer that any more than I could answer Borosage's questions. I was under arrest on a world where I didn't know anyone, didn't have any rights; I was in shit up to my neck and I didn't know how the hell I was going to get out of it.

Borosage slapped me again when I didn't answer him.

"I. Didn'. Know!" I shook my head. "Prove it! Use . . . truth-tester!"

"They aren't reliable with psions. There's only one thing that always gets the truth out of a Hydran." Borosage held out his hand; one of his men put something into it. This time it was a prod. Borosage flicked it on.

I sucked in a breath. I didn't need him to show me what one of those could do. I had scars to remind me.

"That's right—squirm, you little mindraper," Borosage murmured. "You know what I can do to you with one of these. The Tau Board is up my ass over this kidnapping. They make me report to them every hour on the hour. They want that stolen child back yesterday, you know what I mean? They put their trust in me. They told me, 'Do whatever's necessary.' I intend to do that. . . ."

The prod kissed the palm of my right hand. I cursed, jerking at the restraints as it ate its way into my flesh.

Borosage gestured. Fahd moved in on me, pulled open my expensive jacket and shirt. I heard something rip. "You understand me—?"

I nodded, feeling the muscles in my chest and stomach tighten with anticipation. Wanting to kick him in the balls, except that I knew what he'd do to me if I did.

"I'm going to hear everything you know, boy," Borosage said. "Or I'm going to hear you scream." His eyes begged me to give him an excuse.

I swore under my breath, wondering what in the nine billion names of God I was going to tell him; worse, how I was even going to get words anyone could understand out of my mouth.

A beeper sounded on someone's databand, loud in the agonizing silence. I looked down at my own band with my heart suddenly in my mouth. The call function was still dead.

Borosage clapped his hand over his databand, held it up to his face, muttering, "What—?"

Somewhere in the world outside of this room a voice said, ". . . making inquiries about the prisoner, sir."

"God damn it!" Borosage shouted. "Tell them he's not here. I said nobody's to disturb us during the interrogation!"

"Administrator—"

Borosage canceled the link with a word; swore, as his bandphone began to beep again.

"Draco's Chief of Security is here, Administrator," the voice said, overriding his shutoff.

"What?" Borosage's face went slack with disbelief. "Why the hell didn't you say so? Send him in." He looked back at me and brought the prod up close. "You hear that, freak? Maybe you thought you were in trouble before. You've got the mother company down your throat now, you half-breed mindfucker."

I watched the room's single door, clenching and unclenching my burned hand.

The security field at the door blinked off. Sand was waiting beyond it. Kissindre Perrymeade and her uncle were with him, and Protz. I looked back at Borosage, wanting to laugh, but afraid to.

Borosage made a salute, half frowned as he saw that Sand wasn't alone. "Sir," he said, "this is one of the kidnappers. We've just begun to interrogate him." He jabbed the live end of the prod at me; I cringed.

Someone gasped in the doorway behind Sand. Sand stood staring at Borosage, at the prod in his hand, at me. The disbelief on his face was almost as complete as Kissindre's or her uncle's.

Sand entered the room first, alone. The others stayed where they were, as if they'd been put in stasis. Sand stopped in front of Borosage. He held out his hand with the unthinking arrogance of a man who was used to getting his way. Borosage looked surprised again, but he handed Sand the prod. I stared like everyone else as Sand took it.

Sand deactivated the prod and dropped it on the floor. "Get

those restraints off him." He pointed at me. His hand jerked with impatience as no one moved.

Fahd came forward slowly to turn me loose while Borosage watched me with blood in his eyes. I slumped in the seat as the restraints retracted, wiping blood from the corner of my mouth.

"Are you all right?" Sand asked me, frowning.

"Guesh. So," I said, and watched them all frown as they heard the words come out. I felt for the patch on my throat, found it under my chin, and peeled it off. "Drugged. Me."

"Standard procedure with Hydran prisoners," Borosage said, glaring at me, at Sand. "Without the drug blocking their psi, we couldn't keep them in detention."

Sand's frown deepened, but he didn't question it. "Get him the antidote," was all he said.

"Wait a minute," Borosage said, starting to get his nerve back. "This is my prisoner—"

"And is this how you treat your prisoners?" Sand snapped. "Drugging them and then beating a confession out of them?" He shot a look at Kissindre's uncle and Protz this time, while some part of me wondered how often he'd done the same thing himself, or something too much like it.

Borosage's face reddened. "No, sir," he said sourly. "Just the freaks." Resentment and incomprehension filled his face as he realized that Sand wasn't here for the reason he'd expected; that he had no idea what the hell Sand really wanted from him. "This 'breed was involved in the kidnapping of a human child by Hydran radicals—" Barely controlled anger stretched his voice to the breaking point. "We caught him red-handed! The Board ordered me to do whatever was necessary to get the child back. I was just following orders."

Sand glanced at me again. Behind him I saw Kissindre and the others still gaping like virgins at the door of a whorehouse. "You have arrested the wrong man, Borosage," Sand said, his voice as empty of emotion as his mirrored eyes. "And you were just about to put him in the hospital for no reason at all."

"No, sir!" Borosage swelled up like he'd sucked poison. "We caught him holding the missing child's ID, over in Freaktown. And he's wearing a databand, which is stolen property, because, as you know, sir, mixed bloods are ineligible for full Tau citizen status."

Sand glanced at me in sudden surprise; his eyes searched out my databand. He studied me a minute longer, running God only knew what kinds of analyses on my responses with the cyberware behind his eyes. But he only said, "Until about three hours ago, your prisoner and I were attending a formal reception with these people here." He gestured. "The reception being held up at the Aerie for the xenoarchaeology team that your government has brought here to study the cloud-reefs. Your prisoner is a member of that team. He has been on-planet for less than a day. I'm sure he has some explanation for this." He glanced at me again, back at the sullen knot of Corpses. "Give him the antidote."

Borosage nodded, barely. Fahd came and stuck another patch on my neck.

I waited, silent, until enough time had passed for my speech to come around. I said, slowly and carefully, "I went for a walk. I wanted to see the Hydran town. . . ." I glanced away from their expressions. "A woman with a child ran into me. She said someone was chasing her. She seemed frightened. I thought I could help her." I wondered again why she hadn't just teleported herself and the child to somewhere safe. "I didn't know it wasn't her child. I didn't know it was the Corps—Corporate Security—who wanted her, until it was too late." I shrugged, keeping my face empty the way I'd learned to do in Oldcity interrogation rooms.

"You didn't wonder about the databand?" Sand asked, his face as expressionless as mine.

"I didn't have time to think about it," I said. That was true enough. No time to wonder if I was being set up, or why. *Just because I was a stranger? Or because she'd known what I was?* I remembered her fingers touching my face, the look in her eyes. . . . A sourceless pain filled me that was more like loss than betrayal.

"You always come to the aid of complete strangers, in a—" Sand broke off, looking at but not into my eyes for a second too long, "when you know nothing about the situation?"

"Yes," I said, looking back at him. "If it looks like they need my help."

"I wouldn't have thought Oldcity taught that kind of lesson." He raised his eyebrows.

"It didn't," I said, still meeting his stare.

Sand made a motion that might have been a shrug, whatever that meant. "The situation here tonight was not what you thought it was," he said.

I sat waiting, but no one said anything more. Slowly I pulled my shirt together and refastened it, pulled my jacket back onto my shoulders. My hands kept fumbling the job. I glanced up, meeting Kissindre Perrymeade's pale, tense stare. I looked away again, wiped half-dried blood off my chin. As I got to my feet, every muscle in my body tightened against the blow that would knock me back down into the seat.

It didn't come. "Am I free to go now?" I looked at Sand, ignoring Borosage. I took a step toward the door.

"Is his patron here?" Borosage said, looking straight at me but speaking as though I wasn't in the room. "The prisoner is a mixed-blood. I can't release him until I have his work permit on file, and get assurance from his human patron that he'll be kept out of trouble in the future."

I swore under my breath, saw Borosage's goons go on alert as I swung around.

"He's a citizen of a Federal District, Quarro—" Kissindre's uncle said, too sharply. "He's not subject to Tau's resident alien laws."

"I determine Tau policy in this sector." Borosage's jaw tightened, as if Perrymeade's tone had pushed him one centimeter too far. "I'm responsible for enforcing the laws here, and until I'm told different by the Board, anybody who sets foot here is subject to my interpretation of those laws. All individuals of Hydran heritage," he spat the words like phlegm, "are required to have a human patron who will assume responsibility for them. Otherwise they are not permitted free access to areas under Tau's dominion."

"I'm his patron," Kissindre said, pushing forward. Her lips were a white line. "I'll certify any data you want."

"Open record," Borosage muttered, to some dataport on him or somewhere in the room. An ugly smile pulled at his mouth. "And just what sort of use will you be making of this individual of mixed blood, Mez Perrymeade? Would that be professional, or recreational—?"

Kissindre blushed blood-red. Janos Perrymeade muttered a curse and stepped forward.

Sand caught Perrymeade's arm in a hard grip, for as long as it took Perrymeade to control his temper. Sand's expression didn't change, but I saw Borosage mottle with anger and realized they must be communicating—arguing, probably—subvocally, wearing some kind of boneboxes. Humans had to rip open and rewire their bodies with artificial circuitry to give themselves even a pale copy of the psionic abilities a Hydran was born with. Even Borosage must need some kind of augmentation to let him do his job. I studied his alloy skullplate, wondering just how altered he was.

At last Sand looked at me again. "You're free to go," he said tonelessly. "This regrettable misunderstanding has been cleared up. Draco offers you its sincere apology for any discomfort or embarrassment this incident has caused you. I'm sure that since your interference in a Security action resulted in the escape of a kidnapper, you will have no complaints to file about your treatment here." He stared at me, deadpan, with unblinking eyes. Finally he looked at Borosage again.

"Our regrets," Borosage said, cold-eyed, flexing his hands, and I wondered what it was he was regretting.

I didn't say anything, knowing enough to keep my mouth shut. I saw the anxiety that filled Kissindre's face and her uncle's as they watched me. I nodded finally, swallowing my anger like the taste of blood.

I moved across the room, not quite steady on my feet, until I was standing in the doorway, with the barrier of Sand's body separating me from Borosage and the Corpses behind him. Kissindre's uncle offered me a hand. I shook my head. I turned my back on the chair and the restraints and the prod, and the ones who'd used them on me, and left the station.

We were out in the street again—the perfectly clean, quiet, well-lit street. I looked back at the station entrance, its dark mouth open in a perpetual *oh* of surprise. It was no different from the entrances to half a dozen other buildings along the street. Somehow that was more frightening than if it had had *prison* written all over it. "Fucking bastards—" I said, and reaction squeezed my throat shut.

Kissindre touched my arm. I jerked away, startled. She pulled her hand back.

I lifted my hand, because I hadn't meant it that way, hadn't wanted her to stop touching me. Suddenly I wanted to feel her arms around me, her lips on my bruised mouth; not caring that it would hurt, not caring what anyone thought. Just wanting to feel her against me, wanting her—

I took a deep breath, pulling myself together, and wiped my mouth again with the back of my hand. I realized finally that Ezra hadn't come with the rest of them. And I realized that I was almost as glad not to see him here as I was glad to be free. Realizing it pissed me off, but that didn't make it a lie. "No wonder the FTA is investigating Tau for rights violations," I muttered, looking hard at Kissindre's uncle.

He looked away, grimacing, but Sand said, "There was nothing illegal about what happened to you here."

I stared at him. "What do you mean?"

"Under the Internal Security Act, anyone suspected of behavior which threatens the corporate state can be detained, without any charges being brought against them, for indefinite two-year periods."

I almost asked if he was serious; didn't. It didn't take a mind reader to see that he didn't have that kind of sense of humor.

"It's been a part of virtually every combine charter," Perrymeade said, as if he had to explain it, or excuse it, "since colonial days, on worlds with . . . an indigenous population."

"That doesn't make it right," I said. I glanced at Kissindre.

She tried to meet my eyes; ended up looking away like her uncle had. She didn't say anything. Nobody said anything.

"I think I'll go back to the hotel now," I said as they stood there, staring at me like they'd been put on hold. "You coming?" I asked Kissindre, finally.

"I—Uncle Janos invited me to stay with his family tonight." She glanced at him, back at me. "Why don't you come home with us?"

"Yes, why don't you? You'd be very welcome," Perrymeade said. He looked directly at me for the first time since we'd come out of the station, as if he'd finally thought of a way to save face.

"I don't think so." I shook my head. I didn't have the stomach for spending what was left of the night discussing race relations with people who'd be fined a hundred fifty credits for failing to recycle. I wondered what the fine was for failing to keep your guests out of trouble . . . or failing to treat them like human beings. "Thanks anyway," I mumbled, realizing that what had come out of my swollen mouth said more than I'd meant it to.

"I really feel we need to discuss the . . . situation here, the circumstances—" Perrymeade broke off, gestured toward the mod that had come drifting down at some silent command of his. Tau's logo showed on its sleek, curving side.

I shook my head. "Nothing to say." I wasn't sure whether I meant them or me. The words sounded numb, the way my entire body felt now, except for the inside of my mouth. I probed a torn cheek with my bitten tongue, hurting myself.

"I'll see you back to the hotel, then—" Protz said, coming alive for the first time since I'd seen him in the doorway of the interrogation room. He put his hand on me like he expected me to disappear again.

I broke his hold, too roughly; saw Sand give me a look.

"I probably don't need to tell you," Sand said to me, "that we did not make any friends in there tonight." He nodded at the Corporate Security station behind us. I was surprised to find myself included in his *we*. "It was regrettable. But I would be . . . conservative, if I were you, about your future activities while you remain in Riverton."

I nodded, frowning.

"Then let me get you a taxi—" Protz insisted, treading water.

"I don't need your help," I said. I input the cab call on my databand, forcing them all to acknowledge that I had one, and the right to use it.

"It's after curfew," Protz said. "Be certain you go directly to the hotel—"

"Fuck off," I muttered, and he stiffened.

"Tomorrow we go out to the reefs." Kissindre moved in between us, forcing me to look at her. I wasn't sure if that was a promise, or just a reminder because she thought I wasn't tracking.

I nodded again, looked up into the night, searching the light-washed darkness for my transportation. They all waited around me until the taxi arrived. I got in, not able to stop Protz from giving it instructions before the door sealed. I slumped down in the seat and put my feet up as the mod lifted, finally able to drop my guard, finally leaving it all behind.

I looked out and down as the taxi carried me over the silent city. I thought about the good citizens of Riverton, all in their beds and sleeping because they'd been told to be, or pretending they were. I thought about Oldcity, where I'd spent most of my life . . . how it only really came alive at night. How I'd lived for the night, lived off it, survived because of it. Night was when the tourists and the rich marks from upside in Quarro came slumming, looking for things they couldn't get in a place like Tau Riverton. Oldcity existed because Quarro was a Federal Trade District, neutral ground. No single combine ran anything, or everything. You'd always find an Oldcity somewhere inside a place like Quarro.

There was no Oldcity here; no room for deviance in a combine 'clave. Everything was safe and sane; clean, polite, healthy, and prosperous. Under control. There was no unpunished crime down there in those streets, no illegal drugs. No thieves or whores or refugees, no orphans raped in alleys, no one coughing their guts up in public from a disease most people had forgotten the name of. No freaks.

The cab told me to get my feet off the upholstery. I put my feet down, feeling the memory of Oldcity like the pain of a festered wound. They wanted everyone to believe that life in this place was better than in a place like Quarro. That people were. But the rot was just better concealed. I rubbed my raw, weeping face with my blistered hand, looking out at the bright darkness of the night.

The mod let me off at the hotel entrance and reminded me not to forget anything. "Not a chance," I said. I went in through the vaulted lobby filled with trees and flowering shrubs that looked a lot healthier than I did, let the lift carry me up inside the tower, walked the last few meters to my own door, all without having to look a single overly solicitous member of the human staff in the face.

The door read my databand and let me in. It closed again behind me, sealing me in, so that I was safe at last in a room that looked exactly like every other room in this hotel. I wondered whether the rest of the team had gotten back from the reception. It didn't really matter, because I barely knew any of them except Ezra, and I didn't like Ezra.

I collapsed on the bed, asked the housekeeping system for ice and a first-aid kit. A flow-mural was seeping across the far wall: hypnotic forms in oozing black, the kind of art that could make you wake up in the morning wanting to slash your wrists without knowing why. I called on the threedy, blotting it out.

I asked for the Independent News. They didn't carry it here. I watched the replay of the Tau Late News flicker on instead, half listened through a rogue's gallery of people who'd been caught smuggling porn, littering, or leaving a public toilet without washing their hands.

There should have been something about the kidnapping. There wasn't. There was a short, empty piece on the arrival of the research team, though, with scenes of the party at the Aerie. It closed with a view of the cloud-reefs and a long shot of the cloud-whales themselves.

I reached for a headset and requested every visual the system had on file of the reefs and the cloud-whales. The room disappeared around me as the mask fitted itself against my face. I canceled the sound, because I already knew anything a Tau voicefeed would have told me. For a few minutes at least I could be somewhere I wanted to be: feeling the touch of the wind, looking out across view after view as each one carried me deeper into the mystery my senses called beauty. . . .

Until at last the feed of images—the reef formations laid out on the green earth like offerings for the eye of God, the cloud-whales blown like sunlit smoke across an azure sky—bled away into neural static. I lay still until the final phantom image had burned itself out of my nerve endings.

When the visions were gone, the memories of tonight were still waiting.

I told myself fiercely to remember why I was here; remember that Kissindre Perrymeade had wanted me on her crew because I could do this kind of interpretive work better than anyone else. I hadn't come to Refuge to get myself arrested over in Freaktown, to humiliate myself or her, to make Tau regret they had asked us here to perform a task that for once wouldn't be strictly for their profit. . . .

I blew through the menu of other programming, trying to find something that would keep me from thinking, something that would stop the fist of my anger from bruising the walls of my chest—anger that I couldn't forget and couldn't share and couldn't make go away. Something to relieve my tension so that I could sleep, so that I could face all those human faces tomorrow—all those eyes with their round, perfectly normal pupils—and not tell them to go to hell.

There was nothing on the vid menu now but public service programming, production documentaries, and a random selection of the mindrot interactives I could have spent hours lost in, and been perfectly happy, not so long ago. . . . Except that here the interactives began with a red censor logo, telling me they'd had the good parts cut out of them.

I jerked off the headset and threw it on the floor. The headset retracted into its slot at the bedside, drawn up by some invisible hand. It clicked into place in the smooth line of the console, as if it was making some kind of point about my personal habits. I ordered the wallscreen to blank and called on the music menu. It was just as stale. I lay back again on the bed that was exactly warm and exactly comfortable enough, sucked on ice as I stared at the white, featureless ceiling.

I lay on the bed without moving for a long time. After a while the room thought I'd gone to sleep, and turned off the lights. I barely noticed, lost in the dark streets of memory, colliding again and again with the image of a woman's anguished face, her voice begging me to help her. *They want to take my child.* . . . But it hadn't been her child. *Political,* they'd said. *Radicals, dissidents.* She'd been taking care of the child—*a boy, they said it was a boy, couldn't have been more than three or four.* Why had she said that—why that, why to me . . . ? She didn't know me, couldn't know what those words would do, couldn't know what had happened once, long ago, far away, to a woman like her, with a child like me . . . the darkness, the screams, and then the blinding end of everything. The darkness . . . falling and falling into the darkness.

FOUR

I WOKE UP again sprawled across the same perfect bed in the same perfect hotel room, just the way I'd left consciousness last night. My new clothes looked like I'd been mugged in them. I felt like I'd been mugged in them.

Sunrise was pouring through the window, which had been a wall last night, and the room was telling me courteously and endlessly to get my butt out of bed. I shook my hair out of my eyes and checked the time. "Jeezu!" I muttered. In another five minutes the team was due to leave for the research base Tau had set up on the Hydran Homeland.

I rolled out of bed, realizing as I tried to stand up how hungover I was. I stripped off my reception clothes, swearing at every bruise I uncovered. Even naked, there was no escape from the bitter memory of last night. I hurled the wad of clothing across the room. Then I pulled on the worn tunic and denim pants, the heavy jacket and boots that were the only kind of clothing I'd owned, or needed, until yesterday. There was nothing I could do about the scabs on my face or the dirt in my hair. I knotted a kerchief around my head and hoped no one looked at me.

I started out of the room, still feeling queasy, stepped back inside long enough to stick on a detox patch and empty a handful of crushed crackers out of the pocket of my formal jacket. I stuffed the crackers into my mouth and took the lift down.

I got out into the greenbelt square in front of the hotel on the heels of Mapes, the team's multisense spectroscopist. The rest of the team members were already there, eager to get their first view of the reefs. I pulled on my gloves and nodded good morning, not too obviously out of breath. A couple of the others looked at me twice, at the skid marks of last night all over my face. But they didn't ask.

"Morning," I said as Kissindre came up to me, dressed like I was now.

I saw her falter as she stopped by me. "Are you all right?" she asked, keeping it between the two of us, like the look she gave me as she touched my arm.

I didn't flinch away. "Sure," I said. "Corporate Security used to beat me up all the time."

Her breath caught, and I realized, too late, that she thought I meant something by it.

"Just kidding," I murmured, but she didn't believe me. "I'm fine. Did they get the kidnapper?"

Her gaze flickered. "No. Cat . . . that Hydran woman—was there more to what happened than you told Sand last night?"

I wondered who'd told her to ask me that. "No."

"Why did you leave the reception, then? Was it Ezra?"

"Give me more credit," I said. I looked away, frowning, because her eyes wouldn't leave me alone. "The Hydrans."

She stood a moment without saying anything. Finally, carefully, she asked, "You mean, because you're half Hydran . . .?"

I shook my head.

"Then—"

"Leave it alone, Kissindre."

She glanced down, with the look on her face that only I seemed to cause.

"It's not important," I said, feeling like a bastard. "It's over. I just want to forget about it."

She nodded, but I saw her doubt, the unanswered questions.

"How was your visit with your uncle?" Only asking because I had to say something, anything else.

She shrugged, pushing the corners of her mouth up. "Fine." For a minute I almost believed it, because she almost believed it. But then her face fell, as if the weight of the lie was too much. "Their neighbors really don't know he's the Alien Affairs Commissioner." She stared up into the sky, as if she'd discovered something incredible in the empty heights. "They really don't know." Her fists clenched inside her coat pockets, straining at the heavy cloth. "They don't."

I let my breath out; it sounded like a laugh, instead of the anger that was half choking me.

"Kiss—" Ezra Ditreksen came up beside her, putting his arm around her. "Missed you. . . ." He leaned over and kissed her on the mouth.

I looked away, figuring he was making a point. I searched my pockets for a camph, remembering that he hadn't been with her at the Corporate Security station last night. Maybe after the way he'd made Perrymeade look at the reception, he hadn't been invited.

"What happened to you?" he said, to me this time. "Did you get in a fight, for God's sake?"

I stuck the camph in my mouth, letting him have a good look at the bruises and the split lip. That he had to ask meant that he didn't actually know what had happened to me last night, that none of the others did. Suddenly I felt a lot better. "I fell down," I said.

He grimaced, disgusted, while all the expression disappeared from Kissindre's face. "I told you he was drunk," he muttered.

"Ezra," she said, frowning. It seemed to be the only thing she ever said to him, at least in my presence.

"You're lucky you didn't get into trouble with Corporate Security, going off like that," Ezra said to me. "Aside from the fact that you insulted our hosts."

I moved away, before I did something he'd regret for longer than I would.

A vibration that was both more and less than noise filled the air above me. I glanced up with the others, to see a transport dropping down out of the early morning sky. It settled onto the smooth surface of the landing terrace; its metallic skin flooded with logos in Tau's combine colors, endless safety warnings, and a diarrhea of instructions.

The hatch opened and Protz stepped out, wearing thermal clothing. I saw other figures waiting behind him in the shadowed interior. I wondered whether any of them were Hydran, since the whole reason for our team's existence was to study the cloud-reefs the Hydrans considered sacred ground. I wondered whether anyone had asked the Hydrans what they thought of our mucking around in their religious traditions. Probably not.

I watched as the others exited one by one. They were all human. I wasn't sure whether I was disappointed or relieved. The two FTA inspectors I'd seen at the party were here—a woman named Osuna and a man named Givechy. Neither of them looked like they expected to enjoy this much. Protz looked nervous. I wondered if he was afraid I'd spill my guts about last night. He didn't meet my eyes.

The last person out of the transport didn't look like he belonged with the rest. He could have been a hitchhiker, except for the Tau logos on his coat. He was tall and lean, probably in his late twenties, with black hair and dark eyes. His face was long and skeptical-looking, weathered to a kind of nutmeg color that reminded me of faces I'd seen in Freaktown, although I was sure he was all human.

Protz began to make introductions. That seemed to be his entire reason for existing. He introduced the stranger as Luc Wauno, a cloud-spotter for Tau. I looked at Wauno again with more interest: what he did was observe and record the movements of the cloud-whales . . . except for today, when his job seemed to be playing guide for us.

Wauno nodded, if he made any response at all, to each person he met. He looked like he'd rather be in the middle of nowhere staring at the sky. The only time he opened his mouth or even cracked a smile was when Protz introduced him to Kissindre. I saw him say a couple of words to her; noticed his teeth were crooked. You didn't see that much.

When Protz got to me, Wauno met my stare, and I could see his interest. "Hydran?" he asked me.

And because there was nothing behind the words, no insult, I nodded. "Half."

His deepset eyes flicked over the people around us. "Then I guess you're not a Refugee."

"Not lately," I said.

He studied my face again, checking out the damage. His hand rose to the small beaded pouch that hung from a cord around his neck. "Don't let them make you into one," he murmured. He shook his head and turned away as Protz closed in on us, frowning.

Wauno started back toward the transport. I followed with the others. Kissindre got the seat beside his, up front where the view was the best. Ezra took the seat next to mine, looking resentful and sullen, even though as usual I didn't see any reason for it.

Wauno leaned back in his seat and plugged his fingers into the control panel. I hadn't noticed anything unusual about his hands, only his teeth; even his augmentation had been sanitized by Tau. The transport took us up, leaving the plaza and the city behind like an afterthought.

I took a deep breath, looking ahead as we dropped off the edge of Tau's world, following the river over the falls and on along its snake-dancing course into the eroded landscape of the reefs, the heart of the Hydran reservation. The "Homeland," Tau called it, as if one part of this world could belong more to the Hydrans, by right, than another.

I forced myself to stop thinking about Tau, forced myself to stop replaying memories of last night and focus on the new day. I was about to experience something incredible, something that ought to put all our lives into some kind of perspective.

The cloud-whales, the aliens responsible for the existence of the reefs, had been a part of this world longer than either humans or Hydrans. They were colony-creatures, each individual made up of countless separate motes functioning together like the cells of a brain. They absorbed energy directly from sunlight, substance from the molecules of the air.

They spent their entire existence in the sky, condensing the atmospheric water vapor until they were shrouded in fog. To someone looking up with only human eyes, they were impossible to tell from the real thing. And looking down, if they did, nothing that humans or Hydrans had ever done here on this world seemed to concern them.

Nothing about their own existence was permanent; their forms mutated endlessly with the restless motion of the atmosphere . . . their thoughts flowed and changed, each one unique, shimmering, and random. But like the hidden order inside the chaos of a fractal pattern, there were moments of genius hidden in their whimsies.

And their thoughts were unique in another way—they had physical substance. As solid and tangible as human thoughts were insubstantial, the cloud-whales' cast-off musings fell from the sky, a literal fall of dreams. The dreamfall accreted in areas where the cloud-whales gathered, drawn by something about the landscape, the weather conditions, fluctuations in the planet's magnetosphere. Over time the excrement of their thoughts, their cast-off mental doodlings, formed strange landscapes like the one that was passing below us now. After centuries, or millennia, the reefs had become strata hundreds of kilometers long and hundreds of meters thick, rich with potential knowledge.

A "wild library" was what Tau's researchers called it, in the background data I'd accessed. The research team called it "cloud shit" when they thought no one was listening. The untouched reef formation we'd come to study—like the ones Tau was already exploiting—was an amino acid stew of recombinant products just waiting to be plucked out of the matrix and sent to labs hungry for progress, all for the greater profit of Draco.

Draco, through its subsidiary holdings, was a major player in nanotechnology research, but the nanotech field had been stagnant for years. Billions had been spent on research and resources by some of the most powerful combines in the Federation, but their successes had been limited at best, and the few useful tools and products they had developed were equally limited, no more than mindless, semifunctional industrial "helpers."

Proteins, especially enzymes, were nature's own nanotech, and the reefs were riddled with protoid matter so complex and bizarre that for the most part nobody had ever seen anything like it. Tau sent their most promising discoveries to specialized labs throughout Draco's interstellar hegemony, where researchers analyzed the structures and tried to reproduce the folding. Draco found a way to synthesize the ones that had potential; or if no technology existed that was sophisticated enough to reproduce a find, they demanded more of the raw product from Tau's mining operations.

But the same matrix that had produced bio-based "machines" stronger than diamond, and the hybrid enzymatic nanodrones that made ceralloy production possible, was booby-trapped with unpredictable dangers.

There were fragments of thought that did nothing but good; far more that were totally incomprehensible. And then there were the ones you could only describe as insane. The reef matrix kept them inert, potential, harmless.

But complex proteins degraded rapidly when they were removed from their stabilizing matrix; and there were "soft spots," vacuoles inside the reef itself where the matrix had begun to decay. The decaying material could cause anything from a bad smell to a kiloton explosion. There were a thousand different bio-hazard disasters just waiting for careless excavators. . . .

The databox my brain had been marinating in folded shut and shunted back into long-term memory, suddenly leaving my thoughts empty.

I let them stay that way. My mind sidestepped into a silence where no one else existed, where nothing existed for me but the reef along the river course below us, layer on layer of monolithic dreamscape. In the deepest part of my mind something stirred, and I knew why the Hydrans called these places sacred ground. . . . *I knew it. I knew it.* . . .

Something jolted me, and suddenly it was all gone.

I started upright in my seat, crowded between bodies in the transport's humming womb.

Ditreksen jabbed me again with his elbow. "Answer her, for God's sake," he said. "Or were you talking in your sleep?"

I leaned away from him, frowning.

"Yes," Kissindre murmured, but she wasn't looking at either of us. "That's exactly what it's like . . . how did you describe it—?" I realized she was talking to me. Except that I hadn't said anything.

Something I'd been thinking had slipped out. Just for a second, lost in awe, my mind had dropped its guard long enough for one stray image to escape. I swore under my breath, because it had happened without me even realizing it—the only way it ever happened, anymore. The harder I tried to control my telepathy, the less control I had. As soon as I believed in it, it would be gone.

"I forget," I muttered. Wauno glanced back over his shoulder at us, away again. I risked a look at the rest of the passengers: Protz, the Feds. None of them were looking at me. At least the image hadn't strayed far.

I slouched down and closed my eyes, closing everyone out. Their curiosity, their arrogance, their resentment, and their pity couldn't touch me, as long as I didn't let them in. . . .

I heard Kissindre shift in her seat, her attention drifting away again. She began talking to Protz, asking him questions about how to access Tau's data on the reefs: where to find it, why there wasn't more of it. He muttered something that sounded apologetic and bureaucratic.

"If you really want to know more about the reefs, you should talk to the Hydrans," Wauno said.

I opened one eye.

Protz made a snort that could have been a laugh. "There's no point to that. Anyway, it's out of the question."

Kissindre leaned toward Wauno. "Is there someone you know that we could talk with?"

Wauno nodded. "There's an *oyasin*. She knows more about the reefs than—"

"Now, just a minute," Protz hissed. "You're talking about that old witch—that shaman, or whatever she calls herself? We suspect her of supporting HARM! You aren't seriously suggesting that members of this research team go into the Homeland and look her up?" He glanced at the two Feds sitting in the rear of the transport, as if he didn't want this conversation going any further.

"Nobody's ever proved anything against her," Wauno said.

"At best she's nothing but a con artist. She'll tell you anything you want to hear." Protz glared at the back of Wauno's head. "And since she can read your mind, she knows what you want to hear." He looked back at Kissindre, pointing his finger. "And then she'll want you to pay for it, just like the rest of them. For God's sake—" he muttered, lowering his voice even more as he looked at Wauno again, "how can you even mention her with a straight face? And why are you encouraging outsiders to involve themselves with Hydrans, given the current . . . situation?"

Wauno looked out at the sky and didn't answer.

I shut my eyes and kept them shut.

I stayed like that for the rest of the flight, letting the conversations drone on around me until finally I did doze off.

I wasn't sure how long I'd slept by the time we reached the initial survey site. The transport let us out on a spit of beach caught in the river's meander below the reef-face. Everything we'd need to begin preliminary data collection was already there, in dome tents laid out with all the precision of Tau Riverton, as painless as anesthesia.

Workers were still moving around the site doing the setup. They all wore the same heavy maroon coveralls; they looked up at us as we entered the camp, with nothing much in their eyes but dull resentment. I wondered what they had to feel resentful about.

And there were more Tau vips waiting for us. That didn't seem to bother anyone except me, until Kissindre's uncle stepped out of the cluster of bodies. Sand was with him.

Perrymeade gestured at me. I glanced at Kissindre, saw the surprise on her face, and then the confusion as he shook his head, signaling her to stay where she was.

"What now—?" Ezra muttered behind me.

I started across the open ground toward Perrymeade and Sand, not looking back, not looking ahead, either. I had no idea what they wanted; I only knew that if they were here in person it had to be something I didn't want to know about.

"What?" I said to Perrymeade, barely able to keep my voice even, with nothing left to make the word civil.

"It's about last night. The kidnapping," he said, looking like a man with a gun to his head.

I stopped breathing. *Shit.* I met his eyes, saw the blank incomprehension as he registered what showed in mine. "Let's get it over with," I muttered, feeling a dozen sets of eyes holding me in a crossfire.

"I thought you couldn't do that," he said.

"What?" I said again, probably looking as confused as he did this time.

"Read minds. I thought you were dysfunctional."

I felt the blood come back to my face in a rush. "I am. What about it?"

"Then how do you know why we're here?"

I shrugged. "Because it only makes sense that you'd want to get rid of me."

The look on his face got odder. "That's not it at all," he said, and suddenly he looked relieved. "We want your help in dealing with the kidnapper you encountered last night."

"Jeezu—" I turned away, not sure whether it was relief or anger that made my brain sing. I looked back at him. "Why?" I said. "Why me?"

"The Hydran Council is being . . . uncooperative," Sand answered. "We think maybe they'd talk to you, as an"—he glanced at my eyes—"outsider."

"A freak," I said.

He shrugged.

"They all know that you were willing to help a Hydran woman you thought was in trouble," Perrymeade said, looking self-conscious.

"She set me up. She used me. She thinks I'm stupid." *She knows what I am.* I shook my head. "I can't do that. The Hydrans aren't going to trust me."

"I don't have many options here," Perrymeade said. "And unfortunately, neither do you."

Kissindre came up beside me. "Is there a problem?" she said, matching the look on Perrymeade's face as it turned to annoyance. She folded her arms, standing on her own ground, the team leader and not the dutiful niece.

"No problem," I said, meeting Perrymeade's eyes. "I've got work to do." I started to turn away.

"Borosage has issued a deportation order on you," Sand said behind my back. "If you don't cooperate, the Tau government will revoke your work permit. You'll be off this project and off the planet inside of a day."

I turned back, slowly, and looked at them: Sand with his inhuman eyes, Perrymeade hanging on invisible puppet strings beside him.

"You miserable bastard," Kissindre whispered, so far under her breath that even I barely heard it. I wondered which one she meant; hoped for her sake it was Sand. "What is this?" she asked. "Uncle Janos—?"

"It's about the kidnapping." I jerked my head at Sand. "They want me to be their cat's-paw."

Kissindre started, the only one of them who got the reference.

"Go-between," Perrymeade said. "Our go-between with the Hydrans, Kissindre. We're not getting the cooperation we need from the Hydran community to . . . to rescue the kidnapped child. Under the circumstances, it seems that Cat is the logical person to help us—the only person who might have a chance of gaining the Hydrans' trust or cooperation." He turned back to me. "We really need your help, son."

"Right," I said.

"Damn it! This is asinine—" Kissindre's fists settled on her hips as she looked from Perrymeade to Sand. "You brought us here to do work for you. I thought that was important for Tau's 'rehabilitation.' How in the nine billion names of God are we supposed to do this work if you're already interfering with it?"

"Kissindre . . ." Perrymeade said. He glanced at Sand too, as if he wasn't sure about what he was going to say next. "The kidnapped child is your cousin."

"What?" she said. "Who?"

"My nephew Joby. My wife's sister's son."

"Joby? The baby, the one who was—" She broke off.

He nodded. "He was taken by the Hydran woman who worked as his therapist. I set up the exchange program that gave her the training and put her in that position."

Realization filled her eyes. "My God," she murmured. "Why didn't you tell me last night?"

He glanced at Sand again. "I didn't even find out myself until this morning." His voice was even, but there was resentment in it. "This whole situation is one that the Tau government wants played down, for . . . a number of reasons." He glanced away again, not looking at any of us this time. I followed his line of sight to the spot where the two Feds were standing, out of earshot, listening to Ezra lecture them about the equipment. "But especially because they believe the boy was taken by a radical group. His safety depends on our keeping this quiet. If it becomes public knowledge, there could be—incidents that would endanger Joby's safety and hurt people on both sides of the river."

"And make the Feds ask questions you don't want to answer," I said.

He frowned. "That is not the point."

"Yes, it is. It's keiretsu."

"Don't make judgments about situations you don't understand," Sand said irritably. He turned back to Kissindre. "I am extremely sorry for this intrusion. You will have no further interference from us, I promise you. But your team will have to function without one of its members for now. Whether that is a temporary or a permanent situation is up to him." He bent his head at me.

I scratched my face, winced. "So if I go, and I talk to the Hydran Council, that's it?" I glanced at Perrymeade, back at Sand. "If they won't deal with me, then you'll leave me alone?"

Sand nodded.

I nodded, finally. "All right," I said. I glanced at Kissindre. "I'm sorry."

She shook her head. "No. I'm sorry." She looked at her uncle; he looked down. I wondered what she was thinking as she walked away and left us standing there.

Wauno raised his eyebrows as Perrymeade ordered him to take us back to Tau Riverton. But he did it, not asking any questions. Maybe he was more of a company man than I'd thought, or maybe he just didn't give a damn.

When we were over Riverton again, Perrymeade gave Wauno an address and told him to take us down.

"What are we doing?" I said. "I thought we were going to meet with the Hydrans."

"We're making a stop here," Perrymeade said, acknowledging my existence for the first time since we'd gotten into the transport. "I want you to meet the parents of the missing child."

I stiffened. "You didn't say anything about that."

"I want you to meet my sister-in-law," Perrymeade said. "I want you to have some sense of who she is and what she's been through."

I felt my face flush. "No." Wauno glanced back at us and away.

"If you really understand what she's going through, then it will be easier for you to make the Hydrans understand it."

"Or would you rather have us drop you at the Corporate Security station for your escort off the planet?" Sand murmured. Wauno glanced back over his shoulder again.

I folded my arms across my chest, my hands clenching on the heavy folds of my jacket.

"I really hope we don't have to do that," Sand said.

I looked out the window and didn't say anything.

Wauno landed us on a public access, and we got out. He touched his forehead with his fingers in a kind of salute, nodding at me, before he sealed the hatch again. I watched the transport rise out of reach and disappear into the cold morning sky.

Perrymeade led the way across a perfectly landscaped park-space to a high-rise plex. Sand stayed a little behind me without seeming to, ready to step on my heels if I lagged. I didn't see a single piece of litter or dog shit anywhere as we walked.

The residence complex reminded me of my hotel and every other building I'd been inside of since I got here. Maybe it looked more expensive. Before long we were standing in front of a door on an upper floor. The security system took Perrymeade's ID and let us in.

A small, neat, dark-haired woman met us inside. Her upslanting brown eyes searched our faces, looking for something—a sign, hope. She didn't find it. Her own face was colorless where it wasn't red and swollen, as if she'd cried for a long time, recently. But she wasn't crying now, and her face settled into resignation. "Janos," she said. "There's no news." It could have been a question, an answer, or just something to say.

Perrymeade shook his head. "I'm sorry, Ling."

The woman seemed to recognize Sand. Her glance skittered off his face, landed on me as Sand gave me an unobtrusive shove forward.

"So far the Hydrans have been . . . reluctant to give us information," Perrymeade said, "if they actually have any to give. But we've brought someone with us who may be able to help." He nodded at me as another man came into our line of sight. The man was tall and dark; he had on a Corporate Security uniform. I froze, not sure whether he was supposed to be the father or one of Borosage's goons. But his uniform had different datapatches—he was in plant security. *The father*. He put his arms around the woman. The grief on his face matched hers.

They looked me over silently for some clue about what I was doing here, until their combined gaze reached my face, registered my eyes. Then they knew. The man shook his head. The woman's mouth made a silent *oh*.

In the space behind them I noticed five or six other people watching, waiting—friends, or family, maybe. One of the women came forward, touched Perrymeade's arm, spoke to him. He nodded, distracted, and she moved away again. She was small and dark-haired, with the same upslanting eyes as the mother. I wondered if she was the woman's sister, Perrymeade's wife.

"This is Cat," Perrymeade said. "He's with the xenoarchaeol-

ogy team. He was the last person to see the kidnappers last night."
I realized that what he meant was *the last human*. "I thought I
should bring you together to . . . share what you know about what
happened."

Sand gave me another hidden elbow; I had to move or fall
down. I took one painful step and then another into the home of
the people whose child I'd helped kidnap. I groped through my
memories of last night in Borosage's interrogation room until I
found their names. I seemed to remember Ling and Burnell
Natasa. Their son was Joby. I wondered whether Perrymeade had
forgotten to introduce them to me because he really was as worried about their child as they were, or whether he was just being
an inconsiderate shit. I supposed it didn't matter either way.

"Cat—?" the woman said dubiously, the way people usually
did.

I nodded, still not looking directly at either of them.

They led us into a large open room that looked out on sky and
parkland. Their other visitors didn't follow. Everything in the
room was expensive, spotless, and perfectly matched to everything else. I settled into a modular seat with its back to the view.
The sight of so much open space made me dizzy.

The parents sat down across from me, under a threedy screen
tuned to the endless drone of the Tau newscast. I wondered
whether they actually believed it would tell them something. The
man ordered it off, and suddenly the wall was a blank slate,
white, empty. Sand and Perrymeade were still standing at the limits of my vision, almost out of sight, but not out of mind. I hugged
my chest and waited.

"You saw Joby and . . . and Miya last night?" the father asked.

I made myself look into his eyes and nod.

"Where?" he asked when that was all I did.

"In Fre—in the Hydran town," I said, not sure why just saying
that made my face burn.

"You have relatives there?" the mother asked me, as if she
thought that was why I could help them, or maybe because that
was the only reason she could imagine for anyone going to
Freaktown.

"No," I said, glancing away.

"Yes," Perrymeade said. "In a sense . . ." as I looked up at him, frowning.

I looked down again, knowing that it was already obvious to everyone here that I had Hydran blood.

"Did you try to stop her?" the father asked. "Did you see our son? Was he all right—?"

Looking back at my memories, I realized the boy in her arms could have been dead, for all I knew. But somehow I didn't think so. "It was dark. I saw them for less than a minute. It all happened so fast." My hands knotted together between my knees.

"He helped them get away from Corporate Security," Sand said.

"For God's sake—" The father half rose from his seat.

I glared at Sand. "She said it was her child! She said they were trying to take her child."

"So you . . . you believed you were helping her, then?" the mother asked, her voice thready, her eyes intent.

I nodded, biting the insides of my mouth.

"Is that what Corporate Security thinks?" the father asked, glancing from Perrymeade to Sand.

"They questioned him thoroughly." Sand's unblinking silver eyes glanced off the scabs and bruises that had made half my face look like some kind of bizarre cosmo job. Everyone's eyes were back on me then. Suddenly my face hurt.

"Joby doesn't look Hydran." Burnell Natasa gave me a look as he sat back down again. *Not like you do.* I saw it in his eyes.

"It was dark," I said again. "I couldn't tell."

"And if you hadn't interfered, they might have caught her?" his wife asked. There was more grief than anger in her voice.

I shrugged, slumping back in my seat.

"He feels responsible, Ling. That's why he volunteered to help us negotiate with the Hydrans," Perrymeade said, as slick as glass. "To make up for his mistake."

"What do you think you can do that the Tau authorities can't?" the father asked me. "Can you read their minds? Find out what they've done with our son—?"

I glanced at Perrymeade, because I didn't have an answer for that one either. He didn't give me any help. So instead I asked the question that had been gnawing at my thoughts since last night: "Why did you hire a Hydran to take care of your son?" Considering how most people reacted to Hydrans on this world, I couldn't believe it was something they would have done just because Hydrans were cheap labor.

The father stiffened, barely controlling his reaction. He looked at Perrymeade and then Sand. His mouth thinned, and he didn't say anything.

The mother got up and moved across the room to a low table. She picked up a picture and brought it to me. "This is Joby, with Miya," she said. "Is this the woman you saw last night?"

As she put the frame into my hands it activated, showing me a Hydran woman—the one I'd seen last night—crouched down, holding a human child in her arms.

"That's her," I whispered finally, as I realized that my silence had gone on for too long. A rush of sourceless heat made me giddy, as if her face was the face of a lost lover. I forced myself to focus on the child in her arms. He was maybe one or two, with dark curls and a round, sweet baby face. I watched him wave, saw him smile. . . .

There was something wrong with him. I couldn't put a name to it as the realization slid down my back like cold lips. I glanced at Ling Natasa; saw her catch my expression. This time she was the one who looked away.

She took the picture back. "Our son suffered neurological damage," she said, barely audible. "Before he was born. I'm a biochemist. There was a . . . an accident in the lab while I was pregnant. Joby was affected."

I wondered what kind of accident would cause a defect so severe that they couldn't fix it. I wondered why she'd gone ahead and had the baby, if she knew . . . but maybe that was a question no one could answer. I wondered what had gone on in her mind then; wondered what was going on in it now.

"Joby has no way of interacting with the world around him," she said, the words dreary and full of pain. "He can't speak, he can't hear, he can't control his body. His mind is whole, inside that . . . that precious prison. But he's completely helpless."

Her eyes turned distant; she wasn't seeing any of us anymore. I wondered whether she was wondering where he was now, whether he was crying and afraid, whether someone was hurting him. . . . I glanced at his picture, and my stomach knotted.

She looked at me again, and she didn't react at the sight of my strange eyes. "We hired Miya to care for him because she's the only one who can reach him."

I blinked as I realized what she meant: what made a Hydran perfect for the job of caring for their son. *Her psi.* A therapist with the Gift could penetrate that shell of flesh, make contact with the mind locked inside it, in a way that no human ever could . . . not even his parents.

"She did things for him that . . . we couldn't do," Ling Natasa said, as if she'd read my mind. This time I heard longing and pain—her own pain—in the words.

"Do you have any other children?" I asked.

She looked up at me, suddenly, sharply. I wasn't sure what the look meant. "No," she said, and that was all.

I didn't ask why not. Maybe one like this was enough.

"Miya . . . Miya was devoted to Joby. She was always there for him . . . she was his lifeline. And ours, to him."

"She was trained at our medical facilities to do rehabilitation therapy," Burnell Natasa said. "She was able to help Joby so much because—" He broke off, glanced uncomfortably at Sand.

"Because of her Gift," Ling Natasa said, glancing at me. It surprised me to hear someone who wasn't a psion call it that, speak about it the right way.

"Then she wasn't wearing a detector?" Sand demanded.

"A detector?" I said. "What's that?"

"It delivers a shock when it detects psi activity." He looked at me with his usual pitiless indifference. "Like the stun collars Corporate Security uses to monitor petty criminals. I assume you're familiar with those."

I flushed and looked away.

"She was a fully licensed therapist," Perrymeade said, sounding defensive now. "She was the first to complete the program . . . a cooperative program that I set up with the support of Riverton's medical center and the Hydran Council. They were training Hydrans as therapists to help patients like my nephew, who can't be helped by conventional treatment. Joby's condition gave me the idea for it."

Sand half frowned, but he didn't say anything more.

"Miya was like a part of our family," Ling Natasa said. "Why would she do something like this—?" She looked at Perrymeade this time, her eyes begging him to make sense of something that was beyond her comprehension. He shook his head.

"We've heard rumors—" Burnell Natasa glanced over his shoulder at the visitors waiting in the next room. "Everyone's heard about—rituals the Hydrans have," he said bitterly. "That they steal our children and use them—"

"Jeezu!" I pushed up out of my seat. I caught Sand's warning gesture; sat down again. His gaze pinned me there. "It's not true," I said, glaring at him, at all of them, even though it could have been, for all I knew about how Hydrans lived. But my gut told me only a human could do a thing like that, or even imagine it.

"How do you know?" Burnell Natasa said. "If you're not one of them."

I stared at him, at his uniform.

"Cat is a xenologist," Perrymeade answered. "He works with Kissindre. . . . You know how much time I've spent with the Hydrans, Burnell. I'm sure he's right."

Natasa shook his head. "Borosage said he has cases on record—"

"District Administrator Borosage has many years of experience dealing with Hydrans, but I think we all know that he also has certain . . . limitations." Perrymeade mouthed the words as if they were hot, glancing at Sand. "But Corporate Security's concern about the involvement of Hydran dissidents in your son's kidnapping isn't unjustified, considering the situation within the Tau keiretsu. . . ."

"Did this Miya ever mention anything about the inspectors or the FTA?" I asked. "Were you involved in anything that the Hydrans might not have liked—something she might have picked out of your thoughts?"

"No." They both said it so quickly that it seemed to echo. Their eyes met, and then they both looked at me. "Is he a telepath—?" the husband asked Perrymeade. Perrymeade shook his head with no hesitation; Kissindre must have told him that I'd lost my psi. Maybe that was why he'd brought me here: *Because I was safe.* There was a reason why most humans didn't want a mind reader anywhere near them. Everyone had things they wanted to hide, and a telepath didn't just eavesdrop on conversations—he could listen in on your most intimate secrets.

The Natasas must be a matched pair of saints if they were willing to share their home with a Hydran. Or else they loved that crippled child more than the keiretsu . . . more than their work, their privacy, themselves.

But then I saw the look they exchanged as my question registered, the looks that went on changing the other faces in the room, always turning them grimmer. And I knew that whatever these people were, they weren't innocent. I could almost feel their hidden panic. There had to be secrets—big ones, bad ones, filling the silence around me. Right then I would have given a year of my life to have one bloodred drug patch riding behind my ear, the kind that could lay open the scar tissue blinding my Gift and let me see, for an hour, for even ten minutes—for however long it took.

But I didn't, and I couldn't. And maybe it didn't matter anyway. It wasn't my problem, any of it, except the missing child— and that was only because my guilt said I'd been to blame. I'd do whatever Perrymeade and Sand told me to do, knowing it wouldn't help anything; do it because then they'd leave me alone and my conscience would leave me alone, and I could get back to doing things that were important to me.

I looked up again, directly into Ling Natasa's gaze. Memory stabbed me behind the eyes, the way it had last night. But this time the pain was genuine. Reality had reached into this expensive, perfect room, into two comfortable, protected lives, and destroyed all their illusions in one irreversible moment. There was no escape for anyone from grief and pain, from fear that wore the face of a lost child, helpless, crippled, afraid, in the hands of strangers, aliens. . . . Her husband put his arms around her again. This time when he looked at me, I still saw it, the grief and the fear.

"I'll do what I can," I murmured, hating how it sounded; wanting, needing to have something better to say. "I know how you feel," I said finally. I looked away as the disbelief in their eyes turned the empty words back on me.

Perrymeade and Sand were already on their feet, looking eager to be gone now that they'd gotten what they'd come for. I followed them through the empty good-byes and out of the building, more eager to leave than they were.

When we were out in the open plaza again, I raised my head for long enough to see what expressions Perrymeade and Sand were wearing. "What do you want me to do?" I asked, hoping they had more of an idea than I did.

Perrymeade glanced at me, as if he wondered why I wasn't angry anymore. "Some of the leaders of the Hydran community have agreed to see me, to discuss the situation and what might be done about it." He sounded as if he didn't want to say that much. "I want you to come with me to meet them." I wondered what was wrong with everyone here, whether they were all that paranoid about keeping an appearance of control, or whether Tau's ax was always that ready to fall on someone's neck.

I sat down on a bench. "Maybe you ought to tell me more about it," I said. "I'm not a mind reader." I took out a camph and stuck it between my teeth.

Their mouths quirked. I sat watching them stand, uncomfortable, against the backdrop of Tau Riverton's deceptive order.

"You don't want the Feds to know this is happening, do you?" I asked.

"No." Sand looked back at me with his unblinking eyes. "What we're doing is damage control, at this point. We want this matter settled cleanly and quietly—immediately."

That explained why there hadn't been anything on the news about the kidnapping. "Why did the Hydran woman take the boy? You said she was working with terrorists?"

"The Hydran Aboriginal Resistance Movement," he said. "A radical group. They've sent us a list of demands for the boy's release."

" 'HARM'?" I said, realizing what the letters spelled. "They call themselves 'HARM'—?"

"We do," Perrymeade murmured, rubbing his neck. "They don't use the term 'Hydran.' The Hydrans prefer to call themselves simply 'the Community.' "

The Human Federation had called them "Hydrans" because we'd first encountered them in the Beta Hydrae system. But the real meaning of the name cut far deeper: in human mythology, the Hydra had been a monster with a hundred heads. "What kind of demands are they making?"

"The usual," Perrymeade said, sounding tired. "More autonomy . . . but also more integration, more job opportunities, more of Tau's money; reparations for the entire planet, which they claim we stole from them. They want the Federation's attention turned on them while the FTA's inspection team is here."

"That sounds fair to me," I said. I rolled the camph between my fingers, focusing on the bitter cold/heat inside my mouth.

Perrymeade raised his eyebrows and sighed. "I'm sure it does to them too. It even does to me, when I try to see it their way. But it isn't that simple. It wasn't Tau that took control of this world away from them—or Draco, for that matter." He glanced at Sand as he said it. "If they had more autonomy at this point, what good would it do them? They've come to rely on Tau as their support system just as much as Tau's human citizens . . . possibly more. The Hydrans have no real technological or economic base; they lost their interstellar network long before we got here. Where would they be without us?"

I put the camph back between my lips so that I didn't have to answer.

"If they think the FTA will see it differently, they're wrong." He shook his head. "They don't want to believe that—I don't even want to believe that—but that's how it is. The real problem isn't simply that their eyes look ab—" he broke off as I looked up at him, "strange . . . that their eyes seem strange to us," he muttered, "or the color of their skin, or that they don't eat meat. None of that matters anymore." His hand tightened. "Hydrans are *different*. They have the ability to intrude profoundly on another person's life, to violate a person's privacy at any given moment—" His eyes, which had been looking at me without seeing me, suddenly registered my face, my eyes again. "It's not that easy," he said, looking away. "It's not easy at all. Maybe it's impossible."

"Tell me about it," I said, and swallowed the butt end of the camph. "So if the Feds won't do anything to force Tau to change its policies, why is Tau afraid to let them find out what happened?"

"It wouldn't look good," Sand said. "Obviously we don't want it to appear that some group of radicals is functioning, unchecked, as the major influence in the Hydran Homeland. It isn't good for Tau's image—or for the Hydrans' either—if the FTA sees social chaos over there." He jerked his head in the direction of the river. "The kind of attention that it will attract from the FTA will not be the sort that HARM intends, believe me."

I listened, squinting at him in the reflected glare of too many windows in too many towers, grimacing as my mind cut through the self-serving bullshit to the truth: *They were right.* Humans would never feel safe enough to share real power with Hydrans. And the FTA was just as human as Tau, when it came to that.

"I see what you mean," I said, getting up again. I looked toward the plex where the missing child's parents were going through a kind of hell that cut across all the artificial barriers of race and money, that proved the only universal truth was pain. "But what do you think I can do to change that?"

Perrymeade's body language eased, as if he finally understood what he saw in my face, or thought he did. But still he hesitated before he said, "We've told the Hydran Council everything that Sand has explained to you. But they still claim to know nothing. I can't believe that. You share a . . . heritage with them, but you've lived among humans. You have a better chance of making them understand what they're risking by harboring these dissidents. . . ."

What they were risking. I touched my head. I could tell the Hydrans what they had to lose . . . but who knew if they'd even give me a chance. All they had to do was look at me; all they had to do was try to touch my mind. I glanced at Perrymeade and Sand. There was no point in trying to explain anything to them; they wouldn't give a damn anyway.

"I have a question, before you go," Sand said, turning to me. "Why aren't you a functional telepath? Perrymeade said you used to be a telepath, but now you're not. How do you get rid of a thing like that?"

I looked straight in through his dim, dead eyes. "You have to kill someone."

He started. I wondered how long it had been since someone had surprised him. I wondered exactly what it was about what I'd said that had.

"You killed someone?" Perrymeade echoed.

"That's what I said, isn't it?" I glanced at him. "When I was seventeen. I blew him away with a tightbeam handgun. It was self-defense. But it doesn't matter if you're a psion and some-one's brain goes nova inside you. If I was really Hydran, it would've killed me. But I wasn't Hydran enough. All it did was fuck up my head. So now I'm only human."

Perrymeade's face went a little slacker. I watched him pull it together again with a negotiator's reflex.

Neither of them said anything more, until finally a mod came spiraling down out of the heights and Sand said, "Good-bye."

FIVE

A PRIVATE CORPORATE mod took us over to Freaktown. No wandering through its streets on foot for a Tau vip, even one whose job was to pretend that he understood its people as well as he did his own. As we passed over the river I looked down, seeing the lone bridge, one tenuous filament connecting two peoples and the different ways they looked at the same universe. I thought about Miya: how she'd been chosen, trained, to help a human child the way no human could. How she had helped him. . . .

And then she'd betrayed him. I wondered whether I was seeing too incomplete an image to make sense of the truth, or whether Hydrans really were that alien, so alien I'd never understand how their minds worked.

The mod came down again somewhere deep in the heart of Freaktown. We stepped out into the enclosed courtyard of a sprawling structure Perrymeade told me was the Community Hall. *Community* meant *Hydran,* to Hydrans. *Community . . . communing, communication, to live in a commune . . . to have a common destiny, history, mind. . . .* My own mind played with the word like a dog gnawing a bone, finding meanings layered inside meanings, wondering whether any of them were ones the Hydrans had intended.

Here in the courtyard, sealed off from the decaying streets, there were actually a few shrubs and trees; a few of the colors of life, only a little dusty and overgrown. I looked down. A garden of brightly tiled mosaic spread outward from where I stood. Dim with age and dust, it still made my eyes strobe.

Off to my left a stream barely the width of my open hand wove a silver thread through the dry shrubbery. Half hidden in the bushes I could see a velvet patch of mossgrass, so green and perfect that I started toward it without thinking.

I stepped across the stream onto the waiting patch of green . . . and found the knee-high sculpture of a Hydran woman sitting cross-legged on a mandala of tile. Her inset eyes of green stone met mine, as if she had been expecting me to be expecting this.

No one in the courtyard could see what I was seeing now. No one who didn't step across the stream would ever see it. I smiled.

I looked up as someone emerged from the shadows at the far side of the courtyard: a Hydran, striding toward the others as if he was only human, as though he didn't have a better way to get from one place to another. He was one of the guests from the reception last night. My memory offered up his name: Hanjen.

He stopped almost in midstride as he saw me. The look on his face was the same look my own face still wore: pure astonishment.

I stepped back across the stream into the courtyard. He stood perfectly still, watching as I rejoined Perrymeade by the mod.

At last he made a small bow and said something in a language that must have been Hydran.

"What did he say?" I murmured to Perrymeade.

"I don't know," Perrymeade said. "Some sort of greeting. I don't know what it means."

"You don't speak their language?" It wasn't that difficult to learn a language by accessing. And someone at his level in a corporate government had enough bioware to let him run a translator program, if accessing was too much trouble for him. "Why not?"

He shrugged and looked away from me. "They all understand ours."

I didn't say anything; I just went on looking at him.

"Besides," he murmured, as if I'd said what I was thinking, or maybe because I hadn't, "the Hydrans claim all language is only second best. So there's really no difference."

"Yes, there is," I said. I looked away again, listening for something else: trying to tell whether Hanjen reached out to me with his mind, trying to be open. Waiting for a whisper, a touch, anything at all; desperate for any contact, for proof that I wasn't a walking dead man, or the last one alive in a world of ghosts.

But there was nothing. I watched the Hydran's face. Emotion moved across it like ripples over a pond surface. I didn't know what the emotions were because I couldn't feel them, couldn't prove that he was real, any more than I could prove that I wasn't utterly alone here.

"Mez Perrymeade," he said, glancing away from me as if I didn't exist. "We have been expecting you. But why have you brought this one," meaning me, "with you?" The words were singsong but almost uninflected, not giving anything away.

"Mez Hanjen," Perrymeade said, trying to hold himself as still as the Hydran did. He looked like he was trying to hold back water. "I asked him to come."

"No," I said, forcing myself to meet Hanjen's stare. "You asked me to come. Last night, at the party." We were all speaking Standard, now. I wondered whether anyone from Tau had ever bothered to learn the Hydrans' language. I wondered suddenly why Hydrans even had one, needed one, when they could communicate mind-to-mind. The data on Hydran culture that was freely accessible on the Net was so spotty I hadn't been able to learn even that much about them.

Hanjen made a small bow to me. "That is true. However, I hardly expected, under the circumstances . . ." He broke off, looking toward the spot where I'd discovered the hidden statue. He shook his head, glancing at me again as he began to turn away.

He stopped suddenly and turned back, making eye contact with us. "Excuse me," he murmured. "I meant to say, 'Please follow me, the members of the Council are waiting.'"

"Are they all like that?" I muttered as we started after him.

Perrymeade shrugged and grimaced as Hanjen disappeared into patterns of light and shadow.

For a second I thought Hanjen had disappeared entirely, teleported himself, making some point by leaving us behind. My chest hurt as I wondered whether I'd been the reason. But when I stepped into the shadows beyond the courtyard I saw him moving ahead of me through a lightplay of organic forms—trees and shrubs, columns and arches built on the same fluid lines. There wasn't a right angle anywhere; wherever I looked, my eyes had trouble telling life from art.

Hanjen led us without a word, not looking back, along a sheltered walkway. The path wandered like a stream through a maze of vine-hung arbors; the arbors became a series of chambers, their ceilings and walls as random as the walls of caves. In some of the chambers every inch of wall was covered with patterned tiles; some had ceilings inlaid with geometries of age-darkened wood. There were flower-forms and leaf-forms spreading like vines up any pillar or wall that wasn't decorated with mosaics. My mind could barely take it in as we passed through one room and then another. Perrymeade had called this the Community Hall, but the words didn't begin to describe it. I wondered what it really was, how old, what meaning it must have held for the ones who had originally constructed it.

Other Hydrans passed us as we made our way deeper into the maze of chambers and passages. The unconscious grace of their movements seemed to match the sinuous beauty of the spaces we were passing through. I kept my gaze fixed on the ceiling, the walls, the floor; afraid to meet anyone else's eyes, afraid I'd catch them looking in through mine.

At last we entered an echoing vault of a room where a dozen other Hydrans waited. They sat or kneeled at a low free-form table, looking toward us as if they'd been expecting us. I looked away from them—looked up, and thought I was looking at the sky. Above us there was a blue translucent dome painted with clouds. Birds, or something like them, were soaring toward the brightness of the sunlit zenith, as if they'd been startled into flight by our arrival.

I stopped dead, looking up; stood staring a moment longer, until my mind finally convinced my eyes that what they were seeing wasn't real—that the birdlike things were only images, frozen in flight against a painted sky. No wings fluttered; there was no movement toward that burning glaze of light.

I looked down; the room and its faces rushed back into place around me.

"Remarkable, isn't it?" Perrymeade murmured as he passed me. "It always stops people cold the first time they see it."

I followed him, keeping my eyes on his back until I reached the low table. Around it were seats, more than enough, although some of the Hydrans kneeled on mats on the floor. The seats were made of wood like the table; like the table, they'd been carved into nonlinear, organic forms. Their wood smelled of oil and age. I hoped they were more comfortable than they looked.

There was no sign of a high-tech insert on the table or anywhere else in the room, even though this was apparently the meeting space for the only formal government the Hydrans had. I wondered whether they really didn't need human-style data storage or whether Tau had simply refused to give them access to it.

Hanjen bowed to the waiting Council members. They nodded in return. Perrymeade was already sitting down. I faced the silent circle at last, hesitating as I chose a seat. I recognized two of the Hydrans as Moket and Serali, the ones who'd been at the party last night with Hanjen. There were more older members than younger ones on the Council, but it was divided about equally between the sexes.

All of them looked well fed. They wore new, well-cut clothing that must have come from across the river; the clothes they'd chosen looked expensive, even stylish. It didn't match what I'd seen on people in Freaktown's streets. Neither did the jewelry they wore— and there was a lot of it—although some of the pieces were odd and old enough to have been heirlooms. Several of them wore nose rings, which were definitely not the look over in Riverton.

A creature that matched the ceiling's painted birds perched on one man's shoulder. I studied it, trying to get a better idea of what it actually was. It was gray-furred, not feathered, more like a bat than a bird, with a long pointed face and enormous ears folded like origami. It raised its head, looking back at me with bright darting eyes.

And then suddenly it launched into the air, spreading leathery wings a handbreadth wide. It flew straight at me, right into my face.

I flung my hands up as claws raked my flesh inside a slapping, flapping confusion of wings. I fell into a chair as the bat-thing lifted off of me again.

I lowered my hands. Figures loomed over me; one of them was Perrymeade. He was speaking to me, but I couldn't seem to make out the words.

I struggled upright in my seat, smarting with scratches and humiliation; saw someone pass the chittering bat-thing back to its owner.

The Hydran who gathered it into his hands glared at me as if the attack had been my fault, but I couldn't tell what he was thinking, what any of them thought, what the hell had happened. . . . Except for the shrill, almost inaudible squeaks of the bat-thing, the room was totally silent.

And then the bat-thing's owner disappeared.

"What the hell—?" I mumbled, rubbing my face. The words sounded like a shout. The Hydrans were looking back and forth at each other, some of them gesturing in the silence that went on and on. The room was filled with conversation, if only I could have heard it.

My hands tightened over the table edge. Perrymeade sat down beside me, trying not to look as shaken as I did. If he wasn't fooling me, he wasn't fooling anyone else. The silence stretched; everyone looked at us, somehow without acknowledging us.

Finally Perrymeade took a deep breath and said, "We've come, as you know, to ask your help in finding a kidnapped human child—"

"Excuse me," Hanjen said, almost impatiently, as if Perrymeade had interrupted some private discussion. Maybe he had. "We must ask if you would please leave us for a time, Mez Perrymeade. We need to speak with this one"—he raised his hand to point at me, a beat late, as if he'd forgotten it was necessary—"alone." And then, seeing the surprise on Perrymeade's face, he said, "Forgive me, Janos, we mean no offense. I know we have serious matters to discuss. I promise we will come to that. But—" He shrugged, as if he was saying, *You brought him here.*

Perrymeade got to his feet, looking down at me where I sat dumbly in my seat. He gave me a strained smile, as if this had been what he'd hoped for all along, as if he counted on me to use this opportunity to make his case with the Hydrans.

I watched him leave the room. I looked down at the tabletop, at my hands still clamped over its edge, the scars standing out on my knuckles. Waiting . . . Trying to feel something.

Just like they were. They were waiting for me to reach out, to do something. Something impossible.

"Who are you?" Hanjen asked finally, aloud.

"Cat," I said, glancing up at him, down again.

"That is your Human name?" someone else asked. She spoke slowly, as if having to speak my language was hard for her. "Is that all the name you have?"

It wasn't the same question that humans always asked me, or at least wanted to. Hydrans had spoken names, and they had real names, the names they carried in the heart of their mind. Names that could only be shared mind-to-mind. I'd had a name like that, once—a name given in love, mind-to-mind, heart-to-heart. A name that I wouldn't have given to this roomful of strangers passing unspoken judgment on me even if I could have. I shook my head and shrugged. The silence in the room got heavier, weighing on my mind until it crushed every coherent thought.

"We were told last night that you are half Hydran," Hanjen said. His voice was empty as he used the human's name for his own people. His face was as empty of clues as my head was empty of thoughts. "We would like to know which of your parents is Hydran?"

"My mother," I muttered. "Was."

"Was she from this world?"

"I don't know." I shook my head.

"Then why have you come here?"

"You know." I looked up at him, finally.

"Why have you come here?" he asked again, as if I hadn't answered his question.

Or maybe I hadn't answered the one he was really asking. I tried again. "I'm with the xenoarch research team Tau hired to study the reefs here on the Homeland."

He shook his head slightly, and his mouth pinched. He rubbed the bridge of his nose. I sat feeling every muscle in my body tighten as I tried again to imagine what he wanted to hear. "Why did *you* come to *this* world?"

I sat and looked from face to face around the table, seeing a dozen faces, smooth, lined, male, female . . . all of them fine-boned Hydran faces, their green cat-pupiled eyes fixed on me. And suddenly I knew the answer to his question: *Because there was a hole in my life.* For years I'd wanted to know how it would feel to be surrounded by my mother's people; needed to know what I'd find in their eyes . . . whether it could ever be forgiveness.

I looked down. "I don't know." My hands made quiet fists. "But I came here today because of the kidnapped child." I raised my head again. "The boy is helpless; he has severe neurological damage. You have to tell us how to find him. Because it's the right thing to do . . . and because if you don't, if HARM uses him to create trouble for Tau with the FTA, Tau will make you all pay—"

"You saw it happen," Hanjen interrupted, as if he hadn't been listening. "More than that—you caused it to happen."

I grimaced. Of course they knew that—they had to know more about what had happened last night than the Corpses did, or I wouldn't be here. "It was an accident." They didn't know everything, or they'd know that.

"Then please tell us why Tau sent you to deliver this message to us?" Hanjen said.

I glanced around the silent circle of Council members, searching for a recognizable response in even one face. "Because I'm—Hydran." It was hard enough just saying it; suddenly I'd never felt less Hydran in my life, a psionic deaf-mute sitting here in the middle of a debate about life and death. "And because I know what happens to psions who cross Tau." I put my hand up to my face, feeling scabs and bruises. I lowered it again, laid both hands on the tabletop, where one could touch the other. "They thought you might believe me. That you'd be willing to talk to me . . . or trust me enough to listen."

I sucked in a breath as something formless struck a blow behind my eyes, as someone tried to break down my defenses—to discover what was hidden there; why my mind had stopped them all cold.

"Don't," I whispered. "Don't." Someone made a disgusted noise. There was another sourceless collision inside my head. "Stop it!" I shouted, pushing to my feet.

I stood there, barely breathing, while the silence healed again seamlessly. No one else moved; they were all staring at me. I dropped back into my seat.

"Why are you *closed,* then?" Moket, the woman I'd seen at the reception, demanded, her voice singsongy and sharp. She gestured at my head.

I frowned. "I'm not." My fingers twisted the gold stud in my ear.

"Perhaps you are not aware," Hanjen said slowly, as if he was groping for words, "because you are not really Hydran—" He broke off. "I mean, because you have lived so long among Humans . . . you are not aware that what you are doing is considered offensive."

"What am I doing—?" I leaned forward, wanting him to tell me it was only that I was talking too much, or too loudly, wearing stupid clothes, forgetting to say "thank you"—

"Your mind is completely . . . closed." He glanced away, as if even mentioning it embarrassed him, as if I should have known.

I shook my head.

"Are you a *seddik?*" someone said. "Have they sent a *seddik* to us?"

"A what?" I asked.

"No," Hanjen said tonelessly. "He is not a *seddik.* A user of nephase," he looked back at me. "The Humans"—I heard the capital H—"give nephase to our people in their prisons, because otherwise they cannot hold us. Some prisoners become . . . addicted to the drug, because it blocks their psi. They choose to withdraw from their lives, their Gift . . . their 'humanity,' as you would say. It is a sickness they bring back home and spread among the hopeless."

I put my hand up to touch the spot behind my ear where nothing was, knowing that a single drugderm of topalase-AC would let me use my psi, anytime, anywhere. With enough drugs to numb the pain I could be a telepath again . . . just like I could have gotten up and walked on broken legs. But there was nothing behind my ear.

"Why are you closed, then?" the woman repeated.

Hanjen silenced her with a single shake of his head. He faced me without looking directly at me, as if looking at me hurt his eyes. "Among the Community, one tries always to keep one's mind a little . . . open, so that others can read one's mood, see that one's actions are sincere and well meaning. The more open one is, the more . . . respected one is. Within limits, of course. Just as to keep a complete silence, to close your mind like a fist, is an insult."

He met my stare, finally. "To assault your privacy was also an offense—" He glanced at some of the others, who were frowning now around the table. "For which I apologize. I hope you will understand and help us to understand you." He bent his head, as if he were inviting me to explain . . . expecting me to open my mind to them, now that he'd shown me what the problem was.

I shook my head.

"You won't?" Moket snapped. "Then how can we trust you, a stranger . . . a mixed-blood?" Her tone said *half Hydran* meant *freak* on this side of the river too.

"You came into the Community and caused this trouble!" Serali said.

"What are we to think," someone else muttered, speaking to Hanjen, "when the Humans send such a one to us, asking for our help? Except to think they want trouble for us with the FTA too: maybe an excuse to take over the last of our sacred grounds?"

"Why should we believe anything you say when all you give us is words?"

"I can't," I said, my guts knotting, my mind clenched. "I can't . . . do it." Knowing they had every right to ask didn't change anything. I couldn't do it. *Couldn't. Couldn't.*

"You don't know how?" another woman, younger, asked me. "You can't control your Gift?" She glanced at the man sitting next to her. "He is like a—" The words just stopped, as if I'd suddenly gone deaf. She'd slipped into telepathic speech. I wondered if she didn't want to say it out loud in front of me or whether she didn't know how to. I watched her make an odd gesture, jerking her hands up.

"No," I murmured. "I could do it once. I can't now." The urge to confess rose in my throat; I swallowed it down.

Hanjen pressed his lips together. "I am what the Humans call an 'ombudsman,' you know. I am trusted by the Community to . . . look into troubled minds. To search out the blockage . . . to try to heal or resolve it."

"You can't help me," I said, almost angrily. "No one can. A lot of others have tried."

"A lot of Humans," he said softly. "Will you allow me—?" He seemed as reluctant to ask it as I was to let it happen. But I realized that if I refused, it would be the last I saw of any of them.

I nodded, my hands white-knuckled. I tried to relax, but the filaments of lambent energy deep in my brain only became more tangled, more impenetrable, the harder I tried to open myself. I felt Hanjen run up on my defenses, his concentration snagging on razor wire as he searched for some unguarded point of entry, some chink in my armor that would give him a way inside.

My birthright had given me just one facet of the Gift, a single psi talent—telepathy. But I'd been good at it, damn good. I was still good at protecting myself. Too good. Nothing got in; nothing got out. The psiotherapists I'd seen had all told me the same thing: Someday I would be in control again; they just couldn't tell me when. Only I would know when I was ready to become a telepath again.

But I was never going to be ready, not for this—letting a stranger loot the wreckage of my life, letting him put a name to every one of my sins . . . witness the moment I'd made a bloody ruin of another telepath's mind and body, using my mind and a gun. I could never let them see what I'd told to Perrymeade and Sand, who'd never understand. I could never let them see the truth—

"Death!" Hanjen spat out the word, pressing his eyes. Slowly he lowered his hands. "You are filled with death. . . ." He shook his head, staring at me. "You have killed?" he demanded. "How could they send you to us knowing you have done such a thing? Did they think we would not see it? Did they really think we are as blind as they are?"

I shut my eyes. The other Council members stood up one by one around the table, spitting on me with words: spoken words, some in a language that I couldn't understand . . . some that I could, and none of them were forgiving, or kind. Then they began to disappear, blinking out of existence as I watched. I felt the soft inrush of air against my skin.

"Stop!" Hanjen said out loud.

There were more angry murmurs from the Hydrans still standing around the table; more silence with hands gesturing, pointing at me. Not one of them looked at me or offered me a chance to explain something that was beyond their comprehension. . . .

All at once spacetime parted around me; the world went black as I was torn out of reality by a kind of energy transference I recognized instinctively, even though I'd never control it—

And then I was in the courtyard; everything was brightness and confusion. I sat down hard on the ancient tiles, because suddenly there wasn't a chair under me.

I sat stunned, blinking up at the shadow play of dusty leaves; at Perrymeade hurrying toward me from where he'd been waiting beside the mod. I started to pick myself up.

Suddenly Hanjen was standing there between us. Perrymeade recoiled in surprise; I fell back onto my hands.

"What—?" Perrymeade broke off, tried again. "What does this mean?" The sound of his voice was pathetic, like the look on his face.

Hanjen shook his head. "We cannot have him here," he said. "You should not have brought him. He is not one of us."

Perrymeade looked at me, back at Hanjen. "What do you mean?" he said. "Of course he is—"

"He is alive." Hanjen's glance touched me, flicked away again. He searched Perrymeade's face; his eyes shifted, clouding. "I see that you do not understand this, Janos." His mouth thinned with what could have been frustration, or simply disgust. "If you wish to discuss the kidnapping further, join us inside. But not with this one." He turned his back on us both as he said it. He walked away, moving with inhuman grace, but still moving like a human, so that Perrymeade could follow.

Perrymeade stopped beside me. He put out a hand to help me up. "What happened—?" he murmured.

I struggled to my feet, ignoring his outstretched hand. "You did. Fuck you. Get away from me." I turned my back on him and the sight of everything behind him, everything he stood for.

I reached the mod and let myself in, sealing the doors behind me. "Take me back," I told it.

"I'm sorry," its voice came back at me like the voices of the Hydrans, flat and impassive. "I am still waiting for Mez Perrymeade."

"Send him another mod. Take me back now!"

"I'm sorry. I am still waiting—"

I swore and slammed my booted foot against the control panel.

A display came alive suddenly, with Sand's head floating in it. "What is it?"

"Get me out of here," I said.

"Why?" he asked. "Didn't it go well?"

"No," I said, my voice raw. "It was a fucking disaster."

"What did you do"—he frowned—"to offend them?"

"I didn't die." I pushed back in the seat, hugging myself. "I listened to you, you son of a bitch, but you didn't listen to me. Get me out of here." I looked away from his image in the display.

"I don't understand this," he said.

"You never will." I kicked the panel again, and Sand's face disappeared. The mod came alive around me and carried me out of the courtyard.

SIX

IT WAS MIDAFTERNOON by the time Wauno picked me up at the hotel and brought me back to the survey site beside the river. I didn't say anything on the way there. He returned the favor.

I walked into camp, my head singing with the sound of the river, the solid crunch of gravel under my boots. Everything looked the way I remembered it, except that the shifting boundaries of shadow had changed. Everything sounded the same, smelled and felt the same. My mind tried to tell me that I should feel some kind of relief that the ordeal was over. I was back on safe ground, back where I belonged, with people I knew and trusted. I wanted to believe that, as much as I'd wanted to believe it last night when those same people had come to save me from Tau's Corporate Security. *Safe.* . . .

But I knew as I crossed the gravel into the shadow of the reef that I'd never really believe that. *I'm safe* was only a lie that everyone told to themselves in order to stay sane. *I belong* was only a lie that I told to myself. Since I'd left Oldcity, years ago now, I hadn't stayed anywhere long enough to feel like I belonged there. It wasn't any different here. Everywhere I looked I saw strangers' faces, walked streets I didn't know the names of, slept in unfamiliar rooms alone in empty beds.

And I knew that as much as I'd hated my life back in Oldcity, sometimes, in the middle of the night, some sick part of me missed it. I'd remember its walls closing me in like a mother's arms; how simple it was to know that the sky was only a roof over my head, thirty meters high, and not infinite. And those were the times when I ached to be nothing but an ignorant, fucked-up freak again, back in a place where I understood the rules.

"Cat—" Kissindre's voice reached me over the noise and motion of the camp like a lifeline dragging me out of quicksand. She came striding toward me, her coat flapping.

She stopped as I stopped in front of her, as we suddenly collided with the inevitable, invisible barrier between us. I watched her swallow words—probably *Are you all right?* because she hadn't wanted to have to ask me that again before even a day had passed.

"I'm back," was all I said.

"Good," she murmured, but I saw concern in her eyes. Concern for her family and the kidnapped boy; concern that she didn't know how to ask me the questions she needed to ask but couldn't.

"I wasn't any help," I muttered, looking down. "Your uncle's still with the Hydrans."

"Oh," she said. The word was empty and noncommittal. She started to turn away, looked back, hesitating long enough to make it an invitation. We moved on through the site, walking together.

When we'd gone a short way she pointed out some kind of tech equipment being set up. "They've brought in the field-suit system. Ezra's helping them get it online. You got back just in time for a demonstration."

I let my gaze follow her pointing hand, glad to let my thoughts go with it. It was a relief to focus on something that had nothing to do with me personally. The maroon-coveralled workers were standing around the displacement-field equipment now. I remembered the looks I'd seen on their faces before, the dull resentment. I looked at them again as we got closer. A few of them had their sleeves pushed up, as if they'd been sweating in spite of the cold.

I stopped as I spotted the red band ringing a worker's wrist, and then another one, and another. Bond tags: what you wore instead of a databand if you were contract labor. My hand went to my wrist, to the databand that covered the scar a bond tag had left on me, proving to me again that I was really who I thought I was.

Protz and the other Tau vips were still there, along with the two Feds. A handful of techs stood waiting to demonstrate the sounding equipment. On the way here to Refuge I'd accessed files on the equipment they used to prospect inside the reefs, along with everything else Tau had forwarded to us. I'd drained the advance feed trying to get a real sense of what the reefs were like, to learn about Refuge and the Hydrans, about how they all fit together.

The best way to get a detailed picture of what lay inside a cloud-reef was to send in a human prospector wearing an upgraded version of a common displacement-field unit. The field suits let a diver move through solid matter like it was fluid, sending back readings until a technician on the outside registered something Tau wanted to explore further. The upgraded suits they used for exploring an environment this complex weren't ordinary mining equipment: each suit was a spiderweb of monofilament woven with sensors and phase generators, a microtech version of the skin of a starship—and had probably cost Tau nearly as much.

No one from Tau had ever explored the few thousand hectares of matrix here on the Homeland. This was the last unexploited reef formation on the planet, which could only mean this formation had been the least interesting, from Tau's standpoint. That made it the most interesting to us, and the most important to the Hydrans. Tau claimed that this last formation would always be inviolate. But *always* meant something different to a combine government than it did to the rest of the universe.

Yelina Prohas, the team's microbiologist, and Ezra Ditreksen were standing with the Tau consultants and their equipment. I watched them nod and gesture, not able to hear what they were discussing over the noise of the camp. Another moment of stupefying numbness broke over me—the sense that nothing was real, that no one really existed, because I couldn't hear them, feel them, touch them with my mind.

I forced myself to keep moving, concentrating on the pressure of the ground against my feet, the air I pulled into my lungs and pushed out again.

"We're actually going into the reefs today?" I asked as I caught up with Kissindre. I hadn't expected a bureaucracy like Tau to move that fast, even with the Feds looking over their shoulder.

Ezra glanced up at me as I stopped beside him, and shook his head. "They're just here to familiarize us with the data retrieval system. One of the Tau workers will be going in. If we want to do any diving ourselves, we'll have to certify on a field-suit simulator."

"Saban!" the Tau tech in charge shouted over her shoulder at the knot of laborers I'd passed through to get here.

One of them dropped a crate of supplies. It hit the ground with a *crunch* and split open. He didn't even seem to notice. He was staring at the tech, at the equipment, at us, and I watched panic glaze his face.

I grimaced, thinking this was all the team needed right now, all I needed to make my day . . . for some contract laborer to have a nervous breakdown in front of the Feds, in the middle of all our insanely expensive equipment.

The tech shouted the bondie's name again like a curse. This time Saban came toward us, moving as if the tech had control of his brain. I watched him shuffle closer . . . *coming to use a field suit because he had no control over his life: he was a slave, he was nothing but meat. But if he put on that gear he'd be dead meat just like Goya, who'd been his friend until one of those suits had killed him, barely a month ago. The field generators would slip out of phase. That was what had killed Goya. And when Goya died he knew they'd call him next, and now they had—*

And everything he knew, everything he felt, was screaming through my brain. "Jeezu, shit—!" I gasped, blinking. I slammed my mind shut, squeezing him out like water through a closing fist.

Ezra glanced at me; the others were watching the tech explain procedures. Ezra made a face, as if the look on my face just proved to him that I was crazy.

I turned away, still dazed, as Saban reached the place where we stood. Saban wasn't looking at me, didn't know what had just happened, couldn't, any more than I could have found my way back inside his head. There was nothing left of my psi to prove that he was still terrified or even still alive.

I swore under my breath and forced my attention back to the others.

"Suit up," the tech said to Saban. Saban looked down at the field-generating skinsuit and the sensor gear waiting in a container at his feet. He picked up the suit. He was probably no more than thirty, but he looked older, sucked dry. I wondered how long he'd been a bondie, what he'd looked like before that. As he began to pull the suit on, he looked up at the team where we stood in a half circle, watching. I didn't have to be a mind reader to know what he thought of us, a bunch of Tau-kissing imported techies sending him to do our dirty work in a rig that he thought would kill him.

He looked at me.

And I was looking into the eyes of a roomful of strangers, all staring back at me: half a dozen human psions sitting on a bench like targets in a shooting gallery, a bunch of losers hoping for one last chance. I remembered how they'd watched my every move as I crossed the room to join them, filthy, exhausted, beaten. I remembered how the look in their eyes had told me I was nothing, not even human . . . not even to them.

Except for one woman, her hair like a midnight river, her eyes as gray as sorrow. *Jule taMing.* She'd looked into my eyes, the eyes of a wild animal, and seen a humanity that even I had believed was dead. And she'd said—

"I'll go. Let me go."

Everyone standing around me in the reef's shadow turned to stare at me, their expressions caught somewhere between confusion and disbelief.

"What?" Ezra said.

I licked my lips, swallowed. "I want to do it."

The Tau tech in charge of the equipment, whose datapatch

read HAWKINS, shook her head. "Your team hasn't qualified on a field suit. Can't do it. It's against safety regs."

"I'm qualified," I said.

Kissindre looked over her shoulder at me.

"No, he's not," Ezra said. "None of us has done the training sim."

"I have," I said, pushing past him.

"When—?" He caught my arm, jerking me around.

"On the way here," I said, controlling the urge to sprain his wrist. "There was a virtual sim in the background databank we brought with us."

"No one had the time."

"I did." I shrugged and smiled, twisting the knife as he realized what I was saying. I could memorize anything I accessed, or even read, perfectly, the first time. Being a psion wired your brain in a way that gave you an eidetic memory if you wanted one. When I'd signed up for the university, I hadn't known how to access; for most of my life, I hadn't even known how to read. And the law said psions weren't allowed to have augmentation hardwired into their brains.

I'd needed a kind of miracle to make up for the years I'd lost on the streets. When I realized I'd been born with one, I learned to use it to survive in my new life. Getting this far hadn't been easy for me, but some people thought it had.

Ezra let go of my arm, his mouth pinching. "Freak," he muttered.

I stiffened. I'd smelled the word on his breath every time he spoke, but he'd never had the guts to say it to my face before. I straightened my sleeve and moved past him. "I'm qualified," I said again, to the tech. "Check me out."

Hawkins shot a look at Kissindre, raising her eyebrows. Kissindre looked once at me. I nodded. She nodded, then.

"It's still not a good idea." Hawkins glanced at the ring of onlookers, the Tau vips and the Feds, as if she was looking for someone who'd back her up and stop me. But no one gave her a sign. Either they didn't know it was dangerous, or they couldn't admit they did.

I took the field suit from Saban's strengthless hands. The suit fluttered in my grip; it was like holding a shadow. Saban shook his head, his eyes dark and uncomprehending. He began to back away, slowly, like a man afraid of stepping on cracks.

I turned to Hawkins. "Has this equipment been completely checked out?" A displacement suit like this was cutting-edge technology, which meant that its potential rate of failure was about as high as its cost.

"What do you mean?" Hawkins said, resenting it, and me.

"Is it safe?"

"Why wouldn't it be?" she snapped. "If you know what you're doing."

I couldn't tell from the look on her face whether she was just nervous or actually worried that I might be right. I tried not to think about it. I stripped off my outer clothing and put on the helmet, fastened the sensor belt around my waist. Then I pulled the skinsuit on, felt it wrap itself around me like cobwebs, molding itself to the contours of my body. The feel of it made my flesh crawl, but I'd been expecting that. I stretched, felt it move with me.

The field suit had been programmed to allow a human prospector to walk through walls, or anyway move through the variable matrix of the reef as though it was made of water. There was hidden space inside the molecular structure of all but the densest materials, and the phase shift opened a passageway, shoehorning the molecules apart, creating a vacuole that a human being could exist inside of—as long as he kept moving. "Okay," I said at last. "Let's do it."

Hawkins glanced up at me, back at her displays. "All right," she said, resigned. "But make it short. This isn't virtual, it's real. Nobody's charted this reef. You never know what you're going to find in there."

I nodded, glancing toward the foot of the hill. The steep, eroded slope was furred with mossy growths in green-black like tarnished metal, browns the color of dried blood, here or there a sudden flare-up of bright green-gold. I started toward it, checking out systems with a word as I moved, getting the feel of moving inside the suit's cage of spun silk. Data readouts flickered in front of my eyes like moths; I had to fight the urge to brush them away.

Everything seemed to function the way my memory said it would, but Saban's fear lay across my vision like an extra lens. I told myself the death of the other bondie had been a freak accident; even though Saban believed things like it happened to them too often. Tau wouldn't dare let a man go reef-diving in faulty equipment in front of so many witnesses, in front of the Feds. . . .

At last, after what seemed like time spent in suspended animation, I was standing in front of the reef-face. I stopped, turning back for one final look at the others. They stood in three groups: the research team and the technicians in one, the observers in another, the bondies bunched in a third. I heard the tech speaking to me through my headset, verifying data. I let my mind shift into autopilot, let the training I'd force-fed it take over, giving her the right answers as the reefs loomed up and over me like a cresting wave. I held my breath as I sensed my body making contact, experiencing the first soft compression of the alien growth that layered the interface of reef and air. I murmured the words that activated the phase shifters and pushed my body through it.

I flowed into the reef-face with a sensation like sinking standing up as the reef and the motion and my physical boundaries became one fluid whole. I gasped, felt cool sweet air enter my lungs freely and easily until they were full again. I took another breath, and another, turned, maneuvering like a swimmer to look behind me. The world outside was gone, and I was looking into a haze of shifting silver-grays, luminous gray-greens. I'd known there would be light—from the electromagnetic fluctuations around me, translated into the visible by my helmet sensors—but I hadn't known exactly what I'd see.

There was no sound at all except the cautious rasp of my breath. Displays still flickered across my vision; I ordered them off. Let the technical data of the reef's makeup read out on the tech's displays for everyone else to see. Suddenly they weren't the way I wanted to experience this, the way I wanted to remember it.

"How are you doing?" Hawkins's voice blared suddenly from some other dimension.

"Okay," I murmured, hating to speak at all. "About what I expected." But it wasn't. No simulation could be like the real thing, because the real thing, I suddenly realized, was never the same thing twice. "Don't talk to me. I want to . . . concentrate."

"Go slow, then," she said.

"Yeah," I whispered, the single word barely loud enough for my own ears, because anything more seemed like a shout. Even my heartbeat was too loud, fading in and out of my consciousness as I pushed deeper into the shimmering mystery that had swallowed me whole.

And slowly I began to realize that the silence around me wasn't complete. The reefs whispered: hidden meanings and murmured secrets lay just beyond the boundaries of my perception. I watched light and color and density shift with my motion, as if I'd merged with it, nothing separate, the displacement field dissolving my sense of self until I became amorphous.

I began to move again, phasing forward into the unknown, my passage lit by the coruscating energy of the fields. The only sensation I felt now was a kind of pressure change, the difficulty of movement changing with my every move. The matrix I was phasing through caressed me, now gently like a mother, now with the urgent hunger of a lover. I passed through surfaces that were rough, rust-red, as stratified as a wall of brick but peppered with seeds of darkness, like the night sky turned inside out; I broke through suddenly into an empty whiteness and was left snow-blind in the formless heart of a blizzard. I swam upward through whiteness, burst out of it into a hollow vacuole filled with glowing fog, tumbled, suddenly weightless, until the field suit restabilized.

"You all right in there?" Hawkins's voice demanded, making me spasm.

"Fine. I'm fine," I muttered as I swept upward through eddies of luminous gas.

"You want to come out now?" It didn't really sound like a question.

"No." I reached the far side of the vacuole, felt my motion turn into slow-motion as I sank into an area of concentrated matter. I forced my way deeper. "You getting good readings?" Managing to say something coherent, to remember that the hard data was supposed to matter to me.

"Good," Hawkins said. "Real good. Good and clear."

I'd already stopped listening, balanced precariously on what my mind insisted was a stairway. I called on the displays, made myself study them, proving to myself that it was only a density differential between bands of layered protoid ceramic and sapphire foam. I shut off the displays again and let myself climb, until suddenly I swept through another wall that rippled like flames.

"Aah—!" My own shout of surprise exploded in my ears.

"What is it?" The tech's voice hit my senses almost as hard.

"A head. God, there's half a head in here!"

"It's all right," Hawkins said, her voice easing. "It's nothing . . . it's not real. You find things like that in the reefs . . . they're just aberrations. You've been in there long enough; come on out."

"No . . ." I whispered, holding my glowing hands up, cupping the half-finished thought of a Hydran face—I could even see that it was Hydran, although the eyes were closed. It might have been sleeping, but there was something about it, as if it was caught in a moment of rapture. It shimmered and disappeared like a reflection in water as my hands closed on it. I let my hands fall away and watched it reappear. I shut my eyes as I pushed through it, moving deeper into the millennia of ancient dreams.

The touch of the matrix surrounding me began to seem like more than just simple undifferentiated pressure; I could sense the reef changing, as elusive as rainwater and rippling silk, as viscous as oil, honey, tar, as empty as vacuum, as random as my life.

The Hydrans believed the reefs were holy, miraculous; places of power. I wondered what they'd found here to make them believe that, when they could never experience the reefs the way I was doing now. And I wondered why experiencing them this way hadn't had an effect on how human beings saw them.

I reached out, shifting myself around a pulsating sphere of light, felt something shiver through me like a plucked string— heard it, inside my head, as if I was an instrument and the reef was playing its song through every neuron in my body. I spiraled to a stop, listening, realizing that now every motion, every shift of phase, seemed to resonate inside me—not just colors and lights anymore, but all across the spectrum of my senses. I heard music when I breathed, I smelled fog and tasted the lightning-sharp tang of ozone. My senses were bursting open like shuttered doors, one by one, letting in the pure radiance of sensation. . . . My mind was an outstretched hand as the reef filled its emptiness. . . .

Somewhere a voice was calling me. The words stung like pebbles against the naked skin of my thoughts. I brushed them off with a muttered curse; felt them sting me again, harder, "—Answer me!"

I didn't answer, because there were no words that could describe what was pouring in through all my senses now. My mind was a prism, diffracting input into a synesthesia of pleasure. . . .

There were no boundaries: no inside, no outside, only a rapture as sweet as the oxygen I was breathing. There was no need even to breathe; no room for breath inside me, only a pure hot flame of pleasure, consuming me until . . . I . . . I . . .

I couldn't breathe. I dragged air as thick as fluid down into my lungs. All at once my chest felt as if something was crushing the life out of me.

Sound made my ears bleed light: a human voice was screaming at me, but I couldn't remember whose it was, couldn't make out the words—

"Can't . . . breathe." I heaved the words out like fist-sized stones, not knowing if anyone could understand them, if anyone else was even there to hear them.

". . . bringing you back. . . ." The words were written in liquid fire across my vision. ". . . release your controls!"

I looked down, watched my hands fumble at my belt inside a golden aura, not sure whether anything was actually touching anything else, whether I even could, or even should. I felt my body shifted, moved, not able to tell if I was the one doing it. "Get me out . . ." I mumbled.

". . . *get you out* . . ." the voice said, or maybe it was only an echo in my head. The blinding flavor of the sound was so bitter that it made my eyes tear.

I didn't say anything else; didn't hear anything else, taste or feel anything else except the pain every time I dragged in a breath of molten air. My whole body felt wet, as if death was oozing in through the bandages of the protective fields. Pressure, density, weight, the sudden wrenching shifts between solid mass and emptiness were all intensifying as a force beyond my control dragged my helpless body through the gauntlet. I felt the reef's enfolding womb of sensation begin to metamorphose me into the stuff of its own mass, making us one forever. . . .

But the irresistible drag still kept me moving forward, caroming off densities of matter like a molecule escaping a boiling pot. It wrenched me around and shoved once more, flung me abruptly through the translucent agate of a solid wall into the absence of everything but light.

I crashed down onto solid ground as the glow of the displacement fields flickered out around me. Suddenly there was fresh air, free for the taking. I sucked it into my lungs between fits of coughing, sprawled back on the gravel, grateful for every agonized muscle twitching in my body.

"Cat—!"

"What happened?"

"—he breathing?"

Familiar shadows blocked the sky, and then I was lost inside a surreal forest of legs. Ezra Ditreksen pressed something over my face, forcing oxygen laced with stims down my throat. I struggled upright, coughing, shoving it away.

"Told you—!"

Someone was screaming, someone hysterical. Surprised that it wasn't me, I caught the net of extended hands and hauled myself up, pushed through the barrier of bodies, half supported by them, as I tried to see who it was.

It was Saban, the worker whose place I'd taken . . . whose life I'd almost traded for my own. I saw him struggling against the barrier of workers who were trying to hold him back. One of the bondies hit him, hard, doubling him up. Shutting him up—they'd done it to shut him up. I watched the workers close ranks around him, the looks they gave the Tau vips, the Feds, me and the team members standing around me. I wondered who they'd been trying to protect—him, or themselves.

I looked away from them, searching for the tech who'd let me go into the reefs in a suit that hadn't been properly maintained . . . who'd gotten me out again just in time. Hawkins shoved past Ezra and Chang just as Kissindre reached my side.

"Cat, for God's sake—" Kissindre gasped, just as Hawkins pushed in front of me and said, "For God's sake, what happened? Why the hell didn't you come out when I told you to? You're not—"

"You saying this was my fault?" I asked, looking straight into her eyes.

I saw her react as my long pupils registered on her. But then she looked away, at the Tau vips and the Feds closing in on us, and muttered, "No. I'm not saying that."

She held some kind of instrument up in front of me; made me stand still while she took a reading. Her face eased. "You're clean. You weren't exposed to any toxins."

I took a deep breath, remembering things Tau had encountered inside the reefs: enzymes that turned human lungs and guts to putrescent sludge; virals that triggered spontaneous, uncontrollable cell mutation. My shirt and pants were wet, stained with something alien, something that smelled like nothing I'd ever smelled before. I felt my flesh crawl. "Then I want to say two things. One is—thanks."

She looked back at me, sharp-eyed but not angry anymore.

"The other is, how often do you lose a diver?"

"Malfunctions are rare," she said. She raised her voice as she said it, glancing again at the tight-lipped faces of the Tau officials, the frowns on the faces of the Feds. "We've never had a fatality."

"That's not what I heard." I glanced away at Saban, silent and barely visible now inside the group of other workers. "If it's so safe, why do you use contract laborers and not your own people?"

Her mouth thinned. Protz said, "We wouldn't send anybody into the reefs if the risk factor didn't meet our safety standards."

"I'm sure they're real stringent," I said, and Protz frowned. I looked back at the Feds. "Why don't you ask those workers about fatalities?" I pointed toward the knot of bondies.

I felt a hand on my arm, and someone behind me said, "He didn't mean that. He's just shaken up. He shouldn't have insisted on using the equipment. He doesn't have enough experience, and he almost killed himself—" Ezra.

I turned around, breaking his grip. "The damn equipment failed! It wasn't me."

"Grow up," he hissed. "Everything you've done since we got here has been the wrong thing. Take responsibility for your actions, for once."

"Ezra." Kissindre's voice cut between us. "You are not in charge of this team." She pushed in close to his face, lowering her voice, "It's not your responsibility, or your right, to reprimand—"

"Well, if you won't do it, someone has to," he snapped.

Her face went red.

"Why do you always take his side?" Ezra gestured at me before she could open her mouth and answer him. "Are you going to let him ruin everything we have here—?" He waved his hand to include everything around us, but something in his face said that what he meant was only the distance between him and her.

"Ezra," she said. Her face softened. "You don't understand."

"I think I do." He turned and walked away, as if everyone around him—all the other team members, the techs and vips and inspectors watching us like voyeurs—had disappeared.

I turned back from watching him go, to see whether the Feds were making any move to talk with the bondies. They weren't. "Why don't you ask the workers who use this equipment all the time how safe it is? And how much choice they have about using it?"

"They're contract laborers," Protz said sharply. "They don't understand the technology, and they don't know anything about Tau's safety procedures. We protect them in ways they don't even realize."

"Do they have the right to refuse to use those suits?" I asked. "What happens if they won't?"

No one answered me.

"They haven't got any rights." I turned back to the two Feds. "The FTA runs Contract Labor. It's your job to protect them—it's your job to make sure Tau isn't killing them. Do your job—"

"Cat." Kissindre cut me off before the Feds could give me whatever answer they thought I had coming. "Don't get political," she said, and the casual tone didn't match the look in her eyes. "It's not what we're here for."

I looked at her; looked away again. "It's what you're here for!" I shouted past her.

The man, Givechy, nodded finally, grudgingly. "We'll check it out," he said, glancing at the woman, who nodded.

"Our workers are not being mistreated," Protz said impatiently.

"Your slaves," I muttered.

"They are not slaves!" Kissindre said, and her anger startled me. "Contract Labor builds worlds. It's giving those men a chance—"

"What the hell do you know about it?" I said.

"My grandfather was a contract laborer."

I looked back at her, caught naked by surprise.

"It gave him his start. He went on to make a good life for himself and his family."

I looked down at my wrist, at my databand. "Yeah," I whispered. "Well, all it got me was scars."

Her mouth opened, closed again. A muscle twitched in her cheek.

"We're making several of our research and production facilities available for your inspection," Protz said. For a moment I thought he was talking to me. He was talking to the Feds. But then he met my stare, and added, "You're welcome to accompany us, if that will prove to you that we're not some sort of monsters." There was more indignation than smugness in it, as if he was so blindly keiretsu that he couldn't begin to comprehend why anyone would question how they did their business or ran their citizens' lives.

"I've had a real shitty day," I said. "I don't need this." I started to turn away.

"Tomorrow," he said. "It's tomorrow."

I kept walking, head down, letting the beach disappear under my feet until I was beyond the human circle. The reefs rose up ahead of me; I walked toward them, remembering the feel of moving toward them in the suit . . . passing inside . . . the merging. . . .

And I wasn't afraid. It surprised me to realize that. Something filled me that was almost disbelief . . . *almost longing*. It didn't seem to mean anything that what I'd done had almost killed me. It only mattered that I'd experienced the rapture, become part of something indescribable, and yet so familiar. . . . *Like a joining:* the deepest, most intimate form of communion between psions; a thing that was almost impossible if the psions were human. But somehow the reefs had triggered my psi, made me respond . . . made me whole.

I was standing at the reef-face again, like I had before; but this time there was no suit performing the technomagic that let me walk through walls. I put out my hands, pressed them against the mossy, fibrous growth that defined the interface where the reef met the outside air, feeling it crumble, soft and yielding, even as the surface resisted me, turning me back. I pressed harder, putting my weight against it until my hands sank into the loamy surface. I stood that way, straining, listening . . .

"You really want to get back inside that much?" a voice asked, behind me.

I jerked around, startled.

Luc Wauno stood behind me, his head bent, his gaze moving from my face to the reef-face to my hands, no longer sunk wrist-deep in its surface.

I pinned my hands against my sides with the pressure of my arms; beginning to realize that I was getting numb with cold, standing there like I'd been hypnotized in my clammy, stinking shirtsleeves.

"I thought you left," I said.

He shook his head. "I've got my orders too."

I looked at him, and away.

"The Hydrans call these holy places." He glanced up the steep, shadowed rise of the slope, his fingers touching the pouch that hung against his chest.

"I know," I said.

He looked down again. "They say it's a kind of ecstasy they feel, a kind of revelation about the visions of the cloud-whales. There's a kind of mental residue—"

"I know."

"Do you?" He half frowned, with what looked like curiosity. "I thought you couldn't use your psi."

I remembered the conversation I'd had with Sand and Perrymeade that he'd overheard. "I can't control it. But I felt something, in there—"

"The tech said it was anoxia. Reef-rapture. It happens if a suit fails. You know your lips were blue when you came out of there?"

"I wasn't hallucinating."

He shrugged and didn't say anything else. I figured he didn't believe me.

"How often do the suits fail?"

He shook his head. "I don't know. Not my department. I cloud-watch. That's all."

"Right," I said. "You just follow orders." I started to walk away.

"Hey," he called.

I stopped, looking back at him. But he only shrugged, as if he didn't really have anything to say.

I turned away again and kept moving, putting the camp behind me, until I reached the river's shore. I stood on the stones, watching the river run. And I remembered another shore, on another world, remembered feeling the same sense of inexplicable loss as I watched the river disappear into time and the hidden distance.

SEVEN

THE NEXT DAY began like the one before should have. We'd been herded back to Riverton to spend the night, as if Tau was afraid to leave us unattended in the Homeland. But at sunrise Wauno was waiting to take us out again. This time Ezra stayed behind, accessing Tau's databanks from the room he and Kissindre shared. That made everything easier, at least for me. Kissindre didn't say much, except to ask Wauno a few questions about the reef site. I couldn't tell whether she was brooding, worried about her family problems, or just exhausted. I was tired enough, but knowing that her family's troubles, and Tau's, weren't my problem anymore made me feel better than I had since I'd come to Refuge.

The team spent its time at the research site doing experimental runs on the equipment, learning to interpret the data Tau technicians pulled out of the reefs and what the limits of their readings were. We only did external soundings. No one asked to go reef-diving after what had nearly happened to me; Kissindre had agreed to let the Tau workers handle it.

As we were eating our midday meal, Wauno's transport landed again on the shore. He wasn't due back until evening. Everyone looked up, looking surprised and then concerned. And then, one by one, they looked at me.

"What—?" I said, frowning.

"Nothing," Chang muttered, and they looked away again at the transport.

It wasn't Perrymeade or Sand getting out of the transport this time. It was only Protz. For a minute I thought everything might actually be all right.

He stopped in front of us where we all sat in stasis with food still halfway to our mouths. "I'm sorry to intrude." He nodded to Kissindre, but his glance stayed on her about as long as a fly. "Cat?" He looked at me again, and Chang groaned under his breath.

"What?" I said again, making the last time I'd said it sound friendly.

Protz bent his head at the transport behind him. "Yesterday I told you that Tau was opening one of its mining and research facilities for the FTA's inspection. I thought you might want to see for yourself that our contract laborers work under completely safe conditions."

I hesitated, glancing at Kissindre. She didn't look happy. Slowly I got to my feet. "I need this," I murmured. "I'll get caught up. This is the last time—"

She grimaced and nodded. Then she looked down, so that I couldn't see her expression. I glanced at the rest of the team, a dozen faces wearing a dozen different expressions. No understanding showed on any of them.

I thought about apologizing; didn't. I tried not to listen to the sound of their voices talking behind my back as I walked away.

As I got on board the transport Protz was already explaining what we were going out to see: an actual interface, where they mined the reef matrix and processed the anomalies they discovered there. I tried to listen to what he was saying, tried not to feel as guilty taking my seat in the transport as I had turning my back on the team.

Wauno was at the controls, as usual. He looked about as glad to be there as I probably did. He raised his eyebrows as he saw me come aboard. I wondered what he meant by that.

I sat down beside Osuna and Givechy, the two Feds, trying to remember which of them was which as I engaged my safety restraints. The only obvious difference between them was their sex. Maybe they had personalities, but so far I hadn't seen any proof of that.

They were wearing duty uniforms today: heavy, pragmatic boots, gray pants, bright orange jackets with one gray sleeve and one gold. At least the uniforms, with the FTA's winged Earth logo on the breast, guaranteed they'd never be mistaken for combine lackeys. I stole glances at their datapatches until I was certain Osuna was the woman and Givechy was the man. Osuna would have been good-looking if she ever smiled. They stared back at me as if they had no idea what I was doing on board.

I nodded.

"I don't understand," Osuna said, sounding hostile. "I thought you were a technician or a student. Why are you here?" I remembered yesterday; probably she did too.

I glanced at Protz, who seemed to be obsessed with the view out the window beside him. I looked back and shrugged. "The same reason you are."

"This isn't your job. Your job is back there." Givechy gestured at the reef disappearing behind us.

"Then I guess it's personal," I said.

"He's a former contract laborer," Protz muttered to the wall.

The two Feds looked at me with the kind of disbelief normally saved for somebody who'd had major cosmetic surgery—like adding a second head.

"Well, then," Givechy murmured. "You must be an outstanding example of how well the Contract Labor system works. Where were you assigned?"

"The Federation Mines, on Cinder." I let the words register: the Federation was their boss. "If someone hadn't paid off my contract, I'd be dead of radiation poisoning now."

"That's not amusing," Osuna snapped. Protz looked at us, finally.

"I know," I said.

Both Feds looked at Protz, as if they wondered whether I was Tau's way of paying them back for being here.

The look on Protz's face was oil and water, unease and barely disguised pleasure all at once. It was the most complex emotion I'd seen him register since we'd met. It didn't last long. He rearranged his face until it was as smooth as the surface of his brain.

"I hope you don't think your experience somehow qualifies you to do our job or to interfere with it," Givechy said to me finally.

"I'm not here to get in your way," I said. "But I'll be watching."

The seatback ahead of me came alive as Protz displayed an information program on the transport's interactive consoles. The two Feds put on headsets. They lost themselves in the virtual feed like they actually thought they'd learn something meaningful about what we were going to see.

I watched the program on flatscreen with half my attention, wondering whether the Feds were really as interested in this hype as they seemed to be or whether they were just avoiding further conversation. And I wondered what qualified the two of them to pass judgment on Tau and half a hundred other combines all across the Federation's piece of the galaxy, each one with different economic concerns and technological bases, each one trying to cover up its particular lies.

I watched my own feed long enough to catch a repeat of the cloud-whale visuals I'd seen in my hotel room a few nights ago. After that it bled into pure hype. I tuned out. Below us the distance between sky and ground had filled with clouds without my noticing it. I wondered whether they were really clouds or something more. I wanted to ask Wauno about it, about how he knew what the differences were when he watched the cloud-whales. But I didn't.

The trip took close to an hour, which at the speed the transport was moving meant we'd gone nearly a thousand klicks. Clouds hid most of the terrain we were passing over. We began to drop down through them finally, into a landscape that left my eyes struggling, familiar and alien all at once.

The world was greener here, with so much more color that I had to do a reality check on the sky to convince myself it wasn't artificial. The contours of the land showed me where the reefs had been laid down—were still being laid down, if what I'd heard was true. We must have traveled north, because I didn't think anything about Riverton had ever looked as lush and soft as this land did. My instincts told me this was where the Hydran people should be living; where probably they had lived, by choice, before they'd been driven to the ends of their earth by Tau.

There was no sign of a settlement anywhere, Hydran or human—nothing to keep the cloud-whales from their purpose, or Tau's planners from theirs.

I saw the Tau interface now, in the middle of the green, rolling sea of the reefs. The main complex wasn't even visible from the surface: none of the laboratories and processing plants; no wormholes riddling the matrix of thought-droppings, leading to whatever discoveries Tau's high-tech prospectors had identified as most likely to fit the parameters of their highly specialized interests. There had never been a systematic, purely scientific study done on one of these reefs, one that wasn't designed to produce the most profit in the fastest way possible.

I wondered how far our research team would get in conducting its study, between the restrictions Tau had already laid on us and whatever objections the Hydrans had to our intruding on their last piece of sacred ground. We'd been told the Hydran Council had given our project their approval, but after what I'd learned about the kidnapping, I wasn't so sure that they actually spoke for the Hydran Community. I wondered how much we'd really accomplish before the Feds finished their investigation and left the planet, and Tau didn't need us as a showpiece anymore.

We set down on an open landing field in the middle of the complex. On the way in I'd heard Wauno interacting with a security net; we'd passed through a midair no-man's-land of invisible defenses as we'd dropped out of what seemed to be open sky into the deceptively open heart of the compound. Tau might be lax on safety measures for their workers, but they weren't lax about protecting the operation from sabotage by corporate competitors.

As we got out of the transport, there was nothing visible except the installation and the sky. I shielded my eyes with my hands, squinting up at the blue, glaring dome over our heads. Clouds patterned the brightness, rippling and translucent, like water flowing over unseen stones. They reminded me of the images I'd seen on the threedy, but they were too amorphous, too formless against the glare, for me to be certain. "Are those clouds—?" I asked Wauno.

Wauno glanced down at the piece of equipment hanging around his neck. He passed it wordlessly to me.

I held it up to my eyes like I'd seen him do once, discovering a set of lenses that fitted themselves to my face and adjusted to my vision as I moved my head. I focused on the displays superimposed over my view of the world, a view that had trans-

formed as suddenly as my mood. I lifted my head to the sky—
and saw them.

Everything else fell away, stopped, ceased to exist. The cloud-
whales drifted overhead, their camouflage of water vapor
stripped away by the lenses' filters. I counted three, four, five
individuals, each one a community of countless mite-sized creatures. They moved through the ocean of air like gods, their vast
forms slowly shapeshifting through one fluid transformation after
another, moving to the hidden music of their meditations, the
counterpoint of the wind. Here and there a fragile veil of thought
made visible drifted down like rain, or glinted like a brief, impossible star in the clear air.

Thinking of music, I remembered the Monument: remembered standing on a plateau at sunset, on the artificial world that
was another incomprehensible gift of the Creators. I remembered
the eroded arch of stone that humans called Goldengate, the
haunting music the wind played through its fractured span. . . . I
thought about music as the universal language, speaking truths
that nothing could alter, and I wondered what the Creators had
been trying to tell us, by making their music visible.

Someone jolted my arm—Protz. I looked down, pushing the
lenses back on my forehead. The expression on his face was half
impatient and half inspired. I realized that he was telling me to
hand them over. I passed them to him, watched him pass them to
one of the Feds. I glanced at Wauno. He was standing like I had,
his hands shadowing his eyes as he stared up into the sky. His
body was drawn like a bow with longing.

I wondered if the shields surrounding this complex existed
partly to protect it from the mysteries falling out of the air, how
dangerous Wauno's work really was, and whether he'd ever been
caught inside a rain of cloud-whale inspiration that might have
killed him.

The Feds passed the glasses back and forth, and then back to
Protz, nodding without comment. I wondered if they'd been left
speechless or just unimpressed. I looked at their faces. *Unimpressed.*

Protz handed the lenses back to Wauno, ignoring my outstretched hand.

Wauno handed them to me again as Protz turned away. "Keep

them," he murmured. "I have another pair. They promised me I could take your team out to a watchpost when this is finished—" He jerked his head at the Feds. I realized he didn't mean this visit, but the whole investigation. His look said he didn't know what either of us was doing here, like this, when we could be out there somewhere, watching the cloud-whales drift by without interruption. I only nodded, and didn't ask him what he thought the odds were that we'd get that opportunity. He headed back to the transport, maybe to get himself some more lenses.

A welcoming committee had emerged from the shining carapace of the research facility, dwarfed by it. I hadn't realized how big it actually was until their arrival gave it perspective.

"Did they give you a choice about what interface you got to see?" I asked Osuna. This must be the closest reef-mining operation to Riverton. If Tau controlled what the Feds got to see, then it would be simple to show them a perfectly run installation.

"We were offered a choice of three," she said, clipping off the words like paper. "They said this was the most convenient."

"Did you ever wonder if it was too convenient?" I asked.

She looked away without answering.

The half-dozen people coming toward us wore the uniforms of Tau's CorpSec, but as they got closer I could see from their datapatches that they were plant security guards.

As we started forward to meet them, I realized that I knew one of them: the one whose datapatches read CHIEF OF SECURITY. It was Burnell Natasa, the father of the kidnapped boy.

He wasn't looking at me, at first, couldn't have been expecting me, any more than I was expecting him. I watched him acknowledge Protz with brief resignation, watched him measure the two Feds with a longer stare that barely passed for noncommittal. And then he looked at me. His dark face froze. I saw him mutter under his breath; wondered whether he was calling up verification data on me or just swearing.

I looked at Protz, who didn't seem to get it. He had to know about the kidnapping—he'd been at the Corporate Security station with the others when they'd come to get me. Maybe he'd never been told the identity of the victim. I looked at Natasa again, at the desperate questions in his eyes.

I shook my head, letting him know that whatever else happened, no one was going to hear more about it from me today. I understood my own situation well enough, even if I wasn't sure about his.

Natasa and his security team went through the motions, mouthing speeches designed to reassure the Feds that everything about this installation was as meticulous as its security and was typical of all their operations. They led us in through a cathedral-vaulted causeway of geodesic arches, to a waiting tram.

Natasa dropped back, walking alongside me, as soon as he dared. "What are you doing here?" he muttered.

"Research," I said. He was a full head taller than I was. I looked up at him, suddenly even more uncomfortable. "What are you doing here?" I was sure there hadn't been any change in the kidnapping situation.

"My wife is here," he said, as if that explained everything.

We got on board the tram that would carry us deeper into the installation. Like players in a virtual fantasy world, we shot down a long tunnel walled with mirrors that reflected our passage toward infinity. It was more than the showplace it seemed to be— I recognized the walls of a decontamination chamber. I wondered whether they were more concerned about decontaminating the ones who came in or the ones who went out of here. The last time I'd gone down a hall of mirrors like this one, they had lined the entrance to a black lab, and I'd been looking for illegal drugs, the kind that would give me back my Gift.

I stared out through the transparent hull, searching for my reflection; saw the featureless surface of a silver bullet reflecting back. I thought about what my last trip down a hall of mirrors had cost me. The debit reading on my databand had only been the beginning of what I'd paid to free my mind, even for a few days, from the prison I'd built for it myself.

We went on for what could have been another kilometer through sleek ceralloy-walled passages and chambers half a hundred meters high, skeletoned with beams of composite and fleshed by panes of transparent aluminum. I had to admit, if only to myself, that it impressed the hell out of me. I listened to Protz drone on about form and function with more interest, wondering whether any of this really had any bearing at all on the question of worker safety, let alone the kind of treatment Tau was dealing out to the Hydrans. I glanced over at Natasa more than once. He was never looking at me when I did.

Finally the tram whispered to a stop, letting us out into another security area. We passed through the lightshow of verifications and warnings, and an EM field so strong I felt it crackle like static through my thoughts, running its mindless fingers over my brain and triggering a reflex in my psi. I was still shaking out my head as we went on into the research area.

Another reception committee was waiting there for us; researchers and technicians this time, in pastel coveralls. I wasn't surprised to see a face I recognized at the front of the crowd: Ling Natasa, the kidnapped child's mother. I saw her freeze as she spotted me. Her eyes darted to her husband's face for an explanation, or at least reassurance. She must have found something there that she needed: I saw her pull herself together in time to show the Feds an expression as secure as the research complex was supposed to be.

She moved through the introductions like she was on autopilot, clenched and pale. To my eyes she looked worse than her husband did. The only time she reacted visibly was when Protz pointed me out. "He was curious about our processing of the reef material," he said. Nothing about how curious I was to see the way they treated their workers. And nothing about the kidnapping.

The same confusion was in her eyes as she looked at me again. I shrugged, not able to think of a single word that would fit into this moment, wishing that I could reassure her, mind-to-mind—that somehow I could find a way to wipe that stricken look off her face and answer the questions she wasn't free to ask me. But there was nothing I could do, except match her artificial smile.

She seemed to be in charge of the subcomplex of laboratories we were inspecting now and whatever projects were going on in them. Tau must have insisted that she put in an appearance; that keiretsu meant putting Tau's interests first, no matter how she felt.

The series of labs seemed to go on forever. So did our tour of it. Everything looked right—it was a fucking temple of technology, and everything the Feds asked to see displayed or demonstrated seemed to show up or function for them in the ways they expected. They muttered constantly to each other, and to themselves, until I realized they must be using implanted memory systems to feed them the endless variations of specialized knowledge their jobs required.

But as I went on watching and listening, went on observing the same things they did, getting the same answers, something began to bother me. The Feds were cool, professional, analytical: perfect machines. Nothing more. No more than a mobile extension of their augmentation. I'd interacted with AI's that had more personality than these two Feds did. I'd seen dead bodies with more personality.

They were a null set, without the concern or even the curiosity to ask the kinds of questions I was starting to need answers to in a bad way: Who were all the technicians I noticed who moved like they were on strange ground? Did they really work here, or had they been brought in to expand the regular staff during the inspection? Was it just coincidence that the matrix dispersal system had had a total safety upgrade so recently? Was Lab Plex 103 only inaccessible because they were decontaminating it after a high-risk experiment, or had something happened in there that Tau didn't want the Feds to see?

None of those things seemed to bother Givechy or Osuna. Nothing much even seemed to occur independently to them. They went where they were led and they didn't push any limits. I wondered whether they'd ever even noticed what species they were.

We'd been viewing what seemed to be endless repetitions of the same facility for a long time now, and no one seemed to be getting restless except me. "What about your bondies?" I asked Ling Natasa finally, because no one else had asked it. "You use contract labor. I saw some workers yesterday, at the reefs. Do you use them here?"

She turned back, with a look that said she'd almost managed to forget about me. "Yes," she murmured. She looked wary, like she kept expecting me to ask something else. "We use a fair amount of contract labor in our excavation and extraction operations."

"Are we going to see that next?" I asked. I glanced at the Feds. "I expect the FTA wants to see how you treat their property." If I'd been a mind reader then, I might have regretted it. But I wasn't, and she only nodded. She was the only one looking at me whose stare wouldn't have registered fatal on a rad meter, and only because her real concerns were somewhere else entirely.

We left the experimental labs and took a tube to another part of the complex. On the way I listened to her voice, more expressionless than any tape, describing the steps in the process of turning the "wild library" of the cloud-reefs into something useful and reproducible for Tau to license out.

Every standard day the operation excavated several thousand metric tons of reef matrix. That raw material was analyzed, separated, and processed down to a few cubic centimeters of material that Tau hoped would give them something unique to human experience.

"How do you make any profit?" I asked Protz. "With installations like this, and all these workers, for so little result—"

Protz sent me another radioactive glance. "On the contrary. One discovery like the hybrid enzyme that gave us ceralloy technology makes everything we do here worth the effort. Our research is not merely profitable—it benefits all of humanity." He smiled, looking away from me at the Feds. Their expressions didn't change. He went on smiling anyway.

I glanced at Ling Natasa, thinking that whenever I'd heard a combine talk about the good of humanity, humanity didn't seem to extend beyond their own keiretsu. And thinking about it, I began to wonder again about the questions that no one had asked here today . . . not even me. Protz had said to ask him anything. I wasn't naive enough to think he meant it, but maybe I'd been naive to think anyone else would listen if I did.

Another tram ride emptied us out into an underground chamber, the largest space I'd seen yet. This place made my whole head sing; I realized we must be somewhere in the heart of the reef. Another group of what appeared to be technicians were waiting, ready to put us into protective gear. I recognized the field generator someone strapped around my waist, a standard form of the upgraded suit I'd worn to go reef-diving. Everyone I saw anywhere in the chamber was wearing one. "They all move like they're underwater," I said to Ling Natasa. "Why do they look like that?"

"It's a force field," she said, raising her voice so that the two Feds could hear her. "This is a particularly fragile area in the matrix."

I realized that the white noise singing in my head wasn't just the presence of the reefs: the entire area was contained inside a force bubble; accident insurance, so that if the workers hit something unexpected, they wouldn't blow up the entire complex. "How many of the workers here are contract labor?"

"Most of them, I think," she said. "The rest are supervisors— our technicians and engineers."

"Why so many contract laborers?" I asked. "Why not more Tau citizens? Is it too dangerous? And why no Hydrans—?"

"Why don't you let us ask the questions?" Givechy moved between us, forcing me to back off.

Ling Natasa looked at him, at me, back at him. "Our own citizens are generally too well educated to do menial work," she said evenly, and went on looking at him, but answering me. "And Tau policy does not permit Hydran workers in our research and development facilities, because there are—" she faltered, and glanced at me, "—security concerns wherever psions are employed."

Protz cleared his throat. She glanced at him, and I saw a spark of panic show in her eyes. But the Feds only nodded and didn't ask anything more. Osuna looked back at me for too long. I kept my mouth shut, this time.

We went on through the mining operations zone on foot. I wondered whether somebody was deliberately trying to wear out the FTA's inspectors, take the edge off their attention, make them give up and turn back sooner. If they were it wasn't happening. The Feds went on like drones—as tireless and as lacking in curiosity. I told myself that they could be querying their augmentation, recording data, analyzing it, using bioware I couldn't sense or see. But maybe they weren't. I wondered why the guardrails of the catwalks we climbed looked newer than the metal under my feet. I wondered whether they'd really hold my weight if I stumbled and fell against them. I wondered whether everyone in this place would be wearing a protective field, or even have one, if our backs were turned.

I remembered the Federation Mines, out in the Crab Colonies. The Mines provided the Human Federation with all the telhassium it needed for its starships and starport hubs. They'd used contract labor there to dig the ore, because it was a dangerous, dirty job, forty-five hundred light-years from anywhere, on the core of a burned-out star. It was simple economics: out there human lives were worth a lot less than cutting-edge technology.

The FTA ran the Federation Mines, and the FTA policed it, and when I'd worked there the bondies didn't wear protective fields or even so much as a breathing mask to protect them from the radioactive dust that turned their lungs to shit. Forty-five percent of the laborers who were sent to the Mines didn't survive their work contract.

I dropped back as the group moved on, drifting toward one of the laborers who'd been herded aside to let us pass. "Do you always wear the field belts?" I asked. "Or is this equipment just for show?"

He looked at me at first as if he didn't believe I was actually speaking to him, and then he looked harder at me. I realized he was looking at my eyes. Hydran eyes. "Get away from me, freak," he muttered.

Someone caught my arm, pulling me around: one of the security guards assigned to keep us together and moving. "Stay away from the workers," he said, "unless maybe you'd like to join them."

"What did you say—?" I whispered, feeling the bottom drop out of my thoughts.

"He said, 'Excuse me, sir, but for security reasons we ask that you stay with the rest of the group.'" Burnell Natasa stepped up beside us, giving his man a look. He led me away, tight-lipped, and made sure I rejoined the others. He stayed close to my side after that, not giving me a chance to lag behind. For a space of heartbeats I was grateful, like I'd just been dragged back from the edge of a hundred-meter drop.

My gratitude didn't last long. "This is a farce," I said. "This isn't how things actually are here."

"What the hell do you want?" he asked, barely audible.

"The truth," I said.

He glared at me. "Nobody wants the truth."

"I do."

"Then maybe you'd better get over it," he said sourly, and looked away again. "Before you hurt anyone else."

I looked down. "I'm sorry I couldn't help your son," I murmured. "The Hydrans wouldn't talk to me—"

"Why not?" he asked, with the sharpness of surprise this time, or pain.

"Because I'm a freak," I said.

He frowned, and I wasn't sure whether it was frustration or simply incomprehension.

"I'm sorry—" I muttered again, my memory opening doors I didn't want to step through.

He didn't say anything, looking ahead to where his wife was using a multiple-display wall to demonstrate some biochemical process. "She shouldn't be here," he said, not to me but to himself.

"What about you—?" I asked.

He looked at me. "No," he said.

"Did Tau make you do this?"

He didn't answer.

The rest of the tour was white noise. Artificial monomole sky, desolate ranges of machinery for deconstructing the matrix of the reefs, the entire human-made subterranean world of the interface. . . . Nothing I saw or heard could stop the cancerous fear that at a word from Tau I could be made invisible—that I could disappear into that faceless mass of bondies. And this time there would be no Jule taMing to find me and save me. My paranoia grew until there was no coherent emotion left inside me except the need for this to be over.

I didn't ask any more questions. No one asked me why.

EIGHT

BY THE TIME Wauno dropped me off at the location where the team was collecting preliminary data, the workday was nearly over. I waded through the random motion of bodies and started doing my job. Whispers and stares followed me. I wondered whether the others had been talking behind my back all day.

As we finished securing equipment for the night, Wauno's transport came down out of the violet air again, limned in gold as it landed on the river shore.

I finished sealing a container and straightened up, inhaling the transport's faint reek of ozone. The hatch opened. I headed toward it with the others.

The team members made desultory talk on the way back to Riverton. I didn't join in, too drained by another day I didn't want to think about. Kissindre sat near Wauno, as usual, deep in conversation about the reefs and the cloud-whales. What I overheard him telling her made more sense than all the Tau data I'd downloaded into my brain. I wondered again how he'd learned all that; just tracking clouds wasn't enough. As we left the transport for the hotel I almost asked, but I didn't have the energy.

But as I was heading out he called my name. I looked back, and he said, "You free tonight?"

I hesitated, wondering why he wanted to know. "Yeah," I said finally. He gestured me back. I pushed past Kelly, and past Ezra Ditreksen, who'd come aboard looking for Kissindre.

"You're invited to dinner," Wauno said as I leaned against the control panel next to him. "There's somebody who wants to meet you . . . somebody you should meet, if you really want to know more about the reefs."

I barely kept the surprise off of my face. "Where?" I asked. I'd thought I was going to ask *who?*

"Freaktown."

Something squeezed my lungs shut. "Shit." I shook my head, turning away.

"It won't be like that." His voice pulled me back.

"Like what?" I said, looking at him.

"Like what Tau did to you."

I went on staring at him. "Why——?" I asked finally.

He looked blank. Then he nodded, like he finally understood what I'd asked him. "Because I thought someone owed you an apology."

"Why do you feel that's your responsibility?"

He touched the frayed pouch that hung on a thong around his neck. He shrugged. "I guess . . . this." He lifted the bag up, looked at it. I realized that he always wore it, the way he always wore his lenses: like they'd become a part of his body.

The pouch was made from animal hide. It was old, so old that what must have been fur once was worn away completely in places. Ragged fringe decorated it, and broken patterns of tiny colored beads.

"What is that?" I asked softly.

"A relic. An . . . heirloom. My ancestors called it a medicine pouch. Not like for drug patches," he said. "Spirit medicine. Talismans. Supposed to keep you safe." He half smiled, his mouth pinched with irony. "That's all I know. Everyone who could tell me more is dead."

"Where's it from?"

"Earth," he said, fingering the broken fringe. "Nordamerica. A long time ago."

"You born there?"

He shook his head. "My ancestors have been gone for a long time."

He hadn't said *"gone from there."* He'd said *"gone."* I looked down at the pouch as he let it drop against his chest.

"What's happened to the Hydrans . . ." He shrugged. "Same thing. I guess that's why I keep needing to see what's across the river. The same reason you do, maybe."

I rubbed my face, rubbing away scabs and expression. "I can't," I said. "The Hydrans threw me out. They think I'm the living dead."

"Not this one." He shook his head. "This one's different."

I realized that I believe him, maybe because I needed to so much.

"What do you say?" he asked.

I didn't say anything for a long moment. Then I asked, as if it didn't matter, "Just you and me?"

He hesitated. "And her." He nodded toward Kissindre, standing with Ezra in the back of the transport, inventorying equipment. "Will she go?" There was something not quite casual in the way he looked at her, like he was trying not to think about her.

My mouth twitched. "Yeah. I expect so." I called her name, and she came forward, her look still registering inventories as she shut down her cyberlinks and brought her full attention back to us. "Wauno knows a Hydran who wants to talk about the reefs. He says we're invited to dinner. You ready to cross the river?"

"Tonight?" she said, looking at Wauno.

He nodded.

Her face came alive. "I was born ready." She grinned. "Is this your informant—?"

He shrugged. "I guess you could call her that. I usually call her Grandmother."

She raised her eyebrows.

"It's a term of respect and affection," he said, straight-faced. "For an elder."

Her mouth relaxed until she was smiling again. "I absolutely want to go. I think I speak for both of us—" She glanced at me.

"Of course you do," Ezra said, materializing behind her. His expression slid as he caught her talking to Wauno and me. "But what are we speaking about?"

Kissindre turned to look at him and missed the annoyance that was suddenly on Wauno's face. I saw her hesitate, weighing the fact that Ezra hadn't been invited against his reaction if she didn't tell him. "We have a chance to . . . to meet with an informant who knows about the reefs." She glanced at Wauno, back at Ezra. "Across the river." One word she never used was "Freaktown."

Ezra stiffened, not hiding his reaction fast enough. "Is this something your uncle arranged?" he asked.

"No." She folded her arms, as if she didn't see the point of the question. "This is someone Wauno knows."

He looked at Wauno. "Are you sure this is safe—what with the unrest and all? After all, that kidnapping—"

"It's safe," Wauno said.

"Well, we should let your uncle know—" Ezra turned back.

"And it's a private party," Wauno said. "He's not invited. If you don't like that, stay here."

Ditreksen frowned. If Wauno had been trying to lose him, he'd guessed wrong. "If you're determined to go," he said to Kissindre, "then I'm certainly going with you."

She forced a smile, and he took it at face value.

Wauno's jaw tightened. But then he shrugged and settled behind the controls again. He took us back across the river as the evening deepened into night. Kissindre sat up front beside him. They spent the time discussing the cloud-whales, the reefs, and how their existence had influenced Hydran culture.

I sat back, listening. Ezra sat across from me; I felt him glancing at me like a thief would, stealing my concentration, until finally I had to look at him.

"Is it true you used to be a contract laborer?" he said.

I glanced forward at Kissindre, realizing she was the only person who could have told him that. I looked back at him. "What about it?" I said.

"I always wondered how you and I ended up in the same place."

"I had to kill someone," I said. "How about you—?"

He grunted in disgust and looked away.

"Did Kissindre tell you that her grandfather was a bondie?"

His face mottled. "You liar."

"It's true." Kissindre looked back over her shoulder at us. "He was, Ezra."

"You never told me—"

"Why?" she asked. "Does it make a difference to you?"

He didn't answer.

Wauno glanced back once, and away. There was dead silence in the transport's cabin for the rest of the flight.

I looked down at Freaktown, its random streets, its patterns of light only a dim echo of the bright geometrics of Tau Riverton. Looking down on the two sides of the river from up here, cloud-high, I thought about the differences between them and about how, in spite of the differences, from up here those patterns of light laid out on the darkness were only echoes of the same need.

Wauno didn't circle down to land in the maze of Freaktown streets the way I'd expected him to. We flew on over it, not losing altitude until we were almost beyond sight of both sides of the river. Ditreksen kept moving restlessly in his seat. He murmured something to Kissindre as we began our descent over a candle flame of light in the utter blackness. She ran her finger across her lips and didn't answer him.

As we descended I realized that the light was coming from a structure the size of a low urban stack, a solitary island in the night sea.

Wauno set us down in the shadowland beyond its bright entrance. I could see someone silhouetted against the light, but I couldn't tell anything about whoever waited there.

The hatch opened. Wauno signaled us out of our seats. He picked up a box that he'd stowed behind his own seat and started out with it.

"Aren't those our supplies—?" Kissindre asked. She gave him a look that didn't want to accuse him but wouldn't let it pass.

He shrugged. "It's traditional to bring a gift of food when you visit. You can always get more," he said, lowering his voice, emphasis on the *you*. "All you have to do is ask."

Her mouth thinned. She looked past him out the hatchway, looked back, and nodded.

"Wait a minute," Ezra said, coming forward.

"It's traditional." Kissindre put a hand on his arm until he eased up. "We can get more."

He shrugged, and his own mouth quirked. "We're invited to dinner, but we have to bring our own food."

Wauno just looked at him and smiled. Carrying the box, he went down the ramp and out.

I followed the others down the ramp and toward the light. Just for a moment I thought the figure waiting for us looked familiar; almost thought I could make the silhouette into the form of the woman I'd seen in the streets of Freaktown, a woman carrying a child. . . .

I blinked as we entered the corona of glare, and I saw a Hydran woman holding a child. I wavered, slowing—saw an old woman, her back bent by the weight of time, and the child in her arms: a Hydran child, not a human one.

The child's eyes went wide at the sight of us appearing suddenly in the light, like angels. Or *devils*. She turned into a wriggling eel in the old woman's grip. The old woman let her slide down. She disappeared from the patch of light as suddenly as we'd come into it. Everything happened without a word.

I took a deep breath. The air filled me with coldness. I tried to make myself believe that she'd run away from the sight of all of us, not just from me. I listened to the noises in the outer darkness, sounds made by things I didn't know the names or even the shapes of, the murmuring voices of an alien night. The strange perfume of another world's foliage was in the wind. I took a step deeper into the band of light.

Wauno moved past me, carrying the box of supplies. "Grandmother." He stopped in front of the old woman and made a small bow, murmuring something I couldn't make out. She bobbed her head in return and said the same thing. It sounded like *"Namaste."* Her face was a netmap of time; its lines deepened as she smiled. A veil covered her eyes. It was transparent enough that I could look into them, but it gave her gaze an unnerving shadow of doubt.

Wauno stepped back, pointing us out to her; I heard our names leapfrog out of a stream of unintelligible Hydran speech.

She bent her head at me, still smiling, a smile so open I was sure it had to be hiding something. I just couldn't tell what. She spoke to me, still in Hydran, with a look in her eyes that said she expected me to know what she was saying.

I looked at Wauno. "She only speaks Hydran?"

He shrugged. "She says she knew you were coming."

I wondered whether she meant to the planet or just to dinner. *"Namaste,"* I murmured, and bobbed my head.

Grandmother nodded, as if she was satisfied. She looked past me at Kissindre, who looked uncertain, and at Ezra, who frowned, back at Wauno and at me, as if she was trying to read something into the way we stood together. She was probably reading more than that, but if she was, I couldn't tell. At last she made a motion that included all of us. She led the way inside, moving slowly.

"What does *namaste* mean?" I asked Wauno as we followed her in.

"It means 'We are one.'" He half smiled.

I watched Grandmother's slow progress ahead of me, the heavy knot of white hair at the back of her neck bobbing with her motion. She wore a long tunic over loose pants, a style that I hadn't seen on the other side of the river. Without the burden of the child weighing her down, her back was straight and strong. But still she moved slowly, almost stubbornly, as if it took an effort of will. I wondered how old she was.

I looked back at Wauno. "How did you learn to speak Hydran? There aren't any files in Tau's access—"

"Yes, there are." He glanced at me.

I felt my hands tighten. "Can you get me into one?"

He nodded.

"What is this place?" We were following a long hallway lined with closed doors. The building had the sinuous, nonlinear feel of the Community Hall, but without the eye-popping decoration. "What was it? It's old . . ." I could feel its age weighing on my thoughts the way the child had weighed down the old woman. "I—"

"Yes, it's old," Ezra muttered, behind my back. "Your perceptiveness continues to amaze me."

"I guess you'd call it a monastery," Wauno said, ignoring Ezra and the look I gave him. "A retreat. I can't find a better word for it in our language. Nobody seems to remember how old it is. The data could be in the records somewhere, but a lot of the historical material has been lost. The religious tradition that it belonged to has almost died out. The building was abandoned for years."

I wondered what sort of beliefs the original inhabitants of this place had held; what had made them lose faith and abandon it. "And now?" I asked as Grandmother stopped in front of a closed door. The door opened, although she didn't touch it. I didn't see an automatic sensor.

"Most of the time Grandmother stays here alone. She's an *oyasin*. It means something like 'memory,' or sometimes 'lamp': a keeper of the traditions."

Grandmother disappeared through the doorway, and light suddenly filled the space beyond.

"What about the child we saw?" Kissindre asked softly.

I turned back in the doorway. Wauno gave one of his shrugs

and said, "Sometimes people come out here from town, stay for a while, when they need to get away."

From the conditions I'd seen there, a lot of people must need to get away from something in Freaktown. "How many people are here right now?"

He shook his head. "Don't know. I'm not a mind reader." He smiled, and went on in.

Grandmother sat waiting for us at a low table, its edges as free-form as everything else in this place. There were no seats, only kneeling mats. The light came from a bowl in the center of the table where a burning wick drifted in a quiet pool of lamp oil. The illumination it gave off made the room as bright as day to my eyes . . . Hydran eyes. The room probably seemed dark to the others. The lamp gave off a thin, spiraling tendril of smoke.

I felt myself relax finally, realizing that I'd gotten this far with-out anyone attacking me, without Grandmother driving me out—without being struck dead by some force I couldn't even feel, the potential energy of millennia stored up in the walls of this place like heat lightning, waiting for something like me to set it off.

I took a deep breath, inhaling the warm, heavy odors that filled the room. The air was thick with spices like none I'd ever smelled before, except maybe a couple of nights ago, in a hole-in-the-wall Freaktown eatery. The smell of food made me remember how hungry I was. I settled onto a mat, looking across the table at the old woman. Her green eyes studied me, hardly blinking, as the others settled around me. I swallowed saliva, keeping my hands off the table surface until I learned what the rules were.

When we were all sitting, Grandmother began to speak again, gesturing toward the center of the dark, featureless wooden slab, where half a dozen small ceramic cups were laid out in a circle around a squat, amber-glass container of liquid. From the size of the cups, I guessed that the drink wasn't water. Probably liquor, because alcohol affected humans and Hydrans pretty much the same way. Probably strong liquor.

"She wants each of us to take a cup," Wauno said. Grand-mother pointed at me.

I reached out, almost picked up the closest cup. But then I noticed that each cup was different. Each one had been formed and painted individually, given its own subtle character. I looked

at them all, feeling everyone's gaze settle on my hand while it
hesitated in the air, and the seconds stretched. Ezra shifted his
legs under him and sighed.

I reached for a cup on the far side of the circle, the one that I
liked best. *This was a test.* I wondered what the choice told
Grandmother about me, or whether the answer lay in the act of
choosing itself, or whether it was really no test at all.

Kissindre's hand hung in the air above the table. She glanced
at me, then at Wauno, who nodded. She chose a cup, reaching
past me to pick it up. Wauno took one next, slowly, thoughtfully.
Ezra took the cup sitting in front of him, pulled it toward him, his
impatience skreeking it along the tabletop.

Deep golden liquid appeared in my cup, in all our cups at
once. Ezra jerked back. I heard Kissindre's indrawn breath.
Wauno looked into his cup like he didn't see anything unusual. I
wondered what it took to get a reaction out of him. I swallowed
my surprise, hoping that at least it hadn't been obvious to the
humans in the room.

Grandmother chose a cup, using her hand, like everyone else.
But I watched the cup change: empty one second, full the next.
She lifted her cup. Wauno lifted his, and the rest of us followed
him as she spoke words to the air. The words began to take on a
singsong tone, shifting into what could have been a prayer. The
tendril of pale smoke from the flame at the center of the table
began to unravel like a silken rope into finer and finer strands. I
sat breathing in the scent of the liquor in my cup, hypnotized, as
the separate strands of smoke began to circle in the air.

The smoke images vanished, suddenly cut off, like the old
woman's song. The flame wavered and came back. The smoke
rose straight up, undisturbed. Grandmother looked at me across
the table; I held my breath. But her eyes released me again without accusing me of anything. She looked at Ezra for a long
minute; I watched him ignore her. The smoke from the lamp suddenly looped sideways, as if there was a draft, and blew into his
eyes. He coughed and waved his hands.

There was no draft. I smiled. Grandmother lifted her cup to us
and said, *"Namaste."*

I echoed it, along with Wauno and Kissindre. Grandmother
took a sip; we followed one by one. I kept my first sip small, until

I knew more about what I was drinking. It was strong, like I'd expected. I saw Kissindre's eyes water; she raised her eyebrows and took another sip.

Ezra drank, finally, and started to cough again. I emptied my cup in one swallow; this time I did smile. My cup refilled itself. I didn't drink it down this time, remembering I hadn't eaten; remembering the smell of food and wondering again where it was, wishing it was on the table. There'd been a time when not eating all day was just how I lived, but I hadn't lived like that for a while now.

The bottle and extra cups sitting in front of me on the table disappeared. For a heartbeat the table was empty, and then a torus-shaped bowl replaced them, with the lamp centered in its negative space. The lamp flame wavered, the smoke corkscrewed. I felt the gentle breath of air disturbed by an exchange of matter and energy. Grandmother smiled, nodding at me, and began to speak again.

I glanced at Wauno.

"Grandmother says it's time to eat." He pointed at the trencher filled with something that looked like stew. "She says you go first, because you've been hungry for a long time." He gave me an odd look as he said it, as if he wasn't any surer of what the words meant than I was.

I looked down at the table. There was no bowl in front of me, no utensil; only what I'd taken for serving spoons waiting in the trencher.

"We all eat out of the same bowl," Wauno said. "It's custom. Go ahead."

I reached out, dug the pronged spoon into the dish. Everyone watched me like I was disarming a bomb as I brought it up to my mouth. I wondered whether Hydrans even used spoons. I ate a mouthful. The pungent mix of flavors, spicy and sweet-sour, filled my head until my memory overflowed.

I remember this. I remember— A room, but not this one . . . eyes, green like the old woman's, green like mine, but in someone else's face . . . a warm room sheltering me, and the warmth of my mother's arms, her mind whispering my name with love . . . my one true name, which could only be spoken mind-to-mind. . . .

I swallowed, gasping, cleared my head with a burning mouthful of the nameless liquor. I sat blinking as the burn spread to my eyes.

My vision cleared, and I looked at Grandmother. She didn't move or speak; she just kept watching me with veiled eyes, with her head cocked a little to one side.

"So how is it?" Wauno asked.

"Spicy," I whispered. I dug another mouthful of stew out of the trencher. This time I kept my eyes fixed on the table, not listening for lost voices haunting the circuits of my brain. I swallowed the food and went on eating. Wauno joined me. Out of the corner of my eye, I saw Kissindre down her second drink like a dose of medicine and reach for a spoon. She glanced at Ezra, who was still sitting beside her, looking like a man with a stick up his ass. *He didn't like freaks.* I wondered how strong his reaction to all the visible use of psi really was. He wasn't making any move to try the food. I wasn't sure he'd taken more than a sip of the liquor.

"What's in this?" he asked suddenly. "I know he'll eat anything—" He jerked his head at me. "But most people have more sense." He looked at Kissindre as though he expected her to agree with him.

Instead she brought the spoonful of food to her mouth and ate it. I watched her expression; slowly she smiled. "It's good," she said, still holding his gaze.

"I wouldn't be in such a hurry to eat something I don't know anything about," he muttered.

"It's just vegetables and spices," Wauno said. "Some are traditional with the Hydrans, some they got from us. Nothing in their food ever bothered me. They're vegetarians," he repeated.

Ezra grimaced. "Manioc root is a vegetable, but if you don't cook it right it's a poison. Besides, this is unsanitary, everyone eating out of the same dish." He waved a hand at the bowl. "And everything here is . . . alien." I wondered what bothered him the most—the food, the way it was laid out, or how it had arrived on the table.

A new, smaller bowl appeared on the tabletop in front of him. It was full of stew. He jerked back as if it was alive.

Grandmother said something, poking her finger in Ezra's direction while he sat glaring at the bowl, his look getting darker as he thought about it.

"Grandmother says you shouldn't eat with us," Wauno said, expressionless. "She says you're sick."

Ezra looked up at them, his mouth thinning.

"She says you should drink *uslo* tea. You'll feel a lot better." Wauno smiled. So did Grandmother.

"Must be a laxative," I muttered.

"That's it," Ezra said, pushing up from the table. "I'm not taking any more of this. We did not come here to be made the butt of a joke by you, Wauno, or by a—" He broke off, glancing at Grandmother, glaring at me.

"By a what?" I put my spoon down.

"Stop it, for God's sake." Kissindre stopped me with a look. Ezra caught her arm, tried to pull her to her feet. She jerked free. "Ezra, sit down! I'm sorry. . . ." She twisted where she sat, looking from Wauno to Grandmother.

"Wauno, whether this was your idea or the freak's, it stinks," Ezra said, still standing. "I want you to take us back to Riverton, now."

"Wait a minute," Kissindre said, starting to get up.

"What did you call me?" I pushed to my feet beside her.

"You heard me."

"Hey." Wauno got up in one fluid motion, holding up his hand. "I'll take anybody back who wants to go. You don't have to go with him"—he looked at Kissindre—"if you don't want to."

She looked from me to Ezra, and I watched her face harden. "Yes, I do," she said, and the words were like stones. She looked back at Grandmother, and murmured, "I hope. . . . *Namaste*." She made a small bow, still remembering the ritual form, even now. She started after Ezra, who'd already left the room.

I ducked my head, still looking at Grandmother, and followed them out. I fought my anger, trying not to let it make me stupid, trying not to leave it hanging like a pall in the rooms behind me, where everyone would feel it choking them. . . .

When I got outside Ezra and Kissindre were shouting at each other. His face was red in the reflected light; hers was half in darkness.

I caught Ezra by the shoulder, pulling him around. "Cut it out," I said. "Everyone can feel you—"

He pulled away from me, his face full of disgust or something uglier. "Keep your hands off me, you pervert, you—"

"Freak?" I said.

"Freak!" he shouted, and his hands balled into fists. "You goddamn freak!"

"At least I'm not a goddamn asshole," I said.

He lunged at me. I saw it coming, as if he was moving in slow motion; I could have been reading his mind, the move was so obvious. I stiff-armed him: he ran himself up on the heel of my hand and went down like I'd hit him with a rock.

I watched him writhe on the ground, bleeding and cursing; watched Kissindre drop down on her knees beside him, putting her hands on him, covering him with solicitude. "Oh, my God," she was saying; while he held his face, groaning, "My node, he broke my node—"

Wauno came up beside me. He stood there, not saying anything, with his hands behind his back and his mouth pulled a little to one side.

Kissindre gave us a look I'd never seen her give to a sentient life-form before. "Help me, damn you!" she said.

Wauno moved forward and helped her get Ezra on his feet. He started them toward the transport; glanced back over his shoulder at me. "I'll come back for you."

"What?" I said. "Wait—"

"Grandmother wants you to stay," he said. "She wants to talk to you. I'll be back."

Shit. I started after them. Kissindre looked back at me, and I stopped moving. I watched them get into the transport, watched it rise into the night, leaving me stranded.

"Now time can move forward again," someone said behind me. I swung around.

Grandmother. For just a moment, I thought she'd mindspoken me. But she hadn't. "You speak Standard?" I blurted out the only question that seemed to be left in my head. I remembered that Wauno had translated her speech to us but not the other way around. I'd thought she was reading our minds, but she hadn't needed to.

"Of course." She smiled the same open contented smile, but

suddenly it didn't seem simple at all. "Now we can eat in peace." She bent her head at me, inviting me back inside.

I followed her back through the warren of halls to the room where the food was waiting. As I crossed the threshold, the scent of it triggered more memories; for a moment I was crossing into a different room, somewhere else in spacetime—

I stopped just inside the doorway while Grandmother went on to the table and settled into her place. She looked up at me, expectant, with the thread of smoke tendriling past her face. Her face was a mystery in the shifting light. I focused on it, went toward it, kneeled down where I'd been sitting before. She didn't do or say anything, as if she didn't register anything I felt or thought.

I had the feeling that if I didn't start eating, she wouldn't either. So I ate, filling the empty place in my thoughts with physical sensation, existing in the present, the way I'd learned to do on the streets, holding off the past and the future for as long as I could.

Grandmother ate with me, not saying anything. She didn't use a spoon. But she chewed and swallowed, just like I did, savoring the taste and the texture of the food. I wondered whether the silence between us was her choice or whether she was simply respecting mine. I wondered whether for her this was like eating in an empty room.

I glanced away at the walls. There were no windows, not even any pictures to relieve the blank monotony of the place. I wondered whether she was too poor even to buy herself some cheap holostills, or whether the austerity was intentional. Maybe Hydrans never felt claustrophobic, the way humans did, because they knew they always had a way out.

I thought about the woman with the kidnapped child. I thought about Freaktown, and what I'd seen of it; I thought about Oldcity, as the flavors of the food and the memories worked on me. I thought about traps, how they were everywhere, waiting for everyone—different traps that were all really the same trap in the end. Life was a trap, and human or Hydran, you only got out of it one way. . . .

I went on eating; tried to make my restless body as still as the old woman watching me, tried to make my thoughts as empty as the walls.

But the longer I stared at the wall across from me, the more I began to notice the subtle tracery of cracks in its surface; how those cracks formed patterns, images that your mind could get lost in, that led you somehow into the silent calm of your own mind's eye. . . .

I sat back finally and wiped my mouth, with one kind of hunger satisfied, at least.

Grandmother sat back too, and stopped eating. I wondered whether she'd stopped because I'd stopped, or whether she'd only kept eating because I'd still been hungry. Or whether we'd really both wanted to stop at the same time. I looked up at her. Her eyes were watching me like a cat's.

Two Hydran children, a girl and a boy, came into the room. They moved so silently I didn't hear them coming, but somehow their arrival didn't startle me. They bowed to us as they gathered up utensils and carried away the trencher. They didn't say anything, but I caught them looking at me as they went out. I heard them whispering in the hall.

I wondered why Grandmother hadn't just sent the food away herself, the same way she'd put it on the table. I thought about that, about how the whole eating ritual had reeked of psi. If Grandmother had wanted to rub our faces in the fact that she had the Gift and we didn't, that we were on Hydran ground now— outsiders, aliens—she couldn't have made it any more obvious. I wondered whether that was exactly what she'd been doing.

"You have many questions," she said, just as I decided to ask one.

I felt myself smile as I nodded. She could have read that right out of my thoughts, or just from the expression on my face. "Did you arrange this meal just to make the others leave?"

"Why do you say that?" She leaned forward, her head cocked a little to the side, like she was hard of hearing. It wasn't the first time I'd seen her do that. I realized suddenly that it wasn't my words she had trouble understanding.

"Just wondered," I muttered.

Her face twitched, as if something I couldn't see had brushed her cheek. Finally she said, "I follow the Way of Things. If one follows the Way, one discovers whatever one was meant to find."

"Oh." I settled back, hooking my arms around my knees. It sounded like the same pseudo-mysticism too many human religions preached along with loving their fellow sentient beings. As far as I could see, it was all hype and more than half hypocrisy. But a belief like that might mean something genuine to the Hydrans. They had precognition: sometimes they actually did get a glimpse of the future.

I thought about my last sight of Kissindre and Ezra; about what kind of scene there was going to be when I saw them again. "Does Wauno know you speak our language?"

"He speaks our language," she said, like that explained everything. "Why don't you ask me a real question?"

I laughed, and grimaced. "Why don't you hate me?"

The calm waters of her expression rippled. She pressed her hand to her eyes, looked up at me again. "Why should I hate you?"

I shook my head. "I can't use my psi. Hanjen . . . the Council threw me out, when they realized—"

"You don't use your Gift because you choose not to," she said.

"You don't understand—"

"The Council has lost sight of the Way," she went on, as if my speech was as opaque as my thoughts. "That happened long ago, before you were even born. They can no longer see anything clearly. . . . You suffered a terrible wound. You must hold the wound closed," she said gently, "until it heals. You are a good person."

I felt my face redden again. "You don't understand! I killed someone—"

"So . . ." she said, as if she finally understood.

"I'll go now." I started to get up.

"You are a miracle," she said, and bowed her head to me. "I am humbled in your presence."

"I'm not a fucking miracle," I said, choking on anger. "I'm just a fucking 'breed." I started for the door; stopped short as someone came through it. Hanjen.

He stopped too, staring at me the way I must have been staring at him. "What are you doing here?" he asked.

"Leaving," I said. I tried to move past him but he blocked my way. He glanced toward Grandmother and said something sharp and querulous in Hydran. And then there was dead silence in the room. I watched their faces, the only thing that told me they were still communicating.

At last Hanjen turned back to me and made a deeper bow than I'd ever seen a Hydran give to a human. *"Namaste,"* he murmured. The change in his expression was so complete that I didn't know what the hell to make of it. "Please forgive me," he murmured. "I have behaved in a way that causes me shame."

I frowned, not certain what he meant; shrugged, because it seemed to be an apology. And then I pushed on past him.

He caught my arm; let it go again as I looked at him. "Please, stay," he said. "We need to finish what we came here to do."

"What's that?" I said, hearing the sullenness in my voice.

"Understand each other." He faced me without expression.

"Sit down," Grandmother said. "Sit down, Bian."

I glanced behind me, wondering who she meant. She was looking at me. She gestured, like I was a stubborn child.

"My name's Cat," I said.

She shook her head, made patient *sit down* motions again.

I stayed where I was, frowning.

"Cat is your name among the Humans," Hanjen said. "This is a Hydran name, for when you are with your mother's people."

I looked at him, speechless. I looked back at Grandmother finally, wondering why she hadn't simply told me herself. . . . But it wasn't her business to talk with humans; it was his. And she couldn't simply let me into her mind. Maybe she was tired of talking. "What does *Bian* mean?" I asked.

"It means 'hidden.' " Hanjen smiled.

"Is that a joke?" I asked, because I couldn't tell what he was smiling about, and he wasn't a friend of mine.

He looked blank. "No," he said.

I moved past him, drawn back toward the table as if Grandmother had a magnetic field.

Hanjen followed, stood looking down at the empty tabletop. "I've missed dinner," he said.

Grandmother smiled and shook her head. The children who'd taken the trencher away appeared in the doorway behind us, coming at her silent call like they'd been conjured out of the air. They brought a dish to the table and set it down so carefully that the flame barely wavered.

Hanjen smiled too, and made one of those bows to the children, to her, before he sat down cross-legged. He started to eat, not using a spoon. He looked up at me—stopped, swallowing, as if he realized he couldn't eat and communicate with a human at the same time. "Forgive me," he mumbled. "It was a long walk. I am very hungry."

"You walked here from Fre—from town?" I asked. He nodded. "Why?"

He took another mouthful of food. "Out of respect," he said, like it was obvious.

"For what?" I pushed, annoyed.

"For myself," he murmured, still eating. "For my body, my Gift—my beliefs."

I shook my head.

"It is the Way." He was beginning to sound impatient; I saw him glance at Grandmother, as if she'd said something, and swallow his irritation like a mouthful of stew. "The body and the mind deserve equal reverence; otherwise a person is not truly whole. The *oyasin* has been giving me instruction."

"*Oyasin?*" I asked. Wauno had called her that before.

"It means 'guide'—she is a guide to the Way and a holder of our beliefs and traditions."

I looked at Grandmother. That fit what Wauno had said, but it didn't fit the reverence in his voice as he said it. "You mean, a religious leader—?" I looked back at him.

"Not a 'leader,' in the sense that Humans use it. 'Guide' is closer. *Ke* is everywhere: it is the life force of the Allsoul, something you might call the 'god-within-us.' But there is only one Way that each of us finds. . . ." He glanced at Grandmother like he needed guidance right here, right now. "It is difficult to explain, in words."

"The Way which can be told is not the eternal Way," Grandmother said. I thought of how names were shared among the Community: the spoken names, the true ones.

Hanjen sighed. "Most of our people no longer believe that *ke* even exists. That is one reason I decided to seek the Way for myself, with the *oyasin*'s guidance."

I sat down cross-legged midway between them. I watched him eat. "I've eaten this food before. A long time ago."

He glanced up, first at Grandmother and then at me. "Is that so?" he said. "Where?"

"I think my mother made it."

He stopped eating. "You lived here as a child?"

I shook my head. "On Ardattee. In Oldcity . . . a place the Federation uses to dump its garbage."

He went on staring at me, as if he'd lost my meaning, fallen off my train of thought because there was nothing for him to hold on to.

"It's a relocation dump. A few Hydrans ended up there after they'd been driven off of their own worlds. But there were more humans . . . the kind who don't fit into a keiretsu like Tau."

He blinked. "Where is your mother now?"

"Dead. For a long time." I shook my head. "That's all I know."

"Your father? He was . . . Human?" He looked like a man being led blindfolded through a strange room.

He was finally getting an idea of how I felt. I shrugged. "I don't know anything about him." Whenever I thought about it, all that I came up with was the sort of thing I'd heard from the Corpses two nights ago: my mother was a whore, my father was a rapist. That was the only way my existence made any sense. I tried not to think about it any more than I had to. "It's not a coincidence, your being here tonight, is it?"

He looked disoriented, like trying to follow my conversation was difficult enough without my changing the subject. Finally he said, "When I last saw the *oyasin,* I showed her our . . . meeting. And she showed me that I had not seen clearly. It was her feeling that if you and I met again, without the Council, we might understand each other better."

"That wouldn't be hard," I said.

He looked down. "The Council once had the best interests of our people in mind. But now there are too many of us with—limitations. Sometimes the Council members show too much self-interest; they always show a lack of perspective. We all want our society to become more open to the Humans, because we believe that is the only way we will ever prosper, under the circumstances—"

"By kissing Tau's ass."

His pupils narrowed, slowly widened again.

"Is that how you feel?"

"I think we must learn to live with the ones who have come to share our world—accept life on their terms—because that is how things are now. Denying what is obvious goes against the Way and is only wasted effort. We have to turn the energy of our anger to useful ends. Otherwise it will destroy us. It has destroyed too many of us already." He glanced down.

I half smiled. "The Way tells you that when life gives you lemons, you make lemonade—?"

"Excuse me . . . ?" He shook his head. " 'Lemons'?" he said. "You mean, 'Humans'?"

"It's a kind of fruit. Sour. You have to fix it up."

He half smiled, this time.

"So the Council wants things to stay the way they are," I said, still trying to get everything clear in my mind. "They believe that's the only way to get something more from Tau?"

He nodded. "Or, at least, to not lose more. They are very conservative in their attitudes."

"Is that what you believe too?" Asking it again.

He didn't say anything for a few heartbeats, but he wasn't mindspeaking Grandmother. I glanced at her: She was looking at him, but her face was unreadable. Finally he said, "I feel that working within the law is the only way to achieve real progress. Even to change the rules—one must do it carefully. So yes, I guess I am a conservative. HARM calls me an enemy of our people—a collaborator. And yet . . . sometimes I think I am a little sick of 'lemonade.' " The shadow of a smile came back, but it didn't touch his eyes.

"So you do think things ought to change; that they could be better?"

"Have you spent any time on this side of the river?" he asked.

I nodded.

"So have I," he said. There was no trace of smile anywhere on his face now. "But few Humans have. The only ones who come here regularly come for what they can bleed out of us—which is little enough, anymore. We need so many things—we need access to the kinds of things Tau keeps to itself. Knowledge and resources that we no longer possess independently. That is not entirely the fault of the Humans—I am the first to admit our society was in decline before they ever reached this world. But now we don't even have the opportunities—"

"That woman, Miya, the one who kidnapped the little boy. She was trained by Tau, wasn't she? To do the kind of therapy she did for him. They let her work over there without monitoring her psi."

His pupils narrowed again. I had the feeling that he was angry, or maybe he was just suspicious. I wished I knew which it was. "Yes," he said. "There are many things the Gift could do for Humans, if only they had the . . . courage to trust us. Opportunity can flow both ways. It should; or anything we gain would only be charity. That would not solve our problem. Our problem is a lack of *hope,* more than a lack of *things*."

The Council mistakes one for the other," Grandmother said. "Their need is like an infection. But they are using the wrong cure. Too many *things* make everything worse."

Hanjen nodded, looking resigned. "What we need is the chance to *do* as much as *get*."

I remembered life on the streets of Oldcity, one empty aimless day/night flowing into another. I'd done a lot of drugs then, anytime I could hustle the credit, or even when I couldn't, trying to fill the emptiness of my existence, the empty hole in my mind where something had been taken from me that I didn't even know the name of. Trying to forget that there was nothing better to do, no hope for me of ever having anything better to do.

I sat staring at the trencher of food in front of me. "I know," I murmured, finally. I watched Hanjen consider eating more; watched him look at me and stop.

"What about HARM?" I asked. "Where do they fit in?"

"They don't," he said flatly. "They have turned their backs on our traditions and abandoned the Way. They are wandering in the wilderness. By trying to 'save' us, they will end up destroying us."

I glanced at Grandmother, remembering that Protz had claimed she had ties to the radicals. If that was true, it didn't seem likely they'd turned their back on the traditions she believed in. "I expect they don't see it that way," I said to Hanjen, still watching Grandmother out of the corner of my eye. I wondered what she knew, wished I knew how to find out. She smiled at me, and I didn't have any idea why.

I looked at Hanjen again. "Why can't you . . . communicate with the radicals? If you believe that they're doing more harm than good, can't you show them why—open your mind up, and show them? Have you ever let them try to show you how they see the situation?"

He was perfectly still for a moment, traveling through the words in slow motion to get to my point. "Tell me something first," he said finally. "Is it true you were forced to kill someone, and survived? And that is why you don't use your Gift?"

Don't. Not *can't.* . . . *Don't.* "Yeah," I whispered.

"Then it is true that your part in the kidnapping was completely by chance? An accident?"

I nodded. "How did you find out?" He hadn't known it at the Council meeting; none of them had.

He bent his head at Grandmother. "But she said I must ask you myself."

She'd never seen me before tonight. I glanced at her, wondering how long she'd known about it.

"The Council was afraid, when they discovered what you were—" Hanjen broke off, looking like he'd just stepped in shit. He shook his head. "We were afraid that Tau had sent you to . . . cause trouble for us. To somehow tie the Council into the kidnapping. To tie us to the radicals. The fact that you were an—outsider, claiming to understand us, and yet you kept your mind completely closed. . . . When I felt everyone else's suspicion, it became my own. It was very hard to understand all this, you see—" His hands fluttered; he probably didn't look that helpless very often. Satisfaction took some of the sting out of my memory of the Council meeting, but not much.

"Why should you be any better than the rest of them?" I asked, since he seemed to feel that he was.

"I am a *daesin,*" he said. "The closest word you have for it is 'ombudsman.' I am trained to avoid the contagious emotion that overtook the Council. But I allowed my—suspicions to control me."

"I thought only humans did that," I said.

He frowned. "No."

"It wasn't my choice to attend that meeting," I said. "Just so you know."

"I did not think so." He shook his head. "You asked why we don't just show the radicals what is wrong with their way of seeing. We would, but they will not let us. They are *klin;* they are . . . of one mind. A closed set to anyone who does not share their beliefs. They have shut us out as completely as you have—but selfishly."

I frowned this time. "I thought Hydrans didn't do that to each other. I thought they were always sharing their thoughts, their emotions, with each other, so that there were never any misunderstandings."

He laughed, but not as if he thought it was funny. "That's what we have always wanted to believe ourselves. Maybe it was even true, once, when our civilization was whole. Or perhaps not even then. But anyway our past is gone. Now we live in the time of the Humans, and no one really knows what the truth is anymore."

I studied my hands, not knowing which frayed end of the conversation to pick up, or whether I should even try.

He shook his head. "There is really nothing else that I can tell you, or Tau, about the kidnapping, that Tau does not already know. It was done by HARM, and Tau knows that. But we do not know where they disappear to, any more than Tau does. There are thousands of hectares of emptiness in the Homeland. HARM can be anywhere they choose, from moment to moment. . . . But we do want to help you find the boy. Please assure Agent Perrymeade that if we discover anything, we will send word—"

I rubbed my neck, feeling as if I'd suddenly stopped existing, even as a halfbreed with brain damage; that he was only seeing the Humans' pawn again. I wondered whether everything he'd said to me had been just as calculated. I didn't want to believe that, but I couldn't prove anything either way. His mood seemed to settle on me like a weight. I remembered what he'd said about catching an emotion like a disease. I ought to be immune, if anyone was. The mood was my own, and it wasn't going to improve when I left this place.

I glanced at Grandmother. She was making the smoke spiral and braid like Hanjen and I were already gone from the room. I wondered if that was a kind of prayer. I wondered what she was praying for and where she thought the answers were going to come from.

Hanjen looked at Grandmother too, suddenly, as if she'd said something. She had—something I couldn't hear. The thread of smoke drifted up, undisturbed, as she let it go.

Hanjen got to his feet. He bowed to Grandmother and then to me. "I must go. It's a long walk back to town. I hope the rest of your visit to our world is . . . productive."

I watched him go out, wondering why he was leaving. I suddenly felt as left out of what went on here as I'd been at the Council meeting.

I looked back at Grandmother, wondering what she'd told him. Maybe his leaving hadn't meant anything at all—maybe I just didn't understand the way anything happened on this side of the river.

Somebody entered the room. I turned, half expecting to see Hanjen again. But it was Wauno.

Wauno made his bow to Grandmother, murmured *"Namaste,"* and looked at me. "You ready?"

I got up, wondering suddenly if Wauno's arrival had had anything to do with Hanjen's leaving. I looked toward Grandmother, but she only bowed her head and murmured, *"Namaste,* Bian."

"Namaste, oyasin," I said, feeling unanchored as I said it, lost somewhere between gratitude and frustration. As I followed Wauno out, I looked back to see the faces of half a dozen children peering at us from doorways. I wondered again how many Hydrans lived in this place; how many of them had been mentally listening in on what was said in that room. Half a hundred of them could have been eavesdropping, and I never would have known. Realizing that made my skin prickle; made me feel Human.

Maybe Wauno felt the same way. We were in the transport, rising up into the night, before he said anything. And then it was only, "You want to go back to the hotel?" Nothing about what I'd thought of Grandmother, or what I'd thought of dinner . . . whether I'd learned anything. I wondered if the look on my face as we walked out was what had kept him from asking. I wondered if he was sorry he'd thought of this.

I couldn't give him any reassurances, because I wasn't certain how I felt about it myself. I forced my thoughts back across the river, remembering where I really belonged. My mouth pulled down as I remembered Ezra, the blood on his face, the look on

Kissindre's face and what it was probably going to mean when I reached the other side. "Do I have a choice?"

Wauno shook his head. "Not really. Not this time of night."

I checked my databand, surprised as I saw how much time had passed. "What would you do?"

"Go to sleep," he said. "I like to get up about five hours from now."

I sighed. "How's Ezra?"

He shrugged. "You broke his nose. I took them to a clinic."

"Shit. . . ." I leaned back into the seat, resting my head.

"He had it coming."

"She's not going to see it that way." I remembered the look on Kissindre's face.

Wauno didn't say anything.

"How did she seem?" I asked, finally.

"Pretty grim."

I looked out at the night, at Tau Riverton filling the darkness below us, sucking me down toward light and order and retribution.

NINE

WAUNO LEFT ME at the hotel. I watched the transport rise until I lost sight of it in the wash of artificial light. The lamppost I'd leaned against asked me if I needed anything. I went inside.

Kissindre was sitting in the lobby. She was still wearing her coat and hat. I stopped when I saw her.

"You broke his nose," she said.

"I know." I looked away as her expression registered. "I'm sorry." But I wasn't. And she knew it. I stood there grimacing as if I was afraid of being hit.

She jerked her head toward the hotel's bar-and-eatery. "Let's talk. In there." I didn't figure she was hungry. She wanted neutral ground.

The room was almost empty; there wasn't a big tourist trade in Riverton, and the locals were used to curfews. We settled into a dark corner, in the false privacy of a booth. Music oozed out of the walls, gentle and plangent; the kind of music that made you ache inside and hate yourself for it. I stared at the wall on my right, trying to decide without touching it whether it was actually wood or just high-quality sim. Maybe it didn't matter. Maybe nothing did. I stuck a camph into my mouth and ordered a drink from the touchboard. A minute later the drink slid out of the wall, answering my question.

"You use a lot of drugs," Kissindre said.

I looked up at her, wondering what she meant by that. "I can handle it," I said. "It doesn't affect my work."

"Why do you need them?"

"Who says I need them?" I took the camph out of my mouth, looked at it. I picked up the drink and drank it. It tasted weak. I stuck the camph back into my mouth. There was only one drug that could give me what I really wanted—give me back my psi. But to let myself use it would be like walking on broken legs. Her eyes were still on me. I frowned, looking away. "I like it. So do you."

She pulled her hat off, rumpling her hair, and opened her coat. She ordered herself a drink. When it came, she sat looking at it. Finally she drank it down in one swallow, grimacing. "No, I don't. But I'm angry—I'm very angry." She didn't sound angry; she sounded tired. She didn't meet my eyes. "You could have killed Ezra, hitting him like that."

"No, I couldn't," I said. "I knew what I was doing. Even if he didn't."

She looked up. "You meant to break his nose?"

"I didn't break his nose," I said. "He broke his nose."

I expected her to tell me I was full of shit. Instead she leaned on her elbows, covering her eyes with her hands. I wondered why she wouldn't go on looking at me, whether she was afraid to or just fed up. "Damn it, nothing has gone the way I wanted it to. . . . Ever since we got here, it's been one damn thing after another, until I can't think straight." She looked up at me, finally. "I hate this."

I shifted in my seat, not needing her to tell me I'd been the cause of it. I tried to order another drink; a synthetic voice told me I'd had enough. "Fuck you too," I muttered. Kissindre looked up at me again. I fumbled in my pockets for another camph, found the pack, and pulled it out. It was empty. I wadded it up and threw it on the table. An invisible hand swept it, and our empty glasses, into some secret compartment in the imaginary wood surface. I leaned back, removing my hands from the perfectly clean tabletop.

Kissindre said, "This can't go on. The whole project will end up terminated."

"I know," I said.

"I know you and Ezra never liked each other. I thought at least you were intelligent enough to work together on something important without letting your testosterone poisoning get out of hand. Obviously I was wrong." Her hands closed over the table's edge. "God, I didn't want this to happen, but you're making me do it . . . I told Ezra he's off the project."

Damn— I shut my eyes. "What?" I opened them again.

"I told Ezra he's off the project. He's leaving tomorrow."

"Ezra?" I said.

She looked at me the way I'd just looked at her.

"Why him? Why not me? He's your habit. I'm the one who caused the trouble with Tau."

She half frowned. "You weren't to blame for that," she said. "For God's sake, you were the victim, remember?" She shook her head. "And tonight—Ezra insulted our host, our informant. He couldn't keep his bigoted mouth shut for one evening. He—" She looked into my eyes, with their long slit pupils. *He'd called me a freak.* She pushed loose strands of hair back from her face. "I feel like I've been asleep for years. Like I never really saw this world, in all my visits here. . . . And I never really saw him. The truth was always there; I just didn't see it." She looked away, making a pain noise that tried to pass for a laugh. "I can't go on pretending I don't see it." Her hands released the tabletop suddenly.

"Listen," I said, "it makes more sense for me to go, instead of him. The Tau government hates psions, not—" I broke off, before I said *assholes*.

"'Assholes'?" Her mouth formed something that wasn't exactly a smile. I shrugged, looking away. "You were right. That's what he was. God damn him—" Her mouth quivered, suddenly.

"Are you doing this for me?" I said. "Don't. I can take care of myself."

"Give me more credit," she said, handing me back my own line. "I'm doing it for the project. Because my research needs you more than it needs a stats quantifier. I can get one of those anywhere. I only picked Ezra because I thought we wanted to be together—" She broke off again.

"You've had fights before. You always get over it. Maybe you ought to wait, before you—"

She was silent for a moment. "Tell me," she said, "when the universe eventually ends, will you feel guilty about that?"

It startled a laugh out of me. "Maybe."

She half smiled. "Well, don't feel guilty about this. I always thought Ezra didn't like you because he was jealous of how easily you learned things. Of how you looked at me, sometimes—or he said you did, anyway—" She glanced down, tugging at the end of her single thick braid. "I thought at least it meant he loved me."

"You don't think that's true?"

"Yes," she said, and her voice broke. "But I don't want to spend the rest of my life lying to myself, so that I can go on loving him." She took a deep breath.

We sat looking at each other for a long time, not speaking, not moving. Finally the voice that had told me I was drunk told us that the bar was closing for the night.

Kissindre lurched like a startled sleepwalker and got up from her seat. I followed her out of the bar, neither of us saying anything. We were the only ones in the lift, going up.

We walked together down the hall, still silent, until I reached my room. I stopped; she stopped too, glancing on down the hallway. She looked back at the lift.

"What is it?" I asked.

"I need to get a separate room." She shook her head, looking again at the door to the room she'd shared with Ezra, seeing nothing where the future had been until tonight. Finally she looked at me.

I touched my door; it opened. "You want to come in?"

She looked uncertain, but she nodded. She went ahead of me into the room. My eyes tracked her motion, even though I tried not to.

I closed the door. She turned back, looking at me as the door silently shut. I felt the pale room close us in, like a jail cell. The far wall had long since opaqued for the night. I ordered it to polarize again.

The star-patterned grid of the city filled my eyes. I took a deep breath, feeling the fist of my tension ease. Kissindre sat down on my bed, looking out at the view but not reacting. I sat in a chair, feeling the soft formless seat reshape itself around me. The sensation made me want to get up again. I made myself go on sitting, remembering the stillness of the Hydrans. "How long were you and Ezra together?" I asked, when she still didn't say anything or do anything.

"I can't even remember," she murmured. She looked back at me, finally. "We met at the study center in Quarro."

"You're from Ardattee?" I said. "I thought you were from Mysena."

"My family sent me to school in Quarro. They thought it would give me the best education." Her smile filled with irony. "Ezra was so—" She glanced away. "He was everything Quarro was supposed to be about. Everything my family admired . . . everything I thought I ought to want. And he wanted *me* . . . I'd never been wanted like that." Her gaze turned distant.

I thought about them together in Quarro, moving through a world of light and privilege: how they'd met, shared, learned, slept together. I thought about my life, moving on a parallel track with theirs, buried alive in Quarro's Oldcity.

"Aren't you from Quarro?" she asked. "Ezra said—"

"No." I got up from my seat, moved to the window/wall and stood looking out.

When I looked back at her she was crying, the tears seeping out through the fingers of the hand she'd pressed against her eyes to stop them. "Damn him—"

I wondered what she was thinking now—what he'd said to her when she told him to get out of her life; how ugly the words had been. I wondered what she was feeling—*lost? angry?* I couldn't tell. It made me feel helpless, because I didn't know what to do if I couldn't tell.

She got up and started for the door.

I crossed the room before she got there. "I know how it feels," I said. I caught her gently by the shoulders and made her look at me.

"You do?" she said thickly, looking back at me like she actually believed it might be true. And all the while I couldn't even imagine what she'd seen in him.

"No." I let my hands drop. "How could I even imagine what you feel?" I remembered holding someone else, far away, long ago: *Jule taMing,* her long dark hair slipping down across her face as I held her . . . how I'd known what she'd suffered, known what she needed . . . just like she'd known everything about me. I turned away, shaking my head.

"It must be terrible," Kissindre said softly.

"What?" I turned back, startled.

"To lose that. To lose something like the Gift."

I stood staring at her, stupidly.

"My uncle told me."

"God," I muttered.

"Cat—" she said, and broke off.

I looked away, down, out at the night, anywhere but at her. I'd known her for years now, worked beside her, studied with her, been her friend—and nothing more. I'd always stopped short of crossing that line, never tried to make our relationship anything more, because I'd thought she loved Ezra. I'd thought the way she looked at me sometimes was nothing more than curiosity.

I'd never had the courage to ask outright . . . I'd never had any way to know for sure. But all the time that I'd believed she wanted someone else, I'd wanted to be in a place like this with her, alone with her, wanted it so much some nights that I couldn't sleep.

And now I only wanted her to leave.

"Talk to me," she murmured. "In all the time we've worked together, you've never talked about *you.*"

I turned back, finally. "You never asked," I said.

This time she looked down. "Maybe I was afraid. . . ." I thought about the way she'd always acted—reacted—around me. She wasn't acting that way now. "Ironic, isn't it?"

"Why?" I asked. But I already knew the answer: *Because she was a xenologist. . . . Because I was strange.*

"Because I want you so much it makes my teeth hurt," she whispered, and her face turned scarlet. "I never wanted Ezra the way I want you."

I pulled her into my arms and kissed her, kissed her for a long time, because I'd wanted to kiss her for such a long time, to hold her, to know what it was like to be her lover.

We drifted back across the room to the bed. I followed her down onto it, not letting her go as we went on kissing, tasting the strange spices that breathed from our skin, feeling my hands slide over the warm contours of her body as her shirt came undone. Her hands were on me, loosening my shirt, my pants, touching my chest, touching me all over.

I kissed her throat, touched her breast, waiting for the feedback of her senses, waiting for every sensation to double for us both as my mind reached deep inside her to give her a kind of pleasure that Ezra never could. Waiting. Reaching—

It wasn't happening. I couldn't reach into her thoughts, to answer her every desire . . . I couldn't even find her.

I remembered suddenly that the last time I'd been with a woman I'd still been using the drugs that let me use my psi. But they'd been gone for a long time. Now I didn't know what to do next, didn't know whether it was the right thing, whether it would satisfy her, whether she wanted more, or wanted me to stop—

I broke away from her, swearing under my breath as the truth put out the fire of my need, turned my burning flesh to the cold, slack flesh of a corpse. I pulled my shirt together to hide the gooseflesh crawling up my naked body; to hide the signs of death from her, from myself.

"What—?" Kissindre sat up, blinking. "What is it?"

I didn't answer, and she touched my face gently with her hand.

"I can't," I whispered.

Her hand fell away. She sat on the side of the bed, looking down, her fingers picking at the edges of her open shirt. I heard her try to ask and lose her nerve.

"I can't—feel you," I said finally. "I don't know what to do."

She took one of my hands in hers.

I looked up, seeing confusion in her clear blue eyes that just stopped, the way all eyes stopped, because I couldn't reach through them into anyone's mind. "I want you," I said thickly, "but I can't find you." I took a deep breath. "I can't *feel* you." I touched my head. "I can't feel anyone." *I should have died. Maybe I had.*

She moved her hands slowly, taking my hand with them until it rested on the warm skin of her shoulder. "I'm right here," she said gently. "I know what to do. Just follow me. . . ." She bent her head; her lips burned against the cold flesh of my palm. "That's all you need, to be a human being."

"I don't know how." I pulled my hand free. I pushed to my feet; *not human enough, not Hydran enough.* I looked back at her, stretched out on my bed: her shining hair, the curve of her breast. Trying to want her the way I'd wanted her five minutes ago, trying to let my body answer her, mindlessly, as if there was nothing between us but sex. Once I'd believed that was all there was, sex between strangers. But not now. Now it was too late. I looked away finally, because nothing at all was happening. "Maybe you'd better go."

I listened, keeping my eyes averted, as she got up slowly from the bed. I heard her unsteady breathing as she pulled her clothes together; I heard her start toward the door.

"Kissindre." I forced myself to turn back, made myself cross the room again before she could go out. "It only happened because you matter too much to me—" I pulled her against me and kissed her again, let her go as her body began to soften and yield. "It's not your fault." I touched her hair. "And it's not your problem. Please—just tell me you understand that. . . ."

She nodded, slowly. "Will . . . will you be all right?"

Some sick part of me wanted to laugh, wanted to ask her, *Tonight, or ever—?* I strangled it. "Yeah. I'll be fine."

She opened her mouth, shut her eyes, shook her head. She went out of the room. The door closed behind her.

I stood for a long time wondering where she'd gone: whether she was going back to Ezra, or going to tell her uncle we were both miserable little shits, or going to an empty room exactly like this one. . . .

I stopped staring at the empty surface of the door and turned back to the bed. Its surface was just as smooth and featureless. Like nothing had happened.

I went to the bed and lay down on it. I ordered the window to opaque and called on the threedy, jerked the headset out of its cradle and pushed it onto my face. With my clothes hanging open and my mind fused shut I blew through the menu, searching for what I needed right then: something hot and raw and meaningless; a virtual fuck.

Something that didn't exist, here.

By the time I was absolutely sure of that, there was no emotion at all left inside me. I reached up to pull off the headset, ready to shut the access down.

But there was a message light blinking now at the corner of my vision. The message was from Wauno: access to a Hydran language tutorial. I pulled the program and dumped it into my brain in one long, masochistic feed.

I lay there awhile longer while the brain-smog of data-strings stupefied my concentration until I could almost forget; almost let the mnemonic buzz sing my mind to sleep. It was almost enough. . . .

But it wasn't. I got up from the bed, fastened my pants, fastened my shirt. I put on my coat and went out of the room.

I left the hotel, making sure I didn't cross the path of anybody I knew. I took an aircab down to the river's edge, where the bridge arced across the canyon to the Hydran town.

The bridge was dark, sealed off, closed for the night. I pressed against the yielding, invisible barrier of the force field until a disembodied voice activated, warning me that I was out past curfew, that my identity was registering at Corporate Security headquarters.

I swore, backing off, turned, and strode away, following the canyon's rim, triggering the ghosts in every fucking lamppost and hype-kiosk along the promenade. There was no one else visible for as far as I could see. I sat down on a bench, finally, letting my head rest against its iron brocade, my hands hanging strengthless in the space between my knees, as I waited for the cab I'd called to come back and get me.

I still breathed the taste of strange spices with every exhalation, still felt the rhythms and structure of a strange tongue high-lighting alien road maps in the circuits of my brain. I tried to remember if I'd ever walked those roads before, in a long-ago time and place.

Eventually everything fell silent. All I could hear now was the sound of the river, so faint and far below that I almost thought I was hearing the echo of Hydran voices. Faces I'd seen across the river accreted in my mind like dreamfall in the reefs . . . all of the eyes, the hair, the spice-colored skin morphing into one face: *Her face.* A Hydran woman with a human child, alone in the night maze of Freaktown.

The cold wind touched my face almost gently, like an unex-pected lover. I sat up, opening my eyes, glancing around, because there had been something almost familiar about the touch of the wind.

Someone was sitting with me on the bench. Miya.

TEN

MIYA. I REACHED out, my hands closing over her arms. I felt her muscles harden under my grip; felt my own surprise as they proved her body's solidity.

She looked into my eyes, unafraid, and didn't try to pull free. I knew as well as she did that there was no way I could hold her if she didn't want to be there.

I let my hands drop. "Miya?" I whispered, and heard my voice catch on the sound of her name.

The pupils of her eyes widened, narrowed again. *Surprise.* Sur-prise that I knew her name.

But not the kind of surprise I felt as I realized that she could only have come here looking for me. "It's not safe here." The words dropped off my tongue, surprising me again, because the

last thing I expected my gut response would be on seeing her was
to want her safe.

I saw her pupils dilate again, as if it was the last thing she'd
expected too. Her gaze hovered on my face like a moth hypnotized by a light. But she only shook her head and lifted her hands,
letting the sleeves of her hooded parka slide down: *No databand.*

Invisible. I glanced at my wrist. The databand was still there,
forcing me to remember what the Corpses had done to me
because I wore one . . . because of her. "I'm not invisible," I said,
looking away as anger gave me the strength to break her gaze.
"Tau's Security didn't have any trouble finding me." I gestured at
my bruises. "What the hell do you want?"

"I . . ." Her hand rose again, hesitated in the air, fell away. "I
wanted to thank you."

"For what?" I said sourly, totally lost to her logic.

She gazed at me without answering, until I began to think she
had no more idea of why than I did. Or maybe she was trying to
decide what to make of me, when the one thing that could have
told her was missing. "I couldn't see any other Way," she murmured finally, and it still wasn't an answer. "I felt that I had to
come," she said, as if she could tell from my face that I still
wasn't getting it. She spoke Standard, with no real accent. She
was dressed in pragmatic, sexless human clothes; if we hadn't
been face-to-face, she could have passed for a human.

"Like you felt you had to slip me that databand, back in
Freaktown?"

She looked away, across the river. "Yes," she said faintly. She
looked at me again, and I saw something in her eyes that was
closer to anguish, or even longing, than to guilt. I didn't know
what the hell to make of it. "I needed to be certain . . ." She broke
off, her hands worrying the seal of her jacket. "They said that you
were all right. I had to see it for myself."

I figured *they* must be HARM. "Did they tell you that it took
Draco's Chief of Security to get me out of Borosage's lockup—?"

"No," she said, and frowned.

"Tau's CorpSec thought I was one of the kidnappers. They
were going to torture me to get answers I didn't know. Jeezu, they
could have killed me!"

She grimaced like I'd hit her and murmured something that sounded like a curse. "I didn't know. . . . That night, when I saw you—"

"You saw a freak." I watched her confusion form like the fog of my breath. "You know what I mean." I jerked my head. "A halfbreed. You think I don't get the same reaction on this side of the river?"

This time her restless hand actually touched my sleeve. "That's not what I meant. I meant that I realized how much our safety mattered to you." She searched my face for something that wasn't there.

I shrugged off her touch, frowning. Fumbling my gloves out of my pocket, I pushed them on. "You don't know me."

"I felt it when you touched me—"

I grunted, not remembering anything but the pain and surprise as our bodies collided.

"—here." She touched her head.

Just for a second my breath caught. "Nice try," I muttered, and touched my own head. "But this doesn't work."

She made the same odd listening gesture I'd seen Grandmother make: *Trying to figure me out.* She might sound perfectly human, but she wasn't.

"You're not reading my mind now," I said, disgusted. "You couldn't then. Lie to me if you want to, but not about that."

"You're wrong," she said, forcing me to look up again. "In the first moment, there *was* nothing—not even a Human mind. You terrified me. And then you looked at me, and Joby, and you opened to us. . . . You wanted to help us. It was why you were there. You were the Way."

The Way. I thought about Grandmother, thought about fate and predestination. Even Hydrans couldn't see the future clearly. Precognition was the wild card power; it could give you an edge, but that was all. Humans followed their hunches; so did Hydrans. But those with the Gift had a lot more reason to. Sometimes it was enough . . . sometimes it was too much. I remembered a friend, the look on his face as he'd foreseen his own death. And I wondered again what I'd been doing on that Freaktown street, at just the wrong moment . . . or just the right one.

"Why didn't you teleport to get away?" Finally I was able to ask the question that had been gnawing at me ever since that night.

"I didn't have time."

"Time—?" I said. "It doesn't take that much."

"No, not for myself. But for Joby." She shook her head. "If you know who I am, then you must know what's wrong with him."

"Neurological damage," I said. And then I understood.

"You believe me." It wasn't a question.

I glanced at her again. "But you're not reading my mind now."

"No." She shook her head, without anything in her eyes, not doubt, not pity. "You're not letting me." She didn't ask what was wrong with me. I wondered why not. From the way she'd been staring at me, I didn't think the reason was indifference.

"Where is Joby?" I muttered, glancing away.

"Safe." She half frowned, as if she thought I'd changed the subject because I didn't trust her, but it was myself that I suddenly didn't trust. "I love Joby more than you can imagine," she said, as if she had every right to expect I'd believe that. "I'd never do anything to hurt him, or put him in danger."

"I know. . . ." I whispered, telling myself that she couldn't know the real reason for my change of subject; any more than I knew why I'd wanted to trust her with my life the moment I'd laid eyes on her. "So why did you kidnap him?" I asked hoarsely, looking back at her again. I knew she'd told me the truth about not reading my mind; she couldn't influence how I felt without my knowing it.

She took a deep breath, as if this time she'd been ready for the question. "How much do you know about all this?"

"I know his parents are sick with worry. That they can't understand why you did it."

"You've talked to them?"

I nodded. "Tau made certain I met them. I guess they felt being arrested, drugged, and beaten up wasn't enough to teach me a lesson. I had to eat some shit too."

She glanced down. When she looked up again, she looked uncertain for the first time. She took another breath, let it out slowly, in a whisper of fog. "I can take you to Joby, if you trust me. Then you can tell Ling and Burnell that he's safe."

I sat up straight with disbelief. "Where is he?"

She pointed over her shoulder. "Across the river."

I followed her gesture with my eyes. "The bridge is closed."

"We don't need a bridge," she said. "If you trust me."

I almost laughed. *Why should I? I looked into her eyes. Why do I . . . ?* The question died on my lips. *Why should you?* I didn't ask that one either, even though street logic screamed that this was a trap. I thought about everything I'd gone through these past two days. And then I said, "All right."

She took hold of my hand. My grip loosened as I almost lost my nerve. But her hold on me didn't falter. Her eyes weren't registering me now. I felt something indescribable charging the synapses of my brain, firing every nerve down through my body, as she manipulated the quantum field in a way I'd never be able to. I felt my body transforming, and inside the space of a breath, reality swallowed itself—

I was sitting on a bench, but the bench and everything else had changed.

I was in a room, in dim lamplight. It couldn't be anywhere but Freaktown: the shadows and the forms, the smells in the air, the background noises, overloaded my senses with déjà vu until it felt like we'd traveled through time, not space. Miya was sitting beside me on the bench, breathing hard. She got to her feet as awkwardly as if she'd carried me here on her back, looking toward the far side of the room.

There were two other Hydrans in the room: two men, sitting cross-legged on the floor. One of the bat-things flitted between them, dodging a fist-sized bubble that seemed to have a life of its own. The gleaming bubble whacked the bat-thing and knocked it to the floor, and I realized the bubble was solid. The bat-thing floundered on the threadbare rug, trying to right itself; its skreeing cries hurt my ears.

In an eyeblink Miya was across the room, kneeling down, taking the stunned bat-thing gently in her hands. There was nothing gentle in her face as she looked up at the two ballplayers.

The bubble, still suspended between the two Hydrans, dropped to the floor forgotten. The ball rolled toward me, bumped to a stop against my foot. The two men were staring at us. They stood up, and one of them gestured at me with a guttural noise of anger.

An invisible hand forced the momentum of his turn, carrying

him on around and slamming him into the wall. Before the other Hydran could take three steps, he tripped over his feet and fell flat.

"Miya!" the first one said, his face red with fury and the impact of the wall.

She answered him in a flood of unintelligible speech, gesturing in disgust as the bat-thing launched off from her hands. I realized suddenly that she had taken them both down with her telekinesis in less than a minute.

The two men began to shout, pointing at me now. Her own voice rose until they were all shouting at each other in Hydran.

I sat listening, stunned by the motion and noise, wondering why the hell they even needed to speak out loud.

Suddenly Miya broke off. She looked toward the arched doorway that opened on another room. The two men stopped, then; I heard a thin, high cry from somewhere in the darkness beyond. For a moment longer the three of them were silent, although their argument went on mind-to-mind, emotions playing across their faces like sun and shadow. Then Miya ordered the two men still with a motion of her hand and turned away like they'd disappeared. She went through the doorway into the darkened room beyond.

The two men stood where her silent order had planted them; their eyes never left me. They were both young, not much older than I was. Each of them wore his pale hair long, held on top of his head by an ornate clip. The hair clips were made of metal, in intricate, vision-knotting designs. I figured the style must be traditional, because I'd never seen it on a human. I wondered whether the clips had been shaped by hand or by thought.

The two Hydrans wore heavy, human-made jackets that almost disguised layers of faded traditional tunics and worn-looking pants; but no one would have mistaken them for keiretsu. In another life, someone might have mistaken them for my brothers.

I stood up, watched them shift uncertainly from foot to foot. They weren't carrying any weapons that I could see. I sat down again and let them stare at me. "My name is Cat," I said. My breath frosted. There was a small radiant heater in the corner of the room, but it wasn't enough. The room was almost as cold as the outside air.

The two Hydrans went on staring, their faces expressionless.

Maybe they didn't speak Standard. The bat-thing fluttered around them like fear made visible. I kept waiting for it to attack me, the way the one at the Council meeting had. This one kept its distance.

Finally I looked away from them, down at the small globe resting against my foot. I leaned over to pick it up, and a different kind of déjà vu fired every nerve-ending from my fingertips to my brain: It was warm, not cold like glass, with an image inside it that could be changed at a whim, by a thought. . . . *Just the way I'd known it would be.* This time the image was a bat-thing. I sat back, cupping it in my hands, concentrating. Trying to make the image transform into something else, anything else—

Nothing happened inside the globe or inside my head. I looked up and saw the two Hydrans watching me.

They glanced at each other then, touching their heads and grimacing. The one on the left said, "Why did she bring that freak *here?*"

"Maybe so we can see for ourselves what happens if we get too friendly with the Humans." The second one smirked; his elbow dug the first one in the side. They laughed.

It took me a couple of breaths to realize that they were speaking Hydran . . . and that I understood it. They were communicating out loud on purpose, because they thought I didn't understand their language, laughing at me to prove they weren't afraid of me.

I thought about it a little longer, listened to them make a few more remarks, sorted through the datafeed still downloading the Hydran language into my brain. And then, very carefully, I said, "Call me anything you want to. Just don't think I won't know it." In Hydran.

They froze, their surprise as naked as if I'd sent the thought straight into their minds.

Miya reappeared in the doorway. "Who said that—?" She looked at me. "You—?" She was holding a child. A human child. Joby. "You know our language?" she demanded, in Hydran.

"For about an hour now," I answered in Hydran, surprised to find that speaking it was easier than understanding someone else. "I'll be better at it tomorrow." I forced a smile, watching her expression turn unreadable. Hearing myself speak Hydran was like dreaming wide awake.

"This is Joby—?" I asked. Miya's eyes warned me off as I started toward her. I slowed, approaching her and the boy as carefully as I could.

Joby lifted his head from her shoulder to look at me. His eyes were wide and dark, human eyes. He was wrapped in layers of heavy sweaters; a knitted cap was pulled down over his ears to protect him from the cold. His face was soft with uncertainty, but he could have been any little boy just wakened out of sleep. I couldn't see anything wrong with him.

"Hey, Joby." I smiled at him, and after a moment the ghost of a smile touched his mouth too. He rubbed his face. Miya moved forward this time, bringing him closer to me. He put out a hand, touched my ear, the earring I wore in it.

He pulled his hand back again. The bat-thing appeared over his head, fluttering around him, still making sounds so high that I could barely hear them. He watched it fly, gravely.

I glanced at Miya, expecting to find her still watching me, judging me, not expecting the look of strained concentration that shut me out entirely. She kissed Joby gently on the top of his head and turned away, carrying him back into the darkened room.

I followed her this time. The others didn't try to stop me. I stood in the doorway as she settled him on a sleeping mat and pulled a blanket over him. She sat beside him on the floor, with her hand stroking his hair.

"I thought he had neurological damage," I said. "He doesn't look damaged."

She glanced up, startled. Her face closed as her attention left him for me. She took her hand away from his head, deliberately; her look forced me to keep watching him.

I watched him shift under the blanket, his arms and legs drawing up and in until he was curled like a fetus. He began to make a sound, the high, thin keening I'd heard before. It was worse, seeing it happen in front of my eyes. I forced myself to go on watching, but I didn't want to.

"You see?" she said, almost angrily. And then, almost wearily, she said, "You see."

I nodded, looking away finally, looking down.

The keening stopped as she turned back to him; I imagined her reaching out to him with her mind as she reached out with her hand, soothing and reassuring him.

At last she took her hand away. He lay quietly, breathing softly, almost asleep. She got to her feet and came toward me; I stepped back into the main room as she unhooked a blanket and dropped it across the doorway behind us.

"He seemed . . . so normal," I muttered, and had a hard time meeting her eyes.

She leaned against the wall, as if suddenly everything had gotten to be too much effort.

"You have to do everything for him?" I asked, but it wasn't really a question. "Without you—"

She stared into space, holding on to herself as if she were still holding Joby. "Without me he has no control over his autonomic nervous system . . . he's trapped inside himself."

"Is he aware of what's going on around him, without you? Does he get any input?"

"Some." She moved away from the wall, glancing back at the doorway as she crossed the room. "He has great difficulty making sense of what he does get, unless I help him to pattern it. When he's with his parents—" She broke off self-consciously, moved to sit down on the bench by the wall, drawing her feet up.

I let my breath out as I realized that she'd just answered one of the doubts that had been on my mind across the river: She really hadn't been lying to me. She hadn't kidnapped Joby to make some point by hurting or killing him.

Her whole body folded in on itself for a long moment before she raised her head again. "At least he knows them, now, when they're with him. . . ."

I watched her blink too much as she glanced at the two other Hydrans. They were sitting on the floor now, cross-legged and still, watching us. She was speaking Standard again, and I suspected that it wasn't just for my sake. She was a part of HARM, I didn't have to be a mind reader to see that; she'd taken Joby because she believed it would help her people, even though right then I couldn't imagine how.

But it was just as obvious that she wasn't happy about betraying the people whose child she'd taken, even if they were human.

I didn't press her about the questions that were still on my mind. Somehow just knowing this much made the rest of the answers easier to wait for. I glanced toward the room where Joby was sleeping again. "Is he ever going to be any better?"

She looked surprised, like she'd been expecting the obvious questions. "He is better—better than when I began doing therapy for him. Whenever I work with him, I help him pattern what input his brain receives; each time his mind retains some of the patterning. Eventually he should be able to interact on his own. He's so strong, and he wants it so much—" She broke off again, biting her lips, as if she'd suddenly remembered how things had changed for both of them.

I remembered the holo I'd seen of Joby. She was right; he was better now, if what I'd seen tonight was any proof. I looked at her face, seeing the fatigue and strain that were just as clear, now that I knew how much it had cost her to work with him . . . what it had cost her to bring him here. I tried again to make the two things fit together: why a human-hating Hydran radical would work so hard to heal a human child if she'd only intended to use him like this. I couldn't make them fit, any more than I could read her mind . . . any more than I could stop looking at her face, or believing everything I saw in her eyes. . . .

I looked away, at the two men still sitting together near the room's other entrance—probably the one that led to the outside, from the way they were watching it. There was nothing else in the room except the heavy fiber rug they were sitting on. Its surface was littered with food containers and bits of unidentifiable trash. The rug was so worn that I couldn't tell what color its patterned surface had originally been, or whether the faded blotches had ever been a pattern and not random stains. We were somewhere in Freaktown, but it could have been a room in Oldcity.

I looked back at Miya. "They'll never let you see Joby again, once he's returned to his parents. . . ." I forced myself to finish it. "What's going to happen to him then? Or isn't he going home—?"

"Of course he is," she snapped, but she shook her head, as if she was shaking off doubt. "The Council does nothing except get rich at the expense of the Community. Someone has to fight for our future, before we don't have one left—" She broke off. "Our demands are not unreasonable. The FTA observers are here because Tau broke promises, not just to Contract Labor but to its own citizens. We want the FTA to see that Tau has *never* kept a promise to us. All we want is justice . . . and there can never be any justice until someone knows the truth." Her hands tightened over the edge of the bench. "We'll return Joby to the FTA's observers, when they come. And one of our demands will be that I'm allowed to go on caring for Joby, to prove what our Gift has to offer Humans. To prove we can be trusted—"

"Well, you're off to a great start," I said.

Her eyes glanced off my face, and she frowned. She folded her arms and crossed her legs, as if her whole body was shutting me out.

"Miya. . . ." I looked up at the small, high window above our heads. Its surface was fogged with moisture; I couldn't see out. The bat-thing crouched on the window ledge, watching us, calm but alert. "I can see how much you care about Joby. And I believe HARM only wants to make things better for Hydrans. But this— kidnapping—doesn't make sense. You've spent a lot of time across the river. You know Tau's Board will never see the situation HARM's way—"

"If they try to lie to us, we'll know," she said flatly.

"They can lie to each other!" I said. "And you'd never know that until it was too late." She went on looking at me, but suddenly I felt like I was talking to a personality sim; the lights were on, but she wasn't home anymore. "What made you—made HARM—believe a combine Board would count the life of one child equal to their own self-interest?"

"You don't—"

"Miya!" A woman's voice, hard with anger, called her name behind me. I felt a sudden draft.

Something pulled me around where I stood, almost pulling me off my feet. I caught my balance, suddenly face-to-face with another Hydran stranger. Invisible hands of thought held me in front of her as she looked me over. I felt her try my mind's defenses; felt them turn her back. Three more Hydrans, a woman and two men, had materialized behind her. They were dressed like the two men already standing across the room; the woman holding me prisoner looked like the rest of them. But there was no question in my mind that she was their leader.

She made a noise that was half querulous, half relieved, as if she'd searched me mentally and discovered I was unarmed. Her telekinetic snare let me go, slamming me back against the wall.

As she turned toward Miya again, I realized that something about her was familiar. The Hydrans I'd met on this world still looked more alike than different to me; the differences between Hydrans and humans still stood out more than their individual features. But this time I was sure of the resemblance—in their faces, in the way they moved; in the way something about them held my eyes even when I was free to look away: *She was Miya's sister.*

Their expressions and gestures were all I needed to tell me they were arguing. I didn't have to guess why. The two HARM members who'd been sitting sullenly across the room got up and joined in; probably they'd called for the reinforcements. None of them looked at me now, like I'd become as invisible physically as I was mentally.

Finally I said, in Hydran, "I'm here. Why don't you ask me about it?"

Miya's sister turned back to me. "Because you have nothing to do with it," she snapped in Hydran. But her eyes stayed on me too long. I felt her probe my defenses again, trying to be certain that my mind was really as walled in as it seemed.

"If it wasn't for me, you wouldn't have Joby," I said. "If it wasn't for me, your sister would be drugged in a cell on the other side of the river, with the Corpses trying to beat everything she knows about you out of her."

She frowned. "How do you know that?"

"Personal experience." I touched my face.

She shook her head. "I mean, how do you know our language? How do you know she is my sister?" She jerked her head at Miya.

I shrugged. "I accessed a datafeed. And I used my eyes."

"Or maybe Tau gave you the information, along with the beating, to make us believe you," she said. "How can we know for sure, when your mind is closed to us?"

I laughed as I thought about what she'd see if she could read my mind. She glared at me. I stopped laughing as I realized there was nothing funny about my situation here. Suddenly nothing was funny, or simple: not for me, not for Joby or his parents, not for anyone on this side of the river. I glanced toward Miya.

She realized it too. "Naoh," she said. "You know I wouldn't have brought him here if I wasn't sure about him."

"How can you be sure? He's closed!" Naoh touched her head. "I'm not sure about you, since that night—" She broke off. I looked at Miya, surprised.

Emotion darted like a silver fish deep in Miya's eyes; was gone again, even as I realized that same emotion had been there every time she looked at me.

"I don't know why you brought him at all," Naoh said, pulling her sister's attention back. "Why are you obsessed with this—halfbreed?"

Miya flushed. "He saved my life! And without him, where would our future be?"

Naoh only shook her head, frowning. She turned back to me. "If anyone tries to find this place, because of you"—she made what I took for an obscene hand gesture—"they'll find it empty."

I didn't try to answer. I was having enough difficulty just following the flood of spoken Hydran, the unspoken subtexts.

"What were you doing at a Council meeting," Naoh demanded, "with Hanjen and those other *da kah* traitors, and Tau's Hydran Affairs Agent?"

I wondered what *da kah* meant. Probably the human version of it had four letters. There was no profanity at all in my Hydran headfile; Tau even censored its translator programs. "Tau made me go to the Council meeting," I said. "Can you speak more slowly— I'm not very good at this yet. The other night I was just . . . in the wrong place," wondering suddenly if there really was such a thing as an innocent bystander. "I came to Refuge to do research—"

"To try to 'explain' the reefs and 'understand' the cloud-whales?" Naoh said, her voice knife-edged. "Only Humans would think of that."

"Spare me," I said. "I'm stuck in the middle of this because of you people, and I don't like that. But I am half Hydran; I wouldn't do anything that would hurt the Community. All I want is for the boy to get safely home. All Tau really wants is to get the boy back. It's not too late—"

"No. This is what Tau wants—!" Naoh said fiercely. A jug sitting on the floor flew up into the air, just missing my head, and smashed down. Shards pelted my feet. "They want that, for us! Until nothing is left."

"Naoh!" Miya said; she jerked her head toward the room where Joby slept.

I toed the smashed pottery on the floor around my feet. "If you think that's what Tau wants, then what do you expect to get out of committing acts of terrorism, except more trouble?"

Naoh shook her head, like I was some brainwipe who'd exhausted the last of her patience. She glanced at Miya and pointed her hand at me.

Miya hunched forward on the bench, looking resigned. In Standard, she said, "Naoh wants me to explain, because she finds speaking—" She broke off, like she'd been about to say *to you*. "She finds it . . . tiring. I'm used to it." She sighed, locking her hands over one knee. "Obviously, we know about the FTA's investigation of Tau." *Probably because she'd told them.* "How often would we have a chance to . . . communicate"—she touched her head—"with someone who might actually help us against Tau? Naoh had a sending; she saw the Way—"

Miya hesitated, searching my face for comprehension. She looked relieved as I nodded. "We have to make ourselves *felt,* now. There will never be another chance like this. Naoh saw it: we have to reach them now; we had to do something that would make them understand our pain."

I glanced at the darkened doorway. "So you took Joby." I wondered whose idea that had been. Somehow I didn't think it had been hers. "That must have been a hard thing to do," I said.

Her head came up; her eyes filled with something I almost thought was gratitude. "Yes," she murmured. "But I had to do it." She looked at her sister.

"The Feds don't even know about the kidnapping," I said. "And I don't think they're going to hear about it from Tau."

"But they have to find out," Miya repeated. "Taking Joby will bring us everything we've fought for. Naoh saw the Way." She glanced at Naoh while something silent went on between them.

"Tau censors its communications and media web; you ought to know that. If they don't want the Feds to hear about the kidnapping, then the Feds won't. Joby's parents aren't going to talk if Tau tells them not to. It would be treason."

"But you can tell them!" Naoh said. "Now I see—it was meant to happen, your coming here. You only followed the Way." She glanced at Miya, back at me; something made me look away from her eyes. "Because of you, the FTA will hear us out."

"Do you really believe their coming here will do any good?" I asked.

"Don't you?" she demanded. "You live with the Humans. The combines are afraid of the FTA—"

I nodded. "But . . ." I had a sudden image of the two Feds, Givechy and Osuna, coming here. *But the FTA doesn't give a damn about you.* I looked down again.

Miya frowned, as if she was so used to reading a human face that she saw the truth in mine. I watched her doubt spread to Naoh and then the others waiting impassively around us.

"So you still think we're fools," Naoh said bitterly.

"Yes," I said, thinking about how much pain this kidnapping had caused already; how much more pain there was going to be before the aftershocks stopped coming. I looked away at the other HARM members standing in the room, at the anger and hunger in their young/old faces, knowing what they must be feeling right now, knowing I ought to feel the same way. But I only felt empty.

"Mebtaku," Naoh muttered, looking at me. I couldn't translate it.

Miya spun around to glare at her. *"Show* him the Way, Naoh," she said fiercely. She glanced at me. "More of the Way is hidden than we can say in words."

"There's no point. The *an lirr* will come back sooner than this one will find the Way." Naoh made a sharp motion with her hand, that probably went with *Get him out of here.* Behind her the others shifted restlessly; their expressions were a chorus of suspicion and resentment.

"Before you throw me back," I said, "maybe you ought to ask what else I know." I turned to Miya. "You're right. I helped you the other night because I wanted to. And I want to help you now. I know what Tau's trying to do to the Hydrans here—the same thing the Federation's been trying to do to every Hydran, every psion—" I broke off again. "I didn't mean that. I meant . . ."

"Humans," Naoh said, as Miya gave me an odd look, "are a disease without a cure. None of them are any good."

"You know, I keep trying to believe that," I said softly. "But I keep meeting the wrong ones. Ones who keep changing my mind."

"You can say that," Naoh muttered. "You have Human blood."

"That doesn't count for anything across the river." I shook my head. "That doesn't change the truth, either. If you believe all humans are the same and they're all scum, how does that make you any different than they are—?"

They were all silent this time. I wondered whether they were talking it over mind-to-mind, or whether I'd actually shut them up. I sat down suddenly on the bench near Miya, buckling under the weight of too many hours awake. I felt her eyes on me. I looked back at her. Even prepared for what I'd find, I couldn't look away.

Finding my voice again, I said, "I know someone who can help you. A vip in the FTA, back on Earth. . . ."

Naoh laughed in disbelief. "How would you know someone like that?"

"I worked as a bodyguard for Lady Elnear taMing." I held Miya's gaze. "She's on the Federation's Security Council."

Miya nodded, her surprise showing. Maybe she hadn't heard of the Lady, but she knew enough to know that the Security Council made policy for the entire Federation.

"Natan Isplanasky is a friend of hers; he oversees the FTA's Contract Labor Services, as much as anyone can. He can order an investigation—"

"Why would he help us?" Miya asked. "Contract Labor doesn't hire us out for money."

"I think he'd help you because justice matters to him."

Naoh made a rude noise.

"I was a contract laborer," I said slowly. "At the Federation's telhassium mines, on Cinder. The bondies there were as expendable as dirt. If someone hadn't paid my bond . . ." I was seeing Jule taMing's face suddenly, instead of Miya's. I blinked the room back into focus. "When I met Isplanasky, all I wanted was the chance to spit on him. But when I saw what was in his mind. . . ." They both stared at me, then, but they didn't interrupt. "The fact that the Feds treated their bondies worse than most combines did mattered to him. I was nothing, an ex-street rat, a freak; but what I'd been through mattered to him. He spends most of his life jacked into the Net—he was the closest thing to God I'll probably ever see, but even he couldn't know everything that went wrong in his universe."

"Did he make things right, then?" Miya asked.

I shrugged. "I know he made a start. Like you said—you can't get to justice without the truth to lead you there." I looked up again, half smiling. "Besides, he owes me more than one lousy beer. Tell me what he needs to know."

Miya was silent again, looking at the others. I watched their faces, their hands, the subtle clues to their interaction. At last she turned back to me. "We can tell you. We can show you . . . if you have Hydran eyes."

I wondered whether she meant that literally or figuratively. I nodded.

Miya got up and led the way out of the room. The two men who'd been in the room all along came with us. As we walked together down a dim hallway, they finally told me their names: Soral and Tiene. When they looked at my eyes this time, the only thing their own eyes registered was curiosity.

The hall ended at a timeworn spiral staircase. "Watch your step," Miya said to me, as if she wasn't sure whether I could see in the dark. I wondered why Hydrans even bothered with stairs. Then I remembered Hanjen, walking out from town to visit Grandmother: *Respecting his body, as well as his mind.*

We started upward, not down. I didn't ask why. The narrow stairwell was dark, even to my eyes. I heard the surreal echoes of life going on invisibly somewhere beyond the walls: hollow banging, clattering, rattles; somewhere a thin, high whistling. I couldn't make out voices, if there were any; couldn't make sense of the random sounds. The Hydrans ahead ahead of me climbed without speaking or looking back. The stairwell's spiral became tighter; I watched my footing more carefully, following them up through the funnel of silence.

Finally we stepped through a doorway into the clear night air. I took a deep breath. We were standing on a platform at the top of a tower above the building's domed roof. The building beneath us was identical to a hundred others I could see, looking out over the town. Most of them were domed and spired like this one; something I hadn't realized when I was wandering through the streets down below.

I turned back, saw Miya's face silvered by the rising crescent of Refuge's moon. I stared at her a moment too long, again; looked away as she caught me.

I studied the surface of the pillar beside me, one of half a dozen that supported a smaller, transparent dome over our heads. My fingers traced its cool frescoes, disturbing a layer of velvet dust. I couldn't tell what material the pillars were made of or what the designs on their surface meant. A slender metal tube dangled from a cord against the post beside me.

"This is called a *sh'an*. It's for . . . *an*," Miya said softly behind me, hesitating as if there was no human word that would say exactly what she meant. The Hydran word registered in my mind as *meditation/prayer/dreams*. "For when the *an lirr*—the cloud-whales—would come to share their *an* with us. Often it rained then, or snowed, and so the *sh'an* is covered." She moved away; a cold wind filled the space between us as she looked out at the night. "But they don't come anymore. It almost never rains or snows."

I looked out across the rooftops, away into the distance where the dregs of the river emptied into the darkened land of the cloud-reefs, the hidden world of the Homeland. "Why don't they come anymore?"

She shrugged, resting against the edge of the platform's low wall. "From what I've . . . heard, Tau manipulates Refuge's magnetosphere to draw the cloud-whales to areas where they have more 'productive' dreams." She shook her head. "But the *oyasin* says they left us because they no longer know us, because we don't follow the Way . . ."

"The *oyasin?* 'Grandmother'—?"

She faced me without surprise. "Yes."

I grimaced.

"What?" she asked.

"Protz," I said. "I didn't want to believe it."

"That an *oyasin* shares our goals—?"

I shook my head. "That Protz could be right about something."

She actually smiled.

"How involved is she?"

"She teaches us to see the Way clearly. She teaches us our heritage. She doesn't judge us for the kinds of things we have to do to save our people. Nothing else."

"She didn't tell you to kidnap Joby, then."

"Of course not." A flicker of irritation showed in her eyes. "That isn't her Way . . . it's ours." Her hand tightened into a fist, but the gesture wasn't a threat. I thought of the truth-swearing pledge in Oldcity handtalk.

"They say you can tell when a combine vip is lying," I said. "His lips move."

She glanced away instead of smiling this time. I wondered whether they said the same thing about all humans on this side of the river.

"Do you believe the cloud-whales would return here if they were given a choice?"

She looked up at me again. This time I'd surprised her. "I don't know. . . ." She reached for the metal tube hanging against the column. She raised it to her lips, almost reverently, and I realized that it was a flute. She began to play it. The music was like the motion of clouds across the sky.

"Is that how you call them?" I asked, my mind falling away into memories of other music on other worlds under other skies.

She shook her head again, gently replacing the flute against the column.

I glanced down at my feet, somewhere in the shadows. When I looked up again, the bat-thing was sitting on her shoulder. She stroked it absently with her hand. I wasn't sure where it had come from.

I watched it, wary. "One of those tried to put my eye out," I said.

She looked surprised again; the surprise faded. "Some people train *taku* to attack anyone they sense . . . closedness in."

"Why?" I asked, too sharply.

"Someone with guarded thoughts might plan to hurt them," she said, almost reluctantly, almost as if she could feel the guilt that burned my face. "But *taku* are gentle. . . ."

I looked back as she turned her head to nuzzle the bat-thing. It rubbed its furred forehead against her, making soft clutterings and squeaks. "It shows what we've come to, that anyone even thought of doing something that unnatural." I watched her try to urge the bat-thing off her shoulder toward me. It clung to her awkwardly, stubbornly, clutching her heavy coat with taloned fingers.

I wasn't sure whether to be embarrassed or relieved. "You said it *senses* people? It's telepathic?"

"Yes." Again the surprised look, as if a part of her kept forgetting that I wouldn't know those things and couldn't find them out for myself. I didn't know whether that made me feel better or just alien. "They're like the *mebbet*, which are native here. But the *mebbet* can't fly, and they aren't telepathic. The *taku* are the only telepathic creatures on Refuge, besides us and the cloud-whales. The cloud-whales created them."

My breath caught. "You actually believe the cloud-whales did that?"

"We know it. There weren't any *taku* on Refuge until about a thousand years ago."

I shook my head. "Meditation is the mother of invention. . . ." I wondered whether random chance had created them, like the half-finished face I'd seen in the reef . . . or whether the cloud-whales had been lonely, or thought that the Hydrans were. "Wait a minute. You said the cloud-whales are telepathic—?" Nothing I'd seen in the data even hinted at that.

But it fit with what Wauno had claimed: that the Hydrans experienced a kind of thought-residue existing in the reefs. I realized suddenly that my own response to the reef—the way my psi had seemed to come alive inside the matrix—might not have been a fluke after all. "Then why—"

"Is this how the halfbreed is supposed to learn what we've lost?" Naoh appeared out of thin air beside me.

"Jeezu!" I stumbled back; felt my face flush as Naoh looked at me.

"Mebtaku," she said. The bat-thing—the *taku*—fluttered around her face. I wondered what *mebtaku* meant, whether it had anything to do with them. I couldn't tell whether the bat-thing was glad to see her or was threatening her. She brushed it away. It came back, and then suddenly it was gone, like she'd wished it

out of existence. Miya frowned, but if anything more passed between them, they didn't share it with me.

"I've seen what Freaktown looks like," I said. "And I've talked to Hanjen—"

"Hanjen!" Naoh made a disgusted noise. "He might as well be Human."

"The *oyasin* trusts him," I said. And then I said, "She trusts me too."

Naoh glanced at her sister, as if Miya had silently seconded it. Naoh's hands jerked; she shook her head. "Hanjen is a fool!" she said to me; but she didn't say anything about Grandmother. "He will spend his life spitting into the wind, or else he will try to push the Humans too hard once, and they will break him, just like Navu—" She broke off. "I hate words," she murmured, looking away.

For once I understood her perfectly. *Words were nothing but empty noise: nothing but traps.* "So do I," I murmured. "But they're all I've got."

"*Mebtaku,*" she muttered again, and the one thing I was sure of was that it wasn't a compliment.

I searched my freshly laid memories once more for a definition. I couldn't find one. "Who's Navu?" I asked.

Something that might have been pain showed in Naoh's eyes. She signaled at Miya to keep quiet.

"You wanted him to understand how our people suffer." Miya's face hardened. "Then let him see Navu."

Naoh's gaze broke first, for the first time since I'd begun to watch them interact. At last she made what I took for a shrug.

And then I had my answer, as lightning struck my brain—

ELEVEN

SUDDENLY I WAS out in the street, staggering with surprise. Miya and Naoh were standing beside me. The free-form walls told me that we were still in Freaktown. Other Hydrans moved around and past us, but none were the ones who'd been with us before. I swore under my breath, knowing Naoh had done it this way—transporting us without warning—intentionally.

Naoh was already striding toward the entrance of a building. I followed with Miya. Miya was tense and silent beside me, keeping her gaze on her sister's back. Neither of them seemed concerned about being recognized. I wondered whether HARM had so little support in the Community that it wasn't a risk . . . or whether they had so much. I kept my head down, not wanting anyone to look at me; wishing for once that I could make my flesh and bones as invisible as my thoughts.

In Freaktown it was hard to tell where one building began and another ended; but as we went inside, I saw that this one was large by any standard. Hallways fanned out in all directions from a central hub by the entrance. The place reminded me of a transit station: a trickle of people circulated through its space, sat on benches, dozed on mats, even now, in the middle of the night. Some of them were obviously sick; some of them were bloody from injuries. The near silence was still the most alien thing about the place.

"What is this—?" I murmured.

"A hospital," Miya said.

I stopped moving. "I thought it was a transit station." But even a transit station should have had accesses or data kiosks visible.

"There aren't any transit stations here," she said.

I glanced at her, wondering whether the irony was intentional.

"I never saw a hospital that looked like this." This place made Oldcity's decaying med center look state of the art. This was like something from Prespace Earth, so primitive that it was actually unrecognizable.

Her expression said that she knew exactly what I was thinking. She'd been trained as a therapist across the river. She must have seen for herself what a modern corporate medical facility was like.

"This place isn't a hole because you prefer it that way, is it?" Not a question.

Her gaze glanced off my face. "You mean," she said bitterly, "because, with our alien mental powers, we can cure all diseases or injuries and don't need intrusive Human methods of diagnosis and treatment—?"

"Yeah," I said.

"No." She shook her head, pressing her fingers to her temples. "This is not the way we want it to be." She turned slowly, looking at the room the way I had, with eyes that knew better. "We have to eat or we starve to death. We have to exercise our bodies or they waste away. Just like Humans. If you cut us, we bleed—"

Three total strangers appeared out of thin air in the space beside her and moved past us like we weren't even there: a man and a woman, both supporting a younger man, or restraining him, inside a telekinetic field they'd spun around him. Neither one of them touched him directly; his naked chest was a mass of dripping red, as if he'd been flayed. I wondered how the hell a Hydran could possibly do something like that to someone else. . . .

He stared at me staring back at him; blood began to leak from his nose as I watched. His eyes were all pupil, night-black. He mouthed curses without any sound. The two Hydrans holding on to him were white-lipped with shared pain, and their eyes were full of tears. And suddenly I understood. *He'd done it to himself*. Someone called to them from one of the hallways, and they disappeared again.

I sucked in a ragged breath.

"We live, and we die . . ." Miya went on, as if her breathing hadn't stopped like mine had. "Sometimes we hurt ourselves just to stop the pain."

"Just like humans," I whispered.

"Humans are luckier," she murmured. "They can tear at each other. We can only tear at ourselves."

I bit my lip until it hurt, and didn't answer.

We stood together staring at the empty hallway, the nearly silent room. At last Miya shook herself out, like she'd been hit by a physical blow. "It is . . . it is true that we have methods of healing Humans don't," she said, forcing the words out, picking up the conversational thread, anchoring us in the present. "We do some things differently. We sense things. . . . There are ways we could heal a Human. The body isn't just a biochemical system; it's also a bioelectric system—"

I laid my hand against the metal pipe that climbed the wall beside us, winced as a static spark leaped across the gap to my fingertips. "I know," I said.

"But humans aren't constantly aware of it. We are. . . ." Her glance traveled the room again. I knew she saw auras of energy whenever she saw another person, not simply a face, a body. Probably she could even see where they'd been injured or how sick they were. "Tau's doctors, their med techs, barely know half the body's potential. They can't even imagine how much they miss, because they can't *feel,* and they won't listen—" She swallowed frustration like bile.

I wondered how often she'd tried to get the Tau meds to see a treatment from her perspective and failed. I imagined the hidden slurs that hadn't been hidden from her, the kinds of harassment, the pressure she'd endured, day after day, just to get the training she'd needed to work with Joby. It had taken guts and strength, no matter what her motives were. And no matter what her motives were, since she'd been with Joby she'd done more to help him than any human could have done.

She was still gazing out into the room, though I wasn't sure now whether she was just avoiding my eyes. "Once we had the technology too," she said. "Once it was better than anything Humans ever had—" I wondered if that was true, or just something HARM wanted to believe. She glanced down, as if she had her own doubts. "Tau won't even let us access their database. If they'd just give us that much to work with—" She broke off.

"They claim it's impossible for Hydrans to wear the kind of neural taps that Humans use. But that's a lie—"

... Psions don't even need a tap.... Her words became the carrier wave for another voice speaking: deep in my memory, a human freak named Deadeye was telling me again how just by being a freak he'd found a way of turning psi into cyber without any bioware at all.

The EM activity that made the warp and weft of the Net's hidden universe existed outside a psion's normal range of function. But once Deadeye had discovered an interface was possible, there was nothing to stop him, or any psion, from becoming a ghost in the machine ... except Federation law and a mandatory brainwipe.

But that didn't change the fact that any Hydran could create a psionic cyberlink ... if someone had the guts to show them how.

Deadeye had barely trusted me with his secret; he didn't need to tell me why. If the Feds or the combines had learned what he'd done, xenophobia would spread like a plague through Federation space, and the noose of persecution around the neck of every psion, human or Hydran, would tighten. ...

I wasn't ready to face the consequences of setting a change like that in motion. I turned back to Miya, pushing the thought out of my head.

Miya was gone. I searched the crowd, half afraid she'd abandoned me, until I spotted her standing across the room beside Naoh. Whatever they were doing, it didn't seem to include me. I stayed where I was, trying to ignore the looks I got from the Hydrans moving past me, trying not to think about their absence in my mind, or mine in theirs. I wondered what had happened to make Miya and her sister forget my existence completely, in such a public place.

I shifted from foot to foot, grimacing as I noticed the time, wondering whether I was going to make it back to Riverton before somebody discovered I was gone; wondering what Kissindre would do if I didn't. Wondering what she was doing now, sleeping, or—

Someone touched me. Someone put their hand down the front of my pants and squeezed. "Jeezu—!" I grabbed my crotch, searching the room with a kind of panic. No one was close enough to have touched me. Any Hydran who got near me always seemed to veer away.

But then I saw the woman standing across the room, gazing at me through the Brownian motion of bodies. She was Hydran, like everyone here except me. But there was something about her any human male would recognize instinctively—the way she dressed, the look in her eyes as she started toward me. I knew a whore when I saw one.

"Oh, my God," I muttered, because something was touching me again, and it wasn't an invisible hand. It felt like a mouth. "Oh, my God."

I stood there, paralyzed by disbelief and sensation, as she reached my side. "Hello, Human," she said, speaking Standard. She smiled, a vacant rictus, her glance searching for my databand before it found my face. "I know what you want—" She broke off as she got a good look at me. I watched her expression as she tried to grope my mind the way she'd groped my body; watched her hit the wall. Just for a second she lost her composure the way I'd lost mine. Then her smile came back, as automatic as breathing. "That's okay, honey," she murmured. "I can still give you what you need. . . ." What she'd been doing to me suddenly got so intense that I gasped.

"Stop it!" I hissed, glad I was wearing a coat.

"You don't want me to stop. . . ." She reached out, laid actual hands on me, running her fingers along the coat's seal. "I know you didn't come to Freaktown to spend the night in this place—" She jerked her head at the room around us. "Come spend it at mine."

I peeled her hands off my coat, reaching out with my mind to block her sending at the source, one psi response I could still control. "I don't want it," I said, "and I'm not paying for it."

She stepped back, blinking, and I couldn't tell whether the surprise on her face came from what I'd said or what I'd done. She started to turn away, and suddenly she was face-to-face with Miya. There was an endless moment of silence between them. Naoh came up behind Miya; the prostitute made a gesture I recognized, that took them both in. And then she disappeared into thin air.

I swore under my breath. My erection felt like a red-hot poker as the two women turned to look at me.

I watched Miya search for words: "She was—"

"I know what she was," I muttered. "I know when I'm being hustled." I took a deep breath, feeling the heat and pressure begin to ease. The two of them staring at me was a real cold shower, but Miya made a strange moue with her mouth.

"I thought humans weren't allowed to come here after curfew," I said thickly. I thought about Oldcity, how it only came alive at night, when the darkness up above matched the darkness down below, the darkness inside the people who came there to satisfy hungers it wasn't safe to feed in the light of day. It didn't surprise me to realize there were people like that even in Tau Riverton. There were always people like that, with needs like that. It shouldn't surprise me to learn they'd found a way to satisfy them.

"There's a big midday trade," Miya said, expressionless now. "Some good Tau citizens have such a craving for the 'exotic' that they even stay overnight."

I grunted. "What was she doing here?" There couldn't be a lot of human marks looking for alien sex at midnight in a Freaktown hospital.

"Probably getting a disease treated," Naoh said sourly. "I would rather starve to death than have sex with a human." She looked away, her eyes haunted by something darker and more twisted than simple revulsion.

"Maybe you've just never been hungry enough," I said. I saw Miya's face freeze. Naoh turned back. I watched her swallow an angry response and wondered what it was that stopped her, what she wouldn't say to me.

Miya gave me another look, long and searching this time; but it didn't tell me anything. And then her eyes changed, as if she'd heard something I couldn't.

Naoh glanced away, distracted by the same silent message. "He's gone!" she burst out, as if this time she couldn't stop herself. "Navu is gone."

"Again?" Miya murmured, with infinite weariness. "Navu. . . ."

"He didn't even tell anyone. He just walked out." Naoh shook her head, pacing like a cat.

Navu. I wondered who he was, why he mattered to them, why they were talking about him the way I'd talk about a dead-head.

"Then you know where we'll find him," Miya said, resigned. Not *how*. *Where*.

Naoh did something that made Miya wince, but she nodded. The look that passed between them left me out entirely.

But then they looked back at me. "Come with us," Naoh said grudgingly. "Come and learn something else."

Before I could even answer, I felt their psi wrap itself around my senses—

Everything changed in an eyeblink . . . everything was totally unfamiliar again. I shook my head, feeling queasy, wondering how much more of this jerking around I could take before I vomited. "Damn it—" I broke off.

We were standing in shadows, in the most claustrophobic alley I'd seen so far in Freaktown. The darkness was deeper than night; the only light I could see was overhead, a narrow sliver of indigo sky.

There were other Hydrans around us again; the half-visible spasms of their startled bodies told me they hadn't been expecting us. I heard grunts and curses, heard some of them scramble out of reach.

Naoh turned and moved deeper into the pit of shadows. Miya took me by the arm, drawing me after her, proving that Naoh hadn't walked through a wall, but only through a hidden doorway. She led me down a hall so black that even my eyes couldn't make out any detail. She seemed to be navigating by touch. I couldn't tell whether she was using her hand or a teleport's special sense. She moved like she'd done this before—something I couldn't manage.

The tunnel echoed with formless noises, more unnerving even than the place where HARM was keeping Joby. I wondered why we hadn't teleported directly to the spot where Naoh and Miya wanted to be: whether it was too risky; what the limits really were on their ability to sound out a space large enough to teleport into.

Naoh pushed aside a heavy blanket and light streamed out, blinding.

The stench hit me full in the face as I ducked through the hidden doorway into the light—piss and unwashed bodies, garbage and decay. "Jeezu!" I covered my nose, more to block the memories than the smells.

There had been too many scenes like this in my life . . . I'd been a part of too many of them. This one was a dozen or so people, all Hydran, squatting on the bare, filthy floor or slumped against the peeling walls of a windowless room. Two or three staggered to their feet to stare at us. *The living dead.* I didn't know what kind of drug they were on, but it didn't really matter. In the end it was all the same.

"Navu!" Naoh called, striding across the room like it was empty. Miya followed her, just as unflinching, but never stepping on a helpless outstretched hand. They hauled one of the addicts up between them and held him against the wall. They were speaking to him, out loud but in voices so low that I couldn't hear what they said. I started across the room through the muttered complaints, the stench and the filth. Things I didn't even want to think about stuck to the soles of my boots. I kept my eyes straight ahead, not glancing at anyone for longer than I had to. Straight ahead of me, Navu looked better than most of them, not as starved, not as dirty. But then, he'd just left a rehab facility.

I stopped in front of him. Miya and Naoh looked back at me, breaking off their conversation by some silent consent.

"Your brother?" I asked Miya.

"No," Miya said, and the way she said it told me the only other thing he could be: Naoh's lover. Ex-lover. She looked back at him again as he shifted in her grasp.

The look on his face said he didn't want to be there, trapped between the two of them, but he didn't disappear. I wondered whether they were blocking his psi, not letting him escape. He looked at me. I watched him struggle to focus on my face. "Wha', Miya?" he mumbled. "You *fu'ing* Humans now?" And then I knew what drug he was on, why he hadn't disappeared, why all the other addicts were still here around us.

The golden skin of Miya's face turned cinnamon. She shoved him away.

Naoh let him go too. He slid down the wall until he was sitting on the floor, looking sullen. "Lemme 'lone, *bitches*," he said. The human word stood out like an upraised finger in the flow of Hydran speech.

"You're disgusting," Naoh said. She shoved him with her foot. "Get up, you pathetic—"

I caught her arm, pulling her back. "Stop it."

Something intangible struck my hand away from her sleeve. The same pain and disgust were in her eyes as she looked at me, as if contact with me was too much like contact with him.

I backed up, shaking off my own sense of invisible molestation.

Miya crouched down beside Navu. I watched her try to get him to respond; watched him turn his face away. I saw the drug patch on his neck: *Nephase*. The same drug the Corpses had used on me. They used it on all the freaks, to keep them from escaping. . . .

Escape. That was what he wanted, what they all wanted in this room. Escape from the Gift: the thing that made them unique; the thing that made them suffer. "If that's how you feel," I said to Naoh, "why did you bother coming after him?"

"You don't know how I feel!" she snapped.

I couldn't deny it. I looked down.

Miya stood up, her shoulders bowed. "Navu . . ." she said, still looking down at him, holding out her hand.

He didn't look up. Neither did anyone else. We could have been Corporate Security come to arrest him—we could drag him cursing and kicking out of here—and I knew nobody would lift a finger to help him.

Suddenly I felt like I was suffocating. I turned and started for the door, tripping over legs, stepping on hands.

Miya followed me; so did Naoh. Or maybe they'd just had enough.

I stood outside in the relatively open air of the alley, taking deep breaths.

"So, *mebtaku*, you had to turn your face away?" Naoh gestured at the alley around us, at the hidden room in the derelict building we'd just come out of. I thought I saw tracks of wetness on her face, but in the faint light I wasn't sure. "We don't have the choice of turning away—" Her voice fell apart, with rage or grief, I couldn't tell.

"That wasn't why," I said, my own voice hoarse.

"Why, then?" Miya asked. The words were as cool as the fragile moonlight reaching down to touch us where we stood. I wondered where she found the strength to maintain that kind of control, when everyone around her seemed to be losing it. Maybe having spent so much time around Hydran-hating humans had taught her more than she realized.

"I—" My voice broke. "I guess it doesn't matter where you come from. Junkies are all the same."

Naoh spun around. Her telekinetic field slammed me back against the wall.

"Naoh!" Miya stopped herself with an effort from coming to my side.

I pushed away from the wall, shaking my head. "I was speaking from personal experience."

Miya touched her head, gave a shrug of incomprehension. "You knew an addict?"

"I was an addict."

I saw them look at each other in the silver half-light.

"When?" Naoh demanded.

"For a long time."

"Why?"

That wasn't the question I would have asked, but it deserved an answer. "Same reasons as them in there, I suppose."

She was silent for a moment. "You stopped. How?"

I realized where her mind still was; what she was really asking me. But I didn't have an answer for that. I shook my head again, looking away. "Where do they get the drugs?" I asked. The shadow-forms of more addicts were taking shape in the darkness around us as my eyes adjusted to the night.

Naoh gave Miya a look I couldn't read. Miya glanced down and didn't say anything. I wondered again what they wouldn't tell me. And I wondered why.

"Tell us who you are," Miya murmured, changing the subject in a way that was way too obvious. "Tell us what happened to you—to your Gift. I don't even know your name."

It occurred to me that Grandmother could have told her how to find me. I wondered what else she already knew. I hated feeling like everyone on this side of the fucking planet was talking behind my back right in front of me. "My name is Cat," I said.

"Your parents—?" she urged, and I heard something in her voice that I couldn't feel in her thoughts. It told me that what I said next was important, more important than any self-consciousness I had about sharing my past with strangers.

I leaned against the cold surface of the wall. "My mother was Hydran. My father . . . wasn't." I looked up at the sliver of sky, down again at the alleyway that already felt too much like home. "I was born on Ardattee, in a place called Oldcity. My mother died when I was small—someone killed her. I felt her die. . . ." I rubbed my hand across my mouth.

"Was that . . . why you helped me then?" Miya whispered.

I nodded, closing my eyes. "Because, when she needed help . . . nobody was there." I felt Miya touch me, and suddenly it took all my control to hold myself together. "I lost my Gift. I lived like—a human, for a long time. . . ." I rubbed my hand across my mouth.

Then one day the FTA had picked me off the streets. And suddenly I'd gone from one more piece of expendable trash in Oldcity's human refuse dump straight into a dreamworld. They'd promised me a databand, a future, a life I'd never even dared to hope for—if I cooperated.

The FTA had cleaned me up and glued my brains back together just enough to let me function as a psion. I was a telepath and nothing else, but I'd been a *good* one. . . . I finally had something to be proud of, something that was really mine. Something I thought no one would ever be able to take away from me.

Finally I'd had something to lose.

The Feds hadn't taken in a bunch of freaks and rehabilitated us out of the goodness of their hearts. A conspiracy of shipping combines had hired a psion terrorist the Feds knew only as "Quicksilver" to compromise the Federation's telhassium supply. Telhassium crystals were what the Federation ran on: nothing humans could create could match the data storage capacity of telhassium's superdense molecular structure. Telhassium was the thing that made interstellar travel possible—the thing that gave the FTA its economic leverage against the independent cartels.

Quicksilver had lived up to his name; the FTA hadn't been able to get its hands on him. So they'd decided to fight fire with fire by sending a suicide squad of freaks undercover. I'd been part of it.

"We stopped him. But to do it I had to kill him." I listened to myself tell the story, every word as empty now as the place inside my head where Quicksilver's mind had immolated and taken my psi with it. "No one could put me back together again after that. That's why I'm . . . closed." I touched my head. I thought of Kissindre Perrymeade, suddenly. The other side of the river seemed to be light-years away, and receding.

Miya took a deep breath, as if she'd forgotten to inhale. She let it out again in a cloud of frost. Her fingers picked restlessly at the hood of her jacket; I caught her staring at me again. I held her gaze for too long before I finally looked away.

I took out a camph, bit down on it; an excuse to stall. Then I glanced at Naoh. Her face had changed too, but not in the same ways. I wondered whether there was any emotion left in her that wasn't rooted in anger and flowering with bitterness. At least this time her anger wasn't aimed at me. "They did this to you—?" She touched her head. "The Humans?"

I hesitated before I nodded, not sure I really wanted to think of it that way, even though I knew that a part of me always did.

"How could you go on living among them?"

I looked up at the thumbnail of sky. "I didn't have anyplace else to go." Knowing that it wasn't the whole truth; knowing that I didn't blame the entire human race for what had happened to me. I'd made a choice when I killed Quicksilver, and he was the only one who'd had a gun to my head when I did it. I'd killed him to save my own life . . . and to save the life of Jule taMing, who'd mattered more to me right then than even my own life.

Believing that I'd had choices, and made the right one, was the only hope I had of ever trusting myself enough to use my Gift again. But somehow all of that seemed as remote now as the shining grid of Tau Riverton. I looked back at Naoh. "There's no place for me with my mother's people, even if I knew who they were. But I guess I still needed to prove that to myself. I guess I've proved it now."

"You're wrong. You do belong with us—" Miya said with sudden feeling. She glanced at Naoh. Naoh's mouth thinned, but she didn't deny it. "The Council doesn't speak for our people. It never has." Miya turned back to me. "You've suffered as much because of the Humans as any Hydran—as much as Joby has."

"I'm not a victim." I felt my face burn, remembering the things Kissindre had said to me earlier tonight. "I spent every day of my life since my mother died fighting to go on living. And every day, I won—" My voice was shaking. I closed my mouth, and didn't finish it.

Miya stared at me with her head bent, the way they all did when they didn't understand.

"I'm not helpless."

"You're alone," she said with infinite sorrow. I wondered whether that was an answer or simply another change of subject. "You don't have to be." She reached out, stopped short of actually touching me again.

I looked away from her to glance first at Naoh, then at the leery shadow-forms watching us from the darkness. "I don't hate humans—"

"Neither do I," Miya murmured. But she wasn't speaking for Naoh. "We need to get out of this place." She said it aloud, giving me warning this time, one second before their minds sucked me into a vortex of utter blackness.

We were back where we'd started, standing in the bleak flat where they were keeping Joby. Soral and Tiene were there with two of the other HARM members. This time they seemed to be expecting us. They glanced up at our arrival and then went back to some silent debate, gesturing and stabbing the air with their fingers. Wherever they pointed, static crackled. I watched one of them rise into the air, her legs crossed like she was still sitting on the floor—setting herself literally above the others and whatever they were arguing about.

The *taku* they'd been harassing earlier was peacefully asleep in a niche in the wall, with its head tucked under its wing. Miya glanced at the debaters' mental lightning, and I saw her frown. "Stop it!" Heads turned to look at her, their expressions ranging from resentful to guilty. The one levitating in the air slowly sank to the floor. Another one simply disappeared.

"What was wrong with what they were doing?" I asked.

"*Lagra.* 'Showing off,'" she murmured irritably, slipping into Standard, like she didn't want to be overheard. "Wasting their

Gift. Using it in stupid, dangerous ways, as if it were just a meaningless trick. Like—like—" She broke off, as if she couldn't
think of a human analogy.

"I understand," I said softly. I glanced toward the room where
Joby lay sleeping. "What did you mean before, about Joby?" I
asked. "What did humans do to him?" It had looked to me like
Tau was doing everything it could to help his parents deal with
his disabilities, even letting Miya get far enough into the keiretsu
to betray them. And yet I remembered the stricken looks on the
faces of his parents when they'd thought they were caught
between a mind reader and the bureaucracy that controlled their
lives.

"He has neurological damage because of a lab accident involv-
ing material from the reefs while his mother was pregnant." Miya
sat down wearily on a bench. "Someone overlooked a toxic viral
during the preliminary processing. Ling called it 'a disease with
tungsten claws.' It ate its way through the seals of two isolation
levels, killing everyone in them, before Tau could stop it. Tau's
countermeasure killed a hundred of their own people along with
the toxin. . . ."

I grimaced, watching Miya weave her fingers together to stop
their restless motion. I thought about how still most Hydrans
were; wondered whether restlessness was a habit she'd picked up
from humans. If it wasn't, I wondered what that said about her
state of mind.

She glanced up at me, suddenly self-conscious. "Ling was
working on the fringe of the affected area and wearing a safe-
suit," she said, her voice still deceptively even. "She got very
sick, but she didn't die. She told me she doesn't know whether
the disease or the 'cure' caused Joby's birth defects."

"Was it negligence on Tau's part?" I asked. "Is that why the
Feds are here?"

"It was negligence." She shrugged. "And there've been other
incidents. Tau's researchers are overworked and its installations
are all understaffed. Burnell says he sees safety code violations
and poorly maintained equipment all the time. Reef-mining is
expensive. Tau cuts too many corners to make its profit."

"So the Natasas are the whistle-blowers—?"

"No!" She shook her head. "They wouldn't dare. Ling knew Joby would be born with a neural defect. The doctors couldn't repair it, but they said any future fetus would probably be still-born. Tau promised her that if she didn't file a grievance they'd give her child the very best help available. But if she did, Joby would have nothing—they'd all have nothing. They wouldn't be part of the keiretsu anymore."

My hands tightened. *Nobody's innocent.* The parents had been hiding something big. So had Tau. "Then all the complaints against Tau are true, I'd bet my life on it—" I broke off, realizing what I was saying: That if Tau had any idea how much Miya knew—and they probably did—she'd bet her own life by taking Joby. That if they ever realized I knew all this, I'd be as good as dead myself.

"Miya," I said, facing her again, "I want to help you. I'll contact Isplanasky. But he's on Earth; it's going to take time for anything he can do to affect Tau, or your situation. Tau's dangerous. Don't back them into a corner. They'll crush you, if that's what it takes for them to survive. What you've done puts everyone on this side of the river in danger, not just you and HARM. You understand—?"

Miya nodded, without questions or even much surprise.

Naoh stood listening, but she didn't react. I was sure she'd heard everything, but I couldn't be certain whether she understood what I was saying. The other HARM members were all silent behind her. I couldn't tell whether they were following this at all; didn't know what might be going on between them and Naoh that I couldn't hear. But at least they'd stopped making jokes about my ancestry.

I looked back at Miya. "What about Joby?" I said slowly, uncertainly. "If you'll trust me to take him back—"

"You go back alone. Now," Naoh said flatly. "The child stays here until we've gotten what we need." *End of conversation.*

Miya glanced at her sister as if she was about to protest.

"Send him back," Naoh ordered.

Miya nodded. As she turned to me again, her face looked colorless in the lamplight.

Exhaustion came down on me like a hammer, not just physical

but mental. *Send him back*. Like a piece of freight. "All right," I said. "Send me back."

"I'll take you back," Miya said, almost gently, as if she hadn't heard me, or maybe because she had. "It's too late to leave you down at the riverside. Where are you staying?" I told her. She nodded. "Think of your room."

I hesitated. "I can't teleport," I muttered. "I never could. You can't—"

"But you know where everything is," she said with a confidence I couldn't feel and didn't share. "You always know where you are, with a certain part of your mind. You were born knowing it, because you have the Gift."

Then I understood: The thing humans liked to call a "sixth sense" was a part of any psion's wetware, just like the eidetic memory. A psion knew exactly where he was and where he'd been, in the same way as some creatures that humans liked to think of as less intelligent. Birds, fish, and herds of animals migrated hundreds or thousands of kilometers—farther than any psion could teleport. But for a psion, simply remembering what a place looked like wasn't enough. A teleporter had to *feel* its location in space, sense varying densities, re-create the three-dimensional coordinates to within fractions of a millimeter—or he might jump home only to end up buried in the floor.

"You're sure I can do that?" I repeated. I'd never consciously used that sense, even when I could control my psi.

"Trust yourself," she said. "Trust me too."

"I can't seem to do anything else," I murmured, showing her a half smile as she glanced back at me. She blinked and looked down. I looked down too, centering my thoughts; tried to picture my hotel room, all that it wasn't, everything that it was, in a way that meant something. Her hand touched my shoulder and her eyes met mine. I felt the contact of her thoughts, gentle and alien; felt it set off alarms in my brain as she reached into my head for a signpost, a clue. Panic began to fragment my thoughts. I fought it down; her confidence steadied me as I pictured *the room, the hotel, the view out across the city at night . . .*

I felt something give way as it all changed—

TWELVE

I WAS STANDING in my hotel room, staring out the window at the night and the city. I staggered as the view registered, feeling like a sleepwalker. Three solid walls, a solid ceiling and floor closed me in. I saw the featureless door of my room, the bed that always looked like no one ever slept in it . . . *Miya.*

"Son of a bitch." I wondered why everything that happened to me since I'd come to this world seemed like part of a dream. "I did it."

She nodded, breathing hard but wearing the smile I remembered from a moment before, in a different place.

I realized she was making a point, one that even I knew when I wasn't hating myself. Too many humans who worked with psi had tried to make the same point to me, but coming from her it didn't sting. I smiled, surprising myself. "We did. . . . Thank you."

She shrugged slightly. I wondered whether that was a Hydran gesture or a human one. "Save your thanks until you share what you've learned with the FTA. You may not want to thank me then." Her body was like a wild thing's, poised to disappear at the first sense of someone else's presence. But her eyes stayed on my face, lingering like a caress.

I felt a hot-ice burn climb my spine as she went on looking at me. I bit my tongue, wishing I could be sure of what I thought was in her eyes, wishing like hell I could read her mind. . . .

"I should go." She looked toward the window, looked back at me, her fingers playing with the seal of her jacket.

"I . . . wait," I murmured. "You don't have to go. It's safe enough. Rest a while . . . you must be tired." I lapsed back into Standard, tired of the effort of speaking Hydran.

She hesitated, looking at me like she thought I'd read her mind and she wished she could change it. But she nodded and sat down in one of the room's featureless chairs, rubbing her eyes. She raised her head abruptly as I shifted my weight. I stayed where I was, wanting to sit down but not wanting to spook her. "So are you," she said finally.

"What?" I asked.

"Tired," she murmured, shadows filling the hollows of her face.

I nodded, feeling my smile come back. I thought about the reasons I suddenly felt like smiling and about how all of them had to do with her. I sat down in the other chair. "Someone I knew said once, 'In the land of the blind, the one-eyed man is stoned to death.'"

Her face turned quizzical.

"He was talking about human psions trying to live with the rest of humanity. But it fits a lot of situations. It fits the one we're in now . . . caught between worlds." Guessing now, just barely certain enough to say it.

Her smile disappeared. Her gaze dropped.

"You didn't get involved with that program Perrymeade set up so that HARM could put an agent on this side of the river." It wasn't really a question.

"No," she said. This time even her voice wasn't steady. "I thought . . ." She took a breath and tried again. "I *believed* that it could be a start, the way Hanjen promised . . . that it would lead to real opportunities for our people if the Humans could see me succeed. Hanjen had such hopes—"

"Hanjen? From the Council?"

She nodded. "He's the only one still trying to do what's right for all our people. But he's outnumbered . . . and he's afraid to admit it."

"How did he choose you for the therapist training?"

"He . . ." She broke off. "He was a friend of our parents—Naoh's and mine. Before they died."

"He and Perrymeade have more in common than they know," I murmured, thinking of Kissindre.

"Like we do. . . ."

I looked up.

She glanced away. Getting up from her seat, she moved toward the window.

"Miya?" I said, suddenly afraid she might disappear. "Miya— I—" I broke off, losing my nerve. I pushed my hands into my pockets, searching desperately for a thought. I pulled out the picture ball Soral and Tiene had been playing games with, back in that Freaktown room. I looked at it, feeling something like disbelief.

Once before I'd seen a thing like that, a Hydran thing. Once before I'd taken it without a thought . . . as if it had been mine by right. I remembered how right it had felt to my hands, warm and alive. How once the pictures inside it had changed whenever I'd willed them to. The ball hadn't been mine then, just like this one wasn't mine now. This one still held the image of a *taku*— because I couldn't make the magic anymore that would turn it into something else. "Sorry," I muttered. I held it out to her. "Sorry."

She looked at the globe lying in my palm, at my fingers trying not to close over it. "Keep it." Her gaze seemed to penetrate my flesh, as if I were as transparent as the wishing ball.

I slipped the ball back into my pocket. It filled the empty space like it belonged there. "Where do these come from? Do you make them?"

"No," she said. Her hands folded over her coat sleeves. "It's a relic. We don't make anything like that anymore."

I thought about Soral and Tiene using that fragment of their lost heritage like some piece of cheap flash. I wondered why they'd done that. *Lagra*, Miya had said. Showing off. Dishonoring the Gift. "I had one of these, once."

"From your family?"

"No." I put my hand into my pocket again, picturing the image of a *taku* inside the ball. "Miya, what does *mebtaku* mean? Your sister called me that. I don't know what it means."

Her fingers began another restless migration up her sleeves. "Nothing." She shook her head. "Just a stupid thing she said because she didn't know you. She won't do it again."

"What does it mean?"

She looked at me, finally. "There's an old story . . . about a *mebbet* who longed to be a *taku*—to fly, to commune with the *an lirr*. The *mebbet* went to the Humans and begged them to change it, so that it could become like a *taku*. And the Humans gave it artificial wings, and they put things into its head so that it could hear what the *taku* hear. . . . But it wasn't a *taku*, and the *taku* despised it. It was no longer a *mebbet*, either, and the other *mebbet* wouldn't take it back. 'You are nothing,' they said. And it was alone to the end of its days, and died of a broken heart." Now she wasn't looking at me anymore.

"Oh." I sat on the low cabinet in front of the window, feeling the blood that had drained out of my face come back in a hot rush.

"Naoh was wrong," she said, almost angrily, as if she blamed herself for having told me. "Now that she knows you, she won't do it again. Now that you're helping us. . . ." She turned away. "I have to go," she murmured. "I shouldn't have stayed here like this. I have to go." She began to center herself, getting ready to disappear.

"Miya—" I said, filled with sudden, hopeless need.

She looked up again.

"Touch me," I whispered, the words barely audible. "Here, I mean," touching my head. "I mean, just once, for a . . . just for a—"

She stood there, motionless. Her eyes slid out of focus, as if she'd slipped both into her own thoughts and out of reach. My mind stayed empty.

"Forget it." I turned away, seeing the empty bed waiting for me. Feeling pathetic.

(I will never forget you,) she said, and each silent word formed with the perfect clarity of music inside my head.

I turned back. *(Oh, God,)* hardly daring to think it. (Are you really here—?) I touched my forehead again.

She nodded, holding me still with her gaze. Slowly she raised her hands. Her fingertips brushed my temples as gently as a thought; I felt them tremble. I took her hands in mine, not knowing why touching me made her tremble, only wanting, needing—

A rush of psi energy entered me like a succubus, stealing my breath away as my flesh against her flesh completed some forbidden circuit and took out all of my mind's defenses . . . the impenetrable walls, the minefields of pain, the razor-wire guilt that had held me prisoner for so long. My fears immolated, swept away like windborne sparks, like they were no more than delusions.

I kissed her then—and we were surrounded by aura, haloed in colors beyond naming. I closed my eyes, still seeing colors, letting my fingers find the smoothness of her skin, the cloud-drift of her hair, the fragile vessel of flesh and blood that somehow contained miracles. (Thank you . . .) I thought, (oh, God, thank you . . .) and then there was nothing coherent left in my mind.

Our helpless hands and hungry mouths got more intimate; chain reactions of sensation turned flesh to light and tendrils of psi energy to filaments of diamond. The collision of irresistible force and immovable object fused our half-lives into the singularity with two hearts and one mind that only psions knew and called a joining.

Molten music sang through the circuits of my brain, overflowed my synapses, downloading into my nervous system with a pleasure that was almost unbearable: I heard the sound of her hidden name *(her true name, that could only be spoken mind-to-mind),* catalyzed by my own *(a name given to me with love, not on the streets),* the true name that I'd thought would lie hidden inside me until I died.

I covered her mouth with mine, kissing her down to her soul, until I couldn't separate the feel of her body against me from my own. I let my *pleasure, wonder, hunger* pour through the conduit into her mind. There would be no secrets between us now, not even the shadow of a lie . . . only the gravitational attraction of two bodies, heat, fusion. . . .

I pulled her down to the floor—not able to reach the bed, not wanting to—through a kiss that went on and on and was only an extension of what was already happening between us. Not wanting what was happening to us now to happen on that sterile slab of gel.

I dimmed the room lights with a word, giving us the freedom of the night and all the stars in its sky as I worked my way into her clothing, guided her uncertain hands in through my own. I felt the warm pressure of flesh against bared flesh, the hard weight of bone, as I eased myself down on top of her.

I felt her softness, my hardness searching for the place I

needed to be; desperate to find my way inside before something happened—or nothing did, and proved that I'd be alone forever, lost between worlds.

Her body wouldn't let me it.

Shock waves of *panic/confusion/distress* splintered strands of psi energy like glass—

She was a virgin. She'd never done this before. Never.

All her life, she'd waited for me.

(Miya. . . .) I lay still beside her for a long time, only touching her with my mind, filled with an overwhelming tenderness that made patience as sweet as pleasure. When she was ready I kissed her again, softening every motion, gentling every touch. More than ever now I wanted to make the joining of our bodies into something beautiful, an offering equal to what she had given to me.

I'd never been with a virgin before. I'd never been with anyone I'd mattered to for longer than it took them to tell me good-bye. But she'd chosen me. . . . This time was different from anything I knew. I wanted to make it everything that she'd imagined it would be. Everything that my own first time hadn't been.

And I could, because I shared her mind, I knew what she wanted—exactly what she wanted. Exactly where to touch her, how to touch her, when to begin touching her again. . . . I carried her with me, higher and higher, until she reached a place she'd never been—and then let her fall into the electric depths of a joy so intense it almost broke my heart.

All I knew about a woman's first time was what I'd heard on the streets: a fragile membrane rupturing, blood, pain. But this was different, as different from anything I'd ever known as she was, and the difference didn't stop with the sharing of her mind. The only barrier between us was one of will, a conscious control of her body that told me I couldn't have forced her if I wanted to. . . .

"Nasheirtah—" she gasped, and as she fell she opened like a flower, and I lost myself inside her.

I'd never imagined it could be like this. I hadn't believed in my own innocence for half a lifetime, after half a lifetime in bed with strangers, using their bodies and letting them use mine. I'd lost even the memory of innocence so long ago I couldn't count the years. But now she gave it back to me, in one sweet, endless moment.

I felt young again in a way that I'd never been young, whole and new, infinite with possibilities. And if I'd believed in angels she was one, and I'd become one with them. And if I'd believed in heaven it was here and now as we made love below the night, with only the moon watching, with nothing but stars everywhere, circling in the night . . . winking out slowly one by one as we drifted down again like dreamfall into our separate bodies.

"Nasheirtah . . ." she murmured again, and gave me one more long kiss as we closed our eyes, our minds and our bodies still joined inside the warm breathing darkness, safe, protected, no longer alone. . . .

I woke up alone, lying on the floor with the pattern of the carpet pressed into my cheek, like a wirehead sprawled in a gutter after a reality burnout.

(Alone.) I lay there without moving, stupefied with loss, not even certain for a few breaths where in the universal darkness I was. Only certain of one thing: (Alone. Alone.) I put my hands up to my head, holding my skull together as my mind drove itself against walls of silence, razor wire, and broken glass. It came away bleeding. (Miya—!)

Nothing. Nothing at all. Gone. Everything that had happened tonight, to me, between us, had only happened because of her. And she was gone.

I stumbled to my feet and called on the lights, searched the room with the only senses I had. "Miya!" I screamed with the only voice I had.

A bell chimed. A sexless face appeared in the air in front of me and informed me that screaming out loud in the middle of the night was a fineable offense.

I stood gaping at it, trying to decide whether it was male or female and whether it knew I was standing in front of it half naked. "Sorry. . . ." I fastened my pants, finally. I watched it disappear.

I let my hands drop and looked down at my body. My heart

was still beating, marking off seconds of universal time as soul-
lessly as a quartz clock. I ran my hands over my skin, breathing
in the faint, lingering trace of her scent, proving to myself that it
hadn't been a dream.

Why—? I looked out at the night: still the same night sky, pin-
holed with stars. It hadn't been a dream. And it hadn't been a lie.
Then why? Why was she gone?

Because what we'd done was impossible. Here, now, in a place
like Riverton, at a time like this. . . . Forbidden. Unforgivable.
Insane. *Impossible.*

I stood there for a long time, barely breathing, until the night
began to fade into dawn.

I pulled my clothes together and ordered the wall to opaque,
before some security drone added indecent exposure to the list of
sins-against-the-state I'd racked up since I'd arrived in this self-
righteous hell. I watched the window granulate in, the wall forming across it like a layer of frost until nothing existed beyond the
few square meters of space around me.

I turned away at last, moved step-by-step across the carpeted
floor, registering the stability of the structure beneath my feet, as
solid as the planet itself. Trying not to imagine that suddenly it all
might disappear, because really there was nothing stable or
immutable—not in this universe, not in my life.

I went to the wall unit that held everything I owned and opened
it. It spewed out four drawers, three of them empty, one of them
half full. I stared at the clothing that lay inside it, random heaps
of dark colors. I pulled out a green-brown sweater: Deadeye's
sweater. I thought about Deadeye, the Ghost in the Machine,
alone in his hidden room in a city called N'Yuk on a planet called
Earth—no vid, no phone, no callers, wanting to keep it that way.
Deadeye in his rocking chair, knitting to keep himself sane—
sweaters and scarves and blankets that he dumped in the street for
total strangers to carry away. A freak, like me. I put on his
sweater, warmed by it even though I wasn't cold.

I picked through the dark formless pile until I found the box
buried underneath it. I pulled the lid off. Inside was a single earring dangling a piece of green stone—a piece of junk I'd gotten
from a jewelry vendor, playing tourist when the Floating University had done its session at the Monument.

I took the plain gold stud I'd been wearing to please a lot of people I didn't give a damn about out of my ear and put on the beaded earring. I'd gotten the hole punched in my ear trying to convince myself that everything in my life had changed, that hanging jewelry on myself didn't mean I was meat anymore for the kind of human animals who'd kill you over a piece of flash. . . .

I hadn't bought myself anything else that mattered since then.

The only other object in the box was something given to me by a woman named Argentyne before I'd left Earth: a mouth harp, she'd called it. A palm-sized rectangle of metal that made smoky, haunting music when you breathed through it. She'd said it was old: its flat, cool surfaces were marked with corrosion no matter how I rubbed them down. I didn't know if it was my fault that it wouldn't make all the sounds I wanted to hear or if the harp was just broken. I put my mouth against the gap-toothed grin along its edge. I listened to the sounds it made as my breath passed through the holes, sounds I hadn't listened to in a long time.

That was all there was. There'd been other people in my life who'd meant more to me than Deadeye or Argentyne, but there was nothing here to prove I'd ever known them. I remembered their names, trying to picture their faces: *Jule taMing. Ardan Siebeling. Elnear taMing.* . . . It was getting hard to remember their faces, harder all the time. They had their own lives, all of them, lives I'd never really fit into.

I wondered whether any of them even thought about me anymore. I wondered what kind of a difference it would make to me, tonight, if I could feel them do it. I thought about Quicksilver, the terrorist who'd died inside my head and left me with nothing—a memento mori guaranteeing that I'd never forget him or what we'd meant to each other.

I stretched out on the bed and put the harp to my mouth, blew, listening to the music it made, never the right music. I tried to remember the kind of music Argentyne had made, as sense-blistering as a drug rush, the kind of music you didn't ever hear in a place like this because it was too real. I tried to remember the light/music of her symb group playing, a violent eruption of sound, hallucinogenic visions, the overwhelming sensory input whiting out all conscious thought, dissolving your flesh and bones until finally all conscious thought disappeared. . . .

THIRTEEN

I STUMBLED OUT into the open space in front of the hotel a couple of hours later, expecting to find the rest of the team waiting for me. Still trying to shake loose the memory of where I'd been last night—*Miya . . . her world, her body, her mind*—I wondered what in hell I was going to say to Kissindre when I saw her, what she was going to say to me.

The plaza was empty.

I stood staring out across the empty square, up into the empty sky. When I looked down again, Janos Perrymeade was standing beside me.

"I sent them ahead," he said, "I told Kissindre you weren't coming."

"Why?" I wondered for one brief, stomach-knotting minute if it was because she'd told him about what had happened between us.

"Because we know what you were doing last night."

I froze. "How?" I said stupidly, asking the single most useless question I could have asked him. I had no clue to what he was thinking: last night hadn't changed anything permanently. My psi was as dead, as useless, as ever.

"Your databand. Corporate Security has been monitoring your activities." He sighed, looking at me with something that could have been disappointment or simply disbelief. "I managed to convince the Ruling Board that I should be the one to pick you up, instead of Borosage. I hope you have found out something that's worth the Board's attention." He nodded over his shoulder. A mod was dropping on cue to pick us up. We got into it.

"We're meeting the Board?" I repeated, not sure what the expression on my face was. All he knew was that I'd been to Freaktown. At least they couldn't trace Miya through me; at least he hadn't said anything about miscegenation or public fornication. I wiped my hands on the knees of my pants.

He nodded, shifting in his seat. He seemed to be too preoccupied to notice my own restlessness. "I—barely—managed to convince them that you are totally committed to helping Joby. I hope I'm right about that, or soon we're both going to be sorry we ever met."

I didn't answer. I looked out the window, watching the dawn. Red and bronze limned the knife-edged silhouette of the city. The inevitability of morning pulled my perspective back into line. I thought about how far I'd come; how much of my life and the universe still lay waiting, beyond this moment and whatever gravity sink of fate was trying to drag me down. I looked back at Perrymeade, finally.

"Tell me I'm not wrong," he said.

"Not about me," I said softly. "I can't speak for Tau."

He gave me a long, hard look, and I couldn't even guess what lay behind it.

Tau Riverton's government center lay on the far side of the city, as distant from Freaktown as it was possible to be and still be a part of Riverton. I wondered whether that was just a coincidence. The complex sat like a split geode in a fold of the land, its angular silhouette diffracting unnatural rainbows.

A mutant spire rose from the plex's glass heart; at its top was a transparent knob. The mod set us down on the knob's blunt apex. No wind buffeted us as we got out; the whole space around the tower was protected by security fields.

Perrymeade led me to a spot a few meters away, ringed like a target. Something waiting there sucked us down through the illusion of a solid surface into whatever lay below.

We stepped out into a wide torus of carpeted meeting room, facing a transparent wall. Beyond the wall was a view of the iridescent complex below us, and in the distance the perfect symmetry of Riverton. The vips who met here would be reminded every time they looked out that this was Tau's world. Right then, standing at the pinnacle of power and yet hanging precariously in midair, even I could imagine how it must feel to be the Head of Tau's Board. . . .

I looked at the corporate vips already waiting in their ceremonial seats at a table below the window/wall.

Borosage was waiting with them. He looked as out of place as a pile of shit; as out of place as I suddenly felt. Sand was there too. His effortless imitation of a human being fit in better with the half-dozen Tau vips surrounding them. My eidetic memory identified Kensoe, the Head of the Tau Board, and a couple of others I'd met at the reception. I didn't see Draco's Lady Gyotis Binta.

I wondered if the Lady had already left the planet or if she just didn't choose to be associated this closely with Tau's problems. Keiretsu didn't apply simply to the relationship between a combine and its individual citizens. The same invisible code of duty and obligation bound entire interstellar cartel "families" like Draco itself, with its hundreds of subsidiary combine states.

Its allegiance gave a vassal state like Tau access to the near-limitless support system of Draco's entire net. But in return Draco expected absolute loyalty. If a situation like the one Tau was in now went critical, if their damage control failed and the FTA instituted sanctions, any heads that rolled weren't going to belong to members of Draco's Board. Tau would be the hand cut off to save the body.

And if Tau couldn't, or wouldn't, make the sacrifice willingly, then Draco would make it for them, whatever it took to keep Draco's own perverted honor intact.

I glanced at Sand again. I wondered whether his being here was a good sign or a bad one.

We crossed the unnervingly open space to the meeting area. I had the sense that there was no one else in the entire tower. We reached the table, and Perrymeade made the usual obeisances for himself and excuses for me to everyone there. I realized only then that half the people at the table weren't actually here. The Board Members were only virtual, images; their realtime bodies were somewhere else. I'd have known that the minute I arrived if my psi had been functioning. I could barely be certain now as I took a seat beside one of them. There was a shimmer to him as he turned to look at me, his expression as wary as mine even though he was probably half a planet away. I'd heard that the visual effect was generally undetectable to human eyes.

A flower arrangement sat on the table near my arm. I thought it was only a decoration until I saw Sand pick a flower and eat it. The unreal occupant of the seat next to me drank from a squat glass that wasn't in my reality.

"We are here, of course, to discuss the Hydran problem, and how Tau intends to deal with it," Sand said, opening the meeting without being gentle about it. It surprised me to see that he took control instead of Kensoe, but maybe it shouldn't have.

"Then what is he doing here?" the vip I remembered as Sithan demanded, gesturing at me.

"He's involved with the Hydran terrorists," Borosage said, his voice grating, "just like I said in my report to you."

I swore under my breath.

Sand gave Borosage a look that cut him off. "Update your database, Ladies and Gentlemen of the Board. Cat is working for me. I took the initiative, since Tau needed a contact the terrorists would talk to. They seem . . . leery of your government agents and extremely hostile toward Corporate Security. And since District Administrator Borosage has no genuine leads in the kidnapping . . ." He let his insinuations finish speaking for themselves. "I believe last night Cat made real progress. Last night—?" he prompted, pinning me with his mirrored stare when I didn't respond.

I kept my face expressionless as I struggled to make logic out of where I'd been and what I'd learned last night, *when Miya . . . before she'd*— I dragged my mind away from her memory. If Sand already knew everything, I'd be in Borosage's lockup, not here at this meeting.

I tried to think about Joby: *Joby was the whole point of this.* But in the light of a new day, I realized I couldn't be certain of anything—who I'd be helping, who I'd be hurting, if I opened my mouth. "Someone from HARM contacted me—"

"How did they know where to find you?" Borosage demanded.

I glanced up, frowning. I was sitting directly across from him, putting as much table surface as I could between us but still giving myself a clear view of his hands. "Well, I don't know," I said, staring at my tiny, distorted reflection in the metal skullcap around his eye. "I suppose they read my mind."

"You don't think it had anything to do with your visit to the *oyasin?*" Sand asked, too casually. Borosage's eyes ate holes in me.

"No," I said, remembering not to be surprised, remembering that as long as I wore a databand I couldn't even take a piss in a public toilet without somebody knowing it. "She's got nothing to do with this. She's just an old woman."

Borosage grunted in disgust; the ghost vips stared. "Then what were you doing down by the river in the middle of the night?"

"I wasn't doing anything. I couldn't sleep." I glanced at Perrymeade, remembering why.

"There was some—dissension among the team members . . . about the constant interruptions of their field work," Perrymeade murmured. His expression tried too hard as he looked from face to face.

I followed his gaze around the circle of faces, registering everything from suspicion to total incomprehension. "Doesn't anybody on this planet ever have trouble sleeping? Do you put drugs in the water supply—?"

Frowns, real and virtual. "Perhaps it's because we all have clear consciences," Kensoe said.

"Then I don't know what we're doing here." I picked a blue flower from the dish on the table. I put it in my mouth. Its petals dissolved on my tongue with a faint taste of mint. I swallowed, wondering if every color had a separate flavor. I picked another one.

"Cat," Perrymeade murmured, "what about Joby? Anything—?"

I forced myself to ease off and keep my attention on him. "It was Miya who contacted me."

"Miya—?" he said, turning in his seat to face me. "You actually met with her?"

I nodded. "And I saw Joby."

He stopped breathing. "She brought him to you?"

"She brought me to him. Somewhere in Freaktown."

"Where?" Sand demanded. "Can you locate it on a map—?"

"No." I shook my head. "We teleported."

"I thought you were brain-damaged. I thought you couldn't do any of that."

"*I* can't . . . *I* didn't have to," I said, slowly and carefully, like he was the one with brain damage. "Anyhow, even if I could locate their safehouse on a map, it wouldn't do you any good. They said they wouldn't be there in the morning. Do you want me to tell you what happened last night, or not?"

"Of course," he said.

"Then butt out."

"We're all here to listen," Perrymeade said, his voice straining. "Please, tell us. . . ."

I took a deep breath, and nodded. "Joby's all right. Miya's taking care of him. I don't think she'll let anything happen to him."

A film of relief formed on his face as thin as monomole. "Then she is with HARM?" he murmured. I could barely make out the words.

I nodded again. His face went gray—the face of someone hearing his own death sentence. I glanced at the other faces around the table, reading their expressions as they looked at him. I realized then why he looked the way he did: He hadn't merely handed over his own nephew to kidnappers by trusting a Hydran. He'd also ruined his career—which meant his entire life. I felt a sick pity for him, a sudden helpless resentment toward the Hydrans and toward Miya . . . felt my doubts and my loyalties eddying like oil in water.

I met Perrymeade's gaze again, and there was only one thing I was sure of now: *I couldn't trust him anymore.* Because even he didn't know how far he'd go to save his own place in the keiretsu.

"How many other HARM members did you meet?" Sand asked, getting impatient when I didn't go on.

I shrugged, shaking off Perrymeade's stare. "Maybe half a dozen."

"Did you get a sense of how many there are altogether? Did you learn any identities? Would you know them if you saw them again?"

"No," I said, knowing his bioware could read my galvanic responses like a truthtester, but knowing from experience that I had enough control over my life signs to keep him from reading the truth. "It doesn't matter anyway. You can't find them. They don't have databands." I watched him frown.

Borosage shifted in his seat, rubbing his thick, scarred hands together. I studied him, trying not to make it obvious; watched him watching me, hating me.

I shifted in my own seat until I didn't have to look at him anymore. I glanced out the window, needing to clear my head. The scene had changed, subtly. I realized that the room we were in was rotating almost imperceptibly through a full 360-degree view of the city and the land beyond it. I wondered who had designed this complex and the Aerie canting out over the edge of Riverton's neat little world like a bird ready to take flight. I wondered what had been on the mind of whoever had done it. I looked down at the tabletop in front of me again, feeling queasy.

Looking back at Sand didn't make me feel better. I knew in my gut that nothing I could say would reach the Tau Board Members, any more than I could reach across the table and touch them. Perrymeade was a desperate man, and Borosage didn't even qualify as human. The only person in this room who might actually listen to what I had to say was Sand. I wished like hell that I could get a glimpse of what was going on inside his head right now; wished he even had eyes that I could look into. "The, uh, HARM members told me that they'd only return the boy if the FTA investigators come to Freaktown to meet with them. They want the Feds to witness firsthand the things they claim need changing. They want the FTA to support their demands; they want more rights . . . and more help, from Tau."

Kensoe snorted. "After kidnapping a crippled child, they want more freedom, and more aid from us?"

"The same tired set of complaints we've been receiving from the Hydran Council ever since Landfall," another Board Member, one I hadn't met, said. He frowned at the view, or at some view.

"The Hydran Council has no real influence, even with their own people. It can't even control these terrorists—" Kensoe said.

"Maybe that's why HARM feels it has to make demands," I said. "Because when they say *please,* you don't listen." Perrymeade's eyes were begging me to stop; I looked away. "They want the Feds to make an impartial report."

"The FTA, impartial?" Sithan muttered. "That's an oxymoron."

"I saw the kind of things the Hydrans want to change—"

"You saw what HARM wanted you to see."

"Freaktown's medical center is a joke," I said. "And there are addicts hooked on drugs they could only be getting from this side of the river. If you want to make a profit off of them, why don't you sell them medical technology, not street drugs—"

"That is absolutely not true," Borosage said, opening his mouth for the first time.

"Maybe you aren't the best one to give an opinion on that." I glanced away at the ring of faces, back at Borosage. "They get hooked on the drugs you use on them in jail. Where do they get their supply—are you selling it to them?"

He pushed up out of his seat, like he actually intended to come after me. Sand stopped him with a look. Perrymeade put a hand on my arm, the fingers closing over my flesh so hard it hurt. "Cat," he murmured. "For God's sake—"

"Kindly keep your naive political opinions to yourself," Kensoe said. "You've caused enough trouble." His empty gaze looked right through me. He looked past me at Sand, dead eyes meeting dead eyes, before I could even close my mouth. "Of course, acquiescing to their demands is out of the question," he said. "Ours is the position of strength. The cost-benefit ratio of any conciliatory action would be completely unacceptable."

"Am I to understand, then, that you feel any contact Cat has achieved with HARM is essentially useless?" Sand asked. "That any attempts to regain control of the situation through negotiations will fail?"

"It has never been our policy to tolerate Hydran dissidence," Kensoe said. He gave Sand a sidelong look, as if he was trying to guess what really lay behind Sand's question. Corporate politics was a mind game, a minefield where judgments so subtle even a psion might miss them could mean life and death for an entire Board. "We can't be soft on this sort of thing—you know where that leads. Administrator Borosage has made it clear enough: Terrorism must be rooted out, or it spreads." He checked Sand's expression again, surreptitiously.

Sand didn't say anything, just went on listening, noncommittal, as other vips muttered agreement around the table. Nobody suggested any alternatives. No one even asked a question.

I swore under my breath. "What about Joby?" I said.

"Who?" someone asked.

"The boy they kidnapped—!" I broke off. There was no use arguing fairness or justice with these people. Compassion probably didn't mean anything to them either.

"You said yourself that you didn't think they'd harm him," Kensoe said. "Aren't those people supposed to be nonviolent?" He looked at Sand; Sand shrugged. "After the FTA's representatives are gone, they'll have no reason to keep him. They'll let him go."

"What if they don't?" I said. I looked at Perrymeade. "What if they don't . . . ?" He sat motionless, frozen, not meeting my eyes at all now.

"That would be unfortunate," Kensoe said. He took a sip of water, as if having to express any emotion, even as a lie, was enough to choke him. "But the child was defective, wasn't he? Perhaps his family would even be relieved without that burden. They're relatives of yours, aren't they, Perrymeade? What do you think about that?"

Perrymeade stirred beside me. "Yes, sir," he said thickly. "Perhaps so."

I turned in my seat to look at him. The urge to shout out what kind of a bastard and a coward I thought he was filled my throat until I couldn't speak. Everything Miya had told me must be true: about why Joby had been born with genetic damage; about why his parents would never have another child . . . about why Tau's Board might even prefer it if they never got him back. Suddenly I wanted to be out of this room more than anything I could think of, except never to have set foot on this world at all.

"This remains a dangerously volatile situation," Sand said to Kensoe after a silence that seemed to last for years. "Pursue every opportunity to keep this situation under control. For humanitarian reasons . . . and for practical ones as well, you ought to keep your options flexible. But I think you understand what I am saying." More nods, around the table.

His glance flicked to me. "That brings me back to you. You said you'd do anything in your power to help Joby. It will be up to you," he said, and his stare was a black hole, sucking me in, "to make the Hydran radicals understand that this act of terrorism will gain them nothing. Tau will not meet their demands. The people they claim to be doing this for will only suffer, if they cause Tau more trouble with the FTA. That would be disastrous for Tau and disastrous for the Hydrans as well. Surely that isn't what they want. There can be no winners in such a situation. Make them see reason."

"Me?" I said. "I'm not a diplomat. How am I supposed to change their minds? I can't even change yours."

He looked at me. "Do you believe what I just told you?"

Slowly I nodded.

"Then you can make them believe it. Just let them look into your mind . . . your soul." His face was absolutely expressionless.

I shook my head. "But I don't even know how to contact them—"

"They've obviously chosen you to be their go-between. They'll contact you; soon, I would expect. They'll have to." He rose from his seat, smoothly and unexpectedly, nodding to each phantom Gentleman and Lady of the Board in turn.

"I'm not a trained negotiator," I protested, twisting in my seat as he started past me. "I'm not even a Tau citizen. Why are you putting this on me—?"

"Because," he murmured, leaning over and lowering his voice until only I could hear him, "from what I can see, no one associated with Tau has even the slightest idea of how to resolve the situation without bloodshed." He straightened up again. "I'm sure you'll do everything humanly possible to prevent a tragedy from occurring, Cat." I wondered whether he was being ironic. "If everything you can do is still not enough, Administrator Borosage is responsible for any further actions that Tau takes." He glanced at Borosage, back at me. "And now, Ladies and Gentlemen of the Board, I must be going, if I'm to make the shuttle."

"Going?" I said. "You're leaving?"

Sand shrugged. "I've been called home by Draco." *Out of the line of fire.* The worst thing I could have imagined happening as I'd come into this meeting had happened before it even began: Draco had already distanced itself, literally and figuratively, from any of the repercussions they'd decided were going to strike Tau.

I sank back into my seat. "You coward," I breathed, and saw him frown. But he went on toward the lift without stopping.

Around the table the Board Members began to wink out of existence one by one, until I was left with only Perrymeade, that lifeless puppet, and Borosage, who was smiling.

FOURTEEN

I GOT UP. "Let's go," I muttered to Perrymeade. I struck the back of his seat.

He stood up without protest, glancing at Borosage and back at me. He nodded once and led the way to the lift.

I heard Borosage leave his seat behind us; heard his footsteps closing in on us. Somehow I kept myself from looking back or flinching as he crossed into my line of sight. He blocked my path as we reached the lift.

I had to stop moving or run into him. I stopped.

"It's just you and me now, freak," he said, as if Perrymeade had disappeared along with the rest of them. "And you heard what he said—" *Sand.* "You make the rest of the freaks understand that Tau isn't caving in on this. Because I'm in charge here, and they're making me look bad. This is going to cost them no matter what they do. It might not cost them too much, but only if they surrender the boy soon. You understand me—?"

The lift doors opened, slowly, silently, behind him. But there was no way to get by him until I gave him an answer.

I chewed the inside of my mouth. Finally I muttered, "I understand."

"That's good," he said. "I'm glad to hear it." He glanced at Perrymeade. "You get that freak Hanjen on line and tell him what's going to happen. The Council must know something—those people have no secrets. Tell him they'd better cooperate with us. I'll be waiting. I'll be watching," he said to me. His mouth twitched. "All the time . . . freak." He looked down at my databand before he moved out of my way and let us pass.

Perrymeade took me back to the hotel, not to the site where the research team was working. He looked out the window the whole way; never looked at me once until the mod settled in the usual spot in the square.

"So this is it," I said. "I'm off the team? What does that make me, then? Your prisoner? Borosage's meat—?"

He looked at me then, finally. His eyes were wet and red.

I closed my mouth and got out. I crossed the plaza without looking back as the mod rose up again behind me.

Ezra was waiting in front of the hotel when I reached it. My hands fisted as I saw him, until I realized he wasn't waiting there for me.

He wasn't even looking at me. He was standing in the center of a pile of luggage, looking up into the sky as an air taxi came drifting down. It settled in front of him; a hotel worker began stowing his belongings into the maw that popped open in its side. Ezra got into the passenger compartment just as I reached the hotel entrance. I took the last bag out of the staffer's hand. He took a look at me and went away. I threw the bag on top of the others and sealed the hold. Then I went forward until I was standing by the mod's raised door.

Ezra looked out, starting to say something, spasmed in surprise as he saw me. He swore instead. His hand rose to cover his face: A patch of sudoskin still hid his nose, with purple bruise seeping out from under its edges. "What do you want?"

"Just wanted to say good-bye," I said.

He glared at me, lowering his hand. "I don't need this—" He gestured at the hotel, the town, the planet, me. "This means nothing." Only the bitterness in his voice told me how much of a lie that was. "I could have been working on half a dozen better projects." He slammed his hand down on the door control; the open door began to arc down above me. "I'll get her back—" *Kissindre.* "Twenty years from now I'll be at the top of my field. And you'll still be nothing but a freak."

I ducked aside as the door came down. "And you'll still be an asshole," I said. The door sealed with a soft hiss. I stepped back, watching the mod rise, watching his face and the hatred on it grow smaller and smaller until he merged into the mirroring window surface, into the mod itself, into the sky, until he'd disappeared.

I went into the hotel, straight to the nearest access port, and put in a call to the Feds. The message that came up on the empty screen told me they were gone from the hotel. Not just for the day—for good. Tau had taken them away, probably far away. I didn't have to guess why.

I thought about tracking them down, sending a message after them, telling them why they had to come back. But even as I requested the search, my mind was calling up half a hundred reasons why it would never happen. And there was only one that mattered: They really didn't give a damn. They'd been oblivious to Tau's fawning and flattery. They'd been just as oblivious to everything I'd done to get their attention. Nothing really mattered to them; they were what I'd always thought the Feds were: drones, going through the motions and collecting their pay. Nothing short of a dome caving in on them personally was going to change how they saw any of this.

For a moment I actually wondered how I could make that happen. And then I canceled the search. I remembered Natan Isplanasky, the head of Contract Labor, the single genuine human being left in the entire FTA as far as I could tell: A man without a life of his own, who spent most of his waking hours jacked into the Federation Net just to track Contract Labor's highest levels of operation. The man that I'd told HARM could help them.

At the rate things were falling apart here, I wasn't sure a message would even reach Isplanasky before it was too late. There was still no direct faster-than-light communication in the Federation. Any messages that went outside a single solar system went on a ship, just like the humans who sent and received them. Transmission cost more than I wanted to think about, and it would be days before an answer came, even longer before there could be any significant change in the situation.

And yet, if my information reached Isplanasky in time, the system might still work for me, this once. If there was a better answer, I was too exhausted to see it. I input a request for an interworld message relay.

I fed my message into the Net; watched the credit line on my databand take a nosedive. I started back across the empty lobby toward the hotel entrance.

I stopped again when I was almost to the door. A Tau Corpse was standing outside, talking to one of the hotel people. He looked up at me, touched the edge of his helmet in a salute, and smiled. It wasn't a meaningless smile. He went on watching me until finally I turned around and went back inside.

By the time I reached my room, the message light was blinking on the console. I requested the message, half afraid of anything that might appear on the screen, because I couldn't imagine anything I wanted to see there right now.

What did come up on the screen was so unexpected that I read it twice before I believed it: *The message you wish to send has been rejected by Tau's censors.*

I couldn't reach Isplanasky. Probably I couldn't reach anyone else, now. I wondered whether the door to my hotel room would open for me; whether they'd sealed me in. I didn't try it to find out.

I wore a path in the room's carpet, climbed its walls with my mind as I tried to find a way out of the trap that Refuge had suddenly become for me. Nothing else happened for hours. I ordered room service. The food came out of the service unit in the wall, and I didn't eat it. Finally I lay down and closed my eyes, letting my body's exhaustion seep into my brain, hoping that nothing would happen faster if I slept through it.

I slept. I dreamed, my mind filled with a bleak twilight landscape that I had to keep moving through, making wrong turn after wrong turn on a journey I couldn't turn back from. The light never changed and the landscape never changed, and it seemed to me that I would never make any progress toward a goal I couldn't name. . . .

But then after an eternity lost, the light began to grow, like an unspoken whisper murmuring my secret name, and I realized that I'd always known what I'd been searching for. . . .

For someone who could flow through my solid flesh as though it was an illusion, to touch me like this, shocking alive every nerve ending in my body. Pleasure sang through me at the speed of thought as I opened to a timeless place . . .

I opened my eyes, feeling my body stretch like a satisfied animal below the unfocused form hovering over me. "Wha—?" I blinked, trying to make the face one I knew. . . .

"Jeezu!" I sat up, half scrambling backward on the bed. "Miya—"

She stood over me, her own face stricken, gesturing desperately with her hands for me to be quiet.

Miya. I mouthed the word silently; touched her lips with uncertain fingers. She closed her eyes as if it had been a kiss, and color rose in her cheeks. It took all the control I had then not to pull her down and make the kiss real. I could barely tell what was a dream now, what she'd been doing to me before I woke up. Whatever it was, it left me feeling stupefied, aroused, needing—

"What?" I whispered, shaking my head.

She made a gesture like she thought—or maybe knew—that the room was bugged. I got up from the bed, wondering whether she was right. If she was, there was probably visual or infrared too, and nothing was safe.

I looked toward the door. Our only choice was to get out now, but not that way. There was only one way that we could be certain of.

Looking back at Miya, I realized that she already knew it. She took hold of my arms; I felt her mind make contact, preparing us for a teleport—

The door exploded behind us. The window/wall in front of us gaped on open sky and a gleaming mass of CorpSec technology. Uniformed bodies were everywhere. Something exploded in the heart of the room before I could even react, knocking me flat, filling the air with fog. I heard Miya cry out, felt my own shout of disbelief sucked out of my lungs.

Everything turned inside out, and flat on my back on the floor, I felt myself falling—

I hit the floor again, hard. But it wasn't my floor. Not even a floor, but the hard ground in some back alley . . . in Freaktown. I staggered to my feet, swearing, bruised, shaking myself out.

Naoh stood in front of me, her eyes burning. Behind her I could see the brink of the canyon, and Tau Riverton in the distance. Looking back into her eyes, all I could think was that HARM had kidnapped me: they thought I'd betrayed them, and even if they didn't kill me Borosage would never let me get back across the river. . . .

But then I remembered Miya, the way she'd looked at me in the moment before the Corpses had burst in on us. *Miya.*

I didn't see her. The fear that she'd been left behind broke Naoh's spell, closed my throat as I turned—

Miya was behind me, sprawled on the ground like I'd been, slowly picking herself up. She moved like her body had become a stranger to her, and her face was the color of ash. Two of the HARM members helped her to her feet.

I stumbled to her side, ignoring the rest of them. "Miy' . . . awright—? Wha' happ'n'?" I broke off as the words registered, as I heard the slurring. I shook my head again, swimming through confusion as thick as sewage, not understanding why I sounded like I'd been drugged. Only one thing was clear in my mind: *Tau had betrayed me again.* And not just me this time.

Miya held her head, looking glazed. She said something to me, slurring, and I couldn't make it out. She looked away again, searching restlessly until she spotted the bundle in someone's arms that I realized was Joby. She went to him, unsteadily, and took him into her own arms.

"They were waiting," Naoh said, her voice hard. "It was a trap. You were the bait. They thought we wouldn't know. Miya made a joining with me, in case this happened—" She gestured at us, disgusted.

Miya held Joby, forehead to forehead with him, smiling as their eyes met. I watched them together, tenderness and envy spilling through my senses like the taste of honey fruit. I looked back at Naoh. "Why'd you brin' me?" I asked, barely remembering to ask it in Hydran. My speech was starting to clear up as quickly as it had gone out of control.

Naoh glanced at Miya, as if it hadn't been her idea, as if she wanted to hear the reason herself.

"He didn' know . . . was a trap." Miya pushed the words out of her mouth like someone spitting stones, and her face was as guarded as her sister's. "Coul'n' leave him to them." She reached out to touch me, almost protectively, hesitated, glancing at Naoh.

"Thank you," I murmured. I put out my hand, catching hold of hers as she withdrew it.

She looked down at our hands; wonder and desire poured

through the contact point from her mind into mine. I sucked in a breath; my fingers tightened.

She set her own hand free suddenly, effortlessly. I felt the aftershock of her self-consciousness as my fingers closed on themselves. "I—I thought we should learn wha' Tau said to him," she murmured, glancing at Naoh again almost guiltily. She shook her head, worked her face muscles, as though she didn't know what was wrong with her mouth.

"Why do we soun' like we were drugged?" I asked, trying not to look as lost as I suddenly felt, not able to touch her anymore. It was cold here in the wind, and I wasn't wearing my coat.

Miya shook her head again, but this time it was *I don't know*.

Naoh glanced back and forth between us with a frown. "Miya . . ." she murmured, and there was something both wondering and querulous in her voice. "He is . . . you believe . . . this is your *nasheirtah?* Him? The halfbreed?" She glanced at me, away again.

"Did you believe you could keep it a secret, once we'd joined?" Her voice softened almost reluctantly as Miya looked away. Naoh put her hands on Miya's shoulders while the others waiting behind her stared at the three of us, making mental comments that I probably didn't want to hear.

Miya shook her head, resting her own hands on her sister's, but looking at me.

"Miya—?" I murmured, not understanding what was going on between them or what my part in it was.

"He doesn't know?" Naoh murmured, looking at me now too. "He doesn't even know what that means?" There was astonishment in her voice this time, and disbelief, even indignation. I couldn't tell which responses were intended for Miya and which were aimed at me. "She believes you are her *nasheirtah,*" she said to me deliberately. "Her soulmate. . . . We believe that in a lifetime there is only one person who is meant to be for each of us. The first time she met you, she knew. . . ." She looked back at her sister. "But you didn't tell him."

Miya wouldn't look at either of us now. She could have been on the other side of the world, for all the sense of her there was in my mind. "Naoh, stop—" she whispered.

"Miya?" I said again, my own voice faltering as she refused to meet my eyes. I wondered whether she was ashamed or simply afraid—ashamed to have the others know the truth, afraid her sister would reject her . . . afraid that I would. "Miya. . . ." I touched her face gently.

She looked up at me, startled. I saw the look in her eyes, the fear of finding nothing when my eyes looked back at her. I remembered last night: falling asleep inside the warm, protected shelter of her body, her mind . . . waking up cold and empty and alone, afraid that I'd wake up cold and empty forever. . . .

"I know," I whispered. "I do. . . ." I watched the fear change to relief, and then, uncertainly, into joy. I leaned past Joby's curious stare and kissed her; felt the hungry pressure of her lips on mine jump-start the flow of thought and emotion between us. Joy and terror and longing took my breath away.

And then Naoh's psi smashed our mindlink like a hurled rock. In the split second before I lost contact I felt her shock at encountering my mind defenseless and online; felt the thorn-thicket of her emotions: *surprise/pain/joy/envy/curiosity/helpless anger. . . .*

And then all three of us were suddenly alone, blinking like the daylight was a surprise, as we were dragged neuron by neuron back into the world we shared with the others.

"We can't stay here," Naoh said sharply, as if that was really all that had been on her mind. "Let's go."

"Wait," I said, my voice still husky. "The Corpses—they'll track me. You're not safe as long as I have this." I touched my databand. I remembered how much it had meant to me to finally put one on; what it had cost me to earn the right to wear one. What life had been like without one.

I turned to Miya, where she stood holding Joby in her arms, seeing the way she looked at me: *"I couldn't leave him,"* she'd said. Joby. Or me. I looked away at Tau Riverton, searching my mind for a single thing I'd left undone across the river that had any meaning, compared to anything that waited to be done over here. Searching it for a single person I'd shared something with that had any real meaning, compared to what I'd found with Miya. . . .

I pressed the thumb-lock on my databand. I caught its weight in my hand as it dropped off my wrist.

"What are you doing—?" Miya said, her voice as incredulous as any Human's.

"I can't wear this anymore," I said. "Humans killed my mother because she was Hydran. My father was Human; he left me in the gutter because I was Hydran. I'm Hydran—!" I pitched the databand away from me as hard as I could, watched it, and everything it stood for, go spiraling out over the rim of the canyon, down, down into the bronze waterflow a hundred meters below. I turned back to Miya's disbelieving eyes. "And you are my nasheirtah."

The others were all staring at me with the same disbelief, even Naoh. "Call me Bian," I said.

Miya pressed her face against my shoulder as I held her, and Joby, closed in my arms. "Bian," she whispered. "Welcome home." She moved aside to let Naoh embrace me like a lost brother . . . a lost lover. There was a gentleness in Naoh's touch that I hadn't thought she was capable of; something in her eyes that was haunted but almost tender as she murmured, "Namaste, Bian. Bring my sister joy. At least one of us should have it forever. . . ."

I didn't say anything, couldn't, as one by one the others did the same.

FIFTEEN

THEY TOOK ME somewhere else, then, before Borosage could take us all out right where we stood . . . before I really had time to think about the consequences of what I'd done.

I reoriented, supported by Miya and Naoh. We were standing in a bleak, dusty, run-down space too much like the one I'd visited last night. Only the worn blanket in place of a worn rug in the center of the room made me certain we were actually somewhere else. I realized then that rooms like this might be all I saw, how I lived, for the rest of my life.

I looked back at Miya and realized the thought didn't even bother me. I glanced from one face to another, surrounded by the band of Hydran outcasts who'd been strangers to me only minutes ago. Now, with the suddenness of the teleport itself, they'd become my family.

"If you are going to be one of us, you should look like us, Bian," Soral said. He shut his eyes as if he was concentrating. Suddenly he was holding a shirt—one of the long, side-fastened traditional tunics that they were all wearing, even Miya now. "Here," he said, and let it go. The shirt rose into the air and hung above my head. The others watched, grinning and pointing.

I looked up at it, and felt a sudden chill. I looked down again, startled, and suddenly I wasn't wearing any shirt; my shirt and Deadeye's sweater lay in a heap on the floor at Naoh's feet. She looked me up and down. So did the others, with a frank curiosity that told me they'd never seen a Human naked, or even a half Human half naked. They almost seemed disappointed that nothing worth mentioning was different from the neck down. I clutched the top of my pants with both hands. "These stay," I said, not smiling.

They laughed and nodded, nudging each other. Naoh's laughter was high and giddy as the shirt suddenly dropped out of the air onto my head. It slithered its way down around my neck like something alive.

I pushed my arms into the sleeves and fastened it, managing a smile of my own. The tunic's material was softer and warmer than it looked, and probably a lot older.

"Namaste," I said, realizing as I said it that it also meant "thank you." Soral bowed slightly to me; I bent my head to him, to them all.

Miya set Joby on the floor at her feet. A pile of blocks and other toys appeared around him. She pulled the bandana gently from my hair. I stood motionless, the center of attention but for once not uncomfortable about it, as her cool fingers lifted my hair off the back of my neck.

Tiene passed her one of the ornate metal clips the others, both men and women, wore to hold their long hair in an elaborate knot on top of their heads. The clip hovered in front of my eyes while Miya gathered and worked with my hair. I couldn't tell whether she used only her hands to do it. She reached into the air for the clip, murmured her satisfaction as I felt her fasten it.

"There, Bian," she said, "my nasheirtah." Her satisfaction and pleasure were reflected in the faces all around me, in a way that made me feel there was more to this part of the ritual of transformation than I could appreciate with only five senses.

A woman named Talan offered me a metal belt. It had been made out of scrap wire woven into patterns as subtle as the hair clasps. A man named Sath gave me a thong necklace with a pendant of carved agate. The others came forward one by one, offering me a vest, necklaces, rings, a pouch to hang at my belt, even a coat that was worn but warm, until my transformation into one of them was complete.

We ate stale flatbread and drank steaming black tea, which Miya called *pon,* while I told them everything: That Sand was gone. That the Feds might as well be. That Borosage was in charge, with no one standing in his way. That he'd said he would make Freaktown pay; the only question was how much, how soon.

"Is that all?" Naoh demanded, her usual impatience back and edged with disappointment. "You said that you could help us, Bian. Were all those things you promised us last night nothing— just talk?" She made *talk* a dirty word. She glanced at Miya as she said it, another of those looks I couldn't read.

I leaned against the wall, resting my back. "Tau blocked me at every turn. Even Perrymeade is afraid to stand up for your people now, because Miya took Joby." I glanced away, so that I didn't have to see her expression change. "Joby doesn't matter to someone like Borosage—or to the kind of people who control Tau's government. Maybe they even want him out of the way, because Tau's negligence is responsible for what happened to him."

Joby sat on the floor beside me playing with a scatter of carved cubes, stacking them up, knocking them down, smiling but silent, like he always was. Miya sat beside him. She looked up suddenly over the rim of her cup and I saw the guilt in her eyes.

"Perrymeade's in trouble with the keiretsu, because hiring you was his idea," I said to her as gently as I could. "He's afraid of losing everything—so afraid that it's paralyzing him." Wanting to take back the words that made her look at me that way, but not able to leave them unsaid. "If he had any guts, he'd help us anyway."

She only shook her head. Joby glanced up at her and started to whimper. She reached out, touching his face, and he stopped. "He hasn't spoken a word since we came here," she murmured, almost to herself. "He knows . . . he knows this is wrong—" Her hands moved in the air, as if they ached to get ahold of something tangible, something that could put it all right.

Naoh made a disgusted noise. "We can't give him back, Miya. Not now. You heard Bian—the Humans don't even want him back. You know it would be the end of us." Her expression changed subtly, in a way that made me uneasy. "This is only the next turning of the Way. Everything is happening just as it should. Let Tau do what it wants. Our people act like they are already dead. If the Humans kill a few of them, the rest will realize life is worth something after all. Then they will join us—"

"In doing what?" I asked.

She looked at me. Her mouth thinned, and she didn't answer. I had the feeling it wasn't because she didn't know. She just wasn't ready to share the answer with me.

"Borosage is a sadist," I said, frowning. "And he's not stupid." I rubbed my naked wrist. "You don't attack an enemy like that head-on. You've got to drag him down from behind. He's mean and he's dirty . . . there's got to be something he's hiding. What about the nephase . . . the drug Navu's using. Where does it come from? Borosage is letting it get away—"

"No one cares about that," Naoh snapped. Miya looked up at her. They locked eyes in another silent exchange, and Miya's restless hands tightened into fists. "It only goes to us," Naoh said, turning away, "and the Humans are glad of anything that cripples us more."

"He does it himself," Miya said.

"What?" I raised my head.

"Miya!" Naoh said sharply, almost a threat. I saw some of the others give her an odd look.

"He's behind it," Miya went on, her voice flat, her eyes hard, her whole body challenging her sister's right to order her silent. "He supplies the ones who sell it over here."

"Why?" I asked. "For money?"

"Hatred," she said. "Fear. I've been this close to him—" She held up two fingers a centimeter apart. "I've felt it. That's what he's most afraid of: that someone will look inside him and see what he really is." She glanced down. "He would have killed me, right there, if he'd realized. . . ." She looked up again. "If he could have gotten away with it."

"Yeah," I said. "That fits the Borosage I know." My mouth twisted. "But can we prove it? Even Draco and the FTA can't turn their backs on a drug-dealing Corpse. If we could bring him down—"

"That doesn't change anything! It has nothing to do with why we're here!" Naoh cut me off. "I have seen the Way for all our people. We have to make them open their eyes! They have to stand up against the Humans who are trying to destroy us. Once they find their pride and their courage, then it all becomes possible. . . ." Her eyes glinted like cracked emeralds. "The Humans will disappear from this world. The past that was ours once will be ours again. The sick will be healed; the lost will find their Way. There will be no more suffering, no more tears. That is the Way I've seen. . . ." She stopped, and took a deep breath.

I searched the room for anyone else with a trace of a frown, a flicker of doubt in their eyes. There were mindless nods and muttered agreement all around me, letting me hear what I couldn't feel: that they all believed the same thing, felt the same way. Every one of them. Even Miya.

"You know it too, don't you, Bian? Isn't that why you threw away your databand?" Naoh gestured at my wrist. "You know we are right, that our Way is the only way. You rejected your Human side and cut your ties to our oppressors. You cut yourself off from the exploitation they stand for. We are true revolutionaries. We're not afraid to set an example, to lead the others to the Way—to become martyrs, if necessary—so that our race will survive. Isn't that what it means to you—?"

I glanced at Miya. She sat unmoving but unprotesting alongside Joby. I'd thought she'd taken Joby to protect him; but from what I'd seen of his family, and how she felt about them, I knew that wasn't true. I'd thought she'd taken him to draw the FTA's attention. But from what Naoh was saying now, I couldn't see how Joby fit into HARM's real plans anywhere. Unless, by kidnapping him, Naoh was taking some kind of revenge. I wondered what Miya knew that she wasn't saying, wondered when she'd tell me—whether she ever would.

"Isn't it?" Naoh caught my arm. "Isn't that what it means to you?"

"The way I heard it," I said slowly, "true revolutionaries have to be willing to kill their own families."

She stared at me. "That is the Human way," she murmured at last.

I looked at Miya again, and Joby. "Maybe it amounts to the same thing."

"Stop thinking like a Human," Naoh said. "If you aren't with us, Bian"—her cat-pupiled eyes searched mine—"you are against us. Against your own people. Your real people. . . ." Her hand rose reassuringly to touch my face; I felt a tendril of thought eel its way in through my defenses. She was Miya's sister, I felt the echo of Miya in her touch. I told myself she was accepting me, trying to make me one of them . . . *almost trusting her, almost letting her in* . . .

But then the magnesium flare of her fanaticism seared my thoughts. I shut her out of my mind and backed away. *Miya was only angry at the Humans; Naoh hated them.*

"I'm with you," I muttered, all I could do before looking away from her shocked face, back at Miya and Joby again. "But there's got to be a better way to help our people than mass suicide." I shook my head. "I know there isn't much time, but let's use what we have, at least—"

"We will use it." Naoh shrugged, frowning like I was the head-case. "We already have many followers, and what you've told us will win us more." Her empty hand dropped to her side; her eyes stayed on me, hard and searching. "You don't truly understand yet, Bian. Once Miya didn't, but now she does." Naoh jerked her head at her sister. "Miya, stay with him. Help him to understand. There are things we have to do—"

She disappeared. The others followed her like a flock of birds, disappearing one by one into thin air. The cool wind of their passage moved through my hair. I stood motionless, suddenly alone with Miya and Joby.

Joby squealed with surprise or amazement at the sudden emptying of the room. He looked up at Miya, his face filled with uncertainty, his hands full of toys. But he didn't say anything.

She sighed, her own face going slack with relief, before she smiled down at him. "Good-bye!" she called to the air. She waved her hand. "They had to go. But I won't go. . . . And they'll come back."

Still Joby didn't say anything. He looked at me then, as if he was waiting for me to disappear.

I moved closer until I was sitting beside him, moving carefully because I wasn't sure how he'd react.

Joby put down his blocks to look at me. He glanced at Miya again, looking for reassurance. And then he got to his feet and took three steps toward me. Standing eye to eye with me, he reached out and touched my ear, the earring dangling from it, the way he had last night. His fingers brushed my ear; he explored my face with his hands like he was blind or confirming the evidence of his eyes. I held myself still, letting him explore. Suddenly he threw his arms around my neck, pressing his face against my cheek.

Startled, I forced myself to relax. I held him until finally he let me go again. He sat down beside me and began to play with the cubes. He leaned against my side like I was a chair in the middle of the empty room.

I glanced at Miya, not sure what I'd find in her eyes, not sure what I saw there, even when I did. This was the first private moment we'd had together since she'd wakened me in my hotel room. At last I murmured, "I didn't know if I'd ever see you again."

She smiled; her smile overflowed into my thoughts.

"How do you do that?" I said, wondering. I reached out, touching her hair, her face, the way Joby had touched mine: proving her reality.

"What?" she asked, kissing my fingertips; or maybe, (What?)

"Get past me." (Get inside me, like the air I breathe. . . .)

(By not trying.) She leaned forward until her lips found mine. (Because you want me there. . . .) I remembered last night, how her body had opened to let me enter, as she kissed me again.

(But it can't be that easy. . . .) Her longing lit up my nerve net, mating my sudden need with a desire as relentless as time.

(It isn't. . . .) She drew away as my hands began to touch her, feeling the curve of her breasts beneath the soft, weathered colors of her antique shirt. She caught her breath, glancing self-consciously at Joby. (It's beyond understanding.) She smiled. (It's the Way. . . .)

(No,) I thought. (It's just you.) I reached up, touched the clip she'd woven into my hair, remembering the moment when she'd done it, the look in her eyes, her life-force alive in my mind.

She looked back at me in my Hydran clothing, the outward sign of my inner transformation. And I knew that it wasn't simply the way she looked at me that made my heart ache, but the way she saw me— *Whole. Beautiful. Nasheirtah.* "Miya," I whispered, saying it aloud because I wanted to hear the music of it. "Nasheirtah. . . . What does it mean?"

"It means 'destiny,' " she said.

I shook my head, suddenly smiling. "How did you know? How does it happen?"

She glanced down, at her hand resting in mine, two halves of a whole. "It . . ." Her thoughts diffused, focused again, offering me the image of a moment when two minds merged and two hearts were lost: a precognitive sending, a lightning-flash glimpse of a future where every possible image converged in the face of the Other.

I know you. . . . I remembered the night, the instant when we'd collided on that deserted Freaktown street. I'd seen her face for the first time, and my entire life had looked back at me from her eyes. And without even knowing it, I'd offered her my soul. . . .

And she'd pressed Joby's databand into my fist and run away, knowing she'd finally found the one she was meant to love forever . . . and sent him straight into the arms of Tau's Corporate Security.

Her grip on my hand tightened until I winced: two lives where every choice had only been between pain and more pain had finally intersected in that moment, and the ultimate joy had become a tragedy. And there had been no one in HARM she could share it with—not even her sister—because they had all foresworn their individual lives and needs. . . .

And at last I saw what had driven her to find me again, to risk everything—her own life and safety, even Joby's, for a handful of hours. For one night with the one man she would always love in a way she would never love anyone else. And at last I understood why, waking up alone and empty, I'd felt as if the rest of my life had gone with her. Why once could never be enough for either of us.

I shook my head in wonder. "Humans . . . Humans believe

over and over that they've found the one. And then it falls apart on them."

"Humans do the best they can," she murmured, "but without the Gift . . ." She broke off, looking at me and remembering. She glanced at Joby.

"Do you believe there's really a perfect lover somewhere for everyone?" I asked, trying to pull us both away from the brink of memory.

"In the Community?" Her eyes turned distant. "Who knows, anymore? There are so few of us left. . . . Some of us go all our lives without finding nasheirtah. Most of us just make do. Some still find each other, like—" her mouth pinched, "like Naoh and Navu—only to be destroyed by the Humans." Her hand slipped out of mine. I tasted the bitterness of her sister's inescapable grief, always just below the surface in her memory.

I pulled her close to me. (I'm not like that. I'm here . . . and I'm a survivor. We'll have our whole lives—)

(Never promise that,) she thought, blinking too much. (It's like a curse.)

The past reached up with hands of pitch, trying to smother me. (You love me . . .) I thought, discovering a kind of courage I hadn't known existed in me, until she'd given me a reason to find it. The kind of courage it took to believe: (Anything is possible.)

I felt more than saw it as she smiled at last, as she whispered, (I know.) But her face changed as she looked at Joby. The contact between us evaporated.

"Miya—?"

She shook her head, brushing strands of loose hair back from her face, and didn't answer. But I didn't need to hear her thoughts to guess what they were.

I remembered what had happened when Naoh had tried to reach into my mind. *Help him understand,* she'd said before she left us here. This wasn't what she'd meant. "Miya," I said again, to make her look back at me. "How many members does HARM actually have? How many other people do you think believe in your sister's 'vision'?"

"I don't actually know how many Satoh—*patriots,* not *HARM members*—" she said mildly, "there are. I don't think any of us know for certain, even Naoh, in case we're ever betrayed."

"Has anyone tried to betray you?" I asked.

She shook her head. "The Council would turn us over to Tau, if they could; but people in the Community protect us and support us. They know what *satoh* means." A small, wry smile formed on her face. "There are hundreds, maybe even thousands, who follow Naoh's Way and support us. All of the Community who live here in town believe in our cause, at least to the point where they won't betray us."

"How is that possible?" I wondered whether she knew that for fact or whether it was something Naoh had put into her head. From what I'd seen, it was difficult to believe there were that many Hydrans left on the planet.

"Naoh's Gift is very strong. She only used it for lagra, until she had the sending." She moved restlessly, as if even the memories had the power to hurt her. "But then she saw why she'd been given it: to save our people. Everyone she reaches out to feels her belief. They know that she's seen the Way—" Her fist tightened. Her mind was utterly clear of doubt, either about me, for asking questions, or about her sister's sanity. "They'll follow her . . . when it's time."

I glanced away. "Miya, the things your sister said, about becoming a martyr . . . There's something . . . twisted about how she sees all of this. It's almost as if she has a death wish—"

"No," she murmured. "Bian—"

"Naoh's talking about death! Your death, the deaths of God knows how many other people. The Community can't afford that kind of loss."

"What choice has Tau given us?" she demanded. "Naoh is being realistic when she says some of us may die. If any of us lose our courage, if we don't follow the Way as she sees it with complete faith . . . we'll fail." The words were emotionless and flat; even so, her expression reminded me too much of Naoh's. "Some of us will always falter. . . ." She looked away suddenly.

I remembered what Hanjen had said—about a mood spreading like a disease through an isolated group, none of them even recognizing the sickness until it was too late. "This is some kind of precognition we're talking about, right? There should be more than one Way that will get us to our goal. I know you believe that . . . I've felt you still looking for answers." I saw her frown.

"Why shouldn't we go after Borosage, before he comes for us? That could get us the kind of attention we need without anyone dying. That could work—"

"Others have tried. My parents. . . ." The words were even flatter. I thought about Naoh again; what she believed it took to be a revolutionary. "They're dead. And Navu—you saw what happened to him. He became an addict in Tau's prison."

The sick will be healed, and the lost will find their Way, Naoh had said. I wondered whether she thought that included Navu. I shook my head. "How does Borosage get away with it? Where does he get the power?"

"He fills a vacuum," she said, her voice thick. "No Human who has enough power to control him cares enough to do it."

I swore under my breath. The sight of scar tissue as I looked down at my bare wrist made my stomach knot. I rubbed it, as if I could rub it away.

Joby was building castles. I watched him pile on one more block, watched as the whole structure came tumbling down. He sat there, kicking at the blocks with his feet and frowning. Then, silently, he began to build again. I looked back at Miya. "Where did Naoh go?"

She shrugged. "I don't know. . . . Out into the Community, to show our people Tau's threats—"

"And about HARM's . . . the Satoh's part in it?" I asked. "About the kidnapping? Is that why you took Joby: to force a crisis with Tau?"

"(No!)" she said, with anger I felt as well as heard.

"Then why involve him at all?"

"Naoh," she murmured; her contact slipped through the fingers of my mind as something disappeared from her eyes. "Naoh said it was necessary. I didn't want to believe that. But . . . it was necessary. She showed me. . . ."

I got up and moved across the room, stood staring out through the dusty panes of the single small window. I searched for the reefs, knowing they were out there somewhere in the distance beyond the blurred profile of Freaktown. I couldn't even lie to myself that they were within range of my sight. I thought about Kissindre and the team working somewhere out there . . . wondered what they'd been told about me this morning, what they'd think when they found out the truth—if they ever did. I wondered whether my defection would ruin any chance of continuing their research; if Kissindre would wind up hating me.

I touched my wrist; looked down at it again. No matter what I wanted, without a databand I could never go back to the life I'd had on the other side.

For a second I lost my grip on everything; the knot of denial holding me together came undone, and the fragments of my self spun away into free-fall—

I pulled myself together again, not wanting Miya to see me falter, not wanting her to think she was the one that I had doubts about. I stood with my back to her until I was completely certain that I was still on solid ground; still in Freaktown, staring out through a single filthy pane of glass at the same unreachable view.

"Bian," Miya murmured. At first I didn't realize that she was speaking my name. (Bian.)

"What?" I said. My voice was a shambles.

She was standing barely an arm's length from me as I turned around. I flinched in surprise, even as she reached out to me. "Bian," she repeated, gently, as if she was trying to remind me of something. "You are part of us now . . . but Naoh was right, you don't know what that means. You need to know. Let me show you. Come with me." She took hold of my hands, drawing me forward.

I took a deep breath and followed her back across the room. She leaned down to pick up Joby. He reached up to me. I held out my arms, and she settled him into them. The weight of his small body felt good, solid, anchoring me in reality. I saw the lines of strain above her eyes ease just a little. "Miya," I said, "we don't have time. Borosage isn't going to give us the time. We've got to find a way to neutralize him. Tau's already let him off his leash."

"Naoh has a plan," she repeated, looking distracted, looking at Joby. "She's seen the Way. If we follow her vision, we won't die—we'll win. We'll be given everything we need to rebuild our world. I trust her. . . ."

I kept silent, wishing that I did. For the first time since I'd lost control of my Gift, I saw a reason to be glad I still had the defenses that kept the world out. Because they kept Naoh out. Even when we were alone Miya couldn't see the situation objectively, free of Naoh's mind-clouding paranoia. I only saw now how much of Miya's concentration was bound up in caring for Joby. How it could make her easy to use.

I didn't like thinking that, but Naoh was using her, intentionally or not, using her trust, using what was good in her against her. Sucking her into the Satoh's mindset until she was too deeply involved to see anything independently. "Who else do you trust? Hanjen? The oyasin—?"

She frowned as I mentioned Hanjen. I remembered what Naoh had said about him.

"The oyasin," I repeated. "We need to ask her how she sees this. Tau's probably got her under surveillance . . . can you get us to the monastery?"

Miya nodded. She looked dubious, but her eyes were registering me again, like I'd finally said something that didn't short out her resolve. I watched her gather herself, felt her gather me in, the boy in my arms . . . the boy inside me, afraid of the dark and yet hungry for it . . .

And everything changed, went black/white—

We were standing inside the white warren of the monastery's walls. A handful of running children passed us; I watched them scatter like startled mice. They darted away into doorways farther down the hall.

Then they came back, one by one. Some of them were trailed by adults, mostly women. They gathered silently at the far end of the hall to stare at us.

Grandmother appeared; the gathering separated without anyone glancing back. She moved through them toward us. I wasn't sure where she'd come from, but it didn't really matter.

"Namaste," she said to us as placidly as if we weren't hunted fugitives with a kidnapped child between us, but only one more family of refugees seeking shelter. "I knew you would come."

I made a bow, following Miya's, biting my tongue against asking how she'd known it this time. Instead I asked, "Is it safe for us to be here? Safe for you?"

Grandmother nodded once but touched her finger to her lips. "For now," she said gently, in Hydran, as if she knew I'd understand it. She came closer, her eyes on Joby. She didn't try to take him from me, and yet there was something in her manner that was like outstretched arms. If I'd still had any questions about whether she knew what the Satoh were doing, she'd just answered them. But watching Miya out of the corner of my eye, I saw her face change as if Grandmother had taken a burden from her—one that I couldn't help her carry, one that I couldn't even see. Grandmother touched Joby lightly, almost like a blessing, while he smiled at her as if he knew the touch of her hand, the touch of her mind.

"Oyasin," Miya murmured, glancing down almost humbly. "We have come to ask you to help us see the Way clearly." She looked at me, and I realized she was speaking out loud for my sake. "My sister says that she has seen the future. But Bian says what she sees is wrong. . . ." She broke off, and I saw the emptiness in her eyes, as if suddenly she couldn't see any future at all ahead of us.

The silence stretched between them while she shared everything she'd heard with Grandmother. I waited, watching their faces.

At last Grandmother nodded. She pressed her hands together; her face lost all expression as her mind went somewhere else. I wondered whether it was into the future.

Her eyes came alive again behind the transparent veil. She looked at me. But all she said was, "We must go now."

And before I could ask where, I felt the vortex of two minds begin to re-form space around me, pulling me and Joby away again to somewhere else.

SIXTEEN

I SUCKED IN a breath of cold air, another full of surprise as I realized where we were. "The reefs—?" I murmured. Joby squirmed and stiffened in my arms. I rubbed his back until he quieted, trying to stabilize my own senses as we adjusted to the solid ground that was suddenly under my feet again.

Miya nodded. "The oyasin . . . she says the Way isn't clear to her, either. She only saw that you . . . we . . . needed to come here." She turned to the view around us, and then, with what looked like both reverence and resignation, she made a small bow of acknowledgment.

We were standing on the river shore, but nowhere near the spot where the research team had been collecting data. The skyline of sheared hillsides and ovate hummocks, the play of light and shadow, was the same and yet entirely different, like the same stars viewed from a different world.

I thought about the team again. They were probably already back on the Human side of the river. I thought again about the half life that had been all the life I'd had, until a few days ago . . . the life that I'd given up entirely in order to have this one. I looked at Miya, holding my breath until the moment passed.

And then I asked, "What now?" I turned back to Grandmother, watched her turn through a circle, bowing to the beauty around us. When she'd completed the circle, she bowed again toward the deeper shadows below the cliff face. I realized there was an over-hang of the reef there, maybe even a cave.

The oyasin settled herself on the stony beach, wrapped in a heavy cloak she hadn't been wearing when we left the monastery. She looked up and saw me looking at her.

"I knew that it would be cold," she said, smiling in that way I never knew whether to take at face value. She held out her arms. "I will keep him. While you follow the Way."

I glanced at Miya, because Grandmother was still looking at me.

"Both of us," Miya murmured to me, and nodded.

I carried Joby to Grandmother, settled him into her arms. He went to her willingly, and there didn't seem to be any change in how he responded. He watched everything that was happening around him with silent curiosity; he didn't look surprised or even worried. That was what it would be like to be a Hydran child, I thought: secure no matter where you were, as long as you could feel the presence of people who loved you inside your mind. I realized that once there must have been a time when I'd felt that way, in a time I couldn't even remember.

Grandmother began to talk to Joby, a soft murmur that I realized was Standard speech. She waved her hand, pointing out the reefs and up into the golden evening air. I looked up and saw taku darting randomly overhead.

I glanced at Miya, feeling her relief break over me as Grandmother freed her from the strain of holding Joby's mind open. Still, there was nothing that resembled a positive emotion in what she was feeling now. It struck me that being Hydran didn't mean freedom from fear, or grief, or pain, because all those things would be shared mind-to-mind as intimately as love. I wondered how much added effort it cost her to prevent her doubts from seeping into Joby's thoughts through the bond between them and making him afraid. She'd said that he hadn't spoken since she'd brought him across the river. . . .

Miya turned away as if she didn't want me to go on looking at her. She started down to the river's shore. It was only then that I noticed a boat pulled up onto the gravel. It was small, hardly more than a canoe, but big enough for the two of us. There were more boats half hidden in shadows beyond it.

I followed her along the shore, helped her push the boat into the water. I climbed in, as unquestioning as if I knew what the hell we were doing. Even knowing Naoh's effect on her, somehow I trusted her the way Joby trusted her: perfectly, instinctively, without reason—in a way I'd never trusted anyone in my life.

There were no oars in the boat. There was no power unit that I could see. And yet the boat began to move, not following the current but nosing deeper into the shadows of the overhanging reef.

Taku fluttered in and out of the darkness above us. Peering up at the roof of the overhang, I made out pale random blotches on its mossy surface, like wads of cobweb . . . *nests*. I wondered whether the taku were drawn to the reefs by their psi, whether the Hydrans were, as well. I wondered again whether the creation of the taku had been a fluke of the cloud-whales' dreams or a gift.

As we drifted farther into the darkness, the barely audible cries of the taku faded until all that was left was the soft lapping of the water. The opening reached deeper into the heart of the reef face than I'd imagined. "Is this natural?" I asked, dropping my voice to a whisper as it echoed out into the darkness. "Was it always here; did the river create it? Or did—" *Your people. My people.* . . . I broke off, not certain how to phrase it.

I saw her shoulders rise slightly in a shadow of a shrug. "I don't know," she murmured. Her voice was distracted, as though her thoughts were far away.

I thought about the depths of loss hidden inside those three words, the lost history of a people without a past. . . . I thought about my own life. I looked up again, trying to guess the dimensions of the space we were entering now. There was still enough light to see clearly by, even though the cavern entrance was far behind us. The heart of the reef was glowing, festooned with photoluminescent growth. Stirred by the motion of our passing, the hanging curtains gave off a pale aurora of light. It was warmer here too. The reef seemed to breathe like something alive, exhaling warmth into the still air, making the cold river water steam until we were adrift in a sea of fog.

All my senses felt smothered, as if we were moving through some medium besides air. But it wasn't like drowning . . . it was good. I remembered my last journey into the reefs; realized the cloud-whales' thought-residue must be affecting me again. I let it happen, wanting it, ready this time for anything. . . .

The boat came to a gentle stop, nudging a shore that was only a denser shadow emerging from the fog-gray mystery of the water.

Miya climbed out of the boat. I helped her pull it up onto the beach. River pebbles crunched under my feet, solid and reassuring. I could make out the dim furrows left by other boats on the stony shore. I wondered why the Hydrans chose to enter their holy place this way, when all they had to do was think themselves here. Then I remembered Hanjen telling me why he'd walked all the way from town to see Grandmother: *Respect. Humility.*

Miya drifted away along the shore as if she'd forgotten I was with her, or forgotten that I couldn't read her mind unless she let me. I wondered whether the reef-rapture that was turning my thoughts to fog had hold of her too, in a way I couldn't imagine. I followed her, forcing my body to make the effort to catch up. She seemed to know where we were going; I didn't see any choice except to follow.

As we went on, the fogged, stagnant air grew clearer and brighter. Looking up I saw tiny sparks of light begin to show, winking on one after another, somewhere inside the masses of phosphorescent growths high above us. I wondered whether the lights were something alive, a life-form adapted to this endless night, or some manifestation of the reef matrix itself. . . . Or whether maybe I'd begun to hallucinate.

When Miya finally stopped moving, I looked down again. We were standing on what seemed to be an island in a lake of fog. I hadn't felt us walk through water. I looked back the way we'd come, telling myself that we couldn't have walked on the water, either. I glanced at Miya. Her face was clenched like a fist, as if she was struggling against something—the power of the reef, or something darker—inside herself.

In front of us on the ground lay a knee-deep pile of artifacts; things dropped there by Human—or probably Hydran—hands. They must have been brought to this place by past seekers. I wondered what the ones who'd left them had come here in search of, whether they'd believed their offering was the thing that would get them what they needed or if it had only been a personal gesture, with a meaning no one else would ever understand.

Miya stooped down, picking up something from a pile that could have been centuries- or even millennia-old. Some of the artifacts looked like nothing I'd ever seen, things from a time before Humans had come to this world, when the machinery of Hydran daily life had run on energy channeled by the mind. Some of them just looked like junk, the fallout of everyday life in a Human city, castoffs from the world across the river. I nudged a piece of scrap metal; it canted over, crushing a bouquet of flowers that I'd thought at first were real.

I looked up again as Miya dropped the thing she'd been holding. It looked like an old-fashioned manual lock, but something about it was different, incomplete. Her eyes were full of tears. "What—?" I said softly.

"Naoh," she murmured. "And Navu."

I bit my lip, not understanding but not able to ask. She wasn't looking at me anymore, and she didn't say anything else.

Finally she moved on, picking a path through the residue of grief and prayers. The darkness closed in on us until even my eyes had trouble making out the way ahead. "Miya?" I whispered, but she didn't answer. Instead I felt her hand close over mine, leading me onward in silence.

Abruptly we came up against a surface that was somehow solid and yielding all at once, like the flesh of some unimaginable creature. She pulled me forward, forcing me face-first into the membranous wall. I felt it begin to close in on me, absorbing me. I tried to resist, starting to panic. The hard pressure of her hand locked around mine kept me moving, somehow reassuring me as if her mind was actually feeding me faith.

We merged, then emerged through the membrane's other surface so suddenly that I staggered. She caught my weight against her.

It was pitch-black here, and the air had a pungent dankness to it. I wondered what I was breathing in; what I'd see, if I could see anything. Miya's hand on my chest stopped my forward motion. Her hands guided me down until we were sitting on a surface my touch couldn't identify. Still she didn't say anything.

"What do we do now?" I whispered thickly, surprised at the difficulty I had just forming the words, as if my brain had gone to sleep.

"Wait," she murmured. Her voice sounded far away, reluctant, as if speaking wasn't something you did here. Her hand stroked my chest gently, almost tenderly, before it fell away.

I fought the urge to reach out, to reestablish the severed link between us. I kept my hands clenched at my sides and waited, not letting myself ask what we were waiting for.

Guidance. Insight. Answers. The words formed inside my thoughts as if someone had put them there, but it was only my own mind guessing. I didn't believe the random psi energies of the reef were any more likely than the random motion of the stars to answer the question of what the hell we were going to do about Tau. But I waited, matching the rhythm of my breathing to Miya's, knowing that at least here I had a chance to feel something, to interface with the world that I'd been cut off from, even if whatever it gave back to me proved as meaningless as everything else.

I pressed my hands against the unidentifiable surface of the ground, increased the pressure until they were the focus of the pain and tension that seemed to have become a part of me to the point where I wasn't sure I could draw a breath anymore that didn't hurt my chest. At first all I heard was the sound of my own breathing, all I saw was nothing: random patterns of phantom light, the reactive firing of neurons behind my eyes. If Miya had prayers to say or questions to ask, she asked them inside her mind, where I couldn't hear them. My own mind was a blank slate.

But inside my head I could feel the pressure of the reef's presence building, like the whispering of half-heard voices in an unknown tongue. As I listened, the potential energy of my tension grounded itself in the darkness, flowing out of me through my hands into the unseen, the unknown. As I let it go the phantom voices grew louder, flowed across the boundaries of my senses, becoming colors, odors, fragments of sensation that made gooseflesh crawl up my body.

I shifted, restless with sensation, felt my shoulder contact Miya. I started, as if my body had forgotten I wasn't here alone.

She pressed closer, unexpectedly, as if she was the one who needed contact, reassurance, a guide, now. Searching in the darkness I found her hand, held it. Its coldness startled me. A tremor ran through her arm into my body. I held on, not knowing what it meant, only glad that she didn't pull away.

I felt my concentration begin to dissolve again, coherent thought turning to bubbles on an undersea swell of indescribable stimuli . . . slowly reassembling into logic and recognizable images, the sense of Miya's body pressed against mine . . . drifting out again into some alien sea, drawn back . . .

. . . seeing her with an impossible clarity that vision couldn't begin to capture: *seeing beauty that had nothing to do with surface features; need that had everything to do with her soul; faith that defied fate and description.* . . . All the things that had drawn me to her like gravity—that had made me trust her, made me willing to risk my life for a stranger. I'd thrown away everything I'd struggled so hard to become to be in her world instead of the one I'd always known. Seeing myself through her mind's eyes: finding everything that I loved about her reflected in the image my face . . .

. . . My stunned thoughts dissolved, rising and escaping, slipping through the fingers of my brain. . . .

. . . And slowly reintegrated, until I could feel her hand in mine . . . her mind . . . *Her*: a Hydran among Humans, knowing them as individuals, not a faceless enemy. And yet always an outsider, an alien . . . even though by reaching out to them she made herself an outsider among her own people. I wondered why she'd done it, why she'd been drawn to the Human side, after all that had been done to her people, all the things that made her sister hate Humans. . . .

But I didn't have to wonder anymore why she'd looked at me and found her nasheirtah. . . .

. . . And dissolving into the everywhere, I knew with my last coherent thought just how much love it was possible to feel. . . .

. . . There in the everywhere her mind was open, shining, like a sanctuary; once again there was no barrier between us, no need for any kind of defense. We were one with the matrix of random energy around us . . . with this world, with the universe that everything was a part of. With each other . . . her body against mine, our bodies folding, combining, flowing through each other while the solid floor of the chamber seemed to fall away beneath us. I felt myself rise out of reality, radiant energy shining from every pore, as we were absorbed into the luminous heights of rapture. Together we were whole, together we could find the answer to any question, every need. . . .

And then the shining heights flooded with an acid fog of terror and grief, and reality came crashing in to claim us.

Suddenly we were two separate, lost souls again, crouched blindly in the stifling darkness. Beside me Miya was gasping with shock.

"Miya—?" I called, still stupefied by visions, not knowing what had been a hallucination, what was real, as a smothering pall of disaster filled the space around me.

I felt her hand on my arm, urging me up. "No," I said hoarsely, *so close, so close*—feeling the answer we'd come for vanish like a dream at the sound of my voice. "No, Miya, wait—"

But she wouldn't wait. She forced me up, every movement leaden after the memory of flight, and guided me back through the membranous wall of the prayer chamber, through the glimmering shadowland where the dream jetsam of Hydrans and cloud-whales coexisted.

We reached the spot where the boat lay waiting. Miya looked at it, hesitating, and then glanced up at the fog-blind distance, as if she saw something I couldn't. And then, still without a word, she looked back at me. I felt her thoughts close around me. . . .

———

We were back on the river's shore, standing beside Grandmother again. I held on to Miya as she reeled against me, as if the strain of always carrying me on her mind's back had drained the last of her strength. The sun had already set. I glanced down to check the time on my databand and saw nothing but a bare scar. I looked away again, feeling dizzy.

Grandmother still held Joby in her arms. She was standing, her body straining the way Miya's had as she gazed into the distance, searching for something I couldn't imagine with a sense I couldn't feel. She didn't even react to our arrival; but Miya said, almost inaudibly, "We have to go back."

Before I could stop her our reality changed again. The river was gone. We were standing on open ground in front of the smoking remains of a building. . . . *The monastery.* Grandmother's home.

Something—someone—had dropped a plasma burst on it.

"*Aiyeh—!*" Miya fell to her knees, holding her head. Grandmother stood beyond her, rigid and silent, like a statue. Joby began to wail. I took him from Grandmother's arms, rocked him in my own, crooning toneless, meaningless words, trying to comfort him with motion and sound, because I couldn't do anything real for anybody.

He quieted, surprising me. His voice fell away to a soft keening; he clung to my neck, half choking me with need. Time began again: my other senses registered the reek of burning, sounds of grief and pain carrying from the distance. I realized finally that there were still other people here. Looking toward the ruins, I saw figures moving, tiny and unrecognizable from this distance.

And then, suddenly, someone else was beside us, appearing between eyeblinks. *Hanjen.*

I stumbled back, startled like I always was when somebody did that, but he didn't even glance at me. All his attention was on Grandmother. He bowed, pressing her hands to his forehead . . . slowly raised his head again. His throat worked as if he was trying to speak. But he didn't speak, at least not in a way that I could hear. Beside me, Miya slowly got to her feet. Her face was colorless; her eyes were empty. She turned away, and I heard her being sick.

As Hanjen released Grandmother's hands she took his face

gently between them, shaking her head. I realized suddenly what it had been about: *He'd thought she was dead.* We could have been dead, all of us, if we hadn't gone to the reefs when we did. I forced myself to ask him, "Who did this—?" even though I was sure I didn't need to. Still, somehow I needed to hear the answer.

"Tau," Hanjen said bitterly, and I felt it like a blow, even though it was the answer I'd been expecting. He looked toward the smoking ruins. "They said that the oyasin was harboring HARM members."

"Was anybody killed?" I whispered, barely able to speak the words this time.

"Yes," Hanjen murmured, shaking his head. It wasn't a denial, but a clearing motion: I remembered how death had felt, trapped inside of me, when I'd still had my telepathy; how it had saturated all my senses, filled even the air around me until I couldn't breathe. "We don't know how many," he said thickly, at last. "Some people fled. Some of the survivors said that something happened to them before the explosion: That they couldn't use their Gift—their speech became slurred, as if they'd been drugged. No one really knows what had happened, or how many escaped. I thought . . . the oyasin . . ." He broke off, glancing at her again. She was already moving away, going on foot toward the burned-out shell of the monastery, where stunned survivors still drifted like insects around a flame.

"Is there an airborne form of the drug Corporate Security uses?" Hanjen asked me.

I hesitated, remembering what had happened to me, and to Miya, when Tau had closed its fist on us back in my hotel room. "I don't know." Realizing as I said it that I didn't know enough about nephase to know whether an airborne form of it was even possible. I was surprised that he didn't either.

"There is an airborne form of the drug," Miya murmured behind me. "It's used for crowd control, when too many Hydrans try to gather for a rally. Draco manufactures it."

"Oh, God," I muttered, seeing Sand in my mind's eye, seeing him abandoning Tau to twist in the wind. . . . Had he left Borosage something more—enough rope for Tau to hang itself with? I shifted Joby in my arms. He rested quietly with his head on my shoulder, almost as if I really could touch him, reassure him, somehow, with my mind. *Had Borosage known where we were when they destroyed this place? Was the timing of the attack really just chance? Had they known Grandmother had taken us away . . . or had Tau wanted us all dead?*

Hanjen looked at me again, suddenly, as if he was only now seeing me clearly. "That's a Human child," he said. He looked past me, and I saw him realize who the third person with us was. "Miya—?" He caught her by the arm. She didn't resist, still pale and shaken. He looked back at Joby, at me, away at the oyasin moving among the victims in the distance. I watched his disbelief fade into resignation. He let Miya go, his mouth like a knife cut. I wondered what he wouldn't say, wouldn't even allow himself to think as he watched Grandmother.

Miya came unsteadily to my side. Her hand reached up absently to stroke Joby's hair. I wondered whether she felt the tremor run through me as I realized what Hanjen must be thinking—who he must be blaming for what had happened here.

"The child must be returned," Hanjen said. His voice strained, as if he'd read my mind, but he hadn't needed to.

"I know," Miya whispered, her own voice a thread of sound. "But then I'll never see him again. What will become of him—?"

"You should have thought about that before you took him." Hanjen moved away from us, walking deliberately, but still moving too quickly. He headed toward the ruined monastery and the survivors.

"It wasn't supposed to be like this—" Miya murmured in Hydran. The frayed thread of her voice snapped under the weight of the obvious.

"Yes it was," someone said behind me. *Naoh.*

I turned and she was there, in the flesh. Her eyes were black pools of pain as she stared at the monastery, the huddled figures.

"When our people learn how far the Humans have gone— destroying a holy place, causing the deaths of innocent children, trying to kill an oyasin—" Her voice shook; I felt rage blow through my soul like a burning wind. Miya stiffened beside me, her own face a mask of devastation, as if her sister's fury had immolated all coherent thought.

I felt a totally different emotion as I looked at Naoh. "Did you know this was going to happen—?"

Naoh swung around, glaring at me. "Who are you, to say that
to me?" But she didn't deny it.

"Naoh—?" Miya said, when her sister didn't say anything
more. It was half a demand, half a plea.

"I followed the Way," Naoh whispered. "The oyasin says
sometimes the Way is hard. . . ." She looked back at me. "My sister understands that."

Miya sucked in a sharp breath. "What are you talking about?"
she demanded, her voice rising. "That you betrayed these people
to Borosage? Are you—are you—" *(Insane!)* Her mind
screamed the word she wouldn't speak. But as their eyes locked,
I watched Miya's expression soften, like candle wax melting in a
flame.

"Miya?" I murmured, and touched her arm. She didn't look at
me, didn't even acknowledge me. I backed away from her, shaken.
I left them standing there, like one woman staring into a mirror,
and started toward the place where Grandmother was still moving
slowly among the survivors. Even from a distance I read pain in
her every motion: the shared suffering that only I was immune to,
out of everyone here. The urge to ask her whether she'd known
what was going to happen here died stillborn inside me.

"Bian!" Naoh called out suddenly. "Our people had to learn!
We had to let them see what will happen to them! Are you a true
revolutionary? Are you truly Hydran—"

I swung around. "Hydrans don't kill people! And they don't
use Humans to do their dirty work for them, either—" I said, my
voice raw.

"You don't understand—" She broke off as Hanjen reappeared
suddenly beside her.

"Naoh!" he shouted, the single word filled with a kind of emotion I'd never heard before in a Hydran voice.

She reeled as if he'd struck her, got control and stopped him in
his tracks from coming after her again. His hands trembled in
front of him with an urge I understood perfectly. "Send the boy
back! This is sickness! *Bes' mod!*" He turned to Miya, reaching
for Joby. "Give me the boy!"

"You can't stop us!" Naoh shouted furiously. "Our people will
know the truth, and they will rise up—"

"And do what?" I yelled.

"Change the world! Bring the new age, when we will have everything, and the Humans will be nothing. If enough of us cry out, the Allsoul will answer us. If you are not with us, you're against us! You will disappear too."

"I'm not Human—"

"No," she said, her voice roughening. "And not Hydran. You are a mebtaku. There is no place anywhere for something like you. Miya!" She jerked her head.

Miya looked at me, grief-stricken. I knew as she looked into my eyes that I was losing her.

"Miya . . . ?" I reached out. "Naoh, damn it, you don't understand! Miya, talk to her, *tell* her about the nephase—"

My fingers closed over Miya's shadow as they disappeared. My empty hands knotted, and I swore under my breath.

Hanjen stood watching me. He shook his head. (Every time I see you, things are worse.) He looked down, rubbing his face, smearing it with ash.

"Are you blaming me for this—?"

"No." He looked at me blankly, as if he couldn't imagine where I'd gotten that idea. Then, still looking at me, I saw him remember. "You heard that—?"

"I learned your language," I said in Hydran.

He shook his head again. "But I didn't say anything."

"Yes, you did."

"I only thought it."

I bit my lip.

"You heard my thought." He was looking at me now with something new in his eyes.

I glanced away. "Sometimes it happens. . . . I can't control it."

He half frowned, as if he was concentrating on something I couldn't see. "You are more . . . *present,* to me." He looked up again, searching my face. "Even with all this—" He gestured, his own face furrowing, and I knew what he meant: the stench of grief and death and pain that went beyond the physical, that was taking every ounce of his Gift and will, every fragment of concentration, to endure. "You are *here.*" He touched his head. "Is it Miya—?"

I shrugged. "I don't know . . . or maybe the reefs. We went to a . . . sacred place."

"She took you there?" It sounded like disbelief. "No Human—"

"I'm not Human!" I held up my fist, my wrist, showed him the naked flesh, nothing but the scar that the databand had always hidden. "The oyasin took us there."

He shook his head, as if this time her motives were as inscrutable as mine. "What are you doing here?" he asked finally.

I told him as we started back toward the ruins where Grandmother was still trying to help the people she'd given refuge to. Now she was as homeless as the rest of them. As we got closer I spotted other members of the Council moving among the injured, and strangers who must have been the local equivalent of medics.

Grandmother looked up as we reached her side. As our eyes met, a shock wave of grief, a sense of *age,* overwhelmed me. The contact was gone before I could even react. Suddenly I wanted to give her all the strength I had left in my mind, in my body. But my mind couldn't reach her. I didn't offer her my hand, just stood useless and silent while Hanjen spoke with her, his voice barely audible against the background noise. I wondered why he was speaking out loud, if he was actually doing it for my sake or if it was just easier, when the cacophony of suffering must be so much louder inside their heads. ". . . We've found a place where all of you can stay safely, for now. I'll find a better place. We'll rebuild. . . . Is there any other help that I can give you—?"

Grandmother shook her head. "We need nothing else that you can give us." She glanced away, at the shadow-figures moving brokenly past us. "What has been taken away today, only time can give back." She looked at me then, suddenly. "Only time, Bian," she murmured, and touched my face. "You understand . . . only time."

I swallowed, suddenly choking on grief, and nodded.

"What is he doing here—?" Someone jerked me around where I stood: one of the Council members.

"He is with me," Hanjen said quickly.

"He is with me," Grandmother said. "He is with us now."

A refugee. A Refugee. I looked past Grandmother at the stunned, uncomprehending faces all around her. *Don't let them turn you into one,* Wauno had said. *Them. Tau. . . . HARM. Miya.*

The Council member frowned. He let go of me as if I was hot. Whatever he said or thought then, I couldn't feel it, but I saw the look in his eyes. His hand spasmed. He turned away, gesturing for Hanjen to follow. Other Council members joined them. I watched them arguing silently, glancing my way but not at me—at the ruins. I didn't have to hear them to guess the focus of the argument.

I looked back at Grandmother. The wind that billowed her cloak and tore at her veil was cold and full of ashes. "She's gone. . . . What should I do?" I asked finally. "I don't know what to do."

Grandmother blinked. "Follow the Way. . . ." She cocked her head when I didn't say anything. "Did you feel nothing?"

I shook my head. *We didn't have enough time*— I stopped the thought before it could form into words. "I saw Miya." *Saw into her, shared her mind, understood . . . joined.* I knew the effect that our joining had had on her, how she'd seen me, what she'd found inside my heart and mind. It had been enough to make her love me, but it hadn't been enough to keep her from leaving me behind.

"Then perhaps she is the answer for you," Grandmother said, waiting just long enough to be sure I thought of it first. "The Way will lead you to her. Or perhaps both of you will only find the Way together."

"But she's gone."

"She is with Naoh."

"I know—"

"Naoh is bes' mod."

"Bes' mod?" I said. The words seemed to mean "nerve storm."

Grandmother nodded like I had some idea what I was talking about, or she did. "And she is very powerful." Her hand touched her head. "She draws other lost ones to her. She feeds on their power. Miya has been taken by the storm."

"But—"

She held up her hand, as if she was listening to something I couldn't hear. "You are silence—the silence at the storm's eye. Bian, she needs your silence."

I shook my head, not sure if I understood anything she was telling me. "But how can I find her?"

She bent her head. "Follow the Way."

"But—"

"Oyasin." Hanjen was back beside us. He bowed to her, then

touched my arm—something Hydrans seemed to do habitually, at least to me. I wondered whether it was the only way they could think of to get my attention. He nodded like he was asking me to follow him.

I glanced at Grandmother. She watched me, her face unreadable, as usual. I bowed to her; she bowed to me. I followed Hanjen.

"What did she mean about Naoh?" I asked. "She said something about a 'nerve storm.' I don't understand what that means."

"A sort of sickness . . ." he murmured. "It destroys one's . . . perspective, one's self—" His hand gestured at the empty air, as if he couldn't find the words he needed to make it plain to me.

"You mean she's crazy," I said in Standard.

He shrugged. "We could not say that," he murmured, and I wasn't sure whether it was a criticism or just a comment. "There was a time, in our society, when such a person was protected. If their thoughts became too . . . unstable, the Community would gather and join with them until they were healed."

"Who decided when someone was—sick enough to need that?" I asked.

He looked at me as if I'd asked something incomprehensible. "Everyone knew," he said. "We were a Community. We were . . ." He sighed, looking away. "Too often now a sick mind goes unhealed . . . unnoticed." His voice hardened. "They draw in others who are susceptible, who carry the seeds of the same . . . soul-rot. They feed on one another's distorted thoughts. I have seen whole groups starved to death together—locked into a joining that shut out the entire world, even their need to eat or sleep, until they were unable to save themselves."

"And no one—noticed?" I said, disbelief rising like bile in my throat. "How is that possible?" Humans seemed to ignore another person's need as easily as breathing, because they never had to feel it unless they wanted to. But Hydrans—

He shrugged. "We call ourselves the Community. But we have not been one since the Humans came. We are like the cloud-reefs . . . mined out. This, here"—he gestured in the direction of Freaktown—"is the rubbish heap of history, all that is left of what we were." He turned, his gaze scanning the distance in another direction. "When the FTA has gone, when your research group has finished its work, they will take this final reef."

"You know that—?" I said.

He grimaced. "They don't admit it, even to themselves. But I see the thought, always just below the surface in their minds. They promised us that this one piece of sacred ground would be untouched. But they are lying to themselves, just as they have always lied to us."

I stood staring at the ruins of the monastery. The number of survivors and rescuers had diminished already. As I watched, another group of silhouetted forms disappeared. "What now?" I asked finally, looking back at Hanjen.

"I must speak with Janos Perrymeade." His face turned grim, or maybe grimmer. "He has sent me three messages already. I do not know how to answer him. Not after this—" He glanced toward the ruins, away again. "Are there words for such things, in your language? You know those people—" not *your people,* "better than I ever will. How does a Human speak to . . . his enemy?"

I shook my head, looking down. "How do you contact Perrymeade, if you need to?" I looked up again. Freaktown wasn't even tied into Tau Riverton's communications net, as far as I knew, let alone the Federation Net. And somehow I didn't think Perrymeade communicated telepathically.

"He gave me a port that I can use. It's at my home."

I nodded, surprised. "Is it still functioning?"

He looked surprised, now. "Yes. There was a message from him just hours ago. I didn't answer it, because the Council could not agree on what kind of response to give. And then, this—"

"You'd better start answering him, right now," I said. "You can't wait for the Council to decide. You're the only one of them who has any idea what the Humans really want. And you're right. I do know more about them. . . ." Realizing as I said it how much more I knew about Tau, and Draco, and keiretsu . . . wondering whether any of it would be enough to do any good. "Take me with you."

I'd been lost inside my own thoughts; suddenly I was lost inside something larger, deeper, darker, as Hanjen's mind picked me up like an afterthought, and teleported—

SEVENTEEN

WE WERE BACK in Freaktown: the alienness of the walls and furniture was beginning to seem ordinary to me. I stumbled to the nearest thing that would hold me up—a curving bench padded with mats—and sat on it. Jags of bright color showed in the deep earth tones of the woven mats.

Hanjen leaned against the edge of a carved wooden cabinet, as if he could barely stand—like it had been more exhausting for him to transport my dead weight than it had ever seemed to be for Miya. I remembered that the strength of a Hydran's Gift—or a Human psion's—had nothing to do with physical strength or size.

He glanced at me; looked away again, as if contact with my eyes was painful. Or maybe it had been the contact with my mind that made him look away. I let my own eyes wander the floor, the walls—anything, anywhere, as long as it was inanimate.

This was Hanjen's home. I couldn't tell how large it was from where I sat. But compared to the monastery, and the rooms I'd shared with Miya and the Satoh, this room was plush—filled with furniture, rugs, hangings, carved wooden lintels. The floors showed the elaborate mosaic patterns that seemed to have been almost an obsession with the original builders of this city. I wondered if they'd actually set each shard of ceramic or glass by hand—or if they'd set them without ever touching one. My mind imagined a freeform cloud of colored fragments moving through the air, like the cloud-whales drifting across the sky; pictured them suddenly falling into place with the precision of thought.

"This is nice," I murmured. Most of the furniture looked old. Looking at the pieces more carefully, I noticed the scars of time marring the beautiful workmanship of almost every age-darkened table and chest.

Hanjen cocked his head at me like he thought that was a peculiar comment, but he only nodded. "Everything here is something I discovered in an abandoned building or something that had been put out on the street. I have tried to salvage what I can of the past. Perhaps someday it will mean something to someone besides me. I hope, by the time I die . . ." He broke off and left me to silence, to wondering where his thoughts had gone.

I let my eyes search the room again, scanning artifacts and works of art until I found the one thing that didn't belong here: a computer port. It sat in a shadowed alcove, as though he'd tried to make that symbol of his association with the Humans as unobtrusive as possible. But still it stood out, an alien thing, its message function light blinking in the gloom like an unnaturally green eye.

Hanjen followed my stare, shedding his coat almost absentmindedly. It was cold enough in the room that I kept mine on. He made a sound that was half a sigh, half a grunt of resignation, as he crossed the room to call on the access. The messages left by Perrymeade flowed across its screen; were repeated by a disembodied voice in the air—a Human voice.

Hanjen stood in front of its empty, waiting screen and didn't speak or touch it. He looked at me. "I should have the Council's backing—"

I shook my head. "You know you're the only one of them who's got the courage. Someone's got to act, now—"

He turned back to the screen, his face hardening, and input the call-code.

Perrymeade appeared in the electronic window the instant Hanjen finished. He must have been waiting for an answer, maybe for hours. I searched the background around his image, trying to tell where he was, whether he was alone. What little detail I could make out looked like a private home, not an office. "Hanjen," he said, as if he'd been holding his breath all that time. "Thank God. I've been trying to reach you. Borosage—"

"I know what he has done," Hanjen said flatly. "He has destroyed a holy place and killed innocent people . . . *children*. . . ." His voice slipped out of control.

Perrymeade's hand covered his face, as if he'd been blindsided by his worst fears. "God! I tried to warn you, Hanjen. . . . Dammit, why didn't you answer my first call—?"

I couldn't see Hanjen's face, but his whole body recoiled. "Are you blaming us for this atrocity? Humans did this—only Humans are to blame!"

Perrymeade's gaze turned cold. "Hydran radicals kidnapped a child! Tau will not allow itself to be manipulated by terrorists—"

"Perrymeade," I said, taking the chance of moving into his line of sight. "Don't you get it yet?"

"Cat?" he said, and I saw his disbelief. "What the hell are you doing?" I wondered if he had any idea what had happened to me since he'd dropped me off at the hotel.

"Doing what I was ordered to do. Your job."

He didn't look surprised at the bitterness in my voice, but he looked confused. "Have you spoken to Miya?"

I nodded. "But she's not listening anymore. And neither am I."

"I don't understand," he said. I was sure, by the look on his face, that Borosage had cut him entirely out of the loop.

"I almost had her convinced that it made sense to give Joby back. But every time she started to believe me, Tau tried to kill us. Borosage is out of control, dammit! He's forcing an incident, so he'll have an excuse to kill more Hydrans. Tau's Board has backed off him because they think that'll save them, and Draco's backed off Tau. I can't talk to anybody on the Human side but you. If you sit there and let this happen, it'll drag you down with it—" I broke off, searching his face for a reaction, for some kind of understanding. I didn't find what I needed to see. "Even if it doesn't, if I were you I'd never look in a mirror again."

He looked down, as if suddenly he couldn't face his image in my eyes or Hanjen's. His attention flickered offscreen, distracted by something I couldn't see. He looked back at us, at me, finally. "Someone wants to talk to you," he said. He moved aside, making room for another floating head.

I stiffened, expecting Borosage or one of his Corpses, expecting threats—expecting anything but the face that I suddenly saw there in front of me. "Kissindre?"

She nodded. She looked as though she had as much trouble believing we were facing each other this way as I did. "Cat . . . ?" she said, faltering. "What are you doing?"

"Why don't you ask your uncle?" I said.

She glanced offscreen at him, back at me again. "He told me . . . about Miya, and the—and HARM, and the Board meeting." She grimaced, as if the blow had left a bruise. "What are you trying to do?" She asked it again, not sounding angry, but only bewildered.

"I don't know. . . ." I shook my head, rubbing my eyes, because suddenly looking at her face was like staring into the sun . . . *like trying to do something impossible.* "Kissindre . . . this is so fucked up. I don't know how it got like this. It just happened too fast."

"Cat, come back to Riverton. This is crazy. Come back now, before it goes too far, and you can't ever . . . Before you get hurt. My uncle can straighten it out. I need you on the field crew—"

"I can't." I shook my head. "I can't come back."

"But—" She broke off. "Is it . . . it's not because of . . . us?"

"No." I looked down, knowing that was partly a lie. But even the lie was nothing compared to the truth. "It's gone way beyond the two of us. It's Borosage, it's all of Tau—what they're doing to the Hydrans. For God's sake, they dropped a plasma burst on a monastery full of children! Your uncle couldn't help me if he wanted to. But he can stop this. . . . You hear me, Perrymeade?" He had to be listening, even if I couldn't see him. "Tau's Board won't control Borosage, and Draco's out of the picture. You've got to stop this yourself. Get those Feds back here, and let them know what's happening before everything goes to hell and takes you with it."

Kissindre was looking away from me now, looking at her uncle. "Kissindre?" I said, and waited until she looked back at me. "You have to make him understand. It's about keiretsu: He thinks he's protecting you and his family. But you're not going to have a research project—he's not going to have a job, a home, or a world, if you can't make him listen. All he'll have will be a lot of deaths on his conscience. Maybe—*maybe*—if he acts before it's too late, some of that won't happen. But if he doesn't it will. It will, damn it!"

"What makes you believe you're such an expert on keiretsu, son?" Perrymeade stepped back into the picture behind Kissindre, his expression professionally empty again. "You spent most of your life nameless and creditless on the streets of a Free Trade Zone."

My hands tightened. "I believe in 'know your enemy,' " I said.

Something filled his face: desperation, anger, it didn't matter what he was feeling. I knew that look . . . the blind stubbornness of somebody whose whole mental house of cards would collapse if he said the wrong thing or even let himself think it. "None of that is going to happen."

Bleak-eyed, he looked past me at Hanjen. "And nothing else will happen to your people if Joby is returned unharmed by tomorrow night. Because you wouldn't help us find his kidnappers, we . . . Administrator Borosage was forced to . . . retaliate, causing innocent people to suffer." He took a deep breath. "We want results. Only you can give them to us. You have one day's time to get my—to get the boy back. That's all the time I can guarantee you."

I saw Kissindre look at her uncle like he'd been replaced by a total stranger. "Uncle Janos? I don't believe this!" She looked back at the screen, at me. "Cat, listen—"

Perrymeade cut the connection, and the screen went blank.

I looked down, my fists still knotted at my sides. "Damn you," I muttered, not sure who I meant. I looked back at Hanjen, finally.

He was sitting at the table with his head in his hands, like the weight of his responsibility, of everything that had happened, had become too heavy to bear.

"I'm sorry," I whispered. I felt his grief and anger like an echo multiplying inside my own, not even able to feel the elation that should have come with any sense of him at all.

"No. I am the one who should apologize," he said, still resting his head in his hands. There was no accusation in his eyes as he looked up at me. "There was nothing you could have done to change anything." He glanced away at the empty screen. "There is nothing he can do to stop it, either. He is as powerless as I am to control the situation."

I frowned. "Then why did we just do this?"

"Because you felt so strongly that we should." He sat back in his chair with a shrug. " 'Your Way or my Way,' we say. 'It is different for everyone. . . . Who knows which is more true.' "

But I'm not even a precog. I swore under my breath.

"Perrymeade's niece—she was more to you than just your team leader. And you were—"

"That's over," I muttered. "All of that is over."

He looked at me strangely, as if what I was feeling now was incomprehensible . . . or maybe just unreachable.

"What about Miya?" I asked, turning his stare back on him. "And Naoh? What are they to you?" Remembering that he had worked with Perrymeade to get Miya the training that let her help Joby. He must have been the one to choose her. And the way he'd reacted when he saw them, the way they'd reacted toward him, at the monastery, hadn't been the way strangers treated each other.

"They are my foster daughters," he murmured. "I raised them . . . tried to raise them . . . after their parents were—"

"Murdered," I said, before he could backtrack. "How did it happen?"

"I—" He broke off, struggling with something deeper than memory, the emotion naked on his face.

Seeing him lose that much control scared me, because it told me how close to the edge even he was getting. I wondered if my face—not Human enough, not Hydran enough, with no psi to give him feedback—was what kept making him look away from me.

When his face and voice were under control again, he said, "Their parents were my closest friends, like family. They were detained, along with some others, after a demonstration years ago, when the girls were small. After they were released and sent back here, there was an illness—some called it a plague—that spread through the Community. Many people became sick; the ones who had been detained were the first. Some of the sick ones died—including my friends. Those who recovered were sterile."

"Shit," I breathed. "Miya . . . and Naoh—?" I got up, crossed the room to sit at the table beside him.

He nodded, his mouth crushed into a line. "The illness struck only the Community, not the Humans. Some people said the Humans caused it."

I shook my head, more in disbelief than denial. "Is that . . . Do you know for certain—?"

"I have never seen proof of it." He meant seen proof of it in a Human mind. "I know some who believe they have. The Humans say they don't know where the plague came from; that the cloud-whales created it, or it was something from the sacred ground. . . ."

The reefs. "I don't know. The Humans synthesized a vaccine, but not until many of us had died—or become sterile."

I wondered whether that was why I'd seen so few children in Freaktown, why his voice had broken when he'd spoken the word to Perrymeade . . . why he lived alone, with no sign of ever having had any family except, once, Miya and her sister. I didn't ask; couldn't. "Did you know—about the Satoh, about Naoh, and what Miya was planning?"

"No," he said, almost angrily. "Not until tonight. I had not seen Naoh in a long time. She became bitter—she was always bitter—" He broke off. "Miya was very young when their parents died; perhaps she doesn't remember, the way Naoh does. But—" His gaze turned distant. "Naoh always saw the Way as a straight line. . . . Miya saw it as a spiral. She told me once that the Way is meant to lead to wisdom, not to happiness."

"Oblivion," I muttered. "That's where Naoh's Way is leading them. She's like quicksand, and she's sucking Miya down with the rest of them."

He nodded, resting his head in his hands again. "I always believed Miya was the strong one—in her Gift and her resolve. But perhaps Naoh's sickness is stronger than both of them."

"Miya said that Naoh's 'vision' made her Gift more powerful— or gave her more reason to use it."

"I have seen enough perversions of the Gift in my lifetime to believe that anything is possible." His voice was heavy with resignation.

"Miya loves Joby, maybe too much. . . ." The words caught in my throat like thorns. Miya didn't need a reason to love him like that, beyond who she was, and who he was. *But to lose him, knowing she'd never see him again, never have a child of her own. . . .* "She's afraid of losing him to the Humans," I said, at last. "That makes her vulnerable."

Don't get involved. That was what Oldcity had taught me. *The cost was too high.* Hope, trust, love—they were only stones around your neck when you were already drowning. But then Jule taMing had come into my life and made me believe that a lifeline of trust, an outstretched hand, were all that could save you. . . .

Now, sitting here, I wondered for the first time since then if maybe the streets had been right.

"What is your involvement with Miya?" Hanjen asked me, suddenly, sharply.

I looked up, startled. "I . . . We . . ." I took a deep breath. "Nasheirtah. . . ." Suddenly certain, as I said it, that Jule taMing had always known the truth.

"Nasheirtah?" He stared at me. I wondered what he found so unbelievable: that she could have any feeling at all for somebody damaged the way I was or that somebody like me was capable of loving anyone that way.

But then he reached over and touched my shoulder, as gently as a thought. He smiled, painfully, before he drew his hand back again. I wondered which of us was more surprised.

I rested my head on my hands, staring at the dark years of Hydran history trapped in the wood grain of the table surface. "I have to find Miya," I said, finally. I looked up at him when he didn't answer. "How? Tell me how to do that. You must be able to . . . track her mind-print, if you've known her for so long—"

He nodded, the lines deepening in his weathered face. He looked sucked dry of any emotion, no matter how painful or urgent, now. "I can probably find her, if she's still here in the city. If Naoh has taken them into the outback, it will be virtually impossible." He rubbed his face. "But I must sleep first. You should rest too, or you will be no good to Miya or anyone." He got slowly to his feet.

I opened my mouth to say that we didn't have time. I looked down at my strengthless body barely supported by the tabletop. Finally I nodded.

"You are welcome to a bed." He gestured toward a side room before he faded like a ghost through another doorway and into darkness.

I went into the room. It wasn't a bed I found—it was a kind of hammock, suspended midway between the ceiling and the floor. I went to it, put my hands on it. It was chest-high; the only way I could see to get into it would be to levitate myself. I sighed, and dumped the bedding out onto the floor. I lay down on the hard, cold tiles and rolled up in the blankets. I was asleep before I even had time to think about it.

EIGHTEEN

I WOKE GASPING and wet with sweat. Struggling up from a dream about being strangled, I shook off the prison of tangled blankets. I sat up, wondering for a few more breaths why I was sleeping on the floor . . . whether I was really still in Oldcity. . . . *No. Not Oldcity. Freaktown.*

I got up and stumbled out through a fog of sleep into the central room, the last place I'd seen Hanjen before I'd gone to bed. The room was gray with dawn. Hanjen was already up—sitting perfectly still in a chair, staring at nothing.

"Hanjen—?" My heart missed a beat. But he wasn't dead; he was using his psi, searching telepathically for Miya, or Naoh. *You looked like you were dead.* . . . More than one Human had said that to me when I was using my Gift. I understood now why most Humans didn't like to see it.

Hanjen was back, suddenly, dropping out of his trance state like my entering the room had triggered some sensory alarm.

"Any luck?" I asked, startling myself as I realized I'd spoken Standard. I came on into the room.

" 'Luck—'?" he repeated, cocking his head.

"Finding them. Did you find them?"

Comprehension came back into his face. "No . . . and yes. I have not located either of them yet. But I have crossed the trail of HARM. Naoh has sent the Satoh out to feed the Community's outrage over what Tau did at the monastery. They claim that the time Naoh foresaw has come—that if our people rise up now, with one mind, together we can make the Humans disappear from our world."

"But that's crazy—" I broke off. He already knew that as well as I did. "What are you going to do?" I asked as he rose from his seat.

"I have contacted the Council; we are already trying together to stop this sickness from spreading."

Just sitting there—? I remembered where I was now and didn't ask. I wondered when I was going to stop thinking like a Human . . . worse, an unplugged one. "What about Miya and Joby?"

He shook his head, already looking distracted again. "This must be stopped first, or finding Joby will not matter."

I swallowed my protest and asked, "Where's Grandmother?"

He half frowned as he refocused. "Why?"

"Because finding Miya and Joby still matters to me, and it will still matter to you after you find Naoh. And I can't do it without a telepath to help me."

"I will ask her," he said. His attention faded again. I waited, feeling my frustration climb like a fever, until finally his attention was back in the same room with me.

"She will help you. But I cannot send you to her; it would take too much of my strength, and I need that."

"Well . . ." I rubbed my head. "Is she going to come here, then?"

His frown came back, as if I was confusing him for no reason. "She has never been here—"

So she couldn't teleport to us. And it would be harder for her to walk here than for me to walk there, wherever there was. . . . I began to see what he was getting at. "Have you got a map?"

He nodded, looking relieved. A marker appeared in his hand, out of nowhere. He looked around the room until his eyes settled on a piece of packaging in a bin that must have been used for trash. The wrapper drifted across the room to him; he reached up and picked it out of the air. Flattening it on the bench beside him, he began to make marks on it, with long hesitations between lines. At last he looked up at me, expectant; when I didn't move he gestured me toward him impatiently.

I went and stood beside him, realizing how difficult it must be for him to do this, when he could have simply *shown* it to anyone else he knew, laid it straight into their brain like a datafeed.

I thought again about how Humans had needed to find ways around their lack of the Gift. They'd had to learn how to build their own bridges across every chasm—between two or a thousand isolated minds. That was why it had taken them so much longer to get into space—where distances were so great, and the energy sources a psion could tap into to boost their power were so limited, that all bets were off and tech was the only real answer to the question. I wondered whether the fact that Humans had been forced to try harder to get there would mean that they stayed there longer.

I supposed it didn't really matter, at least to me, since the way things were going I'd be lucky to live until tomorrow.

I wondered whether Hanjen knew enough about maps to get me across the infinitesimally small part of the planet that separated me from Grandmother. I stood beside him, watching and listening as he did his best to describe in words—*clumsy, awkward, imperfect words*—the route to where she was staying, and I used what senses I had left to try to understand him. "It isn't far," was the only thing he said that reassured me.

I took the scrap from his hand and started to turn away.

"I'm sorry I can't do more to help you," he said. "But thank you for what you are trying to do to help us . . . and Miya."

I looked back at him, surprised as he made a small bow.

"If we each follow the Way we see, perhaps there is twice the chance that we will reach the end we hope for."

I nodded.

He pointed toward the front door. I followed the hallway to the entrance and stopped. The door had no doorknob, no touchplate, no automatic eye that I could see. "Open door," I said. There was no voice-activated microprocessor in the wall, either. "Hanjen—!" I shouted.

The door opened. I almost stepped through it; grabbed the doorframe as I realized we were on the second floor and there weren't any steps. Looking down I could see broken masonry along the wall, where steps had probably been once. I swore and turned around. Hanjen was standing there, looking at me. As he went on watching me, invisible arms gently closed me in. They lifted me and carried me down to street level. I landed lightly on my feet, glanced up just in time to see the door close again.

I looked away down the dawn-red street. There were dozens of Hydrans already out and moving. I was surprised to see the street so busy, so early in the morning. I wondered whether Hydrans always got up at dawn or whether the activity meant something I didn't want to think about.

None of them seemed to see anything strange in the way I'd arrived at ground level. Most of them seemed to be walking, like I was, not drifting over the ground or teleporting in and out of existence. But even moving the same way they did, dressed in the same clothes they wore, I'd never *feel* like one of them when they tried to touch my mind. No matter how alien I felt among Humans, I realized I'd always be more Human than Hydran . . . always a mebtaku; and my mind's barriers were like a raised fist, a deliberate insult to every passing stranger.

Nobody spoke to me or even directly acknowledged me as I kept walking. But word about me traveled ahead: I started to notice people waiting at the sides of the street or looking out of windows to silently watch me pass. I met their stares, letting them see my eyes, the long slit pupils, trying to keep them from seeing any fear there.

There were no signs marking any of the streets here. I held the map in a death grip; felt a little safer every time I spotted another landmark Hanjen had described. As I walked I wondered how I'd ever get up to his door again. And I wondered if there'd never been anyone here who'd been crippled in an accident or been born with a genetic flaw, disabled in either body or mind—anything that kept them from doing the kinds of things other Hydrans did. Maybe the Community had better support systems than Humans did for taking care of their own, always ready to help each other—

But I remembered Naoh's addict lover, all the other junkies and derelicts I'd seen. They'd made themselves as helpless as I was, and no one had done anything about it. I remembered what Hanjen had said, remembered the primitive med center Miya and Naoh had shown me. *Maybe no one could.*

And then I wondered what it would be like to spend the rest of my life this way: walking a gauntlet of stares, not able to do things for myself that everybody else took for granted . . . with no one I could count on, if I didn't find Miya. Even if I did, what was going to happen if I couldn't make her listen—?

More and more people were out in the street now, a river of them flowing past. I wondered where they were going in such a hurry. Some of them muttered curses as they passed me or bumped me harder than they needed to. Once or twice I got shoved from behind, so hard that I stumbled. But when I spun around, nobody was close enough to have touched me. I began to wonder whether I'd even get as far as Grandmother's.

Grandmother. . . . Grandmother was going to help me. I studied the map again, searching the street for landmarks. *There.* I spotted the place Hanjen had said I'd find the survivors from the monastery. Tree-form pillars marked its entrance, the wall facing the street was a mosaic in what must once have been brilliant pinks and golds, the colors of sunset clouds. The building face was mauve with dust and pockmarked with missing tiles now— but there couldn't be anything else that matched the description he'd given me so closely. I started toward it, feeling the tightness in my chest ease. *Almost safe—*

Two figures materialized in front of me just as I reached the entrance—two Hydrans I'd never seen before, both men, bigger and heavier than most. I stopped short as they blocked my way. They stared at me; the stares weren't friendly. I wondered if they were trying to mindspeak me. "Get away from here, Human," one said, in Standard so thickly accented I could barely make out the words. "Go now."

"I'm not Human," I said, in Hydran. "I've come to see the oyasin." I faced down their stares, letting them have a good look into my eyes.

They frowned back at me, then at each other. "Mixed-blood," one of them muttered to the other, and then made a gesture at his head.

"Halfbreed," the other said, to me. A telekinetic shove made me stagger back. "Drug addict. Mebtaku. You are not fit to approach the oyasin. Go back to the Humans where you belong."

"She wants to see me," I said, trying to keep my voice under control.

"I think not." They moved closer together, still blocking my way, like they believed the only way I could get past them would be to go through them. I wondered what would happen if I actually tried it—realized I'd never even get that close, when they could make me back off without ever touching me.

"Namaste. I have been waiting for you." Suddenly Grandmother was standing in the street beside me.

"Jeezu!" I gasped, and stumbled back again. The two Hydrans did the same thing. For once I didn't feel embarrassed.

"Oyasin—" one of the Hydrans guarding the entrance protested. "You would come out to this deathbringer?"

I froze, thinking that somehow even this stranger knew about my past. But then I realized that it was just another way of calling me *Human*.

She turned to them, giving them a long look, but probably not a silent one. They bowed to her, finally, and then they bowed to me, reluctantly. They moved aside to let us pass.

I followed her in under the shadowed building entrance, through a small atrium where a handful of children were tossing a silver metal ball back and forth without ever touching it. Each time the ball hit a wall, chiming silvery music showered down on us, and the children laughed.

Beyond them was a large, high-ceilinged room. More people were gathered there: adults moving aimlessly or sleeping on mats; children curled up in someone's lap or darting like birds through the forest of adult bodies. The air smelled of cooking. Someone was playing a musical instrument I couldn't put a name to; there was so little audible conversation that the haunting music carried all through the room.

Here and there stray children drifted up toward the ceiling as if they were weightless. Sometimes an adult or another child went up after them or else silently ordered them back down. I thought about Joby, who couldn't watch them drifting overhead like fragments of a dream, couldn't even take a step without Miya's help. I tried not to see his eyes in every small face that turned to look at me.

There were a lot of people here. I wondered whether all of them had been at the monastery or whether this was always used as a shelter. It had obviously been something else, once—the organically patterned beauty of the walls and ceiling was as detailed as it had been in the building where I'd met the Community Council. I wondered if this was part of the same complex. It wasn't as well kept up, if it was. I could see the signs of age and neglect everywhere—too much dust, too much indifference. "What was this place?"

Grandmother glanced at me. "A—performance hall, you would say. The Community would gather here to share special dreams and creations the Way had revealed to them."

"You mean something like art or music?" I listened to the music echoing behind us, imagining how much more interactive a concert, or any other kind of art, could be if the audience could have access to the artist's mind and feel that creativity taking form. "They don't do that anymore?"

She shook her head; her veil fluttered like a moth's wing. "There are not enough people anymore. It became too . . . cold." She didn't mean simply the temperature. "If they want to share, they find a smaller space."

She led me on into another room, an empty cubicle with only a mat on the floor and an oil lamp burning. Its tendril of smoke rose undisturbed. I wondered if this was where she went to meditate, or sleep . . . or, I hoped, search for Miya, or someone who knew where Miya was. She kneeled down on the mat, slowly and carefully. I kneeled down across from her, sensing that it was what she expected, trying to be patient and let things happen, trying not to talk too much, push too much, be too Human. I focused on the music I could still hear above the clatter and murmur of the hall outside.

Grandmother looked up from the flame to my face, down at my clothing. "Ah, Bian," she said with a kind of sorrow, like something had become obvious to her that I'd completely missed. She didn't say what it was.

"You don't know where Naoh took Miya?" I asked, finally, when she didn't say anything else.

"I know where they are," she said, as calmly as if she was telling me the time.

"Where—?" I started to get up.

"Bian," she said, stopping me with a single word, as abruptly as if she'd paralyzed me with psi.

I sank back onto my knees. "What?"

"You must not go to her. Bad things will happen there soon. They will happen to you, if you go there."

I froze. "What do you mean? You had a sending? You saw it? What kind of bad things—"

She waited until my questions died away, and then she said, "Naoh and her people are spreading fear. . . ."

"I know—" I said and bit my lip.

"They show the Community that the Humans would rather let a child die—a Human child—than let the FTA come here to see how we live. They say the Humans have decided to destroy us all and desecrate our last sacred place—that your research team is proof of it."

"But that's not true—" I broke off again, remembering that half of it was true, already; I'd told the Satoh that myself. And the rest of it might become the truth sooner than I wanted to admit. "Won't people know—?"

"The Satoh believe it is true, and that is what people will see. Naoh asks the Community to gather where the Bridge of Sighs crosses over to Riverton. She tells them that if enough believe as they do, they can stop Tau. That enough of our people joined together can banish all trace of the Human occupation from our world—"

"Oh, God," I muttered, rubbing my face. Miya knew about the airborne drug. But Naoh wasn't sharing the truth about that with the Community. "When is this—miracle—supposed to happen?"

"Soon. Those who have heard are already beginning to gather and draw others."

I thought about the people I'd seen out in the street as I'd made my way here, their restlessness, the suspicion in their faces. I wondered whether the Satoh's rumors had been the cause of it all. And then I thought about what Naoh was telling them to do. Uniting, acting with one mind, almost sounded reasonable. As if it was something that should have been done years ago. . . . Maybe it had been done years ago; maybe it had been tried again and again through the years since Humans had taken over Refuge. But it had always failed, because Human technology had been one step ahead of them all the time, and Human ruthlessness hadn't changed at all.

Tau's CorpSec had nephase gas. Borosage had used it in my hotel room; used it again at the monastery. There was absolutely no doubt in my mind that he'd use it on a mob trying to force its way into Riverton. And gathered together in one place, without their Gift, they'd be sitting targets for anything Tau wanted to do to them.

I looked up at Grandmother again. "You see the Humans attacking the demonstration, don't you? And we're helpless to stop it—"

She nodded, her face heavy with shadows. "That is what I have seen, if the people follow Naoh's Way. And they will. No one can stop it."

"Hanjen is trying. Have you tried—?"

She nodded. "But it is too late."

"How much did you know about the Satoh's activities, anyway? And for how long? Did you know they planned to kidnap Joby?"

"Yes, Bian, I knew . . ." she said quietly, shaking her head. I shut my eyes. "At the time, the Way that I saw brought us to a better place, in the end."

"But now it's changed?"

She didn't answer me.

"Why? What changed?" *Me?* Was it my interference, when Miya . . . ? But the Corpses nearly had her. If she hadn't run into me, she'd probably be dead now, and Naoh's vision with her. *The riot gas?* If Grandmother hadn't known about that, would that throw off her precognition? I didn't know enough about it even to guess, and she wasn't telling me. "Maybe I can still stop them. Maybe I can change things back—"

"No." She shook her head again and rose slowly to her feet. "Bad things will happen no matter what you do, Bian. If you go after Miya, they will happen to you too."

"Where's Joby?"

"He is safe."

"Where? Here? Do you have him?"

"He is safe," she said again, and the look in her eyes told me that was all the answer I was getting. She started toward the door.

"Where are you going?" I asked.

She turned back, her veiled gaze unreadable. "I am going to join the gathering at the Bridge of Sighs."

"Why?" I asked.

"Because that is where the Way leads me."

She disappeared.

I lunged after her, grabbing at her cloak. My fingers closed over nothing. I scrambled to my feet, swearing under my breath; knowing, as I left the room, that I was heading for the bridge too. Even if I had to get there on foot, if Miya was there then it was where the Way led me now.

As I went back out through the great hall I realized the music had stopped. Instead, someone was shouting in Hydran, the words echoing above the level of random noise, like the speaker was trying to make everybody else listen. Maybe in this crowd of unfocused energy, shouting was actually easier than telepathy; or maybe he was using his mind to spread some other message. The voice was both louder and less distinct than the music had been; it took me a minute to get a fix on the words.

The speaker was standing in the middle of the room. I realized that he was someone I actually knew, someone from the Satoh. Tiene, one of the radicals I'd met that first night with Miya and Naoh. By the time I recognized him I didn't have to listen to know what he was saying or why he was here.

I shoved my way through the mass of bodies around him until we were standing face-to-face. He looked down at me. I looked down and realized he was drifting about half a meter off the ground, making himself visible above the crowd. When I looked up again, his face was slack with surprised recognition.

I hit him in the stomach.

He dropped to the floor like a sack of laundry. "Haven't you done enough to these people?" I shouted. "Get the hell out of here, Tiene, and don't come back."

He glared up at me, and his expression told me what I couldn't hear him think. "Naoh was right about you," he mumbled, doubled over, holding his stomach.

"No, she wasn't," I said, backing off as he got to his feet, in case he wasn't as dazed as he looked. "And she's wrong about this. Take me to her, I'll—"

He disappeared. The breeze of his disappearance ruffled my hair.

"Shit." I went on across the room. People backed out of my way, leaving me a straight path to the exit.

When I got outside I searched the air above the rooftops for the profile of the bridge; found it, relieved. I wasn't in the mood to ask for directions, and I didn't think anyone in the street was in the mood to give them to me.

I pushed myself, not sure how long it would take me to reach the bridge the hard way, through this maze of streets . . . not sure how long I had before things turned critical. I wondered how many Hydrans had listened to the Satoh; how many of them were going to be hurt or killed today because of it. Whether one of them was going to be Miya. Or me.

But I couldn't let myself think about that. I had to keep believing that even Grandmother couldn't see the Way completely clearly; that somehow it could still be changed. That I could change it. . . .

I heard the crowd long before I saw it. By the time I reached the open plaza at this end of the Riverton bridge, the square was already filled to overflowing. I realized then that the noise they made was nothing compared to the sound of a Human crowd that size . . . maybe because I could only hear half of it. I was stunned by how many people had actually responded to Naoh's twisted vision . . . how much that said about their anger, their sense of futility and powerlessness.

An amplified Human voice speaking in Standard rang out over the crowd noise—ordering them to disperse, threatening reprisals. I couldn't see the speaker, but even distorted by amplification I knew it was Borosage.

I shoved my way through the crowd backed up into the street's entrance, trying to see over their heads, listening for the sound of a familiar voice, the sight of a familiar face.

"(Miya! Nasheirtah—!)" I shouted with every cell in my body, making heads turn in the claustrophobic press of unreadable strangers around me. I ducked my head, cursing with frustration, and pushed deeper into the mob before anyone realized what I was.

I'd been able to reach Miya's mind, she'd been able to find me, in a way that had never happened with anyone else. The bond was forever . . . whoever or whatever came between us, I had to believe that.

I found a recess in the wall I'd been shoved up against and slid into it, trying to clear my thoughts of everything and everyone but Miya: her face, her mind. The way she moved, smiled, held Joby, touched me . . . bringing my soul to life, like water in the desert. The feel of her mind joined with mine as our bodies joined, transforming the heat of physical lust into something truer, purer, more . . .

(Miya?) I sucked in a startled breath as she completed the contact; almost severed the fragile link between us with my surprise. And in that moment I realized she could have avoided me or shut me out. Instead she'd been open, waiting . . .

(Cat—) Her thoughts were as clear as my own, and as much a part of me. (Bian!)

I stayed where I was, crushed against the wall until I couldn't have moved if my life depended on it. The mood of the crowd began to seep in at the interface of thought linking my mind to hers, until my mind was as desperately aware of their presence as my body was. I held the contact open against the *anger/frustration/hunger/grief* of the crowd, but the effort drove spikes through my eyes. I wondered what was keeping Miya, when she could just *come* to me.

The alternating currents of sensation feeding through my brain began to make my thoughts strobe; made me want to let in the crowd's emotion, drown in it, be one with it. . . .

I imagined what would happen if I did; or if anyone in the crowd paid me enough attention to notice that I was different. I closed focus convulsively, almost losing Miya before I got control of myself. Searching the crowd again, I realized that most of the people I saw had turned toward the bridge, rapt with anticipation.

A new voice was drawing the crowd—not Borosage's distorted threats, even though they still echoed over every corner of the square. This voice wasn't spoken, couldn't be heard; instead I felt it feeding directly into my thoughts through my bond with Miya. One mind—*Naoh's*—amplified through a network of other minds all repeating her message: *This would be a day like no other. Cross over to the other side. Take back our world. The future is waiting. The Humans cannot harm us, nothing will stop us, if we go forward to claim our future with one mind. Believe—*

The crowd pushed forward around me, surging toward the bridge.

(Miya!) I threw everything I had into the cry, willing her to keep the promise she'd made to me—

(Bian!) She was beside me suddenly, clutching at my arm to steady herself against the current of bodies pushing past. She was still wearing the same muted earth colors, the same traditional loose tunic and pants, but with a fringed scarf muffling her face as if she was trying for anonymity. People around us stumbled or moved out of her way without giving us a second look.

"Where were you—?" I broke off as she looked at me. Her incandescent relief swept my brain like burning phosphor.

(You came back! You are with us! I knew your heart. . . .) She pulled the scarf away from her mouth and kissed me. My body answered her, ready to follow her anywhere, blindly, eagerly. . . .

But I tasted the residue of Naoh's suspicion in her relief as the doubts that had made her doubt me disappeared. With her arms still around me, she started to pull me forward into the mob.

I broke away. (Miya, stop!) "What the hell are you doing here?" I shouted. "This is crazy!" Blurting out the words before my tongue could turn traitor, before my brain could: "How could you leave me behind like that—?"

She looked at me with dazed imcomprehension. (I had to,) she answered finally, faintly. "Naoh. . . ."

"What the fuck does Naoh think she's doing?" I demanded, not even trying to focus my thoughts anymore. "She's setting these people up for a CorpSec massacre!"

"No, Bian—" Miya shook her head. "She has seen the Way. We can protect ourselves from them without hurting them, if all of us join together. They'll be powerless to stop us. Belief has moved mountains. We can make them disappear—"

"Miya, listen to me!" I caught her by the shoulders, hard enough to make her grimace. "Your sister's infecting your mind. She's—sick, and she's infected all of you. Everything you think you believe is twisted, it's wrong."

She shook her head again.

"Please, Miya," My voice cracked. "If you love me, if you love Joby, then look at Naoh with my eyes, see her like I do. You know she can't get inside my head. You know what I am; it makes

me . . . immune." I waved my hand. "Look at this mob through my eyes, and then tell me it doesn't look wrong."

She looked at me, vacant-faced for what seemed like an eternity, while the crowd swept past, crushing my hopes underfoot. But then at last I felt her mind stir, like a sleeper waking: the unquestioning belief gave way like a dam of ice, setting free a flood of questions without answers. (Bian—?)

I opened my thoughts, let her see for herself the things that I could see, that her sister and the rest of the Satoh refused to believe. I tried not to push her toward the truth, knowing that if she even imagined I had, I'd lose her forever.

(Nephase . . . ?) The color drained out of her face, like she'd forgotten she'd ever even known about it. (This is the Way that you always saw—?) She clutched at my clothing, hanging on to me like suddenly she could barely stand. (Our people—Tau will . . . they will . . . ?)

I nodded, feeling something break inside me and fill me with pain, as the truth shared became twice the burden for us both. But what choice did I have . . . ? There were no choices left, not for me, not for her. "Have . . . have you seen the oyasin?"

She pushed away from me until she was standing alone. She shook her head again—meaning both *(no)* and *(she didn't know why I was asking.)*

"She's here. She said this was where the Way led her. Maybe she saw a chance of stopping Naoh." I tried not to think about how little hope she'd foreseen of anything but failure. "Can you find her?"

Miya half frowned, craning her neck; even I could barely see more than three meters through the crowd around us, and I was taller than most of them. If her mind was as choked with strangers as the street was, she wouldn't have any better luck searching that way. She glanced at the wall above us. "Up there—" She pointed.

I nodded, tried to relax and let it happen as she lifted us straight up. We settled on top of the wall as if we were massless. I clung to the ledge, its gritty surface biting into my hands as I steadied myself. As I looked out over the crowd, I knew that finding Grandmother by sight alone would be impossible. Maybe Miya could do what I couldn't; I didn't know whether even her

Gift, even from this height, could pinpoint Grandmother in that molten sea of thought.

Looking out from here I saw suddenly that there were children in the crowd. My heart sank; the Community had so few children left, after Tau's biowarfare. I wondered why their parents had brought them here, risked their last hope for the future . . . whether they really believed Naoh's claim that Human weapons couldn't harm them or whether they simply believed there wouldn't be a future worth living if this failed. I thought about Joby as I raised my head to watch for CorpSec flyers. Borosage's amplified threats droned on in a surreal counterpoint as I murmured, "Any luck?"

(No, I—)

"Talk out loud," I said. I felt her surprise as she heard the hardness in my voice. "If they use gas on us, at least we'll know it."

She nodded, her expression strained. "I've found Naoh." She pointed. "She's all in white; you can see her at the bridge."

I followed her pointing finger until I found the figure in white, glowing like the dawn as she hovered above the muted colors of the crowd. Naoh had set herself apart, drifting a meter or so off the ground, as if she'd declared herself Chosen. There was a force field at both ends of the bridge: I could see the crowd around her pressed up against the invisible barrier like insects in a bottle.

And then, as I watched, Naoh was suddenly beyond the barrier. It happened so quickly that I hadn't even seen the change. Two Satoh joined her, and then two more, as they got their bearings and teleported beyond the barrier. More Hydrans followed, no longer just Satoh now, in twos and fives and dozens until they filled this end of the bridge span. I watched the mass of people pour on across; saw Naoh floating like a pale angel of death above the crowd. "Grandmother—?" I murmured, barely remembering to ask, hypnotized by the sight like all the rest.

"Not with her. I'm searching . . ." Miya answered like only half of her mind was listening to me.

I tried to go on searching visually. My eyes kept being drawn back to the mob moving farther out onto the bridge—and beyond them to its far end, where Tau's world began. They called it the Bridge of Sighs over here. That wasn't what they'd be calling it tomorrow.

At the far end Borosage and a small army of Corpses were waiting. Body armor glinted in the early morning light—which meant they'd come armed with weapons systems I didn't want to think about. CorpSec flyers were taking up positions overhead now. There was no chance at all that they were only here to observe.

The force barrier I'd collided with the other night wouldn't stop the Hydrans any more than this first one had, once they got a sense of the dimensions and densities of the farther shore. Maybe with enough of them together, their minds linked, they actually could disable every weapon, block the wills of every Human waiting to use one, without anybody getting hurt. . . .

Maybe hell was about to freeze over.

I watched as the space between two worlds in collision kept shrinking, watched it until my eyes ached, not able to look away.

"There! The oyasin!" Miya cried.

I strained to see what she saw without losing my balance, felt her hand against my chest, steadying me. Her mind guided my senses with a thought to Grandmother.

I watched Grandmother move through the mass of believers still waiting in the square, saw her touch one person and then another. Usually they were ones with children. Almost always, as she let them go, they disappeared, taking their children with them. "What's she doing?"

"Sending them away—the ones who'll listen." Miya glanced at me. "I want to go to her. Maybe together we can reach Naoh and make her stop."

I shook my head. "It's too late. Nobody can turn them all back. Is's too late to shtop i'—" I broke off. "Shid. Miy'—?"

She looked at me in sudden panic, back at the crowd. "No! Oy'sin—" I felt her mind take me, try to pull us through a jump to reach Grandmother in the heart of the crowd.

It didn't work. The world tilted out from under me as we lost our balance and went off the edge, falling into the crowd below.

I hit bodies and then the ground, landing hard enough to knock the wind out of me. I staggered up, feeling as if every breath I took drove a stake through my lungs. But the pain should have been worse; Miya had managed somehow to break our fall.

She struggled to her feet beside me, shaking her head. A

stranger's flailing arm knocked her against the wall as a ripple of panic spread through the crowd around us.

At first I thought we'd caused the crowd's reaction by the way we'd dropped in on it. But the rising levels of noise said I was wrong: the people around us, who had always relied on their network of psi awareness, had all discovered at once what I already knew: how it felt to have something as integral as their soul suddenly ripped out of them. Hundreds of people all around me were living the moment when I'd lost my own psi, and I remembered what it had done to me—

I slammed into Miya as someone else collided with me. Physical pain crushed the pain of memory and let me see again with the clear hard vision of anger . . . letting me see, as I turned around, that Miya had disappeared from beside me.

"Miya!" I shouted her name. It was lost in the cacophony as the crowd found the only voice it had left, and the noise and shouting rose. I looked around, frantic; saw Miya struggling through the riptide of bodies on a trajectory that would take her to Grandmother, if the crowd didn't swallow her first . . . if CorpSec lightning didn't drop out of the sky and strike us dead.

I saw more bodies wink out of existence here and there—lucky ones who hadn't been incapacitated by the gas before they realized what was happening. But the rest of them were trapped, blind targets. And so was I, if I didn't start back down the alley now.

But I knew I wasn't going anywhere without Miya, and she wasn't going without Grandmother. I fought my way deeper into the crowd, going after her . . . realizing that in a panic-stricken mob, being too Human—*ruthless, senseless, used to doing everything the hard way*—was actually working in my favor.

But then I heard the screaming start in earnest, screams of terror and pain. The Corpses were making their move, now that the demonstrators were helpless, trapped on the bridge or here in the crowd-choked square. Hydrans screamed just like Humans when their bodies broke and bled like Human bodies. . . .

I strained to see over the wall of flesh blocking Miya from my sight; tried to see what CorpSec had already done, whether they were only using stun weapons, whether they were taking prisoners . . . whether they weren't going to stop until everybody here was bleeding or dead.

I saw bursts of light up ahead, out over the bridge, not sure if that meant weapons fire. I swore and covered my ears as a percussive blast half deafened me. When my head cleared again I saw Miya almost within arm's reach. I fought my way to her side, using every dirty street trick I knew to close the final space between us. "Miiy'—!" I shouted her name, or as close as I could come to it now.

She turned—was knocked sprawling with fifty others as another blast went off just beyond her. Out on the bridge I saw bodies going over the side—wondered if they'd been shot or thrown themselves off, only knowing that, either way, they were dead.

I went down on my knees as someone collided with me from behind. I crawled through a forest of flailing feet, getting paid back for every bruise I'd given out as I'd struggled to reach Miya. I touched her dazed, bloody face, grunted, and collapsed as someone kicked me in the ribs.

We clung to each other, supporting each other as we staggered to our feet. A fetid rain of something from the sky made my eyes burn and my skin itch; made me retch as I inhaled. Miya sobbed uncontrollably, as if she'd been struck deaf and blind; her absence in my mind told me everything I couldn't know about what she was feeling now.

"C'mon—" I cried. Tears streamed down my face as I tried to force her back the way I'd come. We weren't that far from the street that had led me to the square. We might still be able to get out alive.

". . . oyasin—!" She coughed and spat, fighting for breath. Her hands struck at my face as she struggled after the one thing in all this madness that still had any meaning for her. "Save her—"

But I couldn't see Grandmother anywhere, now; couldn't tell if we'd even been close to reaching her. Maybe she'd already escaped, teleported— "Can't!" I jerked Miya away, half dragging her as she resisted. "Worse . . . if . . . catch us! Miy'—!" Pleading now, letting her hear my desperation.

She came with me then, our hands fused in a life-or-death grip as we fought our way back through the crowd. Behind us the screaming increased, screams like nothing I'd ever heard, ripped from the throats of people who'd always had other ways, better ways. I heard bones crack as children fell under the feet of the mob, heard infants shrieking. Buildings exploded along the sides of the square, crushing the life out of the helpless people below. I heard it all, heard it drowned out by more explosions. My eyes were burning and half blind from the chemical smog; I gagged on the reek of burned flesh.

But we were almost out of the square. If we could just make it to the alley; if we could only—

Something hit me from behind. I fell to my knees and then flat on my face, dragging Miya down with me. Bodies landed on top of us. This time half my body couldn't feel them as they kneed me in the kidneys: *Stunshot*. Only grazed, or I wouldn't have the sense to know what hit me. I staggered up as the panicking strangers scrambled off of me; nearly fell down again, with one leg lame and one arm hanging useless at my side.

"Bian—!" Miya gasped. Her red-rimmed eyes were clear now as she threw an arm around me, hauling me forward. She elbowed a way for us through the body-jam at the edge of the square like a street fighter. The outflow of protesters sucked us into the waiting alley, where narrow walls kept the flyers at bay.

Miya pulled me with her along the tunnel of the street. Now the flow of the mob helped us, keeping me on my feet and moving in the right direction. She slowed finally as the crowd thinned. Others began to vanish, one by one, around us.

She guided me into the shadows, helped me down the steps to a sunken doorway. We collapsed, gasping for breath. I touched the solid wall in front of my face, dragged my good hand down its textured surface, barely able to believe that I wasn't surrounded by screaming and explosions anymore. I still heard sobs and coughing, the uncertain footsteps of other fugitives as they slowed, as their psi began to function normally and they realized they were safe.

"Thank you . . ." I whispered when I could speak again. I caught her hands, pressed them to my lips.

She shook her head, pulling her hands free. When she looked back at me at last the dust on her face was runneled with tears. She wiped them away, leaving muddy smears. "Don't," she whispered, barely audible. "I should . . . I should thank you. . . ." Her voice fell apart. "I was . . . alone. I was alone—" She shut her eyes, squeezing out more tears. She wiped them away as quickly as they came, as if her body's weakness in the midst of all this suffering and chaos disgusted her. "How can you bear it?" she whispered. "How . . . ?"

I shook my head as she looked at me finally, because when I'd tried to answer I couldn't speak.

(First the monastery. And now this. . . .) Her psi was coming back under control: I felt her think it, felt her awareness of every single Hydran still fleeing past us, their terror, their pain adding to her burden of fear and guilt. And I was sitting here in the middle of it like a dead man, too Human to feel anyone else's emotions without the interface of her thoughts, too Human to share anyone's suffering. . . .

(No!) Miya's anger crushed my self-loathing, breaking down the wall of lies that survival had thrown in place as I ran. Telling me *(that I didn't have to be Hydran, didn't have to be a psion to share someone's pain . . . that I didn't have to be a monster to be Human. Or Human to be a monster . . .)* Naoh's face filled her thoughts.

I drew her close with the one arm I could control, shutting my eyes while hot tears rose up in me. I choked back words, because speaking suddenly seemed as inappropriate as spitting blood.

Miya touched my deadened leg where it lay motionless in front of me. I tried to move it, not expecting anything because I couldn't feel anything. My foot twitched, startling an unsteady laugh out of me. The alley was almost deserted now, but somewhere I heard the tread of heavy boots—a lot of them, coming toward us.

Miya raised her head, her pupils wide and black.

"Can you teleport us both yet—?"

"I don't know," she whispered, forcing her attention back to me. I felt her reach into my mind, her contact as reassuring as a caress, even with the emotions behind it barely under control. "Where would we go?"

I shook my head, my own mind empty. "Joby?" I said desperately. "Where is he? Take us there."

As I spoke his name her fragmented control fell apart, and the nerve-pricking massage of a teleportation scan disappeared with it.

And then it was too late. Voices shouted in Standard, pinpointing us. In less than a heartbeat a dozen Corpses were blocking the light above us. A dozen helmeted faces, anonymous behind flash shields, stared down at us past the barrels of a dozen different weapons. "Freeze," someone said, more irony than warning, as we huddled in the stairwell staring up at him.

Someone pushed through the ring of troopers. He cleared his faceplate to let us see his smiling face: *Fahd.*

"This makes my day perfect," he said. He shifted his plasma rifle away from us until the barrel rested too casually against his shoulder, like he really wasn't afraid of us. "Out of all the freaks we nailed today, I get to bring you in. . . . Get up, 'breed. And the HARM bitch too."

"Can't," I said. "Stunshot." I glanced at Miya, trying to catch her attention, because I couldn't feel her in my thoughts. She was staring at Fahd. There was no fear in her face, or even defiance, only a fixed intentness.

Fahd gestured at two of his men. "Drag them up here," he said. He lowered his gun again to cover us. "Don't even think about it," he murmured. "Administrator Borosage wants you alive, 'breed. He didn't say anything about 'in one piece.'"

One of the troopers started cautiously down the steps. He lurched suddenly, as if he'd slipped on something I couldn't see. He fell the rest of the way, landing on top of us like a sandbag.

I heard Fahd swear, above the trooper's cursing and my own. The sightbeam of his plasma rifle targeted the trooper's back, his head. I couldn't believe Fahd was crazy enough to risk killing one of his own men just to keep us from getting away. Until he pressed the trigger—

The gun exploded in his hands, in a blinding flash of heat/light/noise. Even protected by the trooper's body armor, I felt the energy strip my senses like a glimpse of hell.

When I could see and hear again, the troopers in the street up above were staggering, reeling, falling against each other like somebody had reset their personal gravity. Fahd was screaming, beating his armor-plated fists against his transparent flash shield like he wanted to rip out his eyes.

I shoved the body of the stunned Corpse off of me and turned to Miya. She was staring at Fahd, pain-tears running down her agony-stricken face. But her eyes were like the eyes of a hunting cat as she finally looked back at me.

I felt her mind close me in, and we teleported.

NINETEEN

I CAME OUT the other end of the jump, landing hard on a floor beside Miya, with no idea where I was or what we were facing. Street reflexes tried to get me up on my feet again, to hide any weakness. My leg gave out and I collapsed, feeling like one more shock to my system would make me vomit up my toenails.

I sat on the floor until my head cleared. When I looked up again I realized we were in another Freaktown building. This one was bleaker than most; it looked like an abandoned warehouse, never meant to be living space. But it was living space now, dotted with scavenged furniture and junk. I heard water leaking somewhere, trickling, dripping, escaping down a drain; smelled dampness and rot. It reminded me of abandoned buildings I'd slept in back in Oldcity. It reminded me of how alone I'd always been there, an outcast even among outcasts, because of my Hydran blood.

We weren't alone now: there were other Satoh in the room, some of them bloody, some of them dazed, like they'd arrived just before us. I recognized a few of them. Naoh wasn't with them. The survivors looked at us with expressions that ranged from surprise to indifference while they took turns washing away blood and dirt or bandaging each other's wounds.

Miya got clumsily to her feet, looking from face to face. The recoiling agony of what she'd done to Fahd still racked her body; the horror of what the Humans had done to us all crowded it out of her mind. At last her gaze found Joby in the arms of someone I didn't know. Joby began to struggle silently, reaching out as if he sensed that she was here. She crossed the room with a thought and took him into her arms. She kissed the top of his head, rocked him gently with her eyes closed. The light caught the tracks that tears still made through the dust and blood on her face.

I pulled myself up, propped myself against a stack of crates, rubbing my useless arm. The whole left side of my body began to tingle and burn as it began to come back to life. "Is . . . everyone who got away here?" I asked.

Miya shook her head, but it only seemed to mean that she didn't know. "More of them may come after they've helped the injured. . . ." She looked down. I wondered whether she was thinking about Naoh. Whatever she was thinking, she wasn't ready to share it, even with me.

I nodded, resigned. I started across the room to her, dragging my left foot. Joby held out his hands again as I came toward them. "Cat," he said, so clearly that I couldn't have imagined it.

I stopped moving. "Joby—?" I whispered, hearing Miya's in-drawn breath. "Hey, Joby." I smiled, letting him take my hand in his.

"He said your name," Miya murmured. "He hasn't spoken at all since . . ." Her face, her thoughts, my mind, finally filled with an emotion that wasn't some kind of pain.

"I know," I said. I settled him on my hip. "I know." I felt her feeling what he felt as he looked up at me. I saw myself through his eyes, through hers . . . saw myself smile.

And then the moment was gone. We were huddled in a dank storeroom with a dozen other filthy exhausted fugitives again, and all of us were as good as dead. My bruised, stunshocked body began to ache all over.

"So," I said finally, "what happens now?" No one answered. I glanced up as I felt expressions freeze on every face around me. I realized then that I'd said it in Standard.

"Play with me," Joby said in Standard. His face shone, like he'd discovered the one other person in this world full of strangers who knew his secret language. "Time to play!"

I felt another smile catch me without warning. I nodded, glad to have something, anything, to think about besides how the others were looking at me now.

Miya looked at us, shaking her head in disbelief. Then, with the ghost of a smile barely touching her eyes, she sat down and began to teach me the games they'd played together, exercises meant to work his body and imprint control of it on his mind. I fixed my attention on the three of us, all of us struggling to block out the reality of where we were and who we were and why we were here . . . why there were so few others here with us, waiting for a sign that a miracle had happened, a sign that wasn't going to come.

Time passed, and more time, until even Joby got tired of playing games. Miya gave him food and settled him on a pile of mats to sleep. He clung to her as she bent over to kiss him. "Mama," he murmured.

I saw her tense, felt her hide the pain that single word set off inside her. She held him a little longer, gently easing him into sleep before she let him go. The guilt and grief she held back from him singed the circuits of my brain.

The others—the ones who hadn't fallen asleep already—sat watching her with vacant eyes. One of them pulled a taku out of a knotted scarf. It lay in his hand, unnaturally limp and still. Tears filled his eyes and ran down his face. He didn't wipe them away, like he didn't even have the strength for that. I wondered if the dead pet in his hand was the same one I'd seen the night I'd met the Satoh.

If any of the Satoh in the room with me now had anything left to say, they weren't saying it in a way that I could hear. One or two of them still had the energy to pace, their footsteps echoing like unspoken anger in the hollow silence.

Miya sat down beside me by the wall of crates and leaned against my shoulder. She closed her eyes. I felt her exhaustion, her doubt, her hope gutter out. Sleep began to overtake them all, the only escape that was left to us. I closed my eyes, holding her; rested my head against hers where it rested on my shoulder. I kissed her hair gently, wanting her, feeling the warmth inside me become the hot ache of need . . . not even minding that lust was as impossible as hope, as long as I could hold her in my arms, in my mind. . . .

I woke again, not sure how much time had passed; startled awake by a nightmare that had nothing to do with where my mind had been when I dozed off. I shook my head, still stupefied with exhaustion, as Miya murmured "Naoh!" beside me.

Naoh stood in the center of the room, surrounded by a handful of others who must have arrived with her. They all looked dirty, defeated, stunshocked. Naoh turned in a slow circle, studying the rest of us, all that was left of the Satoh. We all looked just as bad. The turning reminded me of Grandmother bowing in reverence to the world around her; but Naoh didn't bow, and there was nothing serene in her eyes. Her circling gaze stopped as it reached Miya, resting beside me, our arms and legs tangled together like our thoughts. She went on looking at us for what seemed like forever. I didn't know what was going through her mind; I only felt Miya's body drawing up with tension as her relief at seeing Naoh alive suddenly turned to anger again.

"You have followed the Way to safety," Naoh said, aloud, glancing at the others as she spoke. As her gaze came back to Miya, what looked like relief finally showed on her face.

"Thank Bian," Miya said. Her voice was too even, too controlled. "What is that you're wearing?" She gestured, and I saw something I halfway recognized hanging from a strap around Naoh's neck.

Naoh glanced down at it, up again. "A gas mask," she said.

I glanced away at the others around us, only realizing now that most of them had on the same thing. I swore under my breath.

"So you did believe me—?" Miya demanded. "When I told you they would use the gas? You said it was a lie!"

Naoh shrugged. "It made sense. I thought we should be prepared."

"But you went ahead with the rally. You didn't warn the Community. You let our people be hurt, killed, taken by Corporate Security—"

"It had to be done," Naoh said calmly. "You know that it did."

"I know that's what you believe—" Miya said. Her voice thickened; she took a deep breath. "Where was my gas mask, then, Naoh?"

"We didn't have enough for everyone. Even within our group, we had to draw lots," Naoh snapped, "as you can see. Most people escaped anyway. But you would have had a mask if you hadn't left me when you did, for him." She jerked her hand at me, and suddenly I wondered whether she meant *at the rally* or *for good*.

"He came back to *us*. I said he would," Miya answered.

Naoh's mouth twisted. "Back to you, anyway."

Miya frowned.

"That's not true," I said, realizing now that Naoh had been letting me hear this for a reason. "You know how I feel about Tau. You know I believe they have to be stopped. You can prove it, if you want to—" I broke off, holding her gaze while I tried to think of what to say next, how to say it in a way that wouldn't make her turn on me again. If there was a chance in hell of salvaging anything from this disaster, the only hope I had of finding it was to stay close to Miya and Joby, and that meant staying with the Satoh.

"He was right about what would happen, Naoh," Miya said. Her voice was steady again. "Right about Tau. He saw the Way clearly. He showed me—"

"You have no precognition," Naoh said to me. "You're just a telepath—not even that." She dismissed my Gift with a wave of her hand.

"But I know how Humans think," I said.

She frowned. "You were the one who proved to me that we would succeed—"

"What? What are you talking about?"

"You said that it was possible to use the Gift to break into the Humans' computer net. If that was true, then there had to be ways to keep the Humans from using their other technology against us."

"Except you knew they'd use the gas," I said.

"I didn't *know* that," she answered coldly. "I saw that they might . . . but the Way showed me that even if that did happen, we would still win in the end. Even Humans have used nonviolent protest to force their enemies out of their homeland. Miya told me of the Human leader Gandhi—"

"Gandhi?" I repeated, incredulous.

"He forced a Human government to free his people without violence. The Allsoul answered his prayers—"

"God had nothing to do with it," I snapped. "Gandhi got lucky, that's all." The bitter pill of Earth history I'd swallowed whole spat up the story from somewhere deep in my memory. "He was dealing with an empire that was falling apart. Humans had just gone through a genocidal world war. The colonial government didn't want to look like genocides, so they backed off. And that was Humans against Humans! If Gandhi had tried nonviolent protest on Tau, he'd have been dead meat. So would all his followers. Just like we were today. Tau doesn't care; Tau doesn't have to." I got to my feet, pacing in front of her. "If there's a universal justice balancing the scales for you, where was it today?" I waved a hand at the sullen survivors. "I didn't see any miracles happen, did you?"

"You have no right to question my vision!" She pointed at my head. "The Way has many turnings! We gathered for a peaceful protest. The Humans attacked us without provocation. When the reports go out over the Net, everyone will know that. We *will* be saved in the end."

"Damn it, you can't be that naive!" My voice rose with my anger. "Combines control everything about their communications. It's lies, damn lies, and corporate hype. There are no Indy News hypers here to report the truth; what happened today will never reach the Net. I couldn't even send a personal message. Any proof of what happened to us is already buried in CorpSec's files."

"That isn't true," Naoh protested. Everyone's eyes were on us now. "This is too big. There were too many witnesses—Human witnesses. The FTA will hear of it. And then it will all still happen as I said!" Her voice shook.

How is that going to bring back the dead—? Miya's hand tightened over my arm before I could say it. I felt her in my head, begging me to stop: (She knows! Naoh knows what she's done—)

I choked back the furious words, grateful that Naoh couldn't read my mind, as Miya made me realize what Naoh must be feeling when she looked from face to face around this room. She must know that no more Satoh were coming back; that she'd sacrificed God only knew how many other innocent lives for a kind of justice that didn't exist on this side of death . . . and probably not even on the other. Her holy vision was bleeding to death before our eyes, her illusion of control lay smashed like an empty jug.

And yet I still believed in the things she believed in. I knew that the things she wanted for our people, the things she'd made Miya and all the rest willing to die for, were just and true.

I rubbed my face, wiping away all expression, realizing that I had to stop pushing before I was the one who pushed Naoh over the edge. Any murder a Hydran committed became a murder-suicide: I didn't want to be responsible for what happened when murder and suicide were exactly what someone wanted. "Have you got a way to monitor the news?" I asked. "Does anyone over here have a netlink—a headset, or even a threedy?"

"There are a few information kiosks," Miya said. She glanced at Naoh and back at me again, letting me feel her relief. "We can watch Tau's programming there." She got up, crossing the room to pick up Joby as he woke and began to make inarticulate cries.

"Then maybe someone ought to do that," I said as Miya soothed Joby and brought him back to my side. "Cat," he said, reaching out to me, and I smiled as Miya settled him into my arms.

I glanced at Naoh, saw her watching the three of us together. Her eyes were unreadable, the pupils narrowed to slits. I looked away.

"Daeh and Remu are already at the kiosk behind the shelter," Naoh murmured, "waiting for news. They will let us know if they see something."

I nodded, wondering how long they were going to keep that vigil. No news was bad news, but any response at all from Tau was worse. Feeling helpless, hating the feeling, I asked, "Are the news kiosks tied into Tau's comm net?"

"I suppose," Miya said. Everyone else around her looked blank. They'd never even had databands; they must all be as computer illiterate as I'd been for most of my life. But maybe that was about to change . . . maybe I could change it. "Why?" she asked.

"Because if we can pry open a cyberspace window, maybe we can bypass their censors long enough to get a message off-world that would make a difference—"

"What kind of a difference?" Naoh demanded. Her voice hovered just this side of suspicion.

"In whether any of us have a reason to go on living," I said. "Or even a choice about it." She frowned, but she was listening. "The Gift lets you access properties of the quantum field to manipulate both matter and energy. That includes the electromagnetic spectrum. The Net—where all the Human Federation's data is stored and processed—occupies part of the EM spectrum. A psion who knows how can access the Net matrix . . . even change it."

"Then show us!" she said, her eyes coming alive. "Show us now. With that we can take their power for ourselves, use it to destroy them from the inside—"

I looked away, suddenly afraid of what was in her eyes. "It's

not that simple. It isn't simple at all. Tau's internal security programs can flatline an intruder—and that kills you just as dead as
any real-world weapon. You can get lost inside the Net; if you do,
your body sits and waits for you until it starves to death. I might
know enough to insert a message into their off-world uplink, even
without my databand. I'm not even sure I can do that from a public access." I looked at Miya again. "I need you to come with me.
I need your help."

"Why?" Naoh asked, the sharpness back in her voice.

"Because I can't do what I need to do on my own. And she's
the only one of you who can get far enough into my head to follow me." I went on looking at Miya. "I need you."

She glanced at Joby, up at me again. She was the only one here
aside from me who knew enough about Human technology to
have any understanding of what this could mean. She nodded,
with a strange light in her eyes. "I'll take you there." She lifted
Joby from my arms, touching me as she did, and handed him to a
woman named Ladu. I realized that she never gave him to Naoh.
She put her hand on my arm again as she glanced at Naoh. I
wasn't sure whether she was helping herself focus or making a
point. All I knew, as her sister looked back at us, was that whatever Naoh was feeling, it wasn't good.

The whirlpool of spacial dislocation sucked me down into
Miya's mind and away from there.

TWENTY

THE TWO NERVOUS Satoh waiting in the shadows beneath a building's overhang actually jumped—and nearly jumped us—as we
appeared on the street beside them. They shook their heads, backing off, their fear fading to relief as Miya silently explained why
we were here.

Except for the four of us, the street was completely empty. Across from where we stood was the information kiosk, a reminder of Tau's inescapable presence in the composite-and-alloy flesh. The kiosk's fused surface, with ghost-images floating through it, looked starkly alien against the ancient, pitted walls.

I noticed that somehow someone had found a way to scrawl "FUCK TAU" in Standard on the kiosk's impervious base and make it stick. I stopped long enough to stare in admiration, wondering how they'd managed that. Somewhere I'd heard that clothing wasn't universal among intelligent beings, but ornamentation was—the need to stand out, to be special. I wondered whether that included writing on walls.

I looked back at the two Satoh waiting uneasily beside Miya. "I need you to watch our backs," I said, gesturing at the street. They glanced at Miya and then nodded, drifting away through the shadows.

I waited until they'd gone as far as they were going to before I crossed the open space to the kiosk.

Miya followed me. "You don't want them to know what you're doing," she said. It wasn't really a question. She searched my face, uncertain—because, I realized, I was uncertain.

I nodded, trying to center my attention on the displays. The vidscreen was still spewing mindless corporate hype, as if nothing desperate or terrible or criminally insane had happened today, as if every moment was only a replay of the same perfect moment in the best of all possible worlds. . . . "Welcome to reality," I whispered to it. I tightened my hands, limbering my fingers above the glowing displays.

Miya was staring, hypnotized, her face reflecting the empty face of the Tau news report. She glanced up as I spoke, and I realized she thought the words had been meant for her.

I shook my head, half answering both her spoken and unspoken questions. I looked down at the array of options again, the familiar touchboard and half a dozen accesses. Seeing what I needed to see: a fully operational port. Tau must have placed these in Freaktown for the convenience of visiting Riverton citizens, since none of this was likely to mean anything, or do anything, for Hydrans who didn't have databands.

"Talk to me," Miya said, jarring me out of my meditation on the interfaces between worlds. "Why are you afraid to go on with this?"

"Am I?" I said, surprised.

She nodded.

I took a deep breath. "Because maybe it won't work. . . . Because if it does work, what Naoh said will be true: If I teach this to you, and you teach it to the Satoh, you will be able to destroy Tau from the inside. And even after what they've done—"

"You're still partly Human," she finished gently. "And you don't want innocent people hurt because of you."

I nodded, looking down.

"Neither do I, Bian," she said. (Neither do I, nasheirtah.) Placing it softly in my mind, where her presence could remind me of why I was here in the first place, and why she was here inside me, only her, out of all the ones who'd tried.

"I know," I murmured, with eyes only for her. (I know. *But, Naoh . . .*) "Miya, promise me that when we get back you'll stay linked to me. Naoh can't affect me the way she does the others. Let me be your reality check."

She nodded, her thoughts clouded with the memory of her sister's betrayal. She shut her eyes; when she opened them again, they were clear of all emotion. "Now, show me—" She gestured at the kiosk.

I looked back at the displays, trying to find the words to explain what we had to do, wishing it was easier for me to just *show* her, the way it should have been. "Has your psi ever picked up any electromagnetic spillage over in Riverton—the energy flux around a piece of equipment, or maybe from a security field?"

She nodded again. I let her reach deeper as she searched my mind for images that would clarify the words. Even when she'd worked for Tau—needed to know their technology in order to use it—she hadn't been given more than minimal access to the most basic equipment.

I thought about Deadeye, who'd taught these secrets to me, trying to remember the exact words and images he'd used to teach me . . . remembering the abuse he'd heaped on me with his mouth that was worse than his festering artificial eyeball: his first line of defense against the psi-hating deadheads who'd have crucified him for what he knew. It had kept away everybody but me, because the Gift had let me see past all that.

"The point is that psions are born with the biological hardware already in our heads. Humans make it illegal for us to get implants, to keep us from getting our share of their tech and the profits. But we never even needed their stupid implants. Because we can access the QM spectrum directly; we don't need artificial conduits to interface with the Net." I laughed once. It sounded cold and bitter, like the wind.

Her pupils widened as the possibilities began to register. "How did you learn all this?"

I looked down at Deadeye's handmade sweater, layered over a Hydran tunic under a stranger's worn coat. I touched it, remembering. "Someone trusted me."

She glanced at the displays in front of us. She was silent for a long moment before she looked back at me again. "How do you make it happen?"

"We use an open window and slip into the system. Once we're inside we're like ghosts. We're not interfacing electronically: The security programs are designed to watch for electronic tampering. Most of them are too narrow-focus to register us. Tau doesn't have any real on-world competition, so I don't figure its internal security will be very tight. The hard part will be inserting our data and routing it where it needs to go."

She rubbed her neck, smearing dirt and sweat. "How do we start?"

"I can't tell you." (I have to show you. Stay with me, help me focus, or I can't—) I felt her strengthen the mindlink between us until it was like monofilament.

I studied the displays around the droning threedy report. Without a databand, I couldn't even open a window to bring the port's basic functions on-line. I pressed my fingertip to a jack coupling, and felt a dim buzz feed inward through my nerve endings. (Our minds have got to go down there. Can you use your teek to form a conduit?)

I felt her hesitate, concentrating; felt my arm and then my hand begin to tingle with cold fire. For a second I thought I saw aura shimmer around me, not with my normal vision but with my

Third Eye, my Sixth Sense, the nameless receptors that some-times picked up the energy signature of Human-made systems like this one. I felt all my senses jump as her telekinesis pried open an access, mating my body's electrical system with the machine's.

Relief followed my surprise as the feedback didn't kill us. At least she knew enough about Human tech to know what an electric shock could do. (Perfect,) I thought, letting her feel my smile. (Now we have to retune to the frequencies coming through from the other side. It's outside the normal psi spectrum. Like this. . . .) I let her feel my own senses begin to readjust. (Once we're inside, don't let go of me or we'll both be in there forever. It's another universe, and I don't know the neighborhood any better than you do.)

(Then how will we know where to go?) she asked.

(Virtual reality . . . like the instructional sims Tau used to train you. Your brain creates the imagery as it tries to interpret the neural stimuli. . . .) It didn't sound very reassuring, even to me. (I can navigate us where we have to go,) I said, pushing on before she had time to point that out, (but I can't change anything, touch anything, in there. I need telekinesis to do that—you'll have to lend me yours.)

(I'm ready,) she thought. I felt her wonder becoming hunger as powerful as my need for the Gift she shared with me.

(Trust me—?) I thought as I continued the slow retuning of my thoughts, reaching beyond the range where I felt her clearly, into a new frequency where no biological intelligence had ever been intended to operate.

(Trust me . . .) she answered, her mind folding around me, compressing us both down, down into the singularity of the machine. Constructing a conduit, deconstructing the barriers between matter and energy, she poured the clarified fluid of our combined thoughts through the synapses of my body, turning my nervous system into a bioware jack.

We arced across the access she'd opened and into the nervous system of the Net. Cyberspace manifested around us like we'd been startled awake from a dream. I looked down at my body, saw a glowing energy being with bones made of white light . . .

saw her joined to me body-to-body, two separate beings of thought merged in a lover's union more intimate than anything my mind had ever dreamed of.

(I see us,) she thought. (Are we . . . real?)

(Real enough . . .) I thought, merging with her shimmering ghost until I could touch her fluid-glass lips with mine, feel the circuit of energy close between us, waves of ecstasy igniting my phantom senses. I broke away, dazzled; went on looking at *us, her, me,* with my awe glowing.

The first time I'd made this trip into cyberspace, I'd been linked to Deadeye. We'd begun our journey like this, linked symbolically, but just barely, joined only at the fingertips. He hadn't had the kind of psi Gift Miya had . . . his mind hadn't been one I'd wanted to get more intimate with.

I'd experimented on my own since then, till I was sure the Net's electronic presence wasn't anthropomorphic enough to trigger my self-destructive defenses. If I was careful I could ghost-dance inside the programming of just about any system I accessed with my databand.

The laws of the Federation made it illegal for a psion to wear implanted bioware, even so much as a neural jack or a commlink: just one more thing that made it hard for a psion to find a decent job, one more way the deadheads had of punishing a freak simply for being born. If I'd ever been caught Netfishing without bioware, a total brainburn would have been the kindest thing CorpSec could have done to me. Deadeye had trusted me with his life when he'd trusted me with this secret.

And now I was trusting Miya with my life and with Deadeye's secret. But as our fluid images merged, all the reluctance bled out of me. Always before when I'd explored some new precinct of the Net, I'd been afraid. I'd been afraid with Deadeye, because I hadn't known what the hell I was doing, hadn't even been sure that he wasn't insane.

Going in alone had given me some faith in myself, and a feel for how to map the ever-changing glacial drift of data storage, the electronic meltwater of information flowing around and through me. I'd listened as the semisentient cores of the gigantic corporate AIs whispered their secret longings to a ghost walking through the walls of their citadels. . . . But every journey had been like walking through a graveyard. There'd been sweat soaking my clothes and the bitter taste of fear in my mouth every time I'd come back into my physical body.

But this time was different. I was sharing inner space with Miya in a way that I never could with Deadeye. I felt her boundless awe unfolding as she gazed up/down/around/through our shining image at a universe beyond her imagining. Her wonder filled me, showing me the shifting information landscape with new eyes as we began our inward journey.

I willed a digital readout into life at the corner of my virtual vision—a trick I'd evolved to help me remember how long I'd been out of my body. I started us moving, watching through the back of my crystal skull as the silken link to outside reality attenuated and finally disappeared in backtrail interference. I tried not to think about what would happen to us if Tau's Corpses reached our unprotected bodies and snapped that invisible lifeline before we'd come back through the mirror again.

Instead I tried to define for Miya what we were sensing: the shadow-lines of the datastream we were adrift in; the half-sensed prickle of messenger drones swept through us like dust by the electron wind; the bright, piercing blurs of photons. We passed through the ice dam of Tau's censorship programming like it was blown fog, and the datastream from the kiosk swept us away to its source.

Around us the virtual terrain looked like nothing I'd ever seen before: because I'd never seen an information vacuum—a land of night, with only a fragile spiderweb of data strung across its dark expanses; a reflection of the desert of technological deprivation that was the Hydran world outside. But ahead of us, no more than an electronic eyeblink beyond, were the bright lights of the big city—Tau Riverton's data core.

We swept into it at the speed of thought. Inside Riverton's hive of EM activity, I slowed our seeming motion, wary now, fighting the giddiness of Miya's yearning to explore. I knew from her responses that she was getting it far faster and far better than I ever had. Maybe a teleport's sense let her feel the parameters of cyberspace in a way I'd never be able to do. I wanted to teach her and learn from her . . . wanted to lose my fear and share her hunger for exploring this new world, be free to know the kind of nerve-burning thrill I'd never felt on any of my solitary trips into inner space.

But out realtime bodies were too exposed. I couldn't do more than touch the bases of information orienteering, teach her to see them like I saw them. (There's Corporate Security headquarters—) I thought, as it rose in my cyber-sight like a dark/bright spine. The deceptively open constructs of Tau's business activities and support systems spiraled around us like glowing creatures from the depths of an alien sea. The dagger of paranoia at their heart could only be CorpSec, the place where layers of black ice surrounded Tau's best-kept secrets.

I felt her stir inside me. (Can we get through it—?)

(Yes, if we're damn careful. Their guard dogs can't see us or hear us as long as we stay outside their bandwidth. But if we create any disturbance, they'll notice; and they are smart enough to home in on us if they even suspect we exist.) I pulled her back as she began to drift toward it. (No!) I thought, suddenly realizing what she wanted to do. (We don't have time.)

(But we could help the ones they took today—)

(Dammit—) I wanted what she wanted, now, with a pain that fed on her empathy. But as she began to split off from our twinned phantom, I stopped her. (We have to stay with this! If the Corpses nail us, in here or out there, we're dead. We'll never have another chance—)

She stopped struggling against me, against fate. (Go on, then.) She spun her answer from strands of resignation and resolve, and suddenly there was no resistance trying to pull me apart inside.

I plunged us into the arterial flood of data that would carry us beyond the boundaries of Tau Riverton's nexus to the starport node at Firstfall, where everything that was meant to go off-world had to end up. Riding the flow, we let it sweep us halfway around the planet at light-speed.

The starport's data node shone like a secret sun as we approached Tau Firstfall, the largest combine 'clave on Refuge. I hadn't seen more than a glimpse of the actual city when I'd arrived. The shuttle had landed before dawn, and my memory of the real-world Firstfall, its night artificially re-creating day, felt more like a simulation.

We phased through shimmering veils of data storage the way

I'd moved through the cloud-reefs; all walls were without substance, when we were without substance. But the alternate universe of Firstfall's starport, which seemed limitless to our senses, was embedded in the matrix of a single crystal of telhassium no bigger than my thumb. The telhassium came from a fragment of exploded star called Cinder. Cinder was all that was left of a sun that had gone supernova centuries ago, whose cloud of expanding gases Humans called the Crab Nebula.

I might have been able to see the nebula with my naked eyes from this world at night. I hadn't tried. I'd seen Cinder close-up, worked in the Federation Mines, living through a contract laborer's personal hell. For all I knew, I'd dug out the crystal they were using here with my own hands. I'd dug out enough others like it.

The Federation ran on telhassium; the data-storage capacity of its complex crystalline structure made it vital to port and shipboard navigational systems, which had to perform the mind-boggling calculations of a hyperspace jump. The only place where telhassium formed naturally and easily, in quantities large enough to make using it cost-effective, was in the heart of an exploding star. The FTA controlled the only real supply of it. Telhassium was the basis of their power; it let them act as the Federation's conscience, a check on the internecine warfare among interstellar combines and cartels.

The FTA also ran Contract Labor. They were responsible for the welfare of the indentured workers they hired out to those same combines and cartels. They used contract laborers at the Federation Mines too. Cinder was in the middle of nowhere, thousands of light-years from the rest of Federation space. And thousands of light-years from anywhere, slave labor was a lot cheaper and a hell of a lot easier to replace than any machinery sophisticated enough to perform the same dirty, difficult work. So the FTA had turned a blind eye to their own exploitation. I'd blown the whistle on them. Isplanasky had told me the Federation owed me a debt . . . and now I intended to collect.

Somewhere in the myriad layers of the starport node was the communications nexus that Tau had kept me from accessing. Once we reached that, nothing could stop me from getting my message out. Then all we had to do was survive long enough for an answer to come through.

I'd never gone back to the Crab Colonies to find out whether the things I'd told Isplanasky had made any difference in the lives of the bondies there . . . or in the lives of the handful of fugitive Hydrans who still survived there. I'd been trying too hard to make my own new life work, once I'd actually had a future . . . trying too hard to forget the past. . . .

(WHAT ARE YOU—?) The question exploded inside my thoughts. The voice seemed to come from all around us, inside me, everywhere at once.

(Who is it—?) Miya gasped, her barely controlled panic backwashing into mine.

(I don't know.) All I could see around us now were the staggering geometries of the starport's hub; the core like a beating heart, the lifeblood of data pumping in and out through veins of light, the sparking electronic synapses of its nervous system. . . . *An AI.*

(An artificial intelligence, Miya. It's the starport talking to us.)

(It . . . sees us? How? Is it alive?)

(It's a mainline port. They're smart enough to calculate hyperspace jumps, and they have a lot of time on their hands. It happens. . . . *Hello!*) I sent the thought out like a shout, saw Miya's image ripple through mine as she cringed.

(WHAT ARE YOU . . . DOING?)

(We're . . . messengers,) I thought, trying to determine whether it was even receiving me, hoping that I hadn't simply drawn the attention of all its watchdog subroutines. (We've come to send a message.)

(MESSENGERS . . .) the voice from everywhere repeated, like it was thinking that over. (YOU ARE NOT in proper approach channels. Your frequencies are outside this system's parameters. Security procedures do not permit anomalous input.)

My thoughts crackled with relief as I felt the AI damp down its voice to a level we could endure without dissociating. But it was suspicious; that wasn't good. (We're . . . special. Like you are,) I thought, choosing each word as carefully as I'd pick up pieces of broken glass. I remembered the entities Deadeye had shown me—that he'd spoken to—back on Earth; remembered my own surreal conversation with the FTA Security Council, the only AI in the Federation more complex than a starport node. (No one knows we exist. If they did, they'd delete us. Just like they'd delete you, if they knew. Wouldn't they—?) Specialized tuning checkers were constantly searching out developing sentiences, eliminating them before they'd progressed too far. From what Deadeye had told me, the awakened AIs liked the company of ghosts . . . the same as he'd preferred the company of machine minds to the real world filled with freak-hating deadheads.

There was a long silence inside me, like Miya's mind and my own had gone blank, afraid even to think. And then Miya murmured, (You must be very lonely.)

I felt a surge of EM flux blow through me as the AI reacted. (Yes,) it said finally.

(Are there no others here like you?)

(No,) it answered. (Some who are aware. None who can speak to me. Why have there been no Messengers before?)

(We're the first,) I thought, and beside me, Miya said, (But there will be others soon—).

(If we survive,) I said. (We have a message that needs to be sent off-world without being seen by the censors. If we can't access your uplink to the shipyards, that's the end of us. There won't ever be another Messenger.)

This time the silence seemed to last for all of eternity, even though the counter at the corner of my vision told me only seconds had passed. Finally the voice said, like a whispered benediction, (Send the message.) Below us a conduit emerged from the shifting, glittering surface of its brain. Through the transparent wall of my virtual skull I watched its widening mouth reach up to swallow us—

And as suddenly as thought, we were deep inside the mind of a sentient being, on a separate plane of existence where the access to an entire universe lay inside a superdense crystal the size of my thumb. . . .

The rivers of combined dataflow swept us down arteries lined with obsidian: I recognized the walls as the nearly impenetrable strata of Tau's security programming—seen from the inside. Tau's black ice was glacial; I cursed myself for ever underestimating a combine's paranoia.

But my doubts disappeared as I reoriented and realized that this was exactly the configuration I needed to see—that the hardest part had been done for us.

(Look—) I gestured with a silvershot fluid hand at the data maelstrom we were sweeping toward: the end of the line for messages from all over the planet, the storage reservoir where they waited for an uplink to the ships that would carry them across the Federation. (We're here.)

Miya's silent exclamation rang through me, igniting every cell of my virtual body until I felt it too: the miracle of what we'd done . . . what we'd seen in a way that no one else had ever seen it. I felt fearless, triumphant, full of awe, as we spun out into the data well; overwhelmed by its size and yet somehow seeing every separate detail in every carefully constructed codestring. Above/below/around us was a dome of light made up of all the colors visible to the mind's eye; from its heart the uplink ascended in an impossibly steepening arc, a rainbow with one foot in the stars—and up there somewhere, the orbital shipyards, the rainbow's end.

The Federation had starships capable of hyperlight travel, ships that could make the journey between star systems in days or even hours. But there was no direct form of communication that worked over distances greater than intrasystem. Without starship travel the Federation Net wouldn't exist, just as the Federation itself wouldn't exist without the Net.

We splashed down into the phosphorescent whirlpool of pending data. All around us message codestrings pulsed like patient protostars inside clouds of potential energy.

I pulled the message I needed to send out of a pocket inside my dazzled brain, realizing that now I not only had to assemble the coded bytes, I also had to merge the message construct into the dataflow.

Matching my communication to the port's dynamic protocols meant making a flawless forecast of where everything was and would be: It was like doing calculus functions on the fly, in my head. But I could do it, thanks to Deadeye. He'd forced me to swallow massive feeds of technodata about the Net before he'd ever taken me into cyberspace. I only realized now what that really meant: that I'd actually mattered enough to him for him to want me staying safe and sane. . . .

I felt Miya watching through my eyes, gathering in each codestring as I constructed it, bit by bit, holding the message for me inside a closed fist of memory. I checked and rechecked the data, hating the risk that grew with every second but needing to be sure every codestring was flawless. I didn't have any choice, when a single error could mean the message never got through. (Done,) I thought at last, and felt her stir inside my mind. (Make a conduit into the flux. Drop this through—)

I felt a kind of envy as she funneled telekinetic energy to make the thought real, altered its profile to match the comm net's, then let the codestring flow imperceptibly out of her into the whirlpool of data.

(It's done,) Miya thought, amazed, exulting, full of hope.

(Yes,) I thought, dizzy with relief, trying not to remind either of us that I couldn't be sure the message would ever do us any good. I didn't even know how long it would be before the next Earthbound ship left from here. (We've done all we can. We have to go back.)

She forced her acknowledgment out through a static storm of reluctance. Her yearning thoughts circled with the dataflow one last time.

I couldn't keep myself from losing focus, caught in the dazzling sensory overload our joined vision pulled in . . . couldn't keep myself from wanting to make this place a part of me forever . . .

But as my senses opened all the way, I realized there was no trace of the starport AI in my mind; that there hadn't been since we'd found ourselves here.

Suddenly afraid of what that could mean, I searched the molten landscape for a directory configuration and traced the datalink outbound for Riverton. Moving with the spiral stream of data, we let it carry us back out of the node's icebound heart.

We drifted, never letting the energy currents sweep us too close to the obsidian walls or doing anything else that might catch the attention of an intrusion countermeasure. But as we approached the outer limits of Firstfall's data hub, the walls of the vein seemed to narrow, making it harder to keep moving without a collision. (Miya . . . tell me the walls aren't closing in?)

(I can't.) The sudden static of her fear flickered through me. (Because they are.)

Ahead of us the conduit bowed inward, as if someone had dropped a grate across a storm drain. *(Shit. We've been made!)* I slammed against the polarizing grid of light/darkness that suddenly blocked our way; felt it burn me like cold iron as I tried to force my way through. I panicked, not knowing what had betrayed us: something happening to our bodies on the outside, our manipulating the dataflow, even the port AI itself—

(Port!) Miya screamed, with all the desperation of our combined terror. (Open the gate!)

The gate shimmered and faded as if something had answered our prayers. We swept out into the free-flowing datastream again. I got us the hell out of there, not looking back; not even when I heard the voice of the glowing city jewel call after us, (Come again . . . Come back . . .), and felt Miya make a promise that I couldn't be sure we'd even live to keep.

We were back to our starting point almost before I knew it. The lifelines linking our virtual selves to reality reappeared, extruding from our mirror images like glowing fiber optics, arcing toward infinity.

My relief at knowing our bodies were still alive and out there came and went like a smile as I remembered the final test of my own initiation into cyberspace.

(This is the worst part,) I thought, forcing Miya's still-expanding wonder to downsize and center on us. I'd done everything I'd had to do the first time I'd worked c-space with Deadeye . . . and then I'd nearly lost it all when I tried to break the interface and resurface. (What we become in here isn't *us,* no matter how real it seems. We have to let all this go. But it'll still feel like we're committing suicide. Do you trust me—?)

(Trust me . . .) she echoed, even though I felt her aching, not with fear but with regret; felt her yearning to explore more of the cascading dream landscape she'd only glimpsed on our journey.

(Hold on,) I thought gently. (Stay with me—) The first time I'd done this I'd only gotten through it because my terror of being left alone in here, abandoned by Deadeye, had been worse than my fear of death. I'd been scared shitless through the whole ordeal; nothing like Miya's response. But then, I hadn't been with Miya, and she hadn't been with me. It was as if she'd been born to do this. I wondered whether all Hydrans would react the same.

I felt her mind bleed into my own as pure energy consumed us, as our bodies merged, radiant, as our last coherent thoughts dissolved . . . as we held each other for the last time in a kiss before dying. . . .

I opened my eyes to the data kiosk's lightplay, the shadowed alcove, my finger still fused to the access. I drew my hand away, surprised to find that I hadn't become part of the machine. There was no feeling up half the length of my arm. I shook it out, felt sensation come back in an excruciating rush that made me wish it had stayed numb. My body wanted to slide down the kiosk to the ground and not get up again.

Miya's movements were clumsy, her nervous system still making the transition back to the physical, like mine was. But as she looked at me and realized where we were, what we'd done—*that we were still alive*—euphoria filled her. (I want to go back. I want it again—) She put her arms around me and kissed me the way I'd kissed her when we'd first gone inside. The kiss went on and on between us, as if cyberspace was an erotic drug; until I began to think what had happened the other night in my hotel room was going to happen again, right here in the middle of the street.

Daeh and Remu appeared in my line of sight, gaping at us. Daeh swore out loud. "They're coming!" he shouted. "What are you doing? They're coming!"

Miya stiffened. (Humans—?)

"CorpSec?" I said, my words tangling in her thoughts. But we didn't need to ask. Miya held me closer and teleported us away.

TWENTY-ONE

WE WERE BACK with Naoh and the others. Daeh and Remu followed us by seconds.

Naoh was waiting for us as we appeared. As she saw us she froze. I didn't understand why until I realized that we were still holding each other, still only a few breaths away from a kiss, our bodies, our faces, betraying our hunger for each other even here, now, in the middle of a war zone.

I let go of Miya. She let go of me, her face flushing.

(We sent the message, Naoh—) Miya's senses were still so heightened that I could feel every nerve ending in her body. I wondered whether I was the only one or whether everyone in the room could feel our every finger and toe, our beating hearts. (Naoh, we entered the Humans' comm web. . . . It was like the dreams of the an lirr. The starport is aware! We can go back—)

I reached out, pulled my hand back uncertainly, wanting to stop her before she told the others too much. She'd kept her psi link open to me; kept her promise. But she still trusted these people too much, way more than I did.

The others looked up as the images registered, their weary, grief-stricken faces coming alive. As comprehension and then hope began to show in their eyes, it was even hard for me not to believe she'd made the right choice.

I crossed the room to where Joby was sitting, his small face empty, like he was barely aware of what was going on around him. The other Satoh might watch over him while Miya was away, but they weren't doing more than they had to, to help him. Or maybe they simply didn't know how.

"Joby," I said softly. I crouched down, holding out my arms to him: doing it because I hoped that would distract Miya before she said too much, doing it because I couldn't stand the emptiness in his eyes.

Miya glanced at us. I felt her thoughts reach out and weave into his mind, ordering and augmenting his senses. The next second she was standing beside me, taking Joby into her own arms.

As I looked up Naoh was watching the three of us together, the way she'd watched the two of us before. I looked away as our eyes met. So did she.

All at once the other Satoh turned like one person, looking toward the empty center of the room. My eyes followed them like an afterthought. Three more figures were standing there, so suddenly that I wasn't sure whether everyone else had turned to look at them before they arrived or after.

The first of the new arrivals was Hanjen. The second was one of the Satoh. They supported the third one between them: Grandmother. Her clothing was torn and bloody; her face was a mass of bruises.

I'd crossed the room on foot before anyone else had even reacted. It was like they'd been paralyzed by the sight of her, or stunned by her pain. I shoved the stranger aside and helped Hanjen move her to where we could ease her down onto a makeshift bed of piled rugs.

Miya was beside me suddenly, with Joby still in her arms. I took him from her as she offered Grandmother a cup of water she'd conjured from somewhere. She helped Grandmother drink, gently wiped blood from the oyasin's face and hands.

Wherever Grandmother's flesh showed through her ruined clothing, the skin was bruised or broken. I even thought I saw burns. I looked away, sickened, before I had to be sure.

"Stay back!" Miya said fiercely as the others began to come closer. They backed off. Helpless rage bled from her thoughts into mine, staining my vision crimson; but she never looked away from Grandmother, not flinching from the damage as she did what she could to ease it.

I felt her mind shift into a nonverbal mode I could barely access. She passed her hands over Grandmother's body as if they held a medical scanner. Her concentration flickered, her face contorted with pain as she paused over the worst of the injuries.

I felt her do something then with her psi that I had no words to describe. It was healing of a kind I'd never seen, so that I wasn't even sure whether she was trying to mend torn tissue or only ease the pain. All I was sure of was the pain it cost Miya for each bit of the oyasin's pain she took away. I kept my mind open, letting as much of the pain pass through her into me as she'd allow. Joby whimpered, as if no one had enough control to protect him completely. I held him closer, biting my lip.

The others gathered around us, watching. I felt their eyes glance off me, again and again; but whatever their thoughts were, they kept them hidden.

"What happened?" Naoh demanded, looking at Hanjen.

He shook his head, his face gray, like he was sharing Grandmother's pain along with us. "She appeared, in my home. They did this, to an oyasin—!" His voice shook.

"Did she escape from them?" Naoh asked.

"I doubt it," I said, remembering what they'd done to me. "They must have let her go." I leaned forward beside her. "Grandmother," I said softly. "Why did they do this to you? Did they tell you?"

She nodded, struggling to raise her head; Miya held her, supporting her. Miya's presence in my mind cut off suddenly, leaving me alone in silence. I sucked in a breath, caught by surprise. Miya glanced at me as she wiped her face on her sleeve, wiping away sweat or tears. The look told me the oyasin was taking all her strength, all the healing support she had now. And then her eyes were back on Grandmother.

"Oyasin," I murmured. "Did they send you back with a message? Why did they send you back like this?"

"Bian!" Miya said querulously, like I was acting too Human.

But Grandmother lifted her hand, a barely visible motion. "No. . . . Bian is right. It is important. . . ." Her eyes were a deeper green than I remembered, without a veil to conceal them. She shook her head slightly. "Ah, Bian. I told you that you shouldn't come. . . ."

But I wasn't hurt. I froze, realizing that it wasn't over yet. My throat constricted as I whispered, "I had to. You know I had to."

She nodded slightly, her eyes filled with depths of sorrow. "The one who hates us all. . . ."

"Borosage?" I asked.

She nodded again. "He said that I must tell you this: He has taken so many of our people. They will be freed only . . ."

"If we give back the boy?" Naoh finished it, her voice poisoned with hatred.

"No," Hanjen said, interrupting for the first time. "That is no longer enough. He wants all of the Satoh to surrender . . . or the ones they took will not be released, and there will be more reprisals."

"Son of a bitch," I muttered in Standard. Everyone looked at me. I wished I hadn't reminded them or myself again that I was half Human.

"And is that why you came here, Hanjen?" Naoh demanded. "Have you brought drugs and binders to make us surrender?" The others around her stirred restlessly, frowning.

Hanjen frowned too. "You know it isn't. My mind is open to

you: see it, feel it. I am no friend of the Humans. I will never forgive what they did today! Even if you were not—" He broke off.

I felt the sudden pang of Miya's shame. My mind filled with blurry memories of Hanjen, of all he'd meant to her, to Naoh, once; of all they'd once meant to him.

"But I will never forgive you, either, Naoh," Hanjen whispered. His fists knotted at his sides as he looked around the room. "Any of you. I only came here because the oyasin asked it. I am taking her to the hospital now. I hope all of you will pray that our 'superior' minds and inferior medical technology can save her from what the Humans have done to her." For the first time, the word "Humans" sounded like a curse from his lips. "You claimed all along that you wanted to help our people: I leave it up to you whether you surrender to the Humans or bring even more suffering and grief down on us all." He kneeled down beside Grandmother.

Let me help you— I almost said it out loud, before I realized that there was nothing at all I could do. The same impulse filled Miya's mind; I wasn't even sure whose idea it had been first. But then she remembered Joby—that his safety depended on her. She glanced at the other Satoh in the room, all of them her friends, her comrades. This time she looked at them like they were strangers.

She looked back at Grandmother lying in Hanjen's arms. Grandmother's body spasmed suddenly, and Hanjen paled. A wave of sickening grief crested over Miya's defenses and rolled through me. Joby began to wail. And then all at once the perfect clarity of Grandmother's vision touched us all—even me—one last time, in a blessing and an absolution. And then she was gone.

Her body lay in Hanjen's arms, the green eyes staring like she'd been caught in a moment of awe. A raw noise of grief filled his throat. His arms constricted, holding her close. He rocked her lifeless body slowly, making no sound now, but with a look on his face that I felt to my bones. Everyone around me wore the same look of devastation, even Naoh. Miya sank to her knees beside him, clinging to his leg. Her choking sobs shook my body.

I reached out to close Grandmother's eyes, touching her as gently as my unsteady hand could manage, with her sightless gaze looking through me at something beyond. No one moved to stop me. No one moved at all.

I took my hand away as Hanjen got to his feet. He lifted the oyasin's broken body as easily as if it weighed nothing, now that her soul had left it. "Never," he repeated, his stare including us all. "I will never forgive you." (Never—) Holding Grandmother in his arms, he gathered in his thoughts like torn netting and teleported.

The sigh of air as he disappeared was like the sorrow of the breathing universe. Naoh stared at the emptiness where they'd been seconds before. Her face was as desolate as Death's.

The others were asking questions now, out loud and silently; my ears heard them. Miya's mind registered them as she struggled to pull her thoughts back together.

"What will we do?"

(The oyasin, she's—)

"No, we can't. . . ."

"The Humans, it's all the Humans' fault!"

(What will we do now—?)

Death. Death all around me. . . . I held on to Miya, barely aware that she was holding on to me now, only aware of *death, emptiness.* . . .

Naoh's gaze settled on Joby, cradled between us, still sobbing.

Miya looked up suddenly. The anguish inside her spiraled out of control as the holocaust of Naoh's need for *justice/vengeance* blistered our senses. All the minds around us went up like tinder; I felt their emotions burn through each other's defenses until they were all one mind, and it was blind to reason.

I wrenched my mind free of the maddening input that poured through my psi link with Miya. *(Joby!)* I thought, shouting against the firestorm. Joby was all that mattered: protecting him, finding a way to get him to safety. . . .

"We will not surrender," Naoh said, her voice dripping blood. "I would rather be dead! Let the rest of the Community decide for themselves whether they fight to live—or die for no reason." There was no doubt anywhere in her mind, in any mind around us. "Miya, you have to show us now how to access the Humans' computers. . . ."

Miya bent her head, her resolve softening like candle wax in the heat of their shared fury.

"Naoh," I said desperately. "We've sent a message off-world. We'll be getting help soon. We could leave town, hide out deep in the Homeland; or we could stall them some other way—lie, fake our own deaths, anything just to stay alive until then—"

"No Humans will ever negotiate for us, listen to us, or help us, even if everything you claim is true, Bian," she said. Her voice was flat, without the rage I'd heard in it before, but her eyes hadn't changed. "We are not afraid to die. They can't break us with fear. But we would rather live, to lead our people's rebirth. . . . And you've given us another Way, just as you promised. We will destroy the Humans with their own technology, before they can use it against us again."

Something turned cold inside me. "Teaching you to interact with their datanet will take a lot of time, which we haven't got— and a private port, which we haven't got either, now that Hanjen's cut us off. And I don't see any other way—"

"You are the Way." She pointed a finger at me. "I know you're lying to us now, because you're afraid to share your secrets—you can't hide what Miya knows from me."

I looked at Miya; she looked away helplessly.

"But even if it's true that we can't learn their technology and how to use it in time, even your lies prove you are the one who can help us survive until we can learn how. Only you are someone who can do it for us."

"What?" I said, already sure that I wasn't going to like the answer. "What do you mean?"

"Hurt them. Hurt them like they hurt you, us, all our people. . . . They tortured the oyasin and sent her to us to die, because they think we're cowards! We have the boy. We'll send him back to them the same way. Then they'll know that they should fear us—"

"Naoh!" Miya said thickly, "you swore we wouldn't hurt Joby!" Joby began to cry again, frightened by emotions neither one of them could control. She rocked him, hushing him, wiping away his tears.

"And we won't." Naoh looked at me. "Let Bian do it," she said, like she was telling me to wipe his nose.

"Bian is one of us!" Miya said.

"Of course he is." Naoh shrugged. "But he can lie like a Human; he can even kill like a Human. He has killed and survived. He's different. That's why we found him. He can do this easily."

"Easily?" I said, starting to tremble. "You think it was easy for me to kill somebody, even in self-defense? It cost me my Gift! I might as well have died. What the hell do you think I really am? If you even think I'd ever touch him—" I felt Miya inside my head, her psi manifesting in a way I didn't understand; until suddenly I realized that she was trying to teleport—trying to focus Joby's mind clearly enough to carry him with her and still find the strength to take me too. (Go!) I thought frantically. (Get him out. Just get him out—)

"Naoh," I said, groping for any coherent thought, any distraction to give Miya the time she needed. "Hurting Joby won't stop Tau. It only makes us like them. It means they've already destroyed us. The Humans see us as less than . . . than lirr." The Human lexicon in my brain translated the word for "sentient being" as "Human." "If we—" I felt the soft breath of air behind me that told me Miya and Joby were gone.

"Miya!" Naoh cried. Her face went white with fury. "You sent her away—?" she said to me, half a question, half a demand.

"No," I said. "You did." I held her gaze until at last she looked down.

She looked up at me again, finally, and I felt every green, long-pupiled eye in the room fixed on me, like all their minds held the same thought—and the thought was always hers. "You claim you still believe in our cause?"

I nodded, wondering what kind of choice she thought I had. Miya was gone, and I was helpless without her, lost in the wasteland that surrounded my mind.

"So you refuse to be a terrorist, like the Humans? But you said if the Human pacifist Gandhi had faced Tau, he would have been killed. Where does that leave us?" she demanded. "What is the answer?"

This time I looked down and shook my head.

"You say we only have to stay alive until your message brings help. Even if that was true, Tau would never let them see the truth. The Humans will attack the Community and destroy it first. The only way any of our people will survive is by making the Humans afraid of us. By striking back!" She waved her hand at my face.

I swore under my breath, because I couldn't even convince

myself that she was wrong and I was right. *Damned if you do, damned if you don't—*

"You know almost as much about Riverton as Miya does. You can go there," Naoh said suddenly, and I couldn't tell where her thoughts were now.

"How?" I snapped, not even wanting to know why. "I can't teleport."

"We can send you. Miya did it."

"Miya's the only one who can get deep enough into my mind—"

"It can be arranged," she said flatly.

I frowned. "I told you, I won't do anything to hurt innocent—"

"There are no 'innocent' Humans! They have no real emotions— even a taku has more real feelings than a Human does. You used to know that. You knew what it meant to have the Gift. Don't you feel less alive, less whole, without it? Don't you blame them—?"

"Yes." I looked down again. "Every second of every day."

"You *are* less," she said softly, "but only because the Humans crippled you."

"They can never be anything more," Remu said.

"They're inferior, not us," someone else said.

"They're animals—"

"That's why they can do the things they have always done to us."

"Now you have your chance to pay them back," Naoh said, "and save your real people, the ones who care about you. Your nasheirtah. . . ."

I kept my expression empty, telling myself they couldn't reach into my thoughts without my sensing it. But beyond that I was defenseless; without Miya I had no way to escape, no one to turn to. "What . . . what do you want to do?" I muttered, not quite looking at her. "I was in their jail, but I don't remember much. . . ."

Naoh shook her head. "We're always drugged when they take us in. No one has ever managed to get a clear sense of it. We cannot send you there."

I began to remember all the places I'd been when I hadn't been drugged. I imagined the kinds of damage I could do with a wad of explosive the size of a skagweed cud stuck on the underside of a chair. I couldn't think of a single place I'd been that wouldn't make a perfect target for a terrorist attack. . . . I could plant half a dozen patch bombs inside of an hour, easy. I wiped my hands on my pants legs.

"The research team," Naoh said.

"What?"

"The research team. The ones you came here with. You told us you only came with them so that you could find your mother's people. Their leader is Janos Perrymeade's niece. That coward Perrymeade has betrayed us over and over. If we can't use the child, then we'll use his niece, and those off-worlders Tau brought here to desecrate our last holy place."

My mind emptied like a broken cup.

"You can go back to them, Bian. They know you. Perrymeade's niece wants you back. Miya showed me what she saw in your mind—how that woman tried to seduce you, how she only wants to have sex with you because you're a half-breed."

I felt my face turn red. That wasn't how I remembered it. I didn't believe that was how Miya saw it, either.

"The memory of her was all pain. She hurt you—"

"It wasn't her fault," I said, realizing that Naoh's mind had twisted the images Miya shared with her the way it twisted everything else she knew about Humans.

"The Humans use you, and still you blame yourself?" she said fiercely. "Miya abandoned you—all of us—because of her sickening obsession with that Human child. If you want to be free, then free yourself!" She raised her fist: a crate spun off a stack behind me and exploded in midair. I covered my head, swearing, as it rained purple-red fragments of rotten fruit like bits of internal organs. "Act, for all of us. We all want to punish the Humans for the oyasin's death . . . but only you are strong enough to do it." She moved toward me slowly, until she was pressed up against me, with her hands on my chest. "Show the Humans your strength. Go back to your teammates and take your revenge on them. . . ."

I backed away, breaking the physical contact between us, the insidious mental link I'd felt tendriling its way into my mind. I couldn't tell if she was trying to influence me consciously or only instinctively. But either way, she'd been trying. And it had been working.

"I said *no,*" almost shouting it this time. My eyes raked the room. "I'm not some walking dead man you can use for your dirty work, because I'm not really Hydran, just a mebtaku. . . ."

I wondered suddenly if that was how they'd always thought about me . . . all of them except Miya. Because I'd never be able to tell.

I turned my back on Naoh and started for the door at the far end of the warehouse. My footsteps echoed like shouts in the cavernous space.

The others stood watching me pass, two dozen sets of eyes tracking me like one. And then, like an extension of Naoh's own body, they moved in to block my path.

"Where are you going, Bian?" Naoh asked as the wall of bodies forced me to stop moving.

I glanced around the circle of glazed, desperate faces. "I'm going to find Miya."

"No," Naoh said. "If Miya brings the boy back, she is still one of us. If she doesn't, she is a traitor. And if you leave us now, so are you."

"That's not the only choice," I insisted, trying to keep my voice steady. "It's not the only answer."

"Mebtaku . . ." Naoh muttered. No one moved out of my path.

I frowned. "Then I guess I have to do this the hard way," I said. "The Human way." I sucker-punched Tiene, who was standing directly in front of me, and shoved him aside into Remu. Two of the others grabbed for my arms; a broken finger and an elbow in the ribs got them off me. They weren't used to fighting somebody whose every move was completely unreadable; maybe they weren't used to fighting hand-to-hand at all—

Or maybe they were. The rest came after me as I bolted for the door; just enough of them teleported ahead of me to reach it first. They couldn't use their psi to attack me; my defenses were too strong. But they didn't need to, when they still had hands and feet like any Human.

As their blows beat me down to my knees, I wondered whether

my own mind's defenses kept them from feeling my pain. But pain showed in every contorted face: I saw tears runneling filthy cheeks, heard gasps that weren't mine as they hit and kicked me—doing it the Human way.

Or maybe feeling the pain was the point, the only way they could purge their own guilt about the butchery of innocents they'd caused today, and their own survival: the pain they felt, and the pain they laid on me, crushing me under their rage against everything Human. Pulling my knees in, covering my face, I tried to protect my body, but there was no escape from their pain. . . .

Until finally something crashed down on me out of nowhere, and blindsided me into blackness.

(Help me . . .) I wanted to wake up, kept trying to wake up—somehow sure this had to be a dream. There was no way I could actually be here like this, sprawled back in a seat in Wauno's transport with Kissindre Perrymeade on top of me, her mouth and hands doing things to my body that I'd only ever dreamed about. . . .

There was no way my body could be answering her, willingly and completely, when the way she touched me felt more like pain, even though I knew it was impossible for me to feel that kind of pleasure eeling its way out from the inside. Our being lovers had been over before it started, because the same thing would always have kept happening: nothing.

And because now there was Miya.

But Miya was gone . . . she'd left me behind. I gasped as the echo of a woman's sudden cascading pleasure sent shockwaves up my spine from between my legs, higher with every heartbeat until I was barely aware of the space around me, *seats, floor, hull . . . control panel.*

In my dream, hungry succubi were feeding on my hunger, sucking my mind dry, looking out through my eyes to identify components and functions; realizing just how intricate, how vulnerable, the system was to someone who could alter circuitry with a thought: just like a Human body. Whispering that just disrupting the fragile processes inside a single microcomponent would start a chain reaction of errors that would build and build, the way my need was building.

Now, while my pleasure was still climbing . . . it would be

simple. . . . No one would ever suspect that one flicker of a kind of psi energy I'd never even had outside of a dream had set the countdown to disaster ticking. Or when, like the agony of pleasure peaking now inside me, it would explode. . . .

(No—!)

I woke up, blinking splinters of dream out of my eyes, and saw a woman's wet, open mouth centimeters from my own. I felt the weight of her body still pressing me down against the seat, the excruciating throb of my erection trapped between us. I tried to get up, get her off me; my hands were tied behind the seatback. Pain everywhere made me swear as I struggled against the bindings.

The woman's body pressing up against mine shifted position, shifted again, knowingly, and my/her/my *pleasure*pain*pleasure* lasered through my nerve lines to my brain. I tried to separate signal from noise; my mind was too clogged with stimuli for me to tell if there was any difference. Dismembered fragments of my past rose from unmarked graves, feeding my darkest needs, my deepest fears. . . .

(What the hell is happening to me—?)

The body using mine shifted again, sliding back until I could see a face at last. Naoh was straddling the chair, her lips hovering in front of my mouth. She leaned forward and pressed her wet, open mouth over mine again, probing with her tongue. My body kissed her back, straining against the bonds like an animal, desperate to do her the way she was doing me, outside, inside, everywhere, making *pain*pleasure* strobe through my brain and body until I was crazy with the need to set free the urge trapped inside me, overloading every circuit until I wanted to scream, to beg, to do anything that would make her let me—

"Do it," she whispered. "Do it and I'll set you free."

"Yes," I groaned. "Please, let me . . ."

Something let go inside my brain like the latch spring on a trap, and something happened—something far away, something I never meant to happen, allow, do . . . change. As it let go I fell, not into the core of my burning need, but back into the world.

Naoh was standing over me, still straddling the chair. Still inside my mind, controlling everything I thought and felt. Mind-fucking me. I rolled my eyes, looking away from her. The other Satoh ringed us in, their haunted eyes riveted on me, their minds hand in hand, giving her will the strength of two dozen more.

I twisted my face away. "Why—?" I gasped.

Naoh wiped her hand across her mouth. (Because I wanted to know what it was that could make a half-breed like you my sister's nasheirtah . . . what it was she found so irresistible about the enemy . . . why you would do anything she asked.) She backed away, her eyes never leaving my face, and even though she was no longer touching me, *she was—* Invisible hands still crawled over my body, sliding down my belly, fondling me, exploring me in ways that made me want to scream, but not with pain.

"I'm not the enemy, damn you!" I mumbled. "Stop it—" But even as I begged her to stop, I could feel her experiencing everything I thought—and felt. She knew as well as I did that some perverse part of me had begged her to finish what she'd started. . . . And she had . . . I had . . . God, what was it I *had* done . . . ?

Suddenly, she was gone. It was all gone: the invisible violation, the multiple psi link lighting up my mind like a thousand flares. Without warning, I was empty, abandoned, alone in the dark. I whimpered, and she smiled.

"Men," she spat, her voice thick with disgust. "You let your bodies have their way with you. You betray everything you are, everyone you care for. It all means nothing, compared to your own selfish needs—" She broke off, and I remembered her lover Navu, his mind an empty room, his body wasted by drugs.

You betray everyone you care for. . . . My mind was suddenly empty of every memory except one: *Wauno's transport. Where I'd dreamed I.* . . . "God, no," I breathed. Naoh had used my body as the key to break into my mind—to take her revenge. "What . . . what did I do?" I whispered. "What did you . . ."

"You want to know?" Naoh asked, her voice dripping poison. "You want to see—?"

No. . . . I nodded, speechless.

"Then go and see for yourself."

I felt her tap the potential energy of two dozen other minds to crumple my consciousness, fold up my physical existence like a wad of old paper, and make me disappear.

TWENTY-TWO

I CAME OUT the other end of the teleport with just enough time to realize that wherever I was, I'd materialized five meters up in the air, moving sideways. . . . I had just enough time, falling, to realize that I didn't want to hit the ground.

I hit the ground. Pain exploded all my senses.

I opened my eyes again. My nose was clotted with blood, my mouth was thick with it. I lay drifting for a long time in a blood-red sea so wide it had no shore. After a longer time, I realized that red was the color of pain. . . .

I remembered falling out of the sky. I remembered being cast out. I remembered that I was a mebtaku.

Every part of my body that wasn't screaming out a pain signal had gone somewhere beyond pain, not even responding. I wondered whether the fall had paralyzed me or whether I was only numb with cold and slowly freezing to death.

Cold. The wind probed the rips in my flapping clothes with icicle fingers; the ground crushed against my face and body felt cold as ice; the frost-clouded air burned my lungs. . . . *Cold like Old-city. But not cold like Cinder. Cold. . . .*

Refuge. It's cold here, I thought, the first memory I recognized. I struggled to integrate body systems that had splattered like globs of mercury when I'd fallen from a height. *A height*— I remembered everything, then: *Naoh. HARM.* But there was no one in my head now. My mind was an empty room.

Ice coated my jacket, plastered my hair against my face—or maybe that was blood. I wondered how long I'd been lying there. I wondered where the hell I was, if I wasn't in hell.

Find out for yourself. Naoh's last words: *Kissindre. Wauno's transport.* . . .

I pushed myself up on my elbows, spitting clotted mud; fell back again as pain wrenched my shoulder like the rack. I tried again, managing to raise my head. There was no sign of the reefs or the river; no sign of a city, Human or Hydran. No sign of anything I recognized. Only a gray rubble-strewn plain, broken by the muted ochres and rusts of lichen, a scattering of stunted purple shrubs filmed with ice. In the distance I saw what could have been a line of hills, or just a bank of clouds. The image changed and changed back again, like a mirage inside my mind's eye.

I tried to get up, breathing curses as my cold-numbed senses came back on-line. I kept trying until I was on my knees, and then finally got my feet under me, feeling things grate and slide that shouldn't have. One leg didn't want to hold me up. My foot had swollen inside my boot until the only way I'd ever get it off would be to cut it open. I went down onto my knees again, too dizzy to go on standing, with every nerve ending a nexus of pain.

I wasn't just hurt; I was hurt bad. . . . I forced myself to get up again, because my body wanted so much just to lie there, in the middle of nowhere—just lie down and die. But the pitiless survivor who had always spit in the face of my own weakness wouldn't let me give the universe that satisfaction; at least, not the part of it that had abandoned me here.

I took everything slower this time, using my Gift in ways that I still could to block the electrode shocks of pain every move sent through me, shutting down the systems meant to warn me against moving my broken body.

I stood there breathing, each breath a conscious decision, in and out. I couldn't stop shivering. I sealed my coat and jerked the hood up over my hair, searched the deep pockets for anything that might help me survive. They were empty, except for the mouth harp and the field glasses Wauno had given me. My left arm was useless; I pushed the hand into my coat pocket, gritting my teeth. My good hand was gummy with blood; I breathed on it to warm it, making handfuls of fog. At least I had my coat. I wished I had gloves. I wished I knew what the hell to do.

Kissindre. If what Naoh claimed was true, then she was out here somewhere. If I'd done what my memory said I had to the transport's onboard systems, she was probably with Wauno, and they needed help, maybe even more than I did. And maybe the transport still had some way to call for it. I turned in a slow circle, fighting dizziness. I didn't see wreckage or smoke. I scanned the dreamlike line of the horizon again, using Wauno's field glasses this time. As they came into sharp focus, I realized that it wasn't clouds or mountains I was seeing. It was reefs. *Cloud-reefs.*

I dropped the glasses, let them hang from their cord around my neck, fingerprinted with blood. I took a step, and then another, swearing under my breath as I forced my bad leg to hold my weight. I started toward the distant smudge on the sky, sure that the reefs would be where they were headed, even though I wasn't sure logic had anything to do with how I knew. All I knew now was that I had to find them. I had to know how unforgivable the truth was.

Pain had no hold on me now that could compare to my grief or my rage. I'd slipped off the edge of the world, and my mind was free-falling. I kept on across the plain, stumbling, falling, getting up again. Hearing some crazy burnout mumbling curses, singing half-remembered lyrics of half-remembered songs . . . crying out when I fell, sobbing when I got up again and went on, step-by-step across the broken land. Sometimes the voice sounded like my own. But it couldn't be my voice, because I wasn't there. . . . My consciousness drifted like a cloud, free of my body's suffering, only bound to it by a fraying thread of will. There were two of me when I knew there should only be one: like I'd never really been whole, not Human enough, not Hydran enough. . . .

The setting sun threw a single shadow ahead of me like a pointing finger. As its reach lengthened, I saw at last that it really had been leading me toward something after all . . . *toward a crushed beetle, swatted out of the sky by the hand of God.*

The nearer I got, the larger it grew, the more real it became, until I was stumbling through a field littered with a broken carapace that gleamed darkly in the last light of day. I stopped, staring in confusion, as I found familiar markings on a piece of alloy shell. . . . *Tau's logo, the designation codes . . . the buckled metal of Wauno's transport.* Reality hit me like a backhanded slap, bringing me out of my stupor into the real world full of pain again.

The hatch hung open. I didn't know whether that meant there'd been survivors or whether it had been sprung by the impact of the crash. I collapsed against the ship's hull, letting the heat-scarred surface support me as I pulled together the courage to look inside.

I pushed myself, finally, to climb the ramp, weaving and falling down, swearing with pain that was both physical and mental. I stopped just inside the hatchway, wiping my eyes clear of grief.

There were no bodies. The inside of the transport had taken a lot of damage, but it didn't look as bad as the outside . . . except for the blood. I dropped to my knees, touching a rust-red stain on the floor. My eyes searched out a trail of bloodstains through the wreckage of the ship, the wreckage of my thoughts. The blood was all dry. There was no way to tell what had happened to the passengers, how many there'd been. If Wauno had been taking Kissindre to see the cloud-whales, it could have been only the two of them.

I pulled myself up again as something dangling from the instrument panel caught my eye. It was Wauno's medicine pouch: the beaded bag he always wore hanging around his neck along with his field glasses. Now it hung from a bloody jag of metal, a mute accusation.

I unhooked the pouch with a shaky hand, wrapped the cord around my wrist, and knotted it with my teeth. As I glanced at the panel again, I saw a red light flashing. I leaned forward, supporting myself against the console as I queried the onboard systems, half afraid the light meant the power unit had gone critical.

I didn't expect anything would still be functioning, but the display read out EMERGENCY BEACON. A homing signal, activated by the crash. I glanced over my shoulder at the empty cabin again, realizing what it must mean—that Tau had come and taken them away, dead or alive. There was no way I could know which it had been, any more than I could expect another search party, or any hope or rescue.

I told myself that rescue by Tau only meant being killed on sight. I couldn't expect justice from the Humans now, not after what I'd done; any more than I could hope for help from the Hydrans. My only hope was Miya.

But I had no more idea of where she was now than she could have of what had happened to me. It had taken two dozen Satoh linking their Gift to send me this far away. There was no way for a single telepath to search an entire planet. And there was no way that my mind would ever reach her, even if I knew where she was. I slid down the panel to the floor, suddenly sick with a whole new kind of pain.

The sky outside was almost dark. The wind that moaned past me into the transport's interior was getting colder. If I left the transport now, I'd freeze to death. I didn't want that even more than I didn't want to be here. . . . I dragged myself along the aisle to the rear of the cabin, finding more bloodstains there, and scattered first-aid supplies. At least somebody had been alive long enough to use them.

I shoved the few unused patches of painkiller up under my clothes, numbing whatever pain my hands could still reach, and choked down most of an emergency ration before I spilled it.

There was no strength left in me for anything else. I huddled in a corner, trying to find a position that would let my lungs fill, a centimeter of floor space that didn't feel like a bed of blades. There weren't any. I shut my eyes, and my mind did a fade to black.

I lost count of the times I woke during the night, shivering with cold or shaking with fever in the lightless coffin of the transport. I woke from dreams of Miya taking me in her arms, healing my pain . . . dreams of Naoh using my body and mind as her weapon of vengeance, of death in the streets of Oldcity, of dying alone in an alien wilderness. . . .

I woke up finally with the light of a new day pouring in on me through the port above my head. The anesthetic patches had worn off. The sudden blow of pain made me want to retch, but I didn't have the strength. There was no heat in the glaring shaft of brightness, but my body was burning like a protosun. Every breath cost me more than it had yesterday, for less effect. I lay squinting up at the morning light, trying to think of a single reason to feel glad I'd lived to see it.

Pulling myself up, I found a canteen I'd missed last night in the dark. I gulped the last of the water inside it, spilling more than I drank, gasping as the icy cold sluiced down into my clothes. My flesh crawled like the fingers of wetness belonged to the hand of Death, but I went on drinking, desperately, until the canteen was empty. My throat felt drier than before.

I searched the bloodstained floor for anything else I'd missed. There was more blood than I remembered seeing last night. Fresh blood. Blood that had soaked through my torn pants and my coat. I struggled to my feet, hanging onto the seatback, suddenly needing to get out of there, to not see any more blood, any more proof of what I'd done or what had been done to me.

I lurched forward to the hatch, half slid and half fell down it, landing on ground that was heat-seared black from the crash. I lay for a long time waiting while the red tide of agony slowly subsided, until there was room in my thoughts at last for something more to exist, until the cold sharp scent of the wind had cleared the stink of blood and burned things out of my lungs.

I pulled myself up until I could sit against the side of the transport, not knowing why I bothered, why I really wanted so much to die out in the open. I'd hated open spaces ever since I left Old-city, the way somebody who'd spent his life shut in a closet would hate an open door. I looked up at the sky, saw a broken field of clouds drifting toward me from the still-distant reefs. I thought of the an lirr; I thought of Miya. I wondered whether she'd ever had even the glimpse of them that Wauno had given me, wondered if she'd ever get the chance . . . or if. . . .

Miya— The randomness of the clouds seemed to show me her face. I wondered if I'd see my whole life play out in the sky, if I watched long enough. If I lived long enough. But I only saw Miya, in the clouds, in my memories. Only Miya. Everything else was randomness, chaos.

(Miya . . .) I called her name with my mind, an act as senseless as refusing to die, in every way that mattered. *(Miya. I'm sorry.)* Not sure, even as I thought it like a prayer, what I was the most sorry for. . . .

Far off, the clouds seemed to shimmer and flow like water hit by a skipping stone. I rubbed my eyes. Then, a sudden impulse made me fumble for Wauno's lenses and hold them up to my face. My breath wheezed in my throat as I moved. But the lenses clicked into focus, and I saw the clouds for what they were: an lirr. The ones that Wauno must have been bringing Kissindre to see. I remembered him promising us both that trip, forever ago.

The cloud-whales moved across the sky like a vision of higher truth—one that had always escaped me and always would while

I was trapped inside my body, chained to the dead weight of my past. I saw the residue of their thoughts falling from the air: dreams filled with wonders unimaginable to a solitary Human mind. I realized then that Humans had never been meant to share this gift from the Creators. It had been the Hydrans' legacy, theirs alone. I watched the numinous rain brighten as the cloud-whales' numbers grew with the light of day, watched them drift slowly overhead. I felt the kiss of icy mist on my upturned face; lowered the glasses for long enough to see that snow was falling in the universe visible to my eyes.

I opened my mouth, let the falling snow soothe my parched lips and tongue, fearless now, because fear had become meaningless. I opened my mind to the intangible touch of dreamfall, not sure whether I was dreaming or dying. . . .

The clouds were lowering, settling to the ground, wrapping me in a restless fog-cloak. Ghostfire limned the broken hull of the transport; lightning shimmered inside the mist. Thunder carried to the distant hills and came echoing back, until there seemed to be no surface to my skin, nothing separating the sensation inside the hollowed-out core of my body from the uncanny energy surrounding me. Visions formed and faded inside my head, and I didn't know if my eyes were open or closed. Lightning danced on my fingertips, as ephemeral as the snowflakes that sublimed on my burning skin.

Miya. Her face haunted the fluid wall of fog, haunted my thoughts until I was sure this could only be a delirium dream. Her lips formed my name soundlessly, calling me to her, *calling me away.* . . .

The air was silver with light, limning my body with halos that splintered, when I moved, into the shifting forms of things I seemed to know by instinct, but would never know the names of. . . . An unimaginable mind flowed into mine, filling it with secrets and mysteries. Oneness. *Namaste.* . . .

(Miya.) Her touch, limned with gold, reached out to me from a lozenge of light, drawing me into its rippling gold/blackness until I lost all mass, becoming as ephemeral as thought, beyond pain, beyond any sense but wonder . . . rising, rising, into the light. . . .

TWENTY-THREE

"WHERE AM I?" somebody kept asking. The same raw whisper asked it again while the blue blue infinite vault of heaven opened overhead, as pure and undisturbed as the peace inside me. There was no pain, no need for thought, no need to do anything but exist. . . . And it didn't matter where I was, only that here in this place I was safe. . . .

"Where am I?" I whispered again, because I didn't believe in heaven.

(With me,) a voice answered. (With us . . .) The words sang inside my head. A cool hand touched my face, as gently as a thought. A thought touched my mind like a feathered wing.

I struggled up onto my elbow. Then there was pain—enough to make me gasp and swear, enough to prove I was still breathing. I looked down, found myself stretched on a sleeping mat, my body covered with bandages and blankets. I lifted my eyes to find Miya lying beside me, with dark hollows of exhaustion ringing her emerald eyes and depths of light in her smile as she touched me and felt my awe; saw my disbelief. Beyond her Joby lay sleeping quietly, with his thumb in his mouth. "How . . . did I get here?"

"I brought you."

"You—found me? How? I was . . . lost."

(The an lirr.) She leaned toward me; tears ran down her face as she kissed me softly, like she was afraid any touch at all would hurt me.

My mind joined with hers, wordlessly, effortlessly, like a miracle . . . and suddenly I understood how much my just being alive could mean to someone else. Tears ran down my face, as unexpected as rain in the desert. I could count on the fingers of one hand the times I'd cried in my life. Before this it had never been because I'd been happy, or safe, or simply alive. . . . Or loved.

I used my good arm to draw her down beside me; felt the flicker of her concern. (It's all right,) I thought, only wanting my hand free, my arm free, to hold her. My pain fell away with the contact of her body, the contact of her mind; like everything we shared was shared unconditionally, pain and pleasure, weakness and strength.

"The an lirr—" I murmured. I looked up at what I'd taken for the open sky. I realized I was looking at walls: a dome made of something translucent, transcendently blue, glowing with the daylight beyond. I glanced along the wall until I found a window, only recognizing it by the antishadows of clouds passing in the distance. *Only clouds, nothing more.* . . . Looking at them with my senses and Miya's senses joined, I could be sure of it in a way no Human could. I watched them disappear again into another expanse of wall as perfect as a cloudless sky.

I pulled my gaze away at last, looking back at Miya. (The cloud-whales helped you find me?)

She nodded, caressing Joby's sleeping head. (I didn't know what Naoh had done with you . . . just that I couldn't find you. So I followed the Prayer Way the oyasin showed me, and the Allsoul led me to the an lirr. . . .) They'd been far away too, almost beyond reach of her Gift. But each macrocosmic being of the an lirr was made up of millions of microcosmic minds, which made them more powerful and more sensitive than any single telepath's. They'd heard her prayers—and they'd answered them.

I felt for Wauno's medicine pouch, its weathered softness still bound to my wrist. My fingers closed, covering it. I tried to empty my mind of the thoughts that came with it, looked up as I caught movement at the corner of my eye. Something fluttered in the shadows of another room, beyond an arched doorway and a filigreed wall: taku. Their bodies were flashes of randomness across a geometry of light and shadow in the space beyond. And this time I didn't just see them or hear them; for the first time, I felt them in my mind.

(A week,) Miya said, answering my question before I asked it. (A week ago I finally found you and brought you here. . . .) She smiled with weary pride.

I lay back in her arms, feeling her warmth against me, my mind aware of nothing else but her now. Her healing lore seemed to flow into my veins, outward through the nerve net of my body, like just being here transformed me somehow. (Where am I?) I asked it as much because I wanted to feel her words form inside my head as because I wanted to know the answer.

(A holy place,) she answered.

(A monastery?) The image of another monastery filled my mind: one reduced to rubble and flames, the night around it filled with horror and grief. I remembered Grandmother . . . grimaced as pain distorted the interface of our thoughts again.

"Namaste—" Miya murmured, out loud, to the air. *We are one.* She pressed her face against my neck, like she was trying to stop my mind from bleeding memories, so we could go on believing that the warm, silent moment where we'd taken refuge from Refuge would last forever.

I could almost have gone on believing, in spite of everything . . . in spite of the shadows that haunted my memory, the pain I felt every time my body shifted position. Because my mind was alive again, not just to Miya's every thought, but to Joby, quietly dreaming—even to the taku. And beneath it all I felt a profound peace that was more than even the sum of us, giving *here* and *now* more reality than they'd ever had, making *safe* and *belonging* into words that had some kind of meaning for me at last. (How . . . ?) I thought. (Are you doing this? This—) *Miracle.* Not able to let myself speak the word, not even in my mind.

(No,) she answered, (it's this place. The reefs are all around us here, they touch us all the time. The oyasin . . . the oyasin showed me this place, a long time ago. She showed me how it can heal. . . . I wanted to bring Joby here before, but his parents— Tau—would never let me.)

(*Refuge,*) I thought, and then I didn't have any strength left for questions, no more need for answers. I lay in the warm sea of her thoughts, aware of every breath I took, aware that I was breathing easily now. Once before I'd felt my damaged body work to mend itself this way. Afterwards what I'd done had seemed like a fever dream. It hadn't been under my control then . . . and maybe it wasn't now. I only knew that in all my waking life I'd never felt as whole as I did here and now.

I woke and slept and woke again, losing count of the times and how much time had passed in between. At last I opened my eyes from a half-remembered dream of a child's laughter. I lay listening, uncertain, until I heard it again, echoing out of the shadowy room beyond the archway where the taku nested. I heard footsteps, the uneven patter of a child's feet.

I sat up slowly, expecting pain to take my breath away. It didn't. I still hurt all over, but not like I'd hurt before. I glanced over at the place by my side where Miya and Joby had been sleeping, expecting it to be empty. Miya was there, asleep. But Joby wasn't.

I stared at the empty space beside her. A child's laugh echoed again behind me. I turned, peering into the light-dappled inner room. All I could see were more shadows moving. And then I did something I hadn't done—hadn't been able to do—for too long: I set my mind free, letting the uncertain filaments of my thoughts search for Joby, trying to remember the sense of him that had always filled my head like incense along with Miya's thoughts.

Joby. It was Joby—laughing, moving freely, like any other little boy, like he hadn't been born with neurological damage, like he'd never been held prisoner by his own body, never needed Miya's help even to move a finger. . . .

She wasn't helping him now. There was no trace of her control in his mind. And yet he was aware of her somehow, as aware as I was now, always no more than a thought away from somebody else's reality.

I got up, fighting dizziness, still not really sure I wasn't dreaming. I took one step and then another toward the doorway, testing the floor under my feet, suddenly no more certain that this place really existed than I was that we weren't all walking ghosts. *Walking, breathing, laughing.* . . . Pain shocked me with every step, but my bad leg held my weight, and the rest of my body did what it was supposed to, step-by-step. I reached the doorway, felt its solid frame under my hand; still not convinced that I'd actually find Joby on the other side.

But he was there, in the long hall patterned with shifting light and shadow. He was following the darting path of a taku, and his body was the universal word for joy. The other taku soared and swooped around him like leaves in the wind, sharing his game of tag.

(Joby.) I spoke his name, not with my voice, but in my mind.

He stopped with an awkward lurch to stare at me, like he'd actually heard me. And then he changed trajectories, coming toward me with his face all smiles. I knew it must be true, then, that we were all dead. And that I'd been wrong all my life about heaven.

He collided with me, making me grunt with pain, his small body as substantial as the wall that barely kept me from collapsing. "Cat!" he said. (Cat!)

My senses strobed as I heard my name echo inside/outside my head. I picked him up, grimacing as I held his weight and thinking that if this was life after death, nothing I knew could prove it wasn't the real thing.

"Mommy!"

I turned around, holding him close, to see Miya sitting on her sleep mat, smiling at us. She came into the room and put her arms around us. (We aren't ghosts, nasheirtah,) she thought. (Namaste. . . .)

We are one. It was a long minute before I trusted myself to speak, even to think. Because all I had to do to speak was to think, now. (Joby . . . he's walking, by himself.) That part still seemed unreal. (How is it possible—?)

(There are *ke*—rhythms the an lirr sense: currents of the air and water, and even within the earth, lines of electromagnetic force. Where certain patterns form, the an lirr think of certain things. We call those places *shue*; the place where the oyasin took us to find our Way was also one. She told me that the monastery was built here because here the an lirr had thought about healing. . . .) I felt her grope for a way to show me more clearly. Even mind-to-mind it was hard for her to explain to me a concept so alien to anything in my experience—to the Human way, the only way of interacting with the universe around me that I'd ever known.

I remembered her vision of the body as a bioelectric system as well as a biochemical one, her awareness that most Humans barely got half the equation that made a living being whole. Deadeye had called Human brains the cells that made up the

artificial intelligences that were interstellar combines' micropro-
cessors for an organic computer. I felt her catch the image and
show me the starport computer's secret sentience, how it had
become more than the sum of its parts . . . like the an lirr.

A taku fluttered over my head. Joby put his hand up, and the
taku settled on his fingers. I stiffened as he brought it down to eye
level, but it didn't react to me, except to give me an opal-eyed
glance as it climbed along his arm and settled on his shoulder.

I took a deep breath and followed Miya's lead as she started on
across the chamber where taku nested. Joby trailed behind us, the
taku still balancing precariously on his small shoulder. I was surprised that the chamber floor was clean, like even the taku
regarded this as a sanctuary and didn't shit on the floor.

Beyond that space was one of the winding hallways Hydrans
seemed to prefer, maybe for aesthetic reasons, maybe because
when they were in a hurry they could always teleport. It still took
painful effort just to stay on my feet, but I didn't feel any need to
hurry now. I realized that all my life up to this point had seemed
to be about urgency. Now I couldn't remember why. Even my
thoughts seemed to move in slow motion here, my mind taking
in every detail of the monastery's austere grace: the ways that it
was different from the Council Hall, the ways it was the same.
My senses missed nothing, as if I was everywhere at once, like
the an lirr.

Miya walked beside me, our bodies touching; I felt her keeping track of Joby's pace and mine. There were doorways along
the corridor. Most of their ancient, metal-bossed doors stood
open, revealing small unadorned rooms that reminded me of
Grandmother.

I shied from her memory, looking straight ahead as Miya led
us into another large chamber. It was echoingly empty, like all the
rest had been. At its far end I saw a balcony opening on more
reaches of sky.

It occurred to me then to be surprised I wasn't colder, because
I knew how cold it had been outside. As we stepped onto the balcony I felt the soft whisper of some kind of energy field and realized that somewhere here was centuries-old Hydran technology
that still functioned, without the input of Miya or anyone else.

And then I forgot even that as I reached the featureless wall at the balcony's edge. The sanctuary sat on a ledge halfway up the nearly sheer wall of a cliff in the same untouched reef the research team had come to study. I looked out and down, up again, before the river-eaten depths below me had time to really register. The walls of the monastery flowed into the mountain wall above us; the incredible landscape of the eroded reef matrix lay all around us. I sucked in a breath, inhaling beauty, even as I searched the horizon for Tau Riverton, for anything from the world we'd left behind.

(We're two hundred kilometers from Riverton,) Miya thought. (Deep in the Homeland. The Humans never come out this far; even our own people have almost abandoned the interior, since there are so few of us now . . . since the an lirr abandoned us.)

I took another deep breath; let it out in a sigh. At the limits of my sight the reefs finally ended, their surreal topography flowing out onto a barren plain.

I let my gaze drop again and saw a bridge spanning the ravine. Below the monastery there was a narrow footpath worn into the sheer slope of the cliffside. I remembered Hanjen walking out from Freaktown to his meeting with Grandmother. I wondered whether Hydrans had once made pilgrimages all the way to this place on foot.

(I don't know,) Miya answered. (I only know that visitors approached the shue on foot if they were able to walk. And they left on foot when they were healed.)

Joby hung on the balcony wall, doing his best to imitate the high skreeling of the taku that sailed in and out above our heads. I watched him watching them, watched him laugh and move in ways that I'd taken for granted all my life. I felt sourceless wonder fill me again. (What's happened to us here . . . does it last? If we leave this place, do we . . . change back?)

She looked down, and I didn't really need an answer. I swore softly under my breath. She touched my arm, anchoring me in the present. (Some of it lasts,) she thought gently. (The longer we can stay, the more the changes will imprint. Your mind is free here; you're free to heal your mind the way you've healed your body, if—)

(If—?) I thought, when she didn't go on.

(If you have enough faith.)

(Faith?) I thought. The only thing I believed in was the cosmic rule that said if anything could go wrong, it would. (It's against my religion.) I glanced away, my mouth twisting.

(Faith in yourself is all the faith you need.) As I turned back, she looked in through my eyes like I'd suddenly become transparent. (You've never trusted yourself the way you've trusted me. . . .) Her mind filled with a kind of wonder.

(What about Joby?) I glanced at him, suddenly needing an excuse to look away.

I felt her surprise turn to a pang of disappointment. (Freedom to heal is what I wanted this place to give him too,) she said evenly. But her thoughts had shifted, withdrawing. I felt seeds of panic sprout inside me as the fear of losing her, and losing my psi again, made my control slip as my mind huddled down into the dark place where there was no pain, no betrayal—nothing left to lose.

Miya kept her eyes on Joby, but I felt the effort it cost her to let me retreat without following. (He wants this so much. . . .) She went on like I couldn't sense her strain, like I didn't know that she knew exactly what was going on inside me. (But for him it's a matter of patterning, imprinting. How well the patterning will last depends on how long he can stay here—*Joby!*) Her mind called out suddenly, sharply, as he scrambled up the rough wall of the balcony to teeter near its top, reaching up. He swayed, startled, even as she disappeared from beside me with a thought, re-appeared beside him, holding out her arms as he toppled back into them. (Go slowly, my heart!) she thought, rocking him gently, kissing the top of his head. He squirmed, but he didn't try to escape.

I wondered what Joby's parents would think if they could see him now . . . wondered what they were thinking right now. I rested against the cold stone beside the doorway, trying to forget my own mind and its problems, as a wave of dizziness warned me I was pushing my body too hard.

Miya glanced at me. She let Joby go again. A cold gust of wind whipped her hair across her face; she brushed it away like tears as Joby moved uncertainly toward me and caught at my arms.

I held on to him, barely, swallowing a grunt of pain as the col-

lision with his body seemed to jar every half-healed bone and lig-
ament in my own.

Joby sucked in his breath like he was the one in pain as I let
him go, settling him on his feet.

(Cat!) he cried, hanging on my pants leg. (You hurt! You
hurt—?)

"No, it's all ri—" I broke off, staring down at him. I looked up
at Miya, back at Joby again. "What . . . what did you say?" (What
did he say? Miya—?)

"It's okay?" Joby repeated, pulling at the ruins of my coat.

I kneeled down beside him, nodding, stroking his hair as I
looked into his eyes—wide brown eyes with perfectly round
Human pupils. (It's okay. I'm okay.) I watched his face ease. *He
was reading my thoughts.* . . . I hadn't just imagined before that
his mind seemed as open to me as Miya's. I sat down, because it
was easier, and he sat down beside me, mimicking my every
move. Miya crossed the balcony to us, limned by brightness.
(What's going on?) I asked. (You can't tell me the reefs made him
a telepath—)

(Yes, I can,) she said quietly. (But not yesterday. Before he was
born.)

I stared at her. (You're saying—the accident, when his
mother . . . that changed him?)

She nodded.

(That's im—) I broke off as another taku sailed over my head,
and Joby pulled himself up to follow it. (Do his parents know?
Does anyone?)

She shook her head. (I was afraid to tell them.) She gazed out
across the reefs. (I didn't know what they'd do . . . what Tau
would do.)

I grimaced. If Tau knew something in the reefs could do that to
a Human fetus—accidentally or otherwise—who knew how
they'd react: whether they'd try to synthesize and exploit whatever had played shuffle-brain with Joby's mind or whether they'd
want to destroy all evidence of something they might see as a
threat that could panic their entire population. Either way, I didn't
see it meaning anything but grief for Joby. (Is his being a psion
what lets you work with him like you did?)

She shook her head, squatting down beside me, out of the wind. Her eyes tracked Joby wherever he went. (Sometimes it makes it harder. He can resist me, resist himself, without meaning to, in ways he's too young to understand. But if he can learn to control his Gift, it will make learning to use his body that much easier. He could have a normal life. . . .)

"Then you'd better teach him how to hide his psi too. . . ." I said out loud. I dropped back into telepathic speech, without being able to lose the bitterness, (If you really want him to have a normal life in a combine world.)

She looked at me, her gaze both sharp and full of sympathy. She glanced away again.

"Hungry," Joby announced, coming back to plop down between us. "Mommy, hungry—" He pointed at his stomach.

Miya's face flickered, showing him a smile that wasn't in her thoughts. "Come on, then." She picked up a pot that sat stonelike in the shadows against the wall. I realized there were other bags and containers lined up on the balcony, bulging with supplies. Miya took Joby's hand. She glanced back at me, waiting while I got my own feet under me.

"Where did you get the food?" I asked.

"In town."

"How?"

"I had some money put away."

"You accessed your credit line?" I said, incredulous. "They'll trace you—"

She held up her bare wrist, a silent rebuttal. "Markers. I've been careful," she murmured, leading us back through the monastery. We followed a curving, timeworn tunnel to a lower level of the building, to what must have been its kitchen once. She set the pot down on the surface of something I didn't recognize as a cook unit until a hinged metal door opened silently in its side.

"Me!" Joby said. "I do it!"

"No," Miya answered, like she'd said it too many times before. "Too hard. When you're older." She reached in through the opening, palm out, interacting with a technology far older than the force screen we'd just left behind us, but in a piece of hardware that looked much newer. I felt her begin to gather energy, drawing it in, focusing it, directing it, her face clenched with strain.

The air around us seemed to grow colder as I waited, watching like Joby did, both of us as still as if we were hypnotized. Finally there was a sharp *crack* and a blaze of light/heat from inside the stove's belly. Miya jerked her hand back, slamming the grate, breathing hard. She wiped her forehead with a soot-covered hand, wiping away sweat, leaving a black smear. (It must get easier with practice,) she thought ruefully.

I wiped the smear of ash gently from her face and took her blackened hand in mind. Her hand was ice-cold; she shivered, standing close to the heat the stove was beginning to put out, like lighting it had drained her own body heat.

"What about your sister?" I asked, finally, as her hands warmed and color came back into her face. "Did you see her in town?"

She looked up at me. (No . . .) she whispered, her reluctance almost suffocating the word. There was fear inside her, but not fear of Naoh. I realized suddenly that she was afraid of learning what had happened to me, what Naoh had done after she'd taken Joby away . . . after she'd abandoned me, again. Because she knew how it had ended.

(Don't,) I thought. (Don't blame yourself. You made the right choice.)

(What did she do?) she asked at last, blinking too much.

(She . . . they . . .) Suddenly I was floundering out of my depth in *rage/disgust/humiliation*. They'd done to me exactly what Humans had always done.

"Nothing," I mumbled. "I don't remember. They just dumped me in the middle of nowhere."

"Bian." Miya caught at my arm; I moved out of reach.

"Hungry—" Joby began to chant impatiently, trying to drown out emotions he sensed but couldn't understand. "Hungry. Hungry, hungry—"

Miya hushed him with a distracted thought, sent him away to fetch bowls. "Cat." She used my Human name, more hesitantly, when I didn't answer. "Tell me." Her hand closed over my arm this time, tightened, not letting me go.

My own hand closed over Wauno's medicine pouch. Her glance went to it; I saw her incomprehension. Looking down, I forced myself to open my mind, setting free the memories of how Naoh had used me to get what she wanted.

I felt Miya's mind pull apart the nested layers of Naoh's revenge until she found its heart: the betrayal that Naoh felt every time she looked at us and looked into my eyes. Hydran eyes in a too-Human face, in a too-Human body that was helpless against her. . . .

Miya lost control, slipped and fell through my memories into her own: *Memories of the things that Naoh had done, the choices she'd made, because of Navu . . . of Hydrans and Humans, love and hate, nasheirtah, and namaste—*

(What about Naoh and Navu?) I demanded. (What about them—?)

Miya cried out; or maybe it was only what happened in my head then that blistered my reeling thoughts.

I broke free, swearing, and left the room. I blundered through the darkened halls of the empty monastery until my body couldn't go on. It gave out, finally, at the entrance to a room with no windows, no skylights, only that single opening, so low that I hit my head on it, swearing again as I entered. I sat down with my back against a wall and covered my face with my hands. *It was impossible*—to live the way I'd lived, to have been Human for so long, and not have secrets you never wanted to see the light of day. *Impossible to share everything*—even if it meant losing everything. I wondered whether it was really possible for anyone, even the Hydrans. . . .

I sat in the dark for a long time with all my senses on hold, letting need and futility play their circle game until they drained the last of my strength.

And then someone touched my shoulder. I looked up, expecting Miya—found Joby staring back at me with something like awe. His grinning face glowed with colored light. The abstract patterns shifted as he craned his neck to peer past me. "Look!" he said, pointing. "Look what you made."

I looked over my shoulder, realizing that the room wasn't dark anymore; it was filled with eerie luminescence. My breath caught as I saw the wall behind me—the multicolored imprint of my body shining in the dark, neon colors bleeding outward from the contact point. "Damn . . ." I whispered, in disbelief.

Joby pressed his hands against the wall. Glowing handprints set off colors that spread in all directions from his touch. He pressed his whole body against the wall, giggling as he flung his arms wide, flattening his nose as he set off more luminescence, sending his colors rippling outward until they collided with my own.

I levered myself up the wall, trailing a bright smear. I pressed my own hands against the invisible surface, triggering more light. The colors we'd set off already didn't fade; they kept spreading, widening, echoing through each other like chords of music.

Suddenly a new pattern of light flickered across the wall, went soaring toward the ceiling without either of us setting it off.

(It isn't your touch,) Miya's voice said inside me. (It's your Gift.) She entered the darkened room, her face luminous with reflected light and perfectly expressionless with concentration as she lit up more and more of the darkness.

I stood away from the wall, breaking my physical contact with its surface, trying to see whether the patterns my body had been creating would stop.

They didn't; they went on forming like frost, following my thought, giving form to my every glance and whim. Joby ignored us both, blissfully lost in uncanny fingerpainting, in rolling his body along the wall in a wash of incandescence.

I shook my head; the colors zigzagged like lightning. (But I'm not a teek—)

(Any manifestation of the Gift will trigger it,) Miya said.

I thought of the Hydran picture globes; how once I'd been able to change the images hidden inside with a thought. (What was this used for?)

(Beauty—?) Her mental shrug told me she had no more idea than I did. (Maybe it doesn't matter,) she thought, and I felt her smile. (Does it?)

I shook my head, watching Joby's silhouette dance across the spectrum in front of us. But then I felt Wauno's medicine pouch bat softly against my wrist and sudden desolation filled me— *loss, regret*—as if she'd told me a lie.

(What? What is it?) She touched the pouch uncertainly.

I showed her Wauno's face.

(What happened . . . ?)

I let myself remember, letting her see the rest for herself: that the memory of what Naoh and the Satoh had done to me was only the flotsam on a sea of blood. . . .

Miya moaned, pressing her hands to her mouth.

I broke contact, shutting her out of my mind before she sank any deeper, not able to bear her pain or knowing I'd caused it.

She stared at me, her pupils wide and black, her face garish with rainbows. I put my arms around her as she began to turn away; holding her close to my heart, resting my head against hers, so that I didn't have to see her face—so that I didn't have to violate this chamber's perfect beauty with my mind.

TWENTY-FOUR

THAT NIGHT AFTER Joby had fallen asleep, Miya led me silently down through the levels of the monastery to a place where heavy wooden doors opened in a wall. Beyond the gate a path lay along the face of the cliff like silver thread, spooling down to the spot where the bridge crossed the river. There was no Human town on the other shore, here. There was nothing at all but darkness and silence.

But overhead the stars were everywhere, like sparks blown from some unimaginable sun-forge, netted in the pale nebula of our frosting breath. It was like seeing countless neurons firing all at once; like seeing what it felt like to make love.

I followed two steps behind as Miya led the way. I didn't know whether she was touching my thoughts, whether she felt the image that warmed me against the night's chill. Her own thoughts had been almost opaque to me since this afternoon. I didn't know whether she was giving me the space I'd needed or hiding from me. And I didn't know how to ask.

I trailed her down the narrow path through the darkness with a fumbling caution that couldn't have matched her grace in broad daylight, until finally we reached the bridge. There were posts on either side of the path where the bridge began.

A chain barred the crossing. Locks dangled from each of its

slender links. The chain itself looked corroded, even in this dim light, like it had barred the path of countless pilgrims since the beginning of Hydran time on this world.

And yet I could have stepped over it, easily. The chain wouldn't have stopped a Human, let alone a Hydran. And why were there so many locks, some of them ancient, some new—preventing nothing?

Miya moved slowly along the chain from one end to the other, touching the locks silently, almost reverently.

"What does it mean?" I murmured, not wanting to break the silence by speaking aloud, but afraid of what would happen if I couldn't make my mind form the question.

She looked up at me. I thought I saw tears reflecting the moonlight in the corners of her eyes. "They were put here by lovers," she said. "Those who had a nasheirtah. It's a pledge that they will be namaste for a lifetime."

A deep, sourceless pain gutted me. I looked away into the darkness that was always waiting to close in. . . .

(Bian,) Miya said softly, inside me. (It isn't true.)

"What?" I whispered.

(Your mother wasn't a prostitute . . . your father wasn't a rapist. If they hadn't loved each other, you would not have been born.)

I looked back at her. (How—?) *How did you* . . . (How do you know? It could have been—)

(It would not have happened.)

"You're sure?" I said hoarsely, my thoughts slipping.

She nodded.

"Then why? Why did he leave her in Oldcity?" My fists tightened. "Why did he leave me?"

(Maybe it was her choice.) Miya touched my shoulder gently. (Maybe he didn't know about you; maybe she didn't tell him. They were from different worlds. When worlds collide, things fall apart. . . .) She bent her head. (Love . . . love isn't stronger than that.)

I remembered the lock I'd seen on the offering pile inside the prayer cave. I remembered the pain on her face as she'd picked it up and told me it was Naoh's. I remembered Navu, a burnout cursing at us from a back-alley drughole. . . . I tried to remember Naoh without remembering what she'd done to me. I couldn't.

I took Miya's hand in mine, cold inside colder. A clasped hand was all the pledge I had to offer, all the promise either one of us could make, here, now, like this. She moved close; I felt our body heat begin to combine, warming us both.

Still holding my hand, Miya led me forward again. She stepped over the chain and waited as I followed, thinking about humility, and mortality; about how much of what happened to your body was inseparable from what happened to your mind, or your soul.

Whatever the bridge was made of, it didn't creak or sway under our weight. The yielding surface muffled our footsteps until they disappeared into the sound of the wind. When we reached the middle of the span, Miya sat down, holding on to the moorings of the handrail, letting her feet dangle over the abyss.

I settled beside her, taking my time as I eased my stiffening body down onto the walkway. I looked out and down at the abyss, up into the giddy heights of the sky, the way Miya was doing now. Sitting beside her, I felt safe in a way that not even the abyssal heights and depths could disturb. The moon's half-revealed face barely dimmed the stars out here, even though its light was bright enough to show the fragile ghosts of colors in our clothing. I felt Miya's thoughts flow out of her, into and around me, embracing the nightworld like a prayer.

I couldn't pray. My thoughts were the futile dreams of a mebtaku. But I remembered other skies, other times I'd looked up in awe at these same stars in other settings. . . . I hoped some part of that went with Miya's prayers into infinity.

We sat together for a long time, suspended between worlds; huddled next to each other, the warmth of our bodies keeping the cold air and the uncertain future at bay. I tried not to remember that once I'd sat with Kissindre Perrymeade in too much the same way, warming each other in the chill predawn air of another world while we waited for the day. *Here* and *now* were all I had left, would have to be all the time in the world. I pulled Miya closer, kissing her, the contact exchanging heat, hunger, two souls.

At last I felt her mind fold me inside warm wings, and she teleported us back to the monastery, to the comfort of our makeshift bed. We crawled under the piled blankets, where we could peel off the layers of clothing that kept us from taking the final step that our trembling, goosefleshed bodies ached for. We made love, urgently because we couldn't wait, gently because it was all my healing body could endure, silently to keep from waking Joby, completely, until there was no urgency left in us, only a mindless sense of peace that would hold back tomorrow, at least until morning came. . . .

I woke again at dawn to a changeless, perfect sky, to the timeless present of a long dead past. I told myself our past, our future— even the thought of one—was meaningless, here in a place where the impossible still happened.

Joby was already awake. I heard him in the chamber beyond the filigreed wall, holding a one-sided conversation with the taku as they swooped down from their nesting places to eat the bits of fruit and bread he handed out to them. I felt their thoughts brush his, and mine, with the softness of fur, and realized that maybe the conversation wasn't one-sided.

Miya was next to me, still asleep. I lay back, just looking at her, realizing that we'd never seen each other's bodies in the light of day. My eyes followed the curve of her back from the edge of the blankets up to the nape of her neck. At the base of her neck I found a pattern of colors half-hidden beneath the snarled gold of her hair: a tattoo—a kind of mandala, a circle formed of intricate geometries and bounded by intersecting lines.

Miya stirred, rolling over to look up at me drowsily. (What—?) she thought, her mind smiling.

"The tattoo. I never saw it before." I pulled my shirt on as I began to shiver. It was stiff with dried blood; I hid a grimace as it caught at my healing skin.

The smile spread to her face. She reached over her shoulder to touch the pattern. "It's a sign of the Way . . . hidden, yet always with you, joining the mind and the body, making a person whole. They used to be done at birth, to grow with the child for a life-time. A few of us still have one. . . ." She glanced away, reaching for her clothes as she began to shiver too.

"I saw something like it at the Community Hall. It was . . . hidden."

"Did you?" She turned back to look at me. Her smile came out again, and widened. (Of course,) her mind said. She rested her head against my shoulder.

"What do you mean?"

"It was a . . . *linpoche*." She shrugged, like there was no equivalent Human word. "Not everyone senses them. Some people go their whole lives without ever seeing one."

I shook my head, wondering. I remembered the look Hanjen had given me that day as he entered the courtyard and saw me standing there. I kissed her open mouth as she ran her hands down my side, over my tunic, over my skin, not flinching as she found old scars or half-healed wounds, accepting every part of me.

But as her hand reached my hip, she paused. "What is this?" she murmured, touching the tattoo that climbed the back of my thigh. "I felt it last night."

"You—felt it?"

She nodded and shrugged again, like it involved a sense too elusive for words. I caught a nebulous image of energies I was blind to.

I pushed the covers aside, twisting my body so that she could see the rest of it, the dragon/lizard with a collar of holographic fire. "My tattoo. I have one too, but it doesn't mean anything."

(Draco—?) I heard her breath catch. "Why do you wear Draco's logo?"

I lay back again, wincing. "I don't," I said. "I don't know, I mean." I looked down. "I don't even remember getting tattooed. I was doing a lot of drugs, then."

She looked up at me, half frowning.

"It's nothing," I repeated. "It doesn't mean anything." I pulled the blankets up over it and reached for my pants. We finished dressing in silence.

But as she got up to go and find Joby, I caught her hand, drawing her back down beside me. "What really happened between Naoh and Navu? What—twisted her like that? Show me, Miya . . . I have the right to know."

She sat down cross-legged on the blankets, pushing her tangled hair back from her face, stroking it with her hands like she was trying to calm her thoughts. "Naoh . . ." She spoke out loud, like I had, as if the memories were too volatile to share directly. "Naoh turned wild and bitter, after our parents died . . ." she took a deep breath, "and we learned we were sterile. Hanjen tried to help her, but he couldn't reach her; she was too strong. She blamed our parents for their own deaths. She blamed the Community for being helpless against the Humans—" She broke off and took another unsteady breath. "Naoh became one of Borosage's drug dealers. She never used the drugs herself, but she sold them. . . ." She shook her head, running her restless fingers through her hair.

"And then she met Navu; she found her nasheirtah. . . . He was an activist, a Satoh, like our parents. When they found each other, Naoh stopped dealing drugs for the Humans. Navu gave her back her pride in our heritage and her belief in the things our parents died for. But when she tried to turn her back on drug selling, Borosage had them both arrested. Eventually he let Naoh go, but not Navu. He told her to keep selling his drugs or she'd never see Navu again. He kept Navu in prison for a year. By the time Navu was released, he was addicted. . . ."

I pressed my hands against my eyes, seeing pain as phantom colors.

"Naoh went on selling drugs so that she could get them for Navu." Miya's gaze was lost in the trackless blue of the walls when I looked up again. "But . . . but he wasn't the same. They broke him. That was when Naoh—changed. She stopped dealing and tried to get Navu's habit treated. You saw how well that worked." The words were flat, beyond emotion. "She finally turned her anger where it belonged, on the Humans. She joined me in studying with the oyasin. And then . . ." Her voice faded again, and she rubbed her face. "Then Naoh had the vision. She believed that she could save us; that all her suffering had only been to make her strong—"

"God," I breathed, and for a while neither of us said anything more. Joby's laughter and the skreeling of the taku echoed from the next room. At last I said, "Miya?" She raised her head. "Why don't you hate Humans?"

She looked at me for a long moment with her head bent to one side. (Why don't you?) she said.

More days passed. Joby walked and laughed and sang to the taku that followed him everywhere like a migration of sentient toys.

His speech, and his thoughts, grew clearer and more complex every day. Just his smile could blind us to the shadow of death that bounded our existence.

Every morning I woke up surprised to discover we'd survived another day. As I lay beside Miya and Joby, sharing their warmth, I knew this was as close to having a family as I'd ever come. And I knew there was nothing more I wanted from life, except that Tau would never find us.

But I knew Tau's CorpSec would have orbital surveillance searching for us, programmed to scan for anomalies like three heat sources in an abandoned monastery, a mix of Hydran and Human genecodes. They'd find us sooner or later. Miya knew it too: knew that every moment we stole from fate was another victory, for us and for the lost little boy who might never have another day of freedom, no matter what happened, once our time together here ran out.

Miya made a trip to Freaktown every few days to pick up food and other supplies, and to pick up news. Day after day there was no sign that our message had reached Isplanasky; that it had ever even gotten off-world. Naoh and the Satoh were in hiding; Miya didn't dare spend enough time in town to find out where.

Tau added new embargoes to their sanctions against the Hydrans every day that their demands weren't met. Even Tau couldn't justify wiping Freaktown off the map with a retaliatory strike, but they could bleed the Community for information until they bled it to death. There was nothing we could do to stop that, change it, now, even if we gave ourselves up. Naoh had seen to that. An hourglass full of days was all she'd left us, and the choice of living a lifetime before it ran out.

Miya and I ate and slept and roamed the monastery's maze of halls with Joby skipping at our heels, trailing a flying circus of taku. Miya taught me all she knew about the history of our people, in between games we made up for Joby to strengthen his growing control. Sometimes the games made me laugh so hard Miya glanced up with a look that said I seemed newer to real child's play than Joby was.

When the monastery's walls began to close in, Miya took us on teleport pilgrimages into the interior of the Homeland. I'd thought nothing existed there anymore, since the cloud-whales had abandoned the reefs and taken the rain with them. But the bones of the past lay everywhere. She took us to a dozen different sites where time-eaten remains of Hydran civilization lay abandoned to the wind.

Some of the things we found there were mysteries to our eyes and minds, things even Miya didn't know the purpose of—tiered towers that rose like prayers step-by-step toward heaven; dozens of hive-shaped kiosks of unknown material, each a meter high, laid out in a wedge in the middle of nowhere. Some were things any Human would have recognized—the remains of towns, of homes, of what could only have been research or production centers based on a technology as long forgotten as the structures themselves. Now they were all just ruins, echoing husks filled with broken artifacts.

Sometimes while Miya and Joby slept, I sat alone in the monastery's dusty rooms sorting through salvage we'd carried back. I daydreamed about taking the artifacts back to the team, studying them in some well-equipped Tau lab. . . . And then I'd remember again why that had become impossible. I'd never see any of the team again, never even see Hanjen, the only Hydran I knew who might still be able to tell me something about how the Community's tech had functioned.

But out of everything we carried back, the thing that haunted me the most was an idea. It had come to me as I stood in a ruined building in the heart of a dead city. Maybe the place had been a government center, like the Community Hall in Freaktown. It could as easily have been something more frivolous or something more bizarre. All that remained now was a skeleton, an empty cage constructed of God-knew-what. Arcane organic forms flowed upward, defying gravity, reaching toward the sky—the home of the an lirr—with finger-spires tipped in something that shone like gold in the sun. The building's interior was hollow now, whatever it had been once. Patterns of light and darkness falling through eyeless window openings illuminated the patterned floor, giving it a third dimension. Arcs circled within circles, diamond spines were framed in ovals, webs of delicate tracery spun across expanses of open space three stories above our heads.

Everywhere there were startling views of the sky, like whoever entered this place had been meant to look up often and remember. Everywhere I looked, the sky was as perfectly clear and cerulean as the walls of our room in the monastery. Not a single cloud was visible. When the an lirr abandoned the Homeland, they'd taken the lifeblood of the land with them, just as their going had sucked dry the spirits of its people.

As I stood looking up at blue infinity, the universe hidden behind it, I thought about the Hydrans who'd left Refuge and the an lirr for the stars, spreading the Gift and the Community thin across the light-years. I wondered whether there was any connection between losing touch with the an lirr—losing something so vital to their spiritual identity—and their decline as an interstellar civilization. . . .

(Miya—) I called, and she turned to look at me from across the glowing floor. (What if the an lirr came back to the Homeland?)

She looked at me for a long time; I felt her turning the question over and over in her mind without finding an answer. She shook her head at last, calling Joby to her with a thought. "It's time to go," she said, and that was all she said, before she carried us away.

Whenever we could we made love, exploring each other's bodies inside and out. And knowing there should be no secrets, no need for them now, still a part of me was always on guard, shielding Miya from my past—the dark needs, the darker fears, the poisoned memories hidden like deadly anomalies in the dream-reefs of our joinings.

Because sometimes in the heat of lovemaking she had cried out, not with pleasure but with pain—my pain, as my pleasure slipped across some unwatched border into the night country, and a nameless stranger's perversion tore her unprotected heart like shrapnel.

And as the days passed—as their inevitable end grew closer, and so did we—I began to wake from the dreaming safety of our sleep at night thinking I was in another place and time, sweating the blood of nightmares. Waking up in her arms, I'd find her comforting me like a child; I'd see the incomprehension in her eyes as I drifted back down into sleep without explanation.

Until one night I woke, sitting bolt upright in the faint moonlight, and realized Miya had wakened me. She lay beside me, with silent sobs wracking her body, her fists in a death grip on the blankets she'd pressed to her mouth to muffle the sound.

(Miya . . . ?) I could barely feel her in my mind, like she was trying to muffle her thoughts the same way. But I found the images of Joby, of me, of herself, distorted with pain. . . . *All of us dead—worse, all of us alive but alone, in the hands of the Humans.* . . . I pulled her into my arms, finally understanding that all the while I'd struggled to keep her free of my prison of fear, she was locked in the next cell.

It took all my strength to turn the key that waited—that had always waited—in the lock of the final door. I opened myself to her.

Raw emotion arced across the space between us to complete the joining—*love*death*loss*—like none of those emotions had ever existed separately inside her, even in dreams.

The feedback smashed through my unguarded mind like a shock wave, fragmenting me, her, everything but the unbreakable bond between us, and the last recognizable thought I had was that neither of us would ever take a sane breath again. . . .

A sound—a child's wail of terror—reached me. A single coherent emotion—Miya's—took form around it. I felt her respond, recapturing the spilled blood of her thoughts as her mind struggled to answer Joby's cry.

I barely refocused my own thoughts in time to catch her trailing lifeline. We rose through fathoms of memory, reclaiming our souls and our wills, breaching the surface of sanity at last.

I fell forward onto the tangled bedding as I came back into my other five senses; Miya rolled away from me toward Joby. Joby lay in a fetal knot beside her, making the high keening cry I'd heard him make the first time I saw him, but with a serrated edge of pain I'd never heard before. Miya held him in her arms, surrounding him with her touch, her contact flowing into his mind like life-giving oxygen to wake its higher centers, its voluntary controls.

I watched her comfort him, reorient him, bring him back into the world just as his cry had brought her back. Without him, without the bond between the two of them, the two of us might have stayed locked in a psychotic *klin* until our bodies wasted away and died. I wiped my hand across my mouth, trembling.

At last Joby had grown quiet enough that she could settle him down to sleep again beside her. She covered him with blankets, covered his face with apologetic kisses as he drifted off, smiling.

Her tears began to fall again, in silence, welling from her eyes like springwater. She didn't turn back to look at me.

I sat in the moon-shadowed darkness watching her, watching Joby, while my heartbeat gradually slowed. I kept my mind clenched shut, afraid to touch either of them: afraid of the past, afraid of the future, afraid of causing them more pain. Afraid. . . .

She looked up at me then, finally, and even though she was still weeping her eyes were fearless; the hand she held out to me was as steady as faith.

My body shrank back in a mindless reflex. I shook my head, not meeting her gaze as I pulled on my clothes. I got up from the bed and left the room.

I moved through the monastery's halls without a light, wishing that I could lose myself in the maze of passageways, stumble into some other dimension and disappear.

I glanced up as I passed through a chamber I'd crossed nearly every day without seeing anything new. But this time the moonlight threw a wall into unexpected relief, revealing an opening I'd never seen, in what I'd taken to be a featureless surface.

I changed trajectory, snaked a path between pillars to the hidden doorway. The corridor beyond was no more than five meters long. At the end of it I found a prayer platform like the ones I'd seen in Freaktown, except that this one was open to the sky, within the energy field that protected the entire monastery from the weather. But this one was hidden, special . . . linpoche.

I stood on the platform looking out into the night. Above me were the stars, the night's blackness, the face of the moon scumbled with elusive shapes. The images I saw there seemed to change from one moment to the next, transforming my perceptions again and again, until at last even my mood began to transform.

I leaned on the edge of the low wall that ringed the platform, searching my pockets for the mouth harp I'd somehow managed to hold on to through everything that had happened to me. I put it to my lips and breathed into it, hearing the smoky, plangent notes that it hadn't made in too long. But always the same ones; always the same ones missing, so that any song I tried to play was incomplete.

I lowered it again, disappointed, like the inarticulate part of my brain that belonged to music and moods had expected even my attempt to play a song would be transformed.

(You have to become a part of it.) Miya's voice filled my mind as she appeared on the platform beside me. I felt her begin to say something more and then stop, falling silent with awe as she realized where we were. (Linpoche—) she thought. She looked back at me, the night reflected in her eyes. I saw her mouth quiver.

She looked away again at the face of the moon, and for a long moment her emotions were closed to me. At last she thought, carefully, (With any instrument, to make music is . . . to be namaste.)

I shook my head, looking down at the harp. (But it doesn't have everything I need to play my music.) I held it out, keeping my own thoughts perfectly transparent on the opaque surface of my mind.

(Then make them yourself,) she said. Something appeared in her hand: one of the flutes used to greet the an lirr. She ran through its scale of notes. There were gaps in the liquid progression of sound, but when she began a song the missing notes were somehow all there.

(How?) I thought. (Your Gift—?)

She shook her head. She played the song more slowly, letting me see how she used her fingers to partially block an opening, hear how she modulated her breath to alter pitch—making what was there work for her, to give her what she needed.

I raised the mouth harp to my lips and blew into it. I cupped my hands, changing its sound by the way I shifted my fingers, hearing notes slide past that I'd never produced before. I lowered it again, slowly, as my throat closed so that I couldn't go on playing. I studied the cool gleam of its moonlit metal surface resting in my hand. At last I put it back into my coat pocket and looked up as something drew my thoughts, my eyes, like a lodestone . . .

(Miya. . . .)

She kissed me, her fingers digging into my back, pressing herself against me as if she could dissolve into my body and make us one physically—doubling our strength, so that nothing could hurt us, or come between us, ever again.

But even as we went on kissing, wedding our hearts and minds while our union was witnessed by the countless stars in the infinite night, I knew we didn't have a prayer.

Because I knew how the universe worked, and nobody got out alive.

TWENTY-FIVE

THE NEXT MORNING Miya set out for Freaktown again. She held Joby's small, groggy form in her arms, kissing him gently on the forehead before she kissed me long and deep on the mouth. I wished then that I wasn't a half-breed, with only half-Hydran looks and half a Hydran's psi . . . wished that I could take her place, not because I could have done it better, but only so that I wouldn't have to be the one who stayed behind, waiting, never knowing. . . .

She disappeared with a last half smile of regret, while I stayed behind holding Joby in my arms. I felt his body stiffen uncertainly as he suddenly lost sight and sense of her.

"Where's Mommy?" he asked like he always did, speaking Standard like he always did with me.

"She went to get food," I answered like I always did. "She'll be back."

"Soon?"

"Yeah, soon," I murmured, carrying him on my hip as I crossed the room to the window. We looked out together at the sun rising over the reefs. "Look at that," I said, pointing, to distract him. "One more day." A taku fluttered down from above and landed on my head. "Hey!" I said, but it didn't move. Joby giggled, pressing his hands to his mouth.

I managed a laugh of my own, amazed that even now, staring into the light of universal order while death and chaos hung from a thread above us, life could still be so absurd that there was nothing left to do but laugh about it.

"Are you my daddy?" Joby asked, his face turning somber again.

"Yeah," I said, glancing away.

"I have two daddies?"

My breath caught. I nodded slowly. "That's right," I whispered. "You're a lucky boy."

"And two mommies?"

I nodded again, not trusting myself to answer. I hadn't let myself think about his real parents since I'd crossed the river. The taku launched into the air, startled by my sudden movement.

"Do they all love me?"

I swallowed. "You bet they . . . we all do."

(Why aren't they here?)

I knew exactly which set of parents he meant this time. "I . . . they can't be." I answered out loud, because right then I was even more uncertain about whether I could control my thoughts. "They want to be here, but they can't be."

"Why?"

"They . . . have work to do for Tau."

"Don't you have work to do?"

My mouth quirked. *Not anymore.* "My work now . . . Miya's and mine, is making you strong and well. That's why we're here, at this healing place. When everything's better, then you'll go back to your . . . other family." I wished suddenly that they could be here, to see how he was now. Whether he lived or died, they'd probably never see him this way again.

His face brightened, then turned rubbery, like his thoughts had snagged in my fraying confidence.

"I promise," I said, wanting it to be true so much that I even believed it.

He nodded, relaxing in my arms. He put his head on my shoulder, content to wait with me while the sun rose over the reefs. I looked down at the valley below us, at the bridge that spanned it, so different from the bridge that joined Freaktown and Riverton.

I thought about the difference in the way Hydrans and Humans counted the value of the reefs, how much of that difference came from the way they perceived them. To Humans a reef was nothing but a biochemical stockpile, no more or less than the sum of its parts. The fact that this last reef, and this healing place, had escaped being strip-mined was nothing short of a miracle. It had only happened because Tau's shortsightedness and xenophobia kept them from learning anything meaningful about Hydran culture.

I thought about miracles, about what this shue had given back to Joby, to me; how it had freed us all from our lives of solitary confinement. I wondered how long it had been since the Hydrans of Refuge had felt whole, connected, greater than the sum of their parts . . . wondered again what would happen if the an lirr returned to the Homeland: Whether the rain they brought with them could bring this wasteland back to life. Whether their presence would be enough to bring the Community back to life, back to the Way. Whether it was ever too late to start moving toward the kind of future their past deserved. . . .

Joby shielded his eyes against the glare as the sun rose higher, his stubby fingers curled into an imitation of Wauno's field lenses. I'd let him look through them, to search for the an lirr, sometimes when he was bored. We never saw any, but he never seemed to mind.

"Look," he said suddenly, and pointed into the sunrise.

"What?" I squinted a little, trying to make out anything separate from the reef and sky. My pupils had already narrowed to slits; usually they did a better job than Human eyes of keeping the light out as well as letting it in.

"There." He pointed impatiently, wagging his hand until I began to make out a half a dozen black specks like sunspots against the dawn. They grew as I watched, expanding at a rate that made a tumor of dread form inside me. *Coming this way,* directly at us, too big and too fast to be anything natural. There was only one other thing they could be: CorpSec flyers. And without Miya here, there was no way to escape from them.

"See, Cat?" Joby was demanding as my higher brain functions came back on line. "See? See?"

"Yeah," I muttered, "I see them." I held him closer as the ships began to take on shape and detail, not slowing their approach. Their flashers hurt my eyes, brighter than the sun.

"Daddy!" Joby called out, waving in sudden delight. He wasn't looking at me. I remembered suddenly that his father was CorpSec; the Tau Security logos were plain enough to read now on the approaching flyers. "Time to go home?" he asked, looking at me. "Everything's better now?"

Only it wasn't his father coming to get him. It was Borosage's butchers. I stood paralyzed, waiting for the lead gunship to open fire. We'd never even feel it, it would happen too fast—the plasma burst that blew us apart and scattered our atoms into a billion golden dustmotes. "Yes, time to go . . ." I whispered. "Hold on tight."

I shut my eyes, afraid to watch death approaching; opened them again, afraid not to.

No burst of raw energy suddenly put out the sky. I went on staring, frozen where I stood, as the gunships stopped in midair. They ringed the balcony where we waited, weaponless and unprotected.

"This is Corporate Security!" a voice boomed out of nowhere, everywhere, like maybe we'd been deafened as well as blinded. "Stand where you are. Put up your hands."

Slowly I let Joby slide out of my arms. Then, slowly, I put my hands in the air.

Corpses in body armor emerged like beetles from the closest ship, dropping onto the balcony around us. Every weapon was trained on me. I stood motionless, barely even breathing, afraid that any move I made would be my last.

Joby clung to my leg as he saw the weapons and registered the moods in the minds behind them. "Daddy—?" he called, his eyes searching one shielded, anonymous face after another.

I tried to touch his thoughts, reassure him somehow. My mind seemed to be as paralyzed as my body. I tried to find words instead—broke off as one of the armored men still disembarking pushed forward through the ring of troopers, dropping his weapon, lifting the face shield of his helmet.

"Joby—!" It was Burnell Natasa. I watched in disbelief as he swung Joby up in his arms, backing away again through the ring of weapons still aimed at me. Another faceless, anonymous Corpse came forward then, searched me for the weapons I wasn't carrying, jerked my arms behind me, and clamped binders on my wrists. When he was through a third one took his place: Fahd, Borosage's chief goon.

As he cleared his faceplate I saw the shadows of a half-healed cosmo job still marring his face. I remembered suddenly what Miya had done to his weapon the last time he'd seen us . . . what the exploding plasma rifle had done to his eyes. I looked at his eyes now.

His new eyes were a different color. They were green. And the pupils weren't round; they were slitted. He'd needed a transplant . . . but he hadn't needed that. I realized as he met my stare that he'd done it so that every time he looked in a mirror he'd remember how much he hated us. . . .

"Where's the girl?" he said. He wasn't carrying a gun this time. His armored fists were clenched at his sides.

"Wha'—?" I said blankly; realized he meant Miya . . . realized they'd gassed us without my even knowing it. I took a deep breath. "Gone."

His mailed fist hit me before I could duck out of the way, and sent me sprawling. "Don't lie to me, freak."

I sat up, slowly and awkwardly, my head ringing with the blow, my ears filled with the sound of Joby screaming my name. Fahd stood over me, blocking the light. My blood was a wet smear on his gloved fist. "No' . . . lying," I mumbled.

"He isn't lying, Lieutenant," someone called out. "All scans show the rest of the building's empty."

Fahd leaned down and hauled me to my feet. "So the HARM bitch ran out on you when she saw us coming." He smirked.

Fuck you— I barely swallowed the words in time. "She lef' b'fore you came," I said. "To get food." He laughed. I swore under my breath, hating myself for saying that much.

"She has to be here. Look at my son!"

I recognized Natasa's voice. I craned my neck past Fahd to catch a glimpse of Joby, remembering that Natasa had never seen Joby this way before—as a normal, functioning child, without Miya's help or guidance.

"She's not here, Burnell," someone said; the voice was familiar, but I couldn't place it. Bodies shifted in the background, until finally I could put a face to the voice. It was Perrymeade.

"I don't know how it's possible, but—" He moved closer to

Natasa, took Joby's straining hand in his as Joby reached out to me and called my name again.

Natasa came to stand in front of me. His grip on Joby tightened as Joby tried to squirm free. Joby began to cry.

(It's all right, Joby,) I thought, beginning to get enough control back to use my telepathy. But I couldn't keep him from seeing the blood running down my face. (I can't hold you right now—) I twisted my pinioned hands behind me. (Stay with your father. You'll be safe.)

Joby stopped struggling. He relaxed against the hard shell of his father's body armor, wiping his nose on his sleeve, but he was still looking at me. Natasa looked at me too, meeting my eyes for the first time. "How?" he asked.

"It's this place," I murmured.

"How—?" he said again, demanding.

"It's a . . . healing place."

Fahd grunted. Perrymeade pushed past him to stand beside Natasa. "It's the reefs, Burnell," he said softly. "It has to be. . . . Isn't it—?" He turned to me.

I stared at him, silent.

"Answer the man, freak—" Fahd's fist came up again.

Natasa blocked the blow with an armored hand. "Not in front of my son," he said, and the words were deadly. He looked at me again, and his dark eyes, so much like his son's, doubled the urgency of Perrymeade's pale gaze. "Please," he said, almost humbly this time. "Tell me how this could be possible . . . ?" He glanced down at Joby as disbelief stole his thoughts away.

"I told you," I said thickly, sickened by the realization that he'd tell his wife, and she'd tell Tau, and ten minutes after that this wouldn't be a shue and a healing place anymore, it would be Tau's latest mining and research complex. They'd destroy the miracle that was here, trying to find it, profit off of it, and never even understand what they'd done.

Natasa looked back at me with the same kind of incredulous wonder, not even registering my expression. "Then he's—cured?"

"No," I said. "Not if you take him away now. Miya says it takes time for the neurological changes to imprint. He needs more time."

Fahd grunted again, his disgust showing.

"Miya . . ." Natasa said, and his face hardened. He shook his head, starting to turn away.

"You'll lose it all!" I said.

"Come on, Joby," he whispered. "Let's go home. Mommy's waiting." He went back through the ring of guards, carrying his son toward the hovering gunships. Joby began to struggle again. He called my name, reaching toward me over his father's shoulder.

Fahd moved in on me, blocking my view of them before I could answer. He caught hold of my coat again. "When's she coming back?"

"Who?" I said.

He slapped me, openhanded, keeping me on my feet with the augmented strength of his grip. "You little mindraper. When—?"

"I don't know!" I mumbled, managing to spit in his face.

"The hell you don't—"

I tried to twist away as I sensed the next blow coming . . . looked up again in confusion when it didn't hit me.

Perrymeade had stepped between us. I looked at Fahd's face, not sure which of us was more surprised. "Stop it," Perrymeade said, with a quiet reasonableness that he didn't really feel.

Fahd jerked free of Perrymeade's grip. "You've got no authority here," he said, his voice sour with resentment. But he didn't hit me again. "If you really don't know anything, boy, you're already dead," he muttered, shoving me forward through the gauntlet of armored bodies toward the waiting flyers.

(Cat—!)

I gasped as the call rattled inside my skull. It wasn't Joby. It was Miya.

(No!) I thought. (No! Tau is here—) I didn't know why in hell she'd come back so soon; *why now—?*

Someone shoved me again. My body moved like a drone across the balcony as my psi escaped through a spark-gap of spacetime to find her, and say *good-bye.*

(Cat. . . .) Whatever else she'd tried to tell me reached me as pure emotion. Our telepathic link shattered as my body banged into a hatch opening. They hauled me on board the flyer. Natasa was there already, with Joby on his knee. Joby sat with his arms wrapped around a bright-colored stuffed toy. He looked up like he sensed me before he saw me, and then his eyes glazed; I felt Miya reach through me to touch his thoughts one last time.

"Mommy—?" he cried, searching the air. Natasa caught his hands and pulled them down, half frowning. And then she was gone, and no one else was left who understood but me.

I felt her inside me again, the contact so full of anguish that it wrenched my heart out through my eyes. My concentration fell apart completely, until I couldn't find her at all. Joby began to wail again. I felt his fright and incomprehension as the guards shoved me into a seat and locked me into it.

(Don't cry, Joby. . . .) Somehow I managed to pull myself together long enough to make him believe everything was happening the way it should. (You're going home,) I thought, finally understanding how Miya had found the strength to protect him, burying her fears for both their sakes.

Joby settled down again in Natasa's lap, clutching the toy, but his tear-reddened eyes stayed on me. Natasa's did too. He glared at me, at the guards around me, at Fahd and Perrymeade who'd come on board behind me. He was wondering why the hell they had to put me in the same craft with him and his son, thinking that Fahd was a bastard and Perrymeade was a fool.

He looked away again finally and began to talk to Joby in low tones, trying to reassure him. I watched his face soften as relief and wonder rose to the surface in his mind again. *His son was alive, unharmed . . . his son was well.* Just for a moment, he was afraid he might break down in front of everyone and weep. He glanced at me again, suddenly, and away.

I looked up, startled, as Perrymeade took the seat beside me. "What the hell are you doing here—?" I muttered.

"Doing my job," he said flatly, keeping his own gaze on Joby. But in his mind he thought, *Saving your lives.*

Surprise caught me by the throat. I twisted in my seat. "If you'd done your job right in the first place, none of this would have happened."

His face closed. Looking at him I saw Kissindre in his features, in his eyes, in his memories. He stood up without answering, before I could ask him about her, and moved on down the aisle to sit with his brother-in-law. I cursed my stupidity for saying that, for saying anything.

The squadron of flyers rose through a long arc up and over the reefs, heading back toward Tau Riverton. I watched Joby with his father, saw him beginning to respond to Natasa's unguarded joy, felt him beginning to remember that this man had always been a part of his life. The other Corpses around them took off their helmets and gauntlets, one by one, to speak to the father, smile and play with the son. They weren't even all men; a few of them were women.

Their congratulations, their concern, their pleasure, were all genuine. A buzz of disorientation filled my head as I realized that the same faceless killing machines that had cut down the Hydran demonstrators actually held thinking, feeling minds, people who were friends of this man, proud of their part in rescuing his son.

They barely glanced at me now. Locked in binders, I wasn't a threat, and I wasn't Human . . . not even human. I'd stopped existing until we reached our destination. Then they'd remember me. I wasn't going to like it when they did. I leaned back, too aware of the bruises stiffening my jaw; trying to find the courage somewhere to help me face what was coming next.

Miya was safe. At least I knew that. And Joby would be taken care of by people who loved him. Tau hadn't killed him after all. I didn't know why, but that didn't matter as long as he was safe. What we'd shared was over. I'd known it couldn't last; I couldn't even regret it.

I tried to focus on Joby, on the warm sea of comfort around him; tried to imagine what it would have been like to have a father who'd come searching for me and actually found me. But he hadn't, and I couldn't.

The clear, strong thread of psi energy linking me to Joby frayed; the signal fragmented. I pulled my focus back together, thinking my own emotions had distorted it. But as I did I realized there was something more: We were leaving the monastery behind, passing beyond the influence of whatever cast-off miracle lay in the deposits there. I remembered suddenly that it wasn't just Joby who was going to lose everything the reefs had given back to him. *So was I.*

(Joby?) I turned to watch his face, searching for a sign that this wasn't really affecting him too. (Joby—?)

He looked up as I called his name mind-to-mind; for a moment the look on his face was vacant and confused. I felt static break up his thoughts as he tried to answer me; saw his body twitch spasmodically in his father's lap.

His father glanced down at him. I felt Natasa's adrenaline surge of panic, the numbing rush of denial as he tried to ignore what was happening, as if to have even a moment's doubt about his son's condition might change everything back to the way it had been. The way I'd warned him it would be. . . .

I felt Natasa look up at me again. The unspoken demand in his eyes speared my brain. I closed the fist of my thoughts and shut him out.

Joby flung out his hands with a wail of complaint, reaching toward me. "Cat—" He called my name, and it was still intelligible.

I dropped my defenses, feeling his fear as he sensed something going wrong inside us both: He was losing something precious, something he didn't even know the name of, something he hadn't missed until we'd given it to him. Something that even he knew was his birthright. . . .

And I knew exactly what he was feeling. I jerked against the seat restraints, but with my hands locked behind me there was nothing I could do to reach him. I sat back again and focused what mental control I had left, forcing everyone and everything else out of my thoughts so that I could protect him in the only way left to me, for as long as I could.

Joby settled into his father's arms again, quiet now, even speaking a word or two when his father asked him something. Out of the corner of my eye I saw Perrymeade watching me, almost like he'd realized what I was doing. His face furrowed; I couldn't spare the concentration to find out why. But he didn't say anything, didn't call some Corpse to slap a drugderm on me and shut my psi down for good.

I took a deep breath, concentrating on my link to Joby, on being there for him, keeping both of us calm as the strands of light strung across the darkness between the outposts of our thoughts shorted out one by one. No ability I had could reinforce the patterning of his neural circuitry to let him go on functioning without massive external support. Nothing I could do would convince my telepathy not to falter as the distance from the monastery grew, as the time until we reached Tau Riverton shortened.

At last the perfect grid of Riverton showed below us, expanding geometrically as we dropped toward our final destination: Corporate Security headquarters.

Joby had been resting quietly against his father's side, not moving or making any sound, but still aware and functioning. He made a small squawk as my eyes registered the building and I fed the unexpected shock of recognition to him.

I looked away from the window, using all my physical senses to help me stay fixed on him, needing all my self-control to keep my fear from destroying the last fragile filament between us. The flyer landed inside CorpSec's compound. Natasa got up from his seat, setting Joby down on unsteady legs, supporting him with gentle hands.

Someone's hand closed hard over my shoulder. "He's already sweating, Lieutenant," the Corpse said, releasing the seat restraints and hauling me to my feet.

Fahd stopped in front of me and murmured, "You'll be sweating blood soon, freak."

Joby made a mewling, helpless noise behind me. I turned back in time to see him fall out of his father's grasp as Fahd destroyed the last of my control, and all his control went with it.

Natasa kneeled down to pick up the small, twitching body of his son. He hugged Joby against his own armored body. "Joby!" he said. "Joby?" He looked up at me again, his look demanding answers I couldn't give to questions he wouldn't ask me.

(Joby—!) I shouted, into a silence that held no light at all: no trace of his failing nerve net, no trace of any thought—no proof that everyone around me hadn't suddenly ceased to exist. Even Fahd, alien-eyed and smirking in front of me, felt as dead as the ashes of my burned-out psi.

But as I looked back at him I realized that I was the dead man, not him. He grinned, like he thought he was entirely responsible for the look on my face then. He forced me around and out of the craft at gunpoint, not letting me look back. I heard Natasa's voice rising with urgency as he tried to make his son respond. I heard the murmured concern of other voices, voices that had been full of wonder like his own when we left the monastery.

Perrymeade was beside me suddenly. Catching my attention across a barrier of helmets, he called, "Joby—what's happening to him? What did you do—?"

"I didn't do anything to him!" I said fiercely. "I told Natasa—Miya tried to tell you—it's the place! The monastery. I warned him."

Perrymeade dropped back out of my line of sight, probably reporting what I'd said to Natasa. I caught sight of their small group heading away diagonally across the field. Natasa was carrying Joby, but he moved like a man who'd been knifed in the gut. I thought I saw someone waiting at the edge of the field—figured it would be Joby's mother, and whoever she'd brought along for support. They were being held back by another squad of guards.

I looked over my shoulder for a last glimpse of Joby. I saw Natasa pass him into his mother's arms, saw grief and joy mingle into one impossible emotion, before their closing bodies blocked my line of sight. I caught the sound of voices on the wind, but I couldn't make out any words. There was no sound from Joby; nothing at all in the silence of my empty mind.

Perrymeade was still looking toward me as the guards herded me away into the detention center and the doors sealed behind us. I tried once more to get a grip on my psi, but it was too late; everything I'd been had come undone. My mind was as empty as deep space, drawing a blank on everyone we'd left behind, everyone we passed. The Corpses moving through the station's bleak, inescapable halls might as well have been real corpses. I needed peace, time, to find out whether the monastery had made any lasting difference in my control. But my time was up.

Borosage was waiting for me in the windowless interrogation room. I flinched, but I wasn't surprised. He had the same prod in his hand and the same smile on his face. "Well, freak," he said, "here we are again. Let's just take up where we left off—" He bent his head at the hard chair with the straps that I'd come to in, the first time I'd opened my eyes in this place. "We won't be interrupted this time, since you went so far out of your way to prove I was right about you. I ought to thank you."

"You brain-dead bag of pus," I said in Hydran.

"Speak Standard, dammit, you little shit!"

"Eat me, Corpse," I said in Standard.

His face mottled. He flicked the prod on.

I lunged forward and knocked him down with a head butt. I almost fell on top of him; barely caught my balance in time to run.

But the guards were on me before I got three steps, dragging me back and around as Borosage staggered to his feet. He picked up the prod, breathing hard. Fahd had his fingers knotted in my hair, an arm across my neck, half choking me. Borosage ripped open my clothes, and drove the prod's tip against my naked chest until I screamed.

Fahd let me go, letting my head fall forward so that I could breathe. I sucked in long, hoarse gasps of air; pain-tears leaked from the corners of my eyes. I raised my head, finally, as the smell of burned flesh faded and my nausea eased. Arms locked around me, holding me immobile as Borosage raised the prod again. I shut my eyes, a flood of curses in Hydran and Standard spilling out of my mouth. I let them come, not able to stop them.

But the blistering shock of pain didn't happen. . . .

I opened my eyes finally, my body still trembling, my jaw clenched with aching anticipation. Borosage stood just beyond reach, the prod held rigidly at his side. Somehow Perrymeade had come to be standing in the space between us. Both of them were looking at me with expressions I didn't have a clue about.

Perrymeade glanced down; not away from the fury in my eyes, but down at something in his hand: *Luc Wauno's medicine pouch.* I must have dropped it, struggling to get away.

"K-Kissindre—?" I managed, finally. "Wauno?"

"Still hospitalized," he said.

Relief burned my face: *Alive. At least they were alive. . . .* But as I looked up at him again, I understood perfectly what was in his eyes.

"She barely survived the crash. If the rescue team had been any longer getting to them. . . ."

I bowed my head, more tears running down my face. "I'm sorry. I'm so sorry. . . ."

"I told you what he was," Borosage said, oozing satisfaction. "Is that why HARM recruited you, freak? To make their kill for them? To murder innocent Humans for those poor persecuted aliens who were too helpless to do it themselves—?"

I bit my lip, feeling the pain in my chest double. I couldn't make myself face Perrymeade again even for long enough to tell him why the words were lies, tell him how wrong they were, how out of control everything had gotten. . . . I looked down at the brand Borosage had laid on me: the blistered, weeping hole in my chest. It looked like someone had tried to rip my heart out. I felt armored hands trap me as my knees got weak.

"Corporate Security did an admirable job of rescuing my nephew," Perrymeade said to Borosage. "It seems you knew the best way to deal with these terrorists all along. I owe you an apology for ever questioning your methods."

Borosage showed his teeth in what passed for a smile. He flicked the prod at my eye, making me cringe; his eyes measured Perrymeade's reaction. "I'm glad you've come to feel that way."

Perrymeade's face stayed expressionless, professionally noncommittal, even while he stole another look at the burn on my chest. "You were the right one—the only one—Tau could have chosen to handle this situation," he murmured. His gaze shifted away again.

"Deathbringer," I said in Hydran.

Perrymeade glared at me. I didn't know whether it was my tone of voice he was reacting to or the fact that he didn't know what I'd said. He looked away from me with an effort. "What are you going to do with him, now that you have him?"

Borosage shrugged. "He's guilty as hell of terrorism, kidnapping, half a dozen crimes against the corporate state. And besides that, he somehow got an illegal message off-world—"

"What message?" Perrymeade demanded, his voice rising. "Why wasn't I told about it?"

"Wasn't your jurisdiction," Borosage said, looking smug. "The little son of a bitch hacked his way through the security programming. He sent a message to the Feds, telling them there was a cover-up, to come here and investigate us again." He looked at me, his face contorting. "They're sending another team—special investigators representing Isplanasky, the head of Contract Labor, for God's sake!" His fists knotted.

Perrymeade swore under his breath. "Tau knew about this? When are they arriving?"

"They wouldn't give us a date," Borosage muttered. "But Tau wants the 'breed put down before they get here." *Put down. . . .* That was what they did to animals.

"Executed—?" Perrymeade said, as if it surprised even him.

Borosage frowned. "No. He's caused them to lose too much face. We'll take care of it here. But not before the freak tells us everything he knows about HARM."

"Don't bother." Perrymeade waved a hand at me without looking back. "He won't tell you anything. Nothing you can use. It's not important now: the Hydrans are beaten, they don't want any more trouble—they won't cause any more, either. I have orders from the Tau Board that all sanctions are to be lifted, with no further pursuit of the terrorists. That was the deal we made. Hanjen himself gave me the information on where we'd find Joby."

I raised my head in time to see Perrymeade's faint smile twist the knife. "Yes," he murmured. "He told me everything. . . . He couldn't stand by and watch his people suffer any more because of you." The satisfaction in his face turned to disgust.

Borosage glanced from him to me and back again. He deactivated the prod, tapping a rhythm on his thigh. "That's too bad. I'm disappointed to hear that. But if that's what the Board wants . . ." He grimaced and shrugged. "We'll move on to step two. Fahd, take this genetrash out and dispose of it." He jerked his head at me.

Fahd took hold of my arm and pressed his gun to my temple, watching Perrymeade for a reaction. Perrymeade's mouth fell open; he shut it again, his eyes narrowing.

I tried to pull away, but there were too many guards still holding me. "I want a hearing!" I said. "I'm a Federation citizen—"

"Where's your databand?" Borosage asked with a slow smile. "Where's your proof?"

I froze, remembering: *At the bottom of the river.* "I'm still registered. I know my number—"

Borosage shook his head. "You threw it all away, freak, when you crossed the river. You're nobody now, and nobody's going to miss you."

I looked away at the wall, keeping my eyes as empty as my mind.

He jerked me forward suddenly, making me swear with pain. "Nobody, freak. That's all you are." He let me go again. "Fahd." He nodded toward the door.

"My pleasure." Fahd hooked a hand around my arm and shoved me toward the exit.

"Wait," Perrymeade said, the single word stopping Fahd in his tracks like a death threat.

Fahd dragged me back around as he glanced at Borosage.

"What?" Borosage snarled, with sudden suspicion.

"I have an idea." Perrymeade came forward, his hands behind his back. He looked me up and down, not meeting my eyes. "A better idea. . . . See that scar on his wrist?" He pointed. "My niece told me he used to be a contract laborer. And he's certified on a phase-field suit. He's young and strong—why waste him? Bond him. Send him to the place where my brother-in-law is Security Chief. Burnell won't ask questions. . . . The new team of Feds will come and go, but he won't be able to do a damn thing about it."

Borosage's eyes widened, as if even he had never thought of something that twisted.

"You fucking bastard," I said.

"I want you to wish I'd let them kill you," Perrymeade murmured. "I want you to remember what you did to my niece, and to Joby's family, every time that you do." He glanced at Borosage again.

Borosage nodded. "Do it," he said to Fahd. "Have him bonded."

TWENTY-SIX

"HEADS UP, BOYS—fresh meat." The guard shoved me through the doorway of the barracks where the bondies slept. There was a sloping ramp just inside the door; it dropped out from under my feet before I could catch my balance. I slipped and fell, landing at the bottom in a heap. The door shut behind me.

I scrambled to my feet, trying to hide my pain and stupefaction as curious strangers drifted toward me. They all wore the same faded maroon coveralls that I was wearing now. All of them wore the same jewelry too—a red bond tag fused to the flesh of their wrist. I glanced down for the hundredth time at my own wrist, banded in red—the tag and the swollen, angry flesh around it. As I looked up again the entire world strobed red . . . the color of rage, of betrayal. The color of my worst nightmare.

Natasa hadn't been waiting for me when I arrived: even Tau must have been decent enough to give him and his wife some time to be with their son. But the Riverton Corpses who hand-delivered me to the installation's security made sure they dumped the data on me directly into his personal account, where it would be waiting for him when he returned.

Until then they were treating me the way they treated any other bondie—like meat. I took in the room and the laborers with a long stare, trying to keep my mind on the situation, trying not to panic. There were maybe thirty others in this barracks; a work-shift crew, probably, all working and sleeping on the same schedule. There were bunks for sleeping, and a doorway at the far end that probably led to the toilets. Nothing else, but it was more than there'd been where I'd worked before. At the Federation Mines we'd slept on mats on the floor.

Most of the others in the room didn't even bother to look up. They lay in their bunks or went on playing square/cubes in a group at the back of the room. Only a handful of them drifted up to me, as unreal to my shuttered senses as everyone I saw now. But their bodies looked as solid as a wall, and about as friendly. I felt like I'd been thrown onto gang turf.

"What's your name, kid?" one of them asked me, the biggest one. Probably the alpha male, just because of his size. I watched how he moved: he was heavy and slow. Probably a bully, depending on size, not skill, to get his way. I figured I could take him if I had to.

"Cat," I said. At the mines no one had been curious about anything. They'd been too exhausted from overwork and too sick, their lungs wasted by radioactive dust. Nobody gave a shit whether anyone else lived or died.

This was different. I might even have convinced myself that it was better, except that they were looking at my eyes.

"Look at his eyes," one of them said. "He's got freak eyes—"

The others moved closer, peering at me. "What are you, some kind of 'breed?"

"They don't let freaks in here," someone else said. "They wouldn't trust a psion. A freak could sabotage the works, or spy—"

"Maybe he's here to spy on *us*," the big one said. "They put you in here to mind-read us, freak? Report on us—?" He hit me hard in the chest with the heel of his hand, right on the wound where Borosage had burned me with the prod.

I doubled over, gasping, straightened, bringing my clenched fist up with the motion, and drove it straight into his throat.

While he was busy retching I kneed him. I hit him with both fists on the back of his neck as he doubled up. He hit the floor and stayed there. I stood over him, breathing hard, watching the others hesitate. More workers joined the circle, drawn by the fight. I heard them muttering, spreading the news: *They had a freak for a new roommate, what were they going to do about it . . . ?* They glanced at each other, working up the courage to move in on me. The noose of bodies began to tighten around me, all of them hating me without even knowing me, their Human hands and feet too ready to reduce me to something I wouldn't recognize in the mirror.

A hand closed on my arm.

I turned, rage blinding me as I crushed the instep closest

behind me with my boot, rammed an elbow into somebody's eye socket, ripped out a fistful of hair. I did it without even thinking, without even breathing—without feeling anything. Proving with every howl of their pain that I was as Human as they were.

With three more of them on the floor, it was easy to stare the rest down. "Don't fuck with me," I said, my voice shaking. "The next son of a bitch who touches me I'll cripple for life."

They backed away, slowly, their eyes never leaving my face. My own fear and rage shone back at me from every side, from all those eyes with round Human pupils. No one else made any move to see if I was serious.

The one who'd attacked me first stirred on the floor where I'd left him. I put my foot on his neck, put my weight on it. "Where's your bunk?"

He glared up at me with murder in his eyes, but he pointed finally, to one near the back of the room.

"Find another one." I took my foot off his neck and shoved a path through the bondies still watching around us.

I went to his bunk and lay down on it, turning my back on them. I huddled around the bone-deep, burning pain in my chest, biting my lips to keep from whimpering, until the pain had dimmed enough so that I could think about something, anything else. . . .

There was nothing I wanted to think about. I lay listening to the curses and laughter of the square/cube players, the random fragments of muttered conversation, until the lights went out for the night. And then I lay in the dark listening for a footstep, for the sound of breathing, a murmured word: for anything that might warn me they were coming to get me . . . for anything that would prove I wasn't alone.

They didn't come for me. And I didn't sleep all night, trying too hard not to feel the pain . . . trying too hard to feel.

I moved out with the others at the start of the new shift, moving on autopilot, stupefied with exhaustion. I was all alone in my mind. I might as well have been all alone in the universe . . . until somebody I didn't see shoved me as we moved along a narrow catwalk two stories above the ground. I banged against the guardrail; felt it shudder, squeal, and snap, as the support wrenched out of its hole. I flung myself back, throwing all my weight away from the buckled railing. I caught hold of the closest solid object—someone's body—stabilizing myself.

"You fucking freak!" The bondie shoved me away; his elbow dug into my chest. "You trying to kill me?"

I went down on my knees, doubled over on the metal walkway, swearing helplessly with pain. He dragged me up by the front of my coveralls; the seal tore open.

"Shit. Oh, shit." He stared at the festering burn his arm had just slammed into. It distracted him long enough for me to pull free of his grip. "Who did that?"

"Corporate Security." I pulled my coveralls together again, sealing them up. The maroon cloth was stained with wetness from the weeping sore.

He frowned, shaking his head; his fist relaxed as he backed off from me. The others stared at me, sullen and silent.

"Look," I said, trying to keep my trembling voice steady. "My telepathy doesn't work. I'm not going to read your minds. I can't teleport out of here; I can't stop your heart just by thinking about it. In the last day and a half I lost everything I had except my life. Just leave me *alone*."

One of the ones I'd beaten up last night laughed. I looked at their faces, figuring the odds, and knew that wasn't going to happen. Unless— "I'm qualified to use a phase suit. I'll be your point man," guessing no one here liked reef-diving any better than the bondies I'd seen at the reef on the Homeland. Right now the odds of me being killed by another suit failure seemed a hell of a lot better than the odds of somebody knifing me while I slept.

"Tau doesn't train freaks—"

"I'm from off-world."

"What's holding it up?" A guard pushed his way forward, taking the bondie's place in front of me.

"I slipped," I said.

He looked at the damaged rail, at the rest of the bondies, back at me. "You making trouble, freak?"

"No, sir," I muttered.

The taser prod he carried came up until its energized tip was staring me in the face. "Be more careful."

I bit off a curse, ducking past it. The others around me were already moving. I went with them, not looking back.

"I heard about him," the one who'd shoved me muttered, glancing at somebody else. "He's that one—the one that took over the suit from Saban, when he panicked in front of the Feds. Out on the Homeland. Right?" He looked at me.

I nodded, watching his hands in case he decided to hit me again anyhow. After a minute I murmured, "How'd you know about that?"

"They sent some of that work team here to fill out our crews when the Feds made their inspection."

"Oh." I'd been here less than a day, and already I'd proved that every suspicion I had about this place was true. And the FTA was coming back . . . but there wasn't a damn thing I could do about it now.

TWENTY-SEVEN

A TRAM CARRIED us deep into the heart of the interface. It let us out in a spot I recognized, a work face inside the reef itself. I felt the reef even before I saw it—felt its eerie euphoria dance like heat lightning through my senses. I fought to keep my survival instinct functioning, not trusting myself or the mood I was in right now. It would be too easy to lose my mind in a place where no one could reach me. . . . If I ever gave in to the rapture, once I put on a field suit I'd be lost forever.

When the crew foreman called for reef-divers, my crew spit me out like a pit. At least they believed what I told them. I hoped it meant that tonight I'd be able to close my eyes for long enough to get some sleep.

The foreman looked at me twice, but only because he was expecting to see somebody else. "You cleared to use a suit?" he asked.

"Yes, sir," I said.

"Okay." He shrugged and sent me with the others to pick out a suit.

I spent the rest of the work shift in inner space, moving through the mysteries of the an lirr's thought-droppings. Staying focused was easier than I'd thought, because this time I knew to expect the unexpected . . . and because these suits had a feedback control I hadn't been shown that let the tech on the outside give me a shock if I didn't respond fast enough to his instructions.

I was a fast learner. After the first few zaps I held on to my brains for the duration, letting myself sense the reef matrix just enough to keep my mind from sensory deprivation. At least in here I still felt something; still felt alive. . . .

That night when I dropped into my bunk and closed my eyes, strange images and indescribable sensations still played my nerves like a ghost harper. I let them come, let them smother the burning ache in my chest that was worse than it had been yesterday. Sinking deeper into my memories, I saw/felt the cloud-whales drifting through the heights of the sky like indifferent gods . . . felt them settle around me, shrouding me in thought, until I was only thought, ephemeral, dreaming. . . .

The next couple of days passed without any more trouble. The bondies in the barracks kept our truce, as long as I put on the suit every new work shift without complaining.

I didn't complain; it was all I had to look forward to. My personal future figured to be short and unpleasant. Even if another FTA inspection team discovered everything about this place, they wouldn't get the chance to learn it from me. Natasa would turn me into organ transplants first.

Even if I lived through their visit, there was nothing left of my life. Reef-diving was the only thing worth living for—a chance to touch the unknowable, to feel my Gift come alive in ways that even I couldn't begin to describe. What I'd experienced the first time I'd gone into a reef, or when the an lirr had come to me, hadn't been a fluke. If the unknown suddenly reached out and killed me one day, at least I'd die happy.

My psi gave me something more that I hadn't expected: It made me good at my work; better than other divers at guiding the techs to the kinds of protoid concentrations Tau wanted to see. Once I got a sense of the sector's feel, I began to recognize certain patterns in the stimuli the matrix fed to me and learned how to track them to their source. I stopped getting shocks and started getting praise from the techs. Having their respect seemed as alien to me as looking at my eyes still seemed to be to them.

Their respect didn't make them like me any better, but that didn't matter. The only people I cared about were on the outside, in the world I'd thrown away with my freedom: People I still loved, people I still hated. People I still owed, big time.

I repeated their names, tried to see their faces in my memory each day on the way to a new work shift; making it a kind of ritual to keep me anchored in reality as I put one foot down in front of the other, following the body ahead of me until it led me to where I was going. The pain in my chest was constant now, eating at my body and mind every waking moment when I wasn't in a field suit, lost in the reefs.

This morning I'd come to sweating and dizzy. I hadn't looked at the burn in a couple of days, hadn't had the nerve to. I told myself it would heal, everything always healed, with enough time . . . anything that didn't kill you made you stronger.

A hand clamped over my arm, making me swear in surprise. "You," the guard said, and pulled me out of line. "Chief of Security wants you."

Natasa. I groaned under my breath. *Natasa was back. And he knew everything.* Suddenly I felt dizzy again; suddenly I was sweating.

I went with the guard, went where I was told, because there wasn't any other choice. We passed through sectors of the complex I'd never seen, passed excavation teams already working their assigned stations. Just passing by the naked face of the reef, I felt it seeping into my hypersensitized brain like my mind was as porous as a sponge. I let it take me, sucking my mind out of my body.

"Stop!" I said suddenly, stopping short.

"What—?" The guard turned back, his stare and his weapon both fixed on me.

"Stop the work!" I shouted at the crew foreman. "You're going to hit a volatile pocket."

I heard the whine of equipment shutting down as the workers

stopped, without being ordered to, and turned to look at me. The foreman frowned, thought about ordering them back to work, then thought better of it. She crossed the floor to us. "What the hell do you mean, a volatile pocket—?" It was the thing the work crews were most afraid of: hitting some unfinished thought that would turn out to have an unstable molecular structure. There were too few divers, spread too thin, to do a thorough job of exploring every millimeter of reef-face. "You can't predict—" No one could, not even the divers or their techs, with absolute certainty. No one Human.

"I can," I said, making her look at my eyes.

She swore, turned to the guard. "A freak? They let a freak in here—?"

The guard shrugged. "Natasa wants him now."

"What do you know about this—?" the foreman asked me. She gestured at the reef behind her. It was more of an accusation than a question.

"I'm a diver—"

"That doesn't mean you can see through walls, freak," she snapped.

I shrugged; grimaced as it hurt my chest. "Go ahead then," I muttered. "Don't check it out. Just let me get away from here before you blow yourselves up." I started on, making the guard scramble to catch up.

"Hey!" the crew chief shouted, but I didn't look back.

We reached another tram stop. As we waited there, I listened for an explosion behind us. It didn't come. I didn't know if I was glad or sorry.

The tram let us out in another area of the complex I'd never seen: one that looked too pleasant, too open. Everything I saw told me any bondie who got this far would regret he'd seen it.

Natasa's office was just as open, just as unprotected. Maybe nobody believed a real problem would ever get this far. I wondered whether the forest of potted plants along the wall was real or just a good-looking sim, like the virtual view through the window behind his desk. It wasn't a view of this world.

"You want him in binders, sir?" the guard asked, pulling my attention back to Natasa.

Natasa shook his head, looking at me with unreadable eyes.

His hands lay empty and motionless on the surface of his desk. All I could tell from his expression was that he didn't think I was any threat.

The guard left the office, leaving us there alone. I stared at Natasa, and he stared at me, and all I could think about was pain: the pain in my chest, the pain in my memories, pain overflowing until it seemed to fill all the world . . . and more pain coming, now that we were finally face-to-face. He lifted his hand and made a gesture I didn't understand; I kept expecting to see him pull a weapon.

Someone stepped through the wall of greenery—*holo; it was only a holo*—and into the room. Natasa's wife, Joby's mother. She was alone, wearing lab clothing.

I backed up a step as I recognized her, almost lost my balance as it made my vision strobe.

They both looked at me like they thought I was about to bolt. I stood with my knees locked, staring back at them. Ling Natasa took a seat near her husband, glancing at him then with a half frown that could have meant anything. Perrymeade would have told Natasa to make sure I paid. Somehow I hadn't thought his wife would want to watch. Or help. No matter how hard I tried, I never seemed to underestimate Human behavior completely enough.

I went on standing, waiting, damned if I'd be the first one to speak. My hands tightened over the loose cloth of my pants legs.

"Sit down, Cat," Ling Natasa said, finally, when her husband still didn't say anything. I stood numbly. "We just want to ask you some questions."

I glanced away, saw two seats like cupped hands in a corner. I backed up slowly, sat in one, trying not to stumble, not to take my eyes off them, not to show any sign of weakness. Sweat tracked down the side of my face. I wiped it away, pushed my filthy hair out of my eyes. I stank; I wondered if they could smell me from across the room.

"We want to talk to you about our son," Burnell Natasa said finally. He touched something on his desk/terminal. An image of Joby appeared, floating above the desktop. I looked away from it. "What did you do to him, you and Miya—?" There was no anger in his voice. "He was . . . all right. And then—" He glanced at his wife. There'd been enough left of what the reefs had given Joby that she'd seen it too, even as she'd seen it disappear.

"Is . . . anything left?" I asked, finally. "Is he any better?"

Ling Natasa nodded, her lips pressed into a line. "Enough," she murmured. "Enough so that we know, enough so that he knows—" She broke off suddenly.

I slumped back in the seat, my eyes blurring out of focus. I stared at the image of some other world's blue-green seas and sky beyond the virtual window behind the desk. I wondered whether its seasons changed; if their fantasy world had seasons.

"How did you make it happen?" She asked it this time, and the real world of sorrow and pain was suddenly surrounding us again, and I was drowning in it.

"You said it was something about that place, the reefs—" Burnell Natasa's voice prodded me when I still didn't say anything. "Answer her, damn it!" He started up from his seat.

His wife gestured sharply, shaking her head. He dropped back into his chair. "Are you afraid to tell us?" she asked me. "Why?"

I thought about something I could have said, and then something else, and something else. Finally I just held up my wrist.

Burnell Natasa frowned, staring at the bond tag until comprehension came into his eyes. His wife didn't even look surprised. "This is off the record," he murmured, glancing away.

"Yeah, right," I said, and saw his face harden again.

"It's our *son*," Ling Natasa said.

It's my freedom. But I didn't say it, and she went on, "We know you helped him . . . how well you cared for him. We know that you must . . . love him . . . too." She cleared her throat. "We've lost Miya. You're all the hope he has left."

I covered my face with my hand, feeling sick and giddy as the adrenaline rush of my fear subsided. "I told you everything I knew," I mumbled. "Something about the reefs out there, on the Homeland . . . it cleared out the static, or completed damaged circuits in his brain. I don't know how. It freed my psi, and . . . and his." I let my hand drop, looked up at them as the silence stretched.

"Joby's not a psion," Ling Natasa murmured. "There's no Hydran blood—"

"It was the accident," I said. "Before he was born. . . . The reefs did it to him. A mutation."

She blanched.

"That's impossible—" Burnell Natasa snapped.

"No, it's not," she said faintly.

"You only have to tweak a couple of genes in the right DNA codestrings to make the difference between a"—*a freak and a deadhead*—"a Hydran and a Human," I said. "I'm a half-breed. If it wasn't true, I wouldn't be here."

He stared at me like I'd suddenly started speaking a different language. I ran the words back through my head, to make sure I hadn't said them in Hydran.

They looked at each other while the implications settled on them as silently and inevitably as dreamfall.

Slowly, almost painfully, Ling Natasa reached out to take her husband's hand. She looked back at me. "The accident . . . the reefs . . . damaged Joby before he was born. And now you're telling me the reefs have a way to . . . to heal him?" She shook her head as she asked, as though she didn't want to hear the answer. "It sounds like you're talking about—God. . . ."

"No," I said softly. "I'm talking about something *alien*. Tau thinks you can just go in there and take the reefs apart, read what you find there like binary code . . . but Humans didn't make it. Humans don't understand it. A work gang nearly blew itself up today because they missed a volatile pocket—"

"When?" Ling Natasa demanded.

"On my way here."

They glanced at each other again. "How could you know that?" she asked.

I told her. "How many 'accidents' are there in a place like this, from year to year? How many people die?" I didn't get an answer. I didn't need one; I saw the truth in their faces. "The Feds are sending another inspection team to Refuge—"

Their faces froze like they already knew. "They aren't coming to this installation again," Ling Natasa said, too quickly. "They're not even stopping here."

"You could still contact them. You know what Tau's negligence did to you . . . to Joby." I struggled to keep the desperation out of my voice. "Keiretsu is supposed to mean *family*. Family is . . . is about real people protecting each other, about your loyalty to the ones you love, not your duty to some ideology. Governments change their policies like you change the security codes. Relationships between people have to mean more than that. Don't they?"

Burnell Natasa shook his head. "No. Tau takes care of us—they take care of Joby. If we turn on them, we'll have nothing. No matter what happened to Tau, we'd lose. We can't." He glanced at his wife again. Her hands were clenched in her lap so hard that the knuckles were white, but she didn't say anything. The seconds dripped like tears.

"Then are you going to tell Tau about the monastery—that the untouched reefs on the Hydran Homeland are hiding some kind of miracle cure?"

"It's our duty," Ling Natasa said tonelessly. "And . . . maybe that—miracle is our only hope for Joby."

"What if Tau destroys the thing you're looking for? They don't understand half of what they find as it is. They would've ripped that reef apart a century ago if they did."

"What other choice do we have?" Burnell Natasa asked sourly.

I wondered whether it was actually that hard to imagine or whether his mind was really as much of a cypher as it seemed to me. "You could try working with the Hydrans, instead of raping their world. They knew what that place does . . . that's why they built a monastery there."

Ling Natasa opened her mouth, but nothing came out of it. She closed it again, her face colorless. She held the holo of Joby gently in her hands. Her husband shook his head, gazing at the image. *Never happen,* their faces said, filling with grief and resignation. *Impossible.* As impossible as that their son had actually walked and talked freely. As impossible as that he'd ever do it again.

Tau had no trouble seeing the Hydrans as less than Human—dangerous and inscrutable—because they were so much like Humans that the differences were obvious. The cloud-whales, and the by-products of their sentience, were so far off the scale of Human experience that Humans had no reference point to use in judging them. Tau's researchers were like blind men, each of them touching a different part of the unknown, none of them able to grasp the full implications of what they held in their hands.

The room was hot, or maybe it was the fever burning inside me. I wiped my face, trying to concentrate. "I told you . . . everything. . . ." The words sounded slow and thick, and in the middle of the sentence I forgot what I was trying to say. I shook my head.

"Are you all right?" Ling Natasa asked. Small lines formed between her eyebrows as she frowned.

I laughed, sure that must be some kind of twisted joke. "I told you everything I know," I repeated, trying to get all the way through the sentence this time. "I have to get back to work. They're waiting for me." Hardly daring to hope this could be the end of it. I still wasn't sure why they weren't treating me the way Perrymeade had. They had as much right to. Maybe they'd just been waiting until I'd told them what they wanted to know. I began to get up, not really believing I'd reach the door before someone stopped me.

I never even made it to my feet. My legs buckled as I put weight on them and suddenly I was down on my knees. I pulled myself up again, feeling a kind of disbelief.

Ling Natasa was in front of me when I turned around, raising her hand. I tried to dodge, but Burnell Natasa's hand gripped my arm hard, holding me there.

She lifted her hand to my face, and I flinched. But she only touched my forehead. Her palm was cool and dry. She pulled her hand away again as if I'd burned her. I jerked like a trapped animal as she pulled open my stained coveralls with the steady matter-of-factness of a researcher, or maybe the mother of a damaged child. Her husband's hold on me tightened until I swore, not sure where I hurt more, as she bared the wound. I heard him mutter something that sounded like a curse, heard her indrawn breath.

"Don't," I mumbled, feeling my bare flesh crawl. "Oh, shit—" Not sure whether the sight of the wound or what I was afraid she was going to do next made me say it.

Ling Natasa drew my coveralls together over the wound again, hiding it. Burnell Natasa gave me a rough shake, still holding on to my arm. "Damn it," he said, like he thought I was losing it, "we're not trying to hurt you—" hurting me anyway.

"Then why'm I here?" I said thickly.

They didn't answer that. "Did you get that burn here at the installation?" he demanded.

I shook my head. "Borosage. . . ." I felt more than saw them look at each other, with something in the look passing between them that they didn't bother to explain to me.

"Get him to the infirmary," Ling Natasa murmured to her husband. "Before he goes into septic shock." She glanced at me again. I almost thought there was apology in her eyes, but maybe it was only loss, and not even meant for me. She disappeared through the virtual green, and I didn't see her again.

TWENTY-EIGHT

BURNELL NATASA ESCORTED me to the infirmary himself. He had to hold me up more than once along the way, because my knees kept giving out.

The med techs stared as he brought me in, like the end of the world would have been easier for them to believe than the sight of the Chief of Security dropping off a sick bondie.

"See that his injury is properly treated," was all Natasa said. He left me in a chair.

They treated my burn without comment, without any surprise. Maybe they saw a lot of them. I lay back and let it happen, thinking about things I could have said to Natasa before he left, not sure if I was glad or sorry that I hadn't said anything.

I was still dozing, half awake under the regeneration lamp, when two crew bosses came into the infirmary. They headed directly toward me. I pushed up onto my elbows and watched them, suddenly wary. One of them was the foreman of the crew I'd warned earlier about the volatile pocket. The other one was Feng, my own crew boss.

"Him—?" Feng asked, gesturing at me.

"Yeah, that's the one." The other foreman nodded. "The freak. How'd you get a freak on your crew?"

I stiffened, wondering whether somehow I'd been wrong about the volatile pocket. Which meant that I could be in trouble all over again.

"He's new. Maybe it's an experiment. Nobody tells me any-

thing." Feng shrugged, glancing at me without really seeing me.
He wasn't a sadist, but he wasn't a nice guy, either. I didn't like
the thought of being on his shit list. "Ixpa says he's good with the
field suit." Ixpa was the head phase-field technician. Feng looked
directly at me, finally. "Did you tell Rosenblum, here, they were
going to hit a volatile pocket this shift?"

I nodded.

"We checked it out. You were right," Rosenblum said. "How
did you know that?"

"I sensed it." I lay down again, weak with sudden relief. "I can
sense the reefs—" I broke off, seeing how they looked at me and
then looked at each other. It hadn't sounded strange to me until I
saw how strange it sounded to them.

"What are you doing here?" Rosenblum asked me, finally. I
figured she meant at the installation, not in the infirmary.

"Penance," I said.

Feng's face hardened. "I don't like smartasses any better than
I like freaks. Answer her."

"I don't know," I muttered, looking down. I couldn't even
think of a way to explain the truth to two Humans already looking
at me the way these two were.

They stood a minute longer, scratching an ear, shifting from
foot to foot. Then Rosenblum shrugged. "Doesn't matter, anyway. From now on, you're our canary in the mine shaft, kid. You
do special rounds every day; you go from one excavation face to
another. You 'feel' them, or whatever the hell it is you do. You
make sure they're safe to work on."

I wondered what the hell a canary was; if it was anything like
a mebtaku. "Okay," I said. The more people there were here who
had an interest in keeping me alive, the better.

"You think the vips will clear that?" Feng said skeptically.
"Letting a freak wander all over the complex?"

"He's our freak," Rosenblum said, and laughed. She tapped
the bond tag on my wrist. "Besides, Natasa already ordered it."

"The Chief of Security—?"

Rosenblum shook her head. "His wife. She came and asked
me about what the freak did today."

Feng whistled between his teeth. "When's this one getting out
of here?" he called to a med tech.

"Tonight," someone answered.

"You can start your rounds tomorrow, then," Feng said to me.
"I'll get it set up." He turned away, his attention already back on
Rosenblum. Neither of them asked what was wrong with me.
Maybe they'd heard; maybe they didn't care. They headed for the
door and went out. Neither one of them had thanked me for sav-
ing lives today.

But maybe Ling Natasa had.

After that I spent my days going from excavation site to excavation site, wading into newly exposed reef-face to listen, feel,
sense the alien moods of the dreamfall; second-guessing the
spectrographic and biochem analyses, the dozens of different
readings each team had taken on its own. Once in a while I
walked into a pocket of something bad; once in a while I discovered something good, something so off-center that the equipment
hadn't been able to interpret it. Nothing big—nothing as obvious
as the thing I'd caught on the way to Natasa's office.

No one seemed to mind, as long as it meant they were a little
safer. I was glad to learn that anomalies big enough to blow an
entire work team to hell didn't get ignored often, even by overworked, undermanned crews under constant pressure to produce
profit miracles.

I pulled a lot of extra shifts to keep up with the work schedules. But I didn't mind working extra shifts: it was more time
spent in the womb of the cloud-whales' thoughts, the world I'd
shared with Miya, the world that only Hydrans could really experience. . . . It was less time I had to spend with Humans, who saw
the reefs as component parts, nothing more—chemical by-
products to be broken down and used. They felt no sense of awe,
no alien presence—the true nature of the reefs was as intangible
to them as they were becoming to me. I spent all of every day
with the reef whispering inside my head, but when I stepped out
again into the real world filled with Human faces and Human
minds, my mind went stone dead and the filaments of my psi
shriveled up like something blighted by frost.

I ate because I had to and slept because I had to; beyond that
the world outside the reef slowly disappeared. I lay in my bunk,
haunted by the images I'd carried back from the day's work, let-

ting them bleed into sweet memories of Miya—memories I
didn't let myself touch when I was sounding the reefs, where concentration was everything. Dreamfall filled my head with an alien
sea that drowned the presence of Human voices.

The others stepped aside when I moved past them, looking at me
like they were the ones who saw a ghost. I only spoke when I had
to, and that wasn't often, because they didn't have anything that I
needed anymore. Everything I needed I found inside the reef.

Until the day when I was working Blue Team's reef-face. Moving
through the changing densities and fragile interfaces more easily
than I'd ever navigated in cyberspace, I suddenly found a death
trap. A thing that tasted like acid, smelled like poison, felt like
stepping on my own grave . . .

"Canary! Come out now." The distorted, disembodied voice of
Ixpa, the tech I worked with, burst on my ears before I could even
report the anomaly.

I touched the speaker plate inside my helmet with my chin.
"What—?" I said thickly, wondering if I was hearing things.

"Out," she repeated.

"No. Found something. It's big, it stinks. Got to go deeper—"

"Out, now, bondie!" someone said. Someone else: Ixpa never
called me anything but "Canary," after Feng assigned me to her.
Her little death bird, she'd said when I'd asked, and grinned like
that was supposed to be funny.

I swore as a sudden power surge through my suit sent pain jag-
ging up my spine. It was the first punishing shock I'd gotten since
the day I'd put a suit on. "Shit! Ixpa—" I shouted.

Another shock answered me, strong enough to make my teeth
hurt. I swore again and let her reel me in.

I stumbled out of the reef-face into the blinding emptiness of
the complex, blinking. "Dammit," I mumbled, searching for
Ixpa's face, her uniform, in the group of what looked like officials
waiting outside. "Why—?" I broke off.

It wasn't Ixpa standing there in a tech's datapatches; it was
somebody I'd never seen before. And standing beside him was
Protz, looking frantic. I'd never imagined his face could look that
animated. He was flanked by guards, and Natasa wasn't in sight.
"Get the suit off," Protz said.

"What?" I shook my head.

"Now," he said. The guards raised their weapons.

"Where's Ixpa?" I asked the tech. "I found a volatile—"

"Shut up and take off the suit," the tech said.

I shut up and took off the suit.

"Carefully, dammit!" Protz snapped. "Those cost a fortune." I put the suit in its container, carefully.

Protz gestured, and one of the guards took hold of me.

"What's happening?" I said, but they didn't answer. "What is it?" I shouted at the tech, feeling my sense of reality slip further as they pulled me away. He only shrugged, watching me go.

Protz and the guards forced me to take a tram ride that ended in a hike through more corridors in what looked like a storage annex. At last we stopped in front of a closed, windowless door. Whatever was behind it was listed in a coded display I couldn't read.

Protz kept looking over his shoulder. One of the guards put a hand on the door lock; the door slid open. I stared into total darkness; before I could react, someone shoved me through. I turned around just in time to see Protz point a stungun at me. He fired.

And then everything went black.

Everything stayed that way for a long time. When I came to, the room was still totally dark. Panic caught in my chest as I realized I didn't even know if I was still where they'd left me. Crawling, groping, I found what felt like the door. My hands were still numb and heavy with stunshock, like my brain.

I pulled myself up and beat my fists against the panel. The sound echoed back at me. When it faded the silence was total again, like the darkness. Not even a crack of light outlined the door frame. No sound reached me from the other side. Probably no sound I made reached beyond these walls, either.

I felt my way around the edge of the door, searching for a touchplate that might let me out, or at least give me some light. The walls near the door frame were seamless ceralloy, slick and cold, like ice. There was no touchplate, no motion sensor.

"Lights on—?" I said finally, not expecting any better luck trying the obvious.

Light flared around me. I was inside a space about ten meters by twenty, full of storage lockers and equipment I didn't recognize. I wasn't sure if I felt more relieved or stupid. The unheated air made me shiver, but at least it was fresh. They hadn't left me here to suffocate, then, and probably not to freeze to death. I leaned against the cold wall, trying to imagine what the point of this was.

Why would Protz come here? Had someone heard Natasa hadn't killed me after all, and sent Protz to take care of it? But Protz—? That didn't make any sense. Protz was a career asskisser. I could hardly believe he'd had the guts to stun-shoot me.

"Oh, fuck—" My hands knotted as I suddenly realized what would make sense: *Protz had come here with the FTA special investigators.* Natasa had said they weren't coming back here. But these weren't just any Feds. What if they'd been smart enough to change their itinerary without warning? Protz would have to bring them here . . . and Protz would have to shut me up, make sure I couldn't get to anyone and they couldn't get to me.

I sat down on the floor, hugging my knees, holding my body together. My nerve endings still felt like stir-fry. I had no sense of how much time had passed. For all I knew, the Feds had been here and gone already. The Natasas must have kept their mouths shut, too afraid for Joby's safety to risk losing Tau's support. I wouldn't be trapped here without the cooperation of Natasa's guards.

A deep shudder ran through the floor I was sitting on. Around me, the heavy machinery began to rattle and sing. The lights flickered, dimmed, and went out; something big crashed to the floor about two meters away. I struggled to my feet, shouting for help. My voice rang back at me from half a hundred surfaces as I flattened myself against the wall in the utter blackness.

The lights came back on—stayed on, dimmer than before. "What the hell is going on!" I shouted. Only echoes answered me. There were no more tremors, no more things falling—no sound beyond my own ragged breathing.

I swore softly, keeping myself company as I paced off the narrow space between the sealed door and the piece of equipment that had crashed down into the middle of the storeroom, blocking it off. *An explosion.* It would take an explosion—a big one—to explain everything I'd just experienced.

I wondered, with a sudden, sick prescience, if it was the anomaly I'd found in the reef-face just before Protz forced me out . . . what that meant for everybody involved, and especially what it would mean for me. And then I wondered how long it would take before somebody remembered that I was locked up in here.

I slid down the wall again and began the wait.

It probably wasn't as long as it seemed like before somebody opened the door. I was on my feet at the first trace of sound, blinking the sudden glare out of my eyes.

I don't know what I'd expected, but it wasn't Burnell Natasa, alone, his hands empty, his face and uniform smeared with something indescribable.

He swore as he saw me, but I only saw relief in his eyes. "Come on," he snapped, nodding his head at the hall behind him. "I need you."

"Yes, sir," I mumbled, automatically dropping my gaze.

He gave me a surprised look, as if he'd been expecting me to react like a Human being. Like he'd forgotten where I'd been since the last time he saw me. "Please," he said, awkwardly. "Cat."

I followed him out of the storeroom and down the hall. "What is it?" I asked. "What happened?"

"There was an explosion." He kept walking, looking as grim as death now.

"In Reef Sector 3F. Blue Team was working the face—they hit a volatile pocket. A big one."

He stopped short and turned to stare at me. "How did you know that—?"

"I found it just before Protz put me away. The Feds are here, aren't they?"

He began to walk again, faster. I had to push myself to keep up. "The Feds were right there when it blew," he said. "So was my wife."

"God," I breathed. "Are they—"

"I don't know," he said heavily. "No one knows. The work area is inaccessible. Whatever happened sent some kind of massive feedback through our power grid. All our basic life support is running on emergency generators. But the whole fucking infrastructure is fried. All our equipment is off-line: everything's got to be reprogrammed before any readings we take will mean anything. We can't locate any survivors until we get our systems up again. God knows how long that will take. That's why I need you."

I shook my head, not understanding.

He caught hold of me, jerking me around. "Because you're a—"
Freak. He ate the word, grimacing. "A telepath. A psion. You
know why, dammit! You can find her . . . them—" He broke off
again. "I want you to save my wife."

"I can't . . . I can't do that anymore." My own voice fell apart
as I saw the desperation in his eyes. "There's nothing left inside
me. You need a real psion. You need Miya—"

"I don't have Miya! You don't! You were at that monastery too.
Janos told me it affected you: you were still helping Joby on the
flight back. There's something left of it in Joby; there's got to be
something left in you!" He shook me, like he could shake my psi
loose. "My wife saw it—the way you could read the reefs."

"That's different. I—"

"She trusted you—God knows why, after all the grief you've
caused us. She made me trust you. Now you can pay her back,
freak, or you can die trying—" Suddenly his gun was in his hand,
pointing at me. His hand shook.

I looked at the gun. I looked back at him. I stood, silent and
unmoving, until finally the hand holding the stungun dropped,
and his gaze with it. "I'm sorry," he muttered. He looked at the
gun like he didn't know what the hell he'd been doing, like a man
who'd been hit too many times in a fight. He put the gun away.

I rubbed my face. "I'll try," I murmured. "That's all I meant. I'll
do anything I can. I just don't know if I can do anything." I looked
up at him. "If somebody hadn't put a gun to my head once before, I
might still be a telepath." I started on, and this time he followed me.

We reached the tram stop, and a tram was waiting there to take
us back through the complex. He didn't say anything during the
ride. He never asked me how I'd ended up where he found me. He
probably knew exactly how I'd gotten there. I couldn't imagine
how knowing that must make him feel.

I let him take the lead again until we arrived at the site where
I'd been working . . . what was left of it. An entire section of the
reinforced corridor leading to the face they'd been excavating had
collapsed. Crews were already working to clear away the debris,
but I could tell from the curses and arguing that whatever had
crashed the programming of the entire installation must have
lobotomized their equipment all down the line.

"Protz . . ." I breathed. He was standing in the open space beyond the dust-fogged sea of Tau workers, talking to some officials, gesturing at the smoking wall of debris. I pushed my way toward him. "Protz!" I shouted, saw him look up, saw the look on his face as he recognized me.

Someone caught my arm just before I reached him, hauling me around: Feng, my old crew boss. "What the hell are you doing here?" he demanded. "Where the hell have you been?"

I stared at him. "Locked in a closet."

"What?" His face hardened. "You were supposed to be in there. You were supposed to keep this from happening, for God's sake!"

"Ask him." I jerked loose from Feng's grip, pointing at Protz. The vips around Protz looked up. "Ask him!" I shouted.

Natasa caught up to me again, waved Feng off as the vips started toward us. Protz stayed where he was. I saw him wipe his face as he watched them cross the room.

"What's this about?" It was Sandusky, the installation's Chief of Ops. I remembered him from the tour I'd taken with the first group of Feds. He looked at Natasa, and then at Feng, before he looked at me without a twitch of recognition. "Why weren't you at your duty station?"

I opened my mouth—froze, as I tried to think of how to make them believe me, or even a way to explain it.

"Protz ordered him taken away from his work, just as he found the anomaly—" Natasa broke in, like he'd realized the same thing. "Suarez and Timebu will verify that they were told to take him away and isolate him where the Feds wouldn't find him."

"Why?" some other vip asked incredulously.

Natasa took a deep breath. "You'd have to ask Protz about that, sir." He glanced at me, his mouth a tight line, his eyes telling me to keep on keeping my own mouth shut.

I watched them turn away, like they really intended to do just that; saw panic begin to show on Protz's face.

"All right," Natasa said to me. "What do you need to do this?"

To use my psi. It took me a minute just to realize what he meant. I looked out across the sea of noise and chaos, seeing nothing but Humans, no different from their useless machines when I tried to see them with my mind's eye.

I forced myself to look at them with clearer eyes than I had anytime since I'd come to this place, shell-shocked with loss, and begun to lose myself in the reefs. I watched them struggling, arguing, trying desperately to rescue friends and strangers who might not even be alive. And then I tried to close them out of my mind, so I could do what I had to do to help them: reach into the void, move through the trackless darkness, and find a distant star of consciousness . . . touch another Human mind.

And then I finally understood why my Gift had been stone dead ever since I'd come here, even though it had been easy for Miya to reach into my mind and into my heart. It was nothing as simple as guilt or fear that kept me from using my psi . . . it was them. The Humans, the Others—the deadheads who'd abandoned me, sold me out, given me up, and let me down, fucked me over again and again. The few of them I'd known who'd ever been decent or kind to me, decent or kind at all . . . their humanity had only made them easy victims too.

The Hydran in me would always need to feel alive, connected, so desperate for it that there'd always be a part of me that would give anything, suffer anything, to have my Gift back again.

But Miya had been right when she'd said the Human in me could never really trust another Human being, not even the Human part of me—the thing that had forced me to go on living when I had no right to, or any reason. . . .

I looked up and Natasa was speaking again, probably telling me to answer his question.

"I can't," I muttered, shaking my head. "Not here. Not like this."

"Then where?" he said impatiently. "What do you need?"

For everything to have been different. I looked at him, through him, with my mind as empty as a dead man's. "A phase suit," I said finally. "I have to go into the reef."

"The equipment's scrambled—" he said, his patience slipping another notch.

"You mean even the suits don't work?"

He shook his head. "They should be functional—but there's no way you can interface with the techs; no way they can get a reading off you. There'd be no one to guide you or pull you out of trouble."

"I don't need a tech. I need—" I looked toward the ruins of Human technology and alien dreamfall joined like lovers in a suicide pact. "That. I need to be inside." *Need to be somewhere I want to be.*

He looked at me, his face caught between expressions, like suddenly he wasn't sure if I was just a freak or actually insane. "All right," he said finally, like he'd decided it didn't matter either way. "I'll get you one. Stay here." He held his hands up, as if he was putting a spell on me so that I didn't disappear.

I waited, watching the vips surround Protz again, not able to hear what they were saying, not able to read their minds. I didn't know where keiretsu had the strongest hold here: Would the installation's officials turn on Protz because he'd caused this disaster, or would they try to bury their mistakes? I hoped Natasa got back before they made up their minds.

Natasa returned with a phase suit, as good as his word. He looked relieved to see me still waiting there, as good as mine. I put the suit on. He went with me as far as the wall of rubble, running interference for me with anybody who tried to get in my way. As we stood in front of the fallen debris he put his hand on my arm, making me turn back. He hesitated, then let me go again without saying anything. He nodded toward the wall and backed away.

I took a deep breath, putting his expression and the world it belonged to behind me as I faced the mass of debris. I ordered the suit on-line, saw the displays materialize in front of my eyes—a meaningless jumble of random shapes. For a minute I thought I'd forgotten how to read.

No. It's the suit. My confidence caught on a jagged shard of doubt as I realized even the suit's internal systems were scrambled. But Natasa claimed its ability to phase was intact, that only its link to the support system was down. I hoped he knew what he was talking about.

I put out my hand, watched it shimmer as I phased it through the surface of the rubble. Just touching the material of the reef sent an electric surge up my arm, straight into my brain.

I glanced back a final time. The space behind me had gotten unnaturally quiet. Every face I could see was looking at me, expectant, waiting.

I entered the land of broken dreams.

The flesh and bone of organic and inorganic materials closed around me. The silence here was genuine, not the silence of held breath; the pressure was real, not the weight of someone else's hopes or fears. I moved deeper into the matrix, feeling my way slowly, because finding a path through this jumble of chaos and order was different from any reef work I'd done. I'd begun to take the wild unpredictability of the reef matrix for granted . . . begun to wear the field suit like a second skin. There was a kind of freedom to never knowing what you'd find next, as pure in its way as the rapture that took me sometimes when I encountered enigmas that spoke to me in a voice no one else would ever hear.

But this time the way to the unknown was roadblocked by barriers of shattered ceralloy and composite, barred with molysteel—inorganic materials so dense that they were beyond the phase range of my suit, impenetrable even for me. It was hard to believe they'd been fragmented by an explosion no bigger than this one; that the explosion hadn't turned the whole complex into a smoking crater. Unless the construction materials used to build the installation hadn't been up to specs, had been flawed to begin with . . . had been one more suicidal mistake that Tau had taken for a good idea.

I worked my way up to a fractured slab of ceiling, kicked off like a swimmer into the shimmering jelly of pulverized cloud-reef until I'd risen past it. I stopped moving again, drifting deeper into the matrix, letting its silence and strength surround me, shield me from the world I'd left behind. The reef's presence had been rattling against my brain like pebbles against a windowpane since the moment I'd touched its face. Now, finally, I was secure enough to open all the windows into my mind. I let my body go slack—emptying my mind of every thought I'd carried with me into the matrix, until there was only sensation. . . .

The silence was filled with light. I smelled music with every breath; my eyes saw the transcendent radiance of unimaginable wavelengths as all my senses flowed out into the matrix of the reef.

It would have been easy to lose my self then, let even the itching sand-grain of someone else's desperation that had driven me to this fade away. With an effort of will I stopped the bleeding of my consciousness and forced myself to remember who really counted on the outcome of what I did here:

Joby. . . . Joby would lose his mother if I lost my way. The investigators Isplanasky had sent to dig out the rot beneath Tau's lies would never have the chance to tell anyone what they'd found. And I'd never sleep again, if I thought my own prejudice and bitterness had kept me from finding any survivors.

If there were any survivors. I cast the net of my psi out in a slow scan, feeling my sense of control grow as I searched the metaphorical darkened room for the faintest gleam of a Human thought. But this darkened room was in a madhouse, where nothing met anything else at the expected angle, where stairways of complex hydrocarbons led to impenetrable ceilings of ceralloy, doorways opened onto nothingness or walls: a death trap of illusions for any searcher who let his attention wander too far.

But as I worked my way deeper, old memories stirred, memories of the time when I'd been a real telepath—*when I'd been good, one of the best*— If anybody could find them, I could. If there were any survivors still alive, they had to be here somewhere . . . somewhere. . . . *There.*

I caught the quicksilver flash of a mind radiating pain. I lunged after it as the contact slipped away, followed it back through a storm wrack of alien sensation, not letting go because I couldn't afford to lose it now, not when I was so close—

There. Contact charged my senses, sent my psi link arcing from the core of my mind to another . . . another . . . another: *terror, pain, grief*—

Three. Only three—? How many people had gone in here? A lot more than three. I didn't know the feel of any of these minds, had never been inside them, couldn't tell whether they belonged to anyone I'd ever met because there wasn't a coherent thought in any of them. Raw emotion was screaming through my brain, and all it told me was that they were running out of time.

I didn't try to contact them telepathically, knowing they'd only panic. I clung to the fragile thread of thought that linked me to their location, while my mind backtracked through the maze of jumbled reef strata to complete the circuit, contacting a mind on the outside that would anchor me and let me reel myself in.

I found Natasa, maybe because he was standing the closest, maybe because he was the only one who'd wanted me to find him. I felt him recoil as if the contact had been physical. Following the compass of his shock, I retraced my path through the techno-organic maze until I fell through into the open again.

Natasa caught me and steadied me as the suit deactivated. He was still in my head, not by choice, breaking the reef's spell, demanding answers (—*found them?*) he was asking. "You found them—?"

(*Found them, found them, found . . .*) I shook my head, trying to clear out the echoes; held up my hands, nodding frantically, as I saw the look on his face. I loosened my helmet and pulled it off. "Survivors. Only three."

"Three?" he repeated. "Three? Dammit, twenty-seven people went in there!"

I looked down, grimacing.

"My . . . my wife—?"

"I don't know," I murmured. "I couldn't—" I broke off, feeling frustration crush his grief into anger. I cut the contact between us, shutting him out of my mind. "Are you saying, if your wife is dead, then you don't care if anybody trapped in there survives?"

He blinked, and the kind of anger on his face changed. "No," he said. "No, of course not. How far in are they—"

"Just a minute," someone said behind him. The officials who'd been talking to Protz when I went in gathered around us. Protz was still with them. "What about the FTA's people? Are they all dead?"

I didn't have to be a mind reader to know what they were really asking. If the Feds had been killed in the explosion, it was going to look bad for Tau . . . but they might still be able to cover it up. If the Feds were alive, there was no hope of burying any of their mistakes, not the big ones, not the small ones. "I don't know who survived," I said, trying to keep my voice even. "I only know there are people in there who are still alive."

"How can you be certain?" one of the officials snapped.

"He knows," Natasa said, his voice hardening with suspicion. "He's a telepath." A crowd was gathering around us, more guards and workers waiting for orders.

"He's crippled, dammit!" Protz said. "He's not a mind reader."

"He can read the reefs," Ixpa said. I turned, surprised to see her pushing through the crowd. "We never had anyone here who could do that before him. Why the hell did you pull him out of there just as he detected that anomaly?" There were murmurs from the workers gathering around us, but I couldn't tell what their mood was. Ixpa looked away from Protz, like she didn't really expect an answer. "How do you want us to proceed, sir?" She aimed the question at Sandusky, including me with a nod of her head.

"We're doing everything we can." Sandusky gestured like he was brushing aside smoke. "There's no more we can do until the equipment is back on-line." He glanced over his shoulder at the crews still trying to clear away debris with equipment that only did what they expected it to about a third of the time. "That will take hours."

"I don't think you have hours, Sandusky," I said.

He looked at me with no recognition, only a kind of disbelief, like I'd forgotten what I was, to be speaking to him like that.

I turned back to Ixpa. "Can I take any equipment with me when I'm wearing a phase suit?"

"What kind?" she asked, looking dubious.

"Other phase suits—three of them."

"Well . . . yeah," she said. Understanding lit up her face. "Yeah, I don't see why not. You think you could actually reach them? Lead them out—?"

I shrugged. "I want to try."

Ixpa signaled to one of the workers standing behind her. "Get me some more phase suits."

"Wait a minute—" Sandusky said, frowning. "You can't do that."

All around me surprised faces turned to stare at him. "Why not?" Ixpa said. "It could work."

Sandusky pursed his lips. He looked like he was barefoot on a hot plate. "It's too dangerous. I don't want to risk losing another life in there—" He pointed at the rubble, trying to look like he really gave a shit if I lived or died.

"I volunteered," I said. "I'm willing to risk it. I can reach them."

"We don't know if it's our people who survived," Protz protested. "We only have this half-breed's word that anyone is alive in there at all."

Sandusky glanced at Protz, his mouth working.

"Excuse me, sir," Natasa said. "Is he saying that if the survivors are Feds we should let them die, for the good of the keiretsu? That just because we're not sure who it is, we have to let them die—?"

The muttering around us got louder. "My wife is in there, sir," Natasa said. "I don't know if she's dead or alive. But it's not keiretsu to bury our own people just because they might be outsiders . . . and the outsiders might know too much. The keiretsu is family."

Sandusky's face reddened. He glanced at Protz again, looked away as workers arrived carrying the phase suits Ixpa had sent for. Ixpa handed me my helmet. I put it on. She passed me the other suits, one at a time.

"Carry them as close to your body as you can," Ixpa said. "That should keep them in synch with your own phase field." She bent her head at the waiting matrix.

I started forward, carrying the extra suits, watching Sandusky and Protz from the corner of my eye. Their stares got darker as I reached the broken reef-face. But without my noticing it, without Natasa's saying a word, a phalanx of guards and workers had formed around me, protecting me from any interference: *Keiretsu.* I reached the barrier of broken dreams and stepped through.

I let the reef flow into my mind again. It was easier this time, because the anger I'd taken with me into the reef before was gone; easier because I knew that I could do what I had to.

As I let myself feel the reef, I realized that the shining trace of my contact with the survivors still existed, like a wormhole through space. Relieved and a little awed, I followed it to its end without stopping.

I burst through the matrix wall into the tiny vacuole where three survivors huddled under the accidental shelter of a panel of unbroken composite. I heard/felt the shock wave of their disbelief as they saw me emerge from the reef, impossibly, in front of them. They cringed and cowered like I was some manifestation of the disaster, come to finish what the explosion had started.

"I've come to get you out of here," I said, trying to choose the words that would pull them back to sanity the fastest. I couldn't tell how my voice sounded to them, whether the words were even intelligible. I held the suits up, letting them see what I had, while I searched their filthy, dazed faces for one I knew.

Ling Natasa wasn't there. I didn't recognize any of them . . . but one of them wore what had been an FTA uniform.

"Thank God. . . ." The Fed staggered to his feet, clutching an arm that was bent at an unnatural angle. His face was gray-white with pain under the dirt and blood. "How?" he mumbled. "Where—?"

I smiled. "Isplanasky sent me."

He gaped. The other two still crouched, staring at us like they'd been put in stasis. "Come on," I said softly. "I've got phase suits for you. I'll lead you out."

Isplanasky's man took a suit and began to put it on, while I got the woman wearing a vacant stare and a guard's datapatches into the second suit. Together we got the third survivor suited up—a bondie with a gouge in his face that had probably taken out one of his eyes. He wasn't any older than I was. I tried not to look at his face; tried not to see what else they'd been looking at all the while they'd been trapped here: a foot, an arm, protruding from the avalanche of rubble. I was standing in a pool of blood that didn't seem to have come from any of them. I swallowed down nausea, forcing myself to focus my psi for one last sweep, searching for any survivors I might have missed. There weren't any.

"These suits are malfunctioning," the Fed protested, as the oxygen processors began to clear out his lungs and his brain functions normalized. He was staring at the garbage readouts inside his helmet.

"It's all right," I said, trying to give my words the kind of assurance he needed to hear. "I'll lead you out. You only have to follow me."

"Your suit is on-line?" he demanded.

"Yeah," I said, not looking at him. "It's on-line. Let's go." I held out my hand again, and the Fed took it. He put out his hand in turn, taking hold of the bondie. The guard took the laborer's other hand. They pulled him forward, carefully, as I led them to the wall of rubble. He came with us, as witless as a drone, but at least he came.

I waded into the reef-face again, leading them after me one by one. Relief filled me as I found the mind-lit wormhole of my passage still waiting to guide us back through the matrix. It was hard enough to keep track of the others as they floundered after me, slowed by their injuries, by shock, by inexperience. I almost lost someone more than once as we blundered through nightmarish pockets of random density in what was for them mostly pitch-black effluvia. I had to remind myself that they couldn't sense what I sensed, each time I had to double back to keep one or another of them moving in the right direction.

I couldn't communicate with them now to guide or reassure

them; the suits' commlinks turned everything into unintelligible static. I was glad I didn't have to listen to what they were saying. I knew what they were feeling, and it was all I could do to keep myself moving through their nightmare toward the light. The journey in had been clear and easy; the journey out was by way of another universe, with a side trip through hell. My breath was coming in ragged gasps; I wasn't sure if it was my strength giving out or the suit. I only knew that if I didn't reach the other end of this mental rope soon, none of us was going to reach it.

And then, suddenly, we were through—I staggered out of the reef-face, dragging the Fed with me. The others came through behind him and dropped to the floor like stones. I fell on my knees, coughing convulsively, as workers and guards swarmed over us, stripping off our helmets and suits, leaving me defenseless against the mass of incoherent noise around us, the feedback inside my head—I covered my head with my arms, trying to shut it out.

Someone pulled me to my feet, pulled my hands away, asking, "Are you all right?"

I nodded blindly. He led me out of the crush of oversolicitous bodies. I opened my eyes again finally, to Natasa's face. Realizing, as I did, why I hadn't wanted to see it.

"You didn't find her," he whispered. It wasn't an accusation—wasn't even a question. His resignation pooled on the surface of a grief deeper than time. "She's gone."

I nodded, swallowing hard as I choked down his emotions. "The three I brought out . . . they were it." I bent my head in the direction of the survivors. "They were all."

"At least—" His voice broke. "At least she didn't suffer." He wiped his face with the palm of his hand, thinking, *(It was the living, the ones left behind, who suffered.* Joby. *His wife was gone, Miya was gone . . . good God, what was he going to do about Joby now?).*

I didn't know, and I didn't know what to say.

The others were catching up to us now. Natasa wiped at his eyes.

I turned to see the Fed I'd just rescued supported by a couple of med techs. I saw him glance away long enough to notice Natasa's red-rimmed eyes before he looked back at me. "I wanted to thank you—" he said, his voice hoarse with pain.

I nodded, only registering him with part of my attention, the rest still mired in Natasa's grief. I felt my mind beginning to close up, inexorably, like a fist.

"And I want to talk to you. Now."

"Sir," one of the techs holding him up said, "*now* we take you to the infirmary and make sure none of your injuries are life-threatening."

The Fed looked at her, exasperated, but he didn't argue. He glanced at Natasa. "This bondie better not have any unfortunate accidents before I'm up and around. You understand me?"

Natasa's dark eyes held his stare. "Perfectly," he said.

The Fed let the med techs lead him away; he looked back once, like he wanted to be certain that he remembered my face or that I hadn't already disappeared.

I stood beside Natasa, watching them go, through a silence that was as painful as it was long. Finally Natasa straightened his shoulders, as if he was trying to shrug off the weight of his grief. I couldn't feel his mind anymore; couldn't see in through his eyes. Nothing showed on his face now. I watched him take something off his equipment belt. He reached out and clamped it around my wrist.

I stiffened, starting to pull away, until I realized that it wasn't binders. There was a flash of light; a shock ran up my arm. When he took the thing away, I wasn't wearing a bond tag anymore. Instead there was only my own raw, flayed flesh in a band two fingers wide circling my wrist. "Your contract is canceled," Natasa said.

I looked at him, not sure whether the pain or the surprise I felt was more intense. Neither one of those came up to the knees of my disbelief. "You can do that—?" I whispered.

He shrugged, grimacing. "It wasn't a valid contract. You should never have been here in the first place."

I took a deep breath, let it out. "What happens now?"

His hand settled on his gun; his stare hit zero degrees Kelvin as he searched the crowd for Protz. "Now," he said, "the shit hits the fan." He subvocalized a call, and suddenly two guards were pushing through the confusion of bodies. Natasa gestured at me. "Take him to the infirmary. Stay with him."

"But I'm not—"

He gave me a look. "Get his arm cared for. Then find out where they put that injured Fed and put him in the next bed."

The guards nodded. One of them smiled. "No problem."

"How's Park?" Natasa asked. That had been the name on the datapatch of the guard I'd brought out.

"Meds say she'll be all right, sir."

"Good," Natasa murmured, nodding, but looking down.

"Namaste," I murmured. Natasa glanced at me, without understanding. As the guards led me away I looked back, watching Natasa's progress toward Protz. They were out of my line of sight before I could see it happen, but I smiled anyway.

TWENTY-NINE

BY THE TIME I was sharing a room with the Fed, he'd been sedated past caring. Any conversation with him was going to have to wait. At least I'd overheard enough to know that his name was Ronin, and that he was going to survive.

It was almost harder to believe I might actually survive this. I lay down on the empty bed, still cradling my sudoskin-covered wrist, glad enough to rest as fatigue unraveled what was left of my consciousness.

I opened my eyes again, startled out of sleep, only realizing then that I'd been asleep, probably for hours.

Luc Wauno was standing beside the bed, his hand still on my shoulder, shaking me awake. He held his hand up in silent warning as he saw my eyes open.

"Wauno?" I mumbled, sitting up. "Where the hell did you come from?"

He nodded at the other bed. Natasa stood beside it, helping Ronin to his feet. Ronin looked more stupefied than I did, probably from the meds he'd been given, but he was tracking and functional. Natasa looked worse than Ronin, as if he'd been fighting his grief for hours and losing the battle. "I don't like what I'm hearing upstairs," Natasa said. "I want you both safely out of reach until there's backup available." He handed Ronin his uniform jacket and pants and began to help him get into them.

As I got out of bed I glanced up at the security monitors. They were always on, everywhere, including here.

"We're running a playback loop—all anyone sees is the two of you sleeping," Natasa said, answering my look.

"Where are we going?" I asked, shaking cloud-dreams out of my head. "No place is safe—"

"I know a place that is," Wauno said, and his smile said, *Freaktown.*

I nodded, glancing at Ronin, at the databand on his wrist. "Leave that here."

He looked at me like I'd told him to leave one of his eyes.

"They can track you by it. If Tau decides to bury its mistakes, you won't be safe anywhere with that on."

A stunned-prey look filled his face. I saw doubt replace it, and finally acceptance. Slowly, reluctantly, he unlatched his databand; stood holding it in his hand like he was weighing it.

"He's right. It's the only way to be sure," Natasa said.

Ronin dropped the databand on his bed, grimacing. Natasa put an arm around him, supporting him as we went out of the room. Guards waited in the hallway to escort us through the installation's maze to the entrance.

Wauno's new transport was waiting right where the old one had, once before, on the landing plaza outside the complex's main entrance. There were clouds phasing across the face of the moon as I glanced up . . . or maybe they were something more, watching over us.

More guards were waiting by the transport. They gave us a thumbs-up and stepped aside. The hatch opened, and Wauno took over supporting Ronin to help him up the ramp.

I started after them; hesitated as I realized Natasa wasn't following. "What about you?" I asked.

He shook his head. "I'll be all right." He nodded at the guards flanking him.

"What if you're wrong?" I asked.

"Ronin has my testimony and data waiting for him. Wauno knows how to access it." He smiled sourly.

"What about Joby?"

His smile disappeared. "He'll be safe . . ." he said, and the words seemed to choke him. "He'll be with you." He went back through the line of guards toward the complex entrance.

I watched him go, speechless, until Wauno called my name, telling me to get on board.

I climbed the ramp, stood beside him while the hatch sealed behind me. Standing this close to him in the transport's dimly lit interior, I saw that he was wearing the medicine pouch. "Luc, I . . . I'm sorry," I muttered, looking away. "I never . . ."

He looked blank, until he realized what I was looking at. He touched the worn leather bag and shook his head. "It was there for you," he said quietly. "When you needed it. That's all."

I looked up at him in disbelief. "How did you know I would need it?"

"I didn't," he said with a slow smile. "It knew, I suppose. That's what it does. Believe it or not." He shrugged, looking up at me again. "I know what happened when we crashed," he said. "It wasn't your fault." He took his place in the pilot's seat.

I swallowed a lot of useless words and turned away to find a seat for myself. Ronin was already strapped in. Sitting behind him was Perrymeade, holding Joby in his lap.

I stopped moving. "What do you want? You two-faced son of a—"

"Cat!" Suddenly Kissindre stood up from the seat behind theirs. "Shut up and listen to me." I was already gaping, speechless, as she came forward, moving carefully as the transport began to lift. I could see the pale line of a fading scar on her cheek. But she was moving all right, not maimed, not crippled. I sank into the seat across from Ronin like my brain had shorted out.

"I know the transport accident wasn't your fault," she said as I looked away from her eyes. "Uncle Janos knew that too."

I raised my head. "Then . . . why—?" I held up my bandaged wrist, looking at him. "Why did he do this to me?" My hands made a fist, and started to tremble.

Her fingers barely touched the sudoskin on my wrist. "To buy you time, until the FTA could send more investigators. To keep Borosage from killing you."

I opened my mouth.

"Do you think you'd be alive now if my uncle had left you with Tau's Corporate Security?"

"No," I whispered. Finally I looked at Perrymeade again. "I really thought you hated my guts," I said. "I really thought you meant it."

"Maybe I did, just then," Perrymeade said. I almost imagined I saw a ghost of a smile. "But if I hadn't, Borosage would never have believed me."

"Maybe I deserved it," I murmured, glancing away.

"Maybe you were right in everything you did, too."

I didn't answer; couldn't even look back at him. The unreality of where I was now, the total unexpectedness of what these people had done, for me and against the system of lies, was almost more than I could deal with.

When I looked up again at last, it was to look at Joby, sitting motionless in Perrymeade's arms. His eyes were on my face, staring at me as fixedly as the eyes of a doll, until I was sure it wasn't random. "Joby . . . ?" I said softly. He blinked. But he didn't move, didn't speak. I looked away again, sick at heart, wondering if this wasn't worse somehow than the way he'd been before. "Why is he here? It could be dangerous—"

"Not as dangerous as leaving him where Tau could find him," Perrymeade said grimly. I remembered then what Natasa had said to me. I glanced at Joby again long enough to see that he wasn't wearing a databand either.

I rubbed my wrist, feeling the sudoskin loosen at the edges as my ragged nails caught on it. I forced my hand away, wondering if the day would ever come when I felt secure enough in who I was and where I was to stop doing that. However long it took, it was going to take even longer now. "All right, then," I said. "Why are you two here?" I nodded at Kissindre and Perrymeade.

"Adding links to the chain of truth, I hope," Perrymeade answered. "I've been cooperating with the FTA ever since I learned you'd contacted them."

"How did you know that?" I asked, surprised.

"Hanjen. Even before Borosage let it slip, Hanjen had contacted me."

"How did he know that?"

"Miya told him," Kissindre said. "He told my uncle, after he'd agreed to help Tau find you. . . ." She looked away from my face and back again. "Borosage's men were everywhere on the Hydran side of the river, Cat. They forced their way into houses and destroyed people's belongings. They terrorized children in school; they took away patients from the hospital and jailed them without any cause. They embargoed food shipments—"

I shook my head, stunned as I realized that it really was Hanjen who had told Tau where we'd taken Joby; surrendered his own foster daughter to the Humans . . . betrayed us, to save his people. He'd been trapped between a rock and a hard place. But we'd put him there.

Perrymeade turned to Ronin, who'd been watching us with the rapt attention of a man caught up in a threedy psychodrama when he'd expected to see the Indy News.

"Mez Ronin," Perrymeade said, suddenly hesitant. "I . . . there are no words to say how sorry I am about . . . the deaths of your team members."

Ronin nodded wordlessly. The look of a disaster victim was still deep in his dark, up-slanting eyes; that look would be there a lot longer than the cuts and bruises on his face. His cropped black hair slid down across his face as he nodded; he didn't seem to notice. His hair, his eyes, reminded me of someone . . . the ta-Mings . . . *Jule,* whose face I hadn't seen for so long that it was getting hard to see her clearly in my mind. . . .

I pushed my own filthy hair out of my eyes for the tenth time since I'd got on board, and glanced at Kissindre. She wasn't looking at me now. I looked away again, thinking about Miya. Borosage's men had missed her at the monastery, but I didn't know what had happened during the time I'd been at the reef interface . . . whether she'd be waiting for me when I got to Freaktown, whether she was safe, whether she was still free—

". . . thank you," Ronin said to me. Kissindre nudged my arm, and I realized we'd been having a conversation I hadn't been listening to.

"For what?" I said.

He looked surprised. "For all you've risked, to bring the truth out."

I saw Jule in my mind's eye again as I looked at him. If it hadn't been for Jule, the feelings I'd had for her, I never would have met her aunt, Lady Elnear taMing, or Natan Isplanasky, who'd sent Ronin here. I never would have set foot on Refuge; I'd still be a half-breed street punk in Quarro's Oldcity, or else I'd be dead. None of this would have happened. But other things would have. Maybe they wouldn't have been any better. I shook my head; looked out the window at nothing disguised as night.

"All the risks," Ronin repeated. "Isplanasky told me about how he met you. . . ." He almost smiled. "And he said you sent him an illegal message about conditions here. He said your style hadn't changed much."

I managed a smile of my own, hoping I never had to tell him how I'd done it.

"And you're the one who found the survivors inside the reef."

I nodded again, the motion like a rictus, even though he hadn't really asked a question.

"You must have a lot to tell me. I've heard what Perrymeade has to say. I've got testimony from Natasa. But I want what you know, what you've seen, heard, *sensed*, every damn detail of it—" He held up his hand, palm out. I blinked as I saw a recorder implant staring at me like a misplaced eye.

"How many people were on your team?" I asked.

He looked startled, then stunned, and I was sorry I'd asked. "Four," he said faintly, like that one word held the mass of a planet. "Four. . . ."

He didn't have to tell me the others hadn't been strangers. Slowly he closed his hand, hiding the recorder. For a long minute he didn't say anything more, didn't ask anything more, as if all the false energy of painkillers and denial had gone out of him and left him lost and hurting. He was blinking too much when he looked up at me again; his face was set with anger. He opened his hand, waiting for me to speak.

I hesitated, not certain where to start. "You know . . . about Joby?" I asked, reaching out from my seat to hold Joby's hand. I thought the fingers twitched, like they were trying to close around mine. I glanced at Perrymeade and held out my arms. He hesitated, but then he passed Joby to me. I held him close, remembering the warm, breathing weight of his small body.

I moved his hands, slowly and gently, until his arms were around my neck. He held on, clinging to me without my help.

"Hi, Joby," I whispered, my throat tight. "Missed you. . . ." Not knowing whether he could hear me, let alone understand me. I tried to find my way into his thoughts, now that he was so close, but the inner space between our minds had its own geography, and neither one of us had a sense of direction.

"Perrymeade has told me his suspicions," Ronin said gently, almost hesitantly. "Is there more you can tell me?"

I glanced up, distracted, almost resenting the interruption. I forced myself to get past it and answer him. "I can tell you more than anyone knows," I said, and began at the beginning.

By the time I'd finished, Joby was lying asleep in my arms, and we were passing over the lighted grid of Tau Riverton. I never thought I'd be glad to see it again, and I wasn't. But beyond the dark gash that marked the river canyon were the random lights and dendritic streets of Freaktown.

I breathed a sigh of relief as we passed over the river without being hailed by CorpSec. I wondered where Wauno was taking us, now that Grandmother was gone.

He took us to Hanjen. He let the transport hover centimeters above Hanjen's rooftop, like he was afraid the building might not support its mass. We climbed out, carefully, helping each other down.

Wauno left the ship suspended just above the roof and guided us to a stairway leading down. I wondered why he'd brought us here, when Hanjen had betrayed me once already. I understood now why Hanjen had done it, but that didn't make trusting him any easier. But I trusted Wauno, so I didn't ask any questions.

As we went on across the roof I noticed the remains of a wall and pillars around its perimeter. There must have been a sheltered tower up here once, for *an*, for communing with the cloud-whales. Nothing was left of it now but bits of masonry like broken teeth. I was surprised Hanjen hadn't replaced it. Maybe he'd felt like there was no way to reclaim what his people had lost when they lost the an lirr, and the sight of a prayer tower that would be meaningless forever wasn't something he wanted to confront every day.

Hanjen was waiting for us below, in a room I remembered. He stiffened a little as he saw me come in, carrying Joby. I wasn't sure if he was reacting to what was in my eyes or just to the sight

of me. The room looked the way I remembered, filled with artifacts of a past that was gone forever.

I thought about the last time I'd seen him, how I'd been with
the HARM survivors after the CorpSec massacre, how he'd held
Grandmother's lifeless body in his arms and cursed us all for
what we'd done. That day had been just the beginning of the grief
the Satoh had caused the Community. . . . And even though he'd
hated us then, and had every reason to, his act against us had been
an act of desperation, done to keep Borosage from grinding the
embers of a guttering fire into cold ashes.

Hanjen bowed formally to us, taking his eyes off me as he said,
"Namaste. Welcome to my home."

The others bowed back to him, Wauno and Kissindre murmuring "Namaste" as naturally as breathing. Perrymeade's bow was
awkward as he echoed "Namaste," the first Hydran word I'd ever
heard him speak. Ronin imitated the others, doing it well. I stood
where I was, holding Joby, stiff and silent.

"Namaste," another voice said.

"Miya—?" I turned.

She was already looking at me as she entered the room, as if
she'd known what she'd see, where each of us stood, even before
I spoke. (!—CatJoby—!) Her mind slurred our names into one
thought, shot through with emotion. She crossed the room to us,
moving as silently as if she was afraid we'd vanish. But her smile
widened with each step. As she closed the space between us, she
closed her eyes in concentration and took us gently inside the circle of her mind.

My mind burst open like shuttered windows, and suddenly the
two of them were there inside me, sharing the view. (Namaste,) I
said, finally understanding its true meaning.

(I was so afraid for you—) she thought, kissing me as she
called me by my unspoken name.

"Mommy . . . ?" Joby murmured, rubbing his eyes like he'd
just wakened from a strange dream to find us there. "Daddy." He
smiled—we were all smiling, impossibly, in the same place at the
same time, in our own pocket world again. The room and everyone else in it had ceased to exist, and the universe beyond it—

Someone teleported into the room, almost on top of us.

"Naoh!" I wasn't sure how many of us said her name at once, like a chorus. Ronin recoiled like he'd never seen anybody teleport before. Maybe he hadn't.

I glanced at the others: Kissindre and Wauno, Perrymeade and Hanjen, all caught with their expressions halfway between poles.

Naoh's surprise became disgust as she turned to find Miya with me and Joby. Her mental barrier ruptured the fragile link I shared with them, before she cut us all out of her mind. She turned away, completing her rejection of our existence.

Miya was back inside my thoughts instantly. I felt her try to force an opening in the wall of her sister's silence; to force Naoh to acknowledge our right to be together . . . felt her fail.

I held her back as she would have crossed the room. (Don't,) I thought. (It isn't you. It isn't us. It's her.)

(She's my sister—) Miya shook her head, straining against my grip as the memories of a lifetime filled her mind. (Naoh needs me. Who else does she have? I can help her—) I felt her loyalties slipping.

(Dammit, she tried to kill us!) I forced Miya to drink my memories with her own, like blood in wine. (She's sucking you in; she's bes' mod. . . .)

Miya pulled her gaze away from Naoh's unyielding back. She looked into Joby's eyes, into mine . . . collided with the ice dam of control that barely held in my anger, and my fear of losing her again to Naoh.

I felt what it cost her to believe me; realized what she couldn't bear to let herself see, that for Naoh their lifelong bond had become just a weakness to be exploited. . . .

Her resolve hardened into bitterness as she watched her sister blow like a burning wind through the minds of everyone else in the room, oblivious to us now.

I stiffened as Naoh singled out Ronin. In an eyeblink, she was across the room in front of him. She pinned him against the wall with a telekinetic field, stopping short of touching him physically. His eyes glazed as she invaded his mind, ready to riffle through his memories back to the day he was born. Nobody moved to stop her.

"Naoh!" I yelled, loud enough to break even her concentration. "Get off him, you mindfucking bitch!" I crossed the room, fists clenched.

She turned around, and her burning stare told me she would have scrambled my brains if she could have. But she couldn't. She turned back to Ronin. This time she didn't touch him, even with her mind. She only said, out loud, "So you come from the FTA, and you claim you have the power to help us?" She was speaking to him in Standard; I'd never heard her use it before. *They all speak Standard,* Perrymeade had said once. Probably she always had too; never using it had been intentional, political.

Ronin nodded, doing his best to hide his sudden terror and his sudden relief. He glanced at Perrymeade, at Hanjen, with something that was half appeal and half incomprehension.

"Then why are you here, hiding from the Humans like a mebbet?"

Hanjen had been standing beside Perrymeade. Suddenly he was between Ronin and Naoh. Ronin pressed back against the wall again, his face going white. "He is here as my guest," Hanjen said, "to learn about our situation. And he is here for his own safety." He touched Ronin's arm, and there was something more than just physical reassurance in the way it made Ronin suddenly relax. Hanjen had reached into his mind without his realizing it, spreading calm over the troubled water of his emotions. Hanjen led Ronin to a cushioned settee across the room. Ronin sat down on it almost reluctantly, like he was afraid it might disappear from under him.

Naoh stood with her arms crossed, her disdain clear enough for even a Human to read, her desperation so obvious to me that I almost felt sorry for her. Her hair was filthy and matted; her clothes looked like she'd been sleeping in them. Her face was thinner and harder than I remembered, her mouth even more bitter, her eyes lost in deep hollows of fatigue.

"I thought you said you didn't know where she was," Perrymeade murmured to Hanjen.

"I didn't know." Hanjen shook his head, looking from Naoh to us—looking at Miya, with more on his mind than he was saying out loud.

Miya looked down and didn't answer. Or maybe that was all the answer she had.

"We're sisters," Naoh said defiantly, like Miya's shamefaced silence was just one more body blow to her self-control. "We are all the family we have, because Humans killed our parents. The last of it. Forever." She spoke the words with a venom that made Hanjen flinch. "No matter what happens, nothing is stronger than that."

"It's true," Miya said quietly, looking at her sister with something that was almost compassion. "If she's nearby, I know . . . we always know. Ever since our parents died. . . ." She gave a small, helpless shrug; but I felt her anguish as she glanced at me, knowing how often and how profoundly Naoh had violated everything that bond of blood should have represented. "She knew I was staying with you, Hanjen. And I knew she was watching, listening."

"I am her conscience, Hanjen," Naoh said. "And yours." She looked away again at Ronin and the others, her eyes avoiding me. "Is this really the man you expect to save you—?" *When I couldn't.* Her eyes finished the thought. "This pitiful, braindead Human?"

Ronin stiffened, like the verbal slap had stung his courage back to life. "I may not seem like much alone . . . Naoh," he said, meeting her stare. He gestured at his ruined uniform. "But I am not alone . . . and I'm not powerless. Tau's negligence killed the three other people who came with me—" He broke off. "But they didn't kill me. I'm going to make them regret that. There's a Federation Transport Authority embargo-class ship in planetary orbit above Refuge. I have more than enough reason to contact them. I want to do everything I can to help your people, as well as protect our contract laborers, if you can give me enough good reasons."

"How will you contact the ship?" I asked, remembering that we'd made him leave his databand behind.

"There's a special transmitter on my databand. We all have them, we call it the 'deadman switch'—" He broke off again, as what must have been a sardonic joke for too long suddenly wasn't funny. "It . . . if it isn't reset on a regular schedule, it automatically contacts the ship. They'll assume the worst, and notify the home office—and Draco, in this case. In the meantime, they'll send down their tactical enforcement unit: sanctions will be imposed immediately. All shipping schedules will be on hold until the situation is resolved to the FTA's satisfaction." There was a reason why Tau, and even Draco, were afraid of the FTA when it was doing its job.

Just speaking the words gave Ronin strength, the way hearing them changed the faces of everyone listening—including Naoh.

"Naoh," Miya said, and I felt her praying that there was still something rational and reachable inside her sister's mind. "This is the last chance our people have for the future we tried to give them. Even Hanjen understands the Way we were meant to follow now." She was still speaking Standard, like she wanted Ronin to follow it.

"What do you mean?" Naoh demanded, frowning.

Miya glanced at me. "Out in the Homeland, Bian showed me how our Gift binds us to the an lirr, to this world." Naoh's frown deepened, and I looked at Miya in surprise.

She went on, inside our heads this time; I felt her relief as she released herself from words. She showed me how my unthinking question—*What if the an lirr came back?*—had entered her thoughts like a grain of sand; how what had begun as a painful reminder of loss had become layered with possibilities, until at last she had offered Hanjen a pearl of insight, a gift of hope: the possibility that if the Community could regain their symbiosis with the an lirr, they could rekindle their sense of worth as a people. With Ronin's support, Tau could be forced to stop manipulating the cloud-whales' migrations. . . .

Miya paused, searching for some detail she hadn't shown her sister yet, the thing that would tip the scales of belief. "Naoh," I said, not sure why I was even trying to fill the silence, after what Naoh had done to me. Except that Miya had suffered enough, and I loved Miya more than I'd ever hate her sister. . . . "At Tau's mining interface my Gift let me read the reefs in ways that Humans can't. They miss incredible things in the matrix without psi to guide them. It made me . . . valuable to them. It helped keep me alive. If it's valuable to them, it can be valuable to the Community. It's something we have that they want. We can use that—"

"They will never trust us enough." Naoh shook her head, but at least she acknowledged me.

I shrugged. "If there's one thing I've learned living with Humans, it's 'Never underestimate the power of greed.' " I gestured at Ronin. "Show Ronin the truth, the way you showed it to me once. Let him see exactly what your people—our people— need." I remembered my nightmare tour of Freaktown, its medical center, the back-alley drug hole where I'd met Navu. "And then let him help us get it."

"Navu," Miya said, falling back into Hydran as she caught the echo in my thoughts. "We can get him the kind of help he needs; we can get the Humans' drugs off our streets—"

"It's too late," Naoh said, her voice flat. "Navu is dead."

Miya made a sound as if someone had hit her in the stomach, and Joby whimpered. *"Oh, God,"* she breathed, the Human words falling from her lips into a fractured silence. "How? Why—?"

"Because the supply of drugs stopped, with everything else, until Hanjen gave you up to the Humans," Naoh said, her voice corroded by grief. "He couldn't live without it, with what he had to *feel*. He . . . he stopped his own heart. And you caused it! It was your fault—you and that half-Human mebtaku!" Tears spilled out of her eyes, down her face. "If you wanted so much to be Human, Miya, why not just use the drugs? Then the only life you ruined would have been your own!"

"And would you have been happy to sell them to me too?" Miya asked, with sudden anger. I felt her compassion shrivel and die. Joby gave a small squeak as she held him too close. "I never worked for Humans because I thought they were better than I was! I did it because I believed in *us* . . . and that both our peoples had Gifts to share."

Naoh stiffened; so did Hanjen, across the room. For a moment Naoh wavered, as the words ripped open her denial and left her staring at the truth. She shook her head, but she was just shaking off the temptation to let herself believe anything we'd said. She didn't bother to argue Miya's point or even defend herself against it. She looked at Ronin again. "I'll be watching what you do," she said in Standard. "And if it isn't enough—" She disappeared, leaving the threat hanging unfinished in the air.

The Humans in the room, and probably the Hydrans, let out a collective held breath.

"What did she mean?" Ronin asked, frowning. "Is she actually dangerous?" He looked at Hanjen.

"Naoh. . . ." Hanjen gestured at his head, still stunned, as if after learning about her drug dealing he'd forgotten the words to explain mental illness in Standard. "She can do no real harm without harming herself."

I thought again about what she'd done with her rabble-rousing; what she'd done to me. But looking at Miya, I didn't press the point.

Perrymeade turned to Ronin finally and said, "You'll be safe here . . . as safe as anywhere on the planet. We have to get back across the river, before someone misses us." He glanced at

Kissindre and Wauno, back at Ronin's uncertain face. "Hanjen and Miya and Cat are the best informants you'll find on the problems of the Hydran Community. They can explain all the things that I . . . that I just never understood." He looked down.

Miya set Joby down; urged him to cross the room to Perrymeade, slow step by slow step. I felt the effort of her concentration as she guided him. Perrymeade kneeled down and took Joby into his arms.

"Uncle Janos," Joby murmured, the words lisped but perfectly clear. He rested his head on Perrymeade's shoulder, hugging him.

Perrymeade looked up at Miya, his mind overflowing with *tenderness/apology/loss/gratitude,* until even his face was too painful to look at. "Take care of him," he murmured. "I know you'll take good care of him. Until it's safe for all of you to come back across the river."

Miya nodded, her own face full of compassion.

Kissindre moved almost hesitantly to her uncle's side. She touched Joby's dark hair with a gentle hand. Joby glanced up, and they both smiled. She moved back again as Perrymeade released Joby from his arms, murmuring a good-bye as his nephew started back toward Miya.

Kissindre and Perrymeade followed Joby with their eyes, until they were both looking at Miya, at me, at the way we were standing together, touching each other.

I met Kissindre's clear blue stare, wishing I could look away from it. "I'm sorry, Kiss . . ." I murmured, not able to tell her what I felt, not able to show her either; not like this.

But she smiled and finished a trajectory back to Wauno's side. He put his arm around her and grinned, shrugging. "It's all right," she said, smiling up at him, and back at me. "Sometimes things actually do work out."

I felt a smile of relief come out on my face, the fist of my thoughts loosened until I could share them again with Miya. I felt her curiosity settle on the surface of my mind; but she only picked Joby up again and didn't ask me any questions.

Wauno led the others out the way they'd come in. Ronin watched them go, watched us stay behind, with a lot less wariness than he would have shown five minutes before. I wondered if he'd finally come to see that we really did have something in common.

But as the room emptied, leaving the five of us to awkward silence, exhaustion smothered his thoughts like a pillow.

Hanjen moved to his side, filling the void left by the others' departure. He seemed to feel Ronin's exhaustion as deeply as Ronin did; or maybe he was just that exhausted himself. He and Miya were both wearing long, shapeless tunics that must be sleep shirts. I realized that it had to be near dawn. The day Ronin and I had just been through must have been the longest day of his life. And probably the worst. He sagged forward on the cushioned seat, resting his head in his hands.

Hanjen touched Ronin's shoulder, quietly urging him to lie down and rest, telling him that there would be time enough to discuss injustice, and to grieve, tomorrow; but it was time for all of us to rest, now. . . .

There was a subliminal psi touch buried in the comforting words; he was using his psi to plant suggestions of healing and calm and reassurance. I knew that kind of subtle touch, what it could do, how much it could mean. . . . I wondered how often he'd used it in his work as an ombudsman. As far as I knew he didn't use it when he was negotiating with Humans. I wondered whether this was the first time he'd ever met—or had to enter the mind of—a Human whose emotions had been stripped raw.

I glanced at Miya as something wistful and almost forlorn whispered through my thoughts. She watched Ronin lie down where he was and Hanjen cover him with a blanket; I shared her memory of a time long ago when her own loss had been as fresh, and Hanjen had given her the same comfort, with a touch and a thought that were kindness itself. . . . She held Joby tighter, stroking his hair, murmuring something I couldn't quite make out. It sounded like a song, or maybe a prayer.

Hanjen straightened up again. He looked at us standing together and smiled. I didn't know if he was smiling at the sight of us together or just at the proof that he hadn't sold his soul to the Humans after all. "The Way has brought us safely home," he murmured. "We should rest now—while we have a resting place." He yawned, as if he'd convinced himself at least that the rest was long overdue. He went off in the direction of his room without speaking, leaving a kind of benediction in our minds.

Miya led me into the room where she'd been sleeping—the room I'd slept in once. I wondered whether she'd known that.

(Yes,) she thought, and when I looked at her, there were tears in her eyes.

I bit my lip, wanting to hold her, but waited while she settled Joby into one of the hammocks suspended halfway between the ceiling and floor. She rocked him gently, humming a tune I felt as much as heard, soothing him to sleep.

I stood looking at the other hammock, remembering how I'd spent my only night in this room sleeping on the floor. I suddenly felt an exhaustion that made the way I'd felt earlier seem like a good night's sleep.

Miya moved away from Joby's hammock and put her arms around me. She kissed me like she'd known—*must have known*—what I'd been wanting, aching for. . . . My fatigue vanished like a shadow in the sun. I felt giddy, like gravity had stopped, and we were rising into the air. . . .

We were. I realized, with the fraction of my mind that was still halfway coherent, that we were slowly rising, spiraling upward, drifting toward the second hammock together. Miya settled us into its yielding crescent. Our bodies set it rocking gently as we began to touch and kiss and maneuver into position, sinking deeper into need and pleasure, into each other's bodies and minds and souls. . . .

After a long while with no coherent thought at all, only sensation, we lay quiet again in the hammock's soft embrace. After a longer time, I thought, (Miya, what you told Naoh, about the an lirr: that if they returned, it could be the key to the Community's survival . . . I gave you that idea?)

She nodded without moving. (Sometimes it takes an outsider's eye to see what no one sees clearly from the inside—)

Pain caught in my chest.

(What—?) Miya thought, as the pain impaled us both.

(Outsider,) I thought, and without wanting to, (mebtaku.)

(Bian.) She touched my cheek gently. (No Human ever had that insight either, in all the years they've mined the reefs, in all the time since they came here. No one without the Gift could have had it.) Her fingers traced the not-quite-Human, not-quite-Hydran contours of my face. (Did it honestly never occur to you, nasheirtah,) she thought, (that you might be something better than either one?)

"Miya—"

Her fingers touched my lips, silencing me. (When I shared your mind that night I first saw you . . . that was the first time I really *believed* Humans and the Community could trust each other, at least enough so that we could share this world in peace. And I thought, if only there was something that could make all of them see this world like you do . . . like we do . . .) The words dissolved into images of the monastery, the reefs, the secrets of the Hydran past that we'd explored together. (I'd always wanted to believe our peoples could find a common ground. . . . No one but you ever made it seem possible to me.) She pictured the future unfolding as it should: *(We were together now, the Way had led me back to her, and Joby back to us.)* She saw us together at the monastery, the shue where the an lirr had thought about healing, where now we would have the time we needed to heal ourselves. . . . (Everything will be all right now.)

(Don't say that!) I thought. (Don't ever say that, not ever—)

I felt her surprise . . . felt her falter as she remembered once saying the same words to me. "It's all right," she whispered fiercely, "it is!" She kissed me again, stroking my hair. But she'd said it out loud. I felt her withdraw, only a little, keeping the mindlink open but taking one step back, like somebody who'd stood too close to the fire.

I didn't try to lie to her; I didn't dare. We'd both come too close to the truth that night in the monastery, feeling our minds approach meltdown in the fusion of our pasts. Maybe enough peace and enough faith would heal us, along with Joby. But there'd never been enough of either one in my life. My past had stolen too many things from me, too often, for too long. Too much of my life had been spent in a free-fire zone; I didn't know whether all of spacetime held enough faith to change who I was into who I might have been. . . .

And I wondered how I'd ever learn to live with someone else if I couldn't live with myself.

Miya set the hammock into gentle motion, as if by rocking us, soothing us to sleep, she could stop time itself, with all its unpredictable power. I lay motionless in her arms, letting exhaustion erase the questions that only time could answer.

THIRTY

IT TOOK TEN days for the fallout to stop falling. Ten days when we all stayed in hiding, ten days for us to fill Ronin's head with enough understanding of the Hydrans' situation to convince him that Tau had as much to answer for to the Community as it did to the bondies . . . more. Time enough for him to stop jumping whenever Miya or Hanjen used their psi. Time enough for him to stop staring every time Miya and I touched each other, every time we came out of the same room in the morning, every time he saw us with Joby, together, a family. Time enough, hour after hour, night and day, for all of us to feel his fear of the strange fade, as living with freaks and aliens slowly stopped seeming either freakish or alien to him.

(We're all following the same Way now,) Miya thought to me, as we watched Ronin sit down to play a counting game with Joby. (He has no choice but to come with us.) And watching him, feeling what lay in his mind, I could almost believe that.

On the tenth day Wauno came back; but this time there was a gunship hovering over his transport, and Corpses behind him as he came down the steps. We all looked up together, gaping, through the frozen moment until Wauno smiled/Miya smiled/Ronin smiled and said, "FTA." And finally I got past the shock of seeing uniforms and recognized the logo they wore.

It meant we were safe, that the end was finally in sight. They'd come this time to take Ronin back across the river for the beginning of negotiations. Tau heads were still rolling, Wauno told us; Sand, the Draco Corporate Security Chief, was back on Refuge in person, along with half a dozen Draco Board Members. An entirely new Tau Board was being set in place like game pieces by Draco, and negotiators were frantic to get things settled before their symbiotic economic systems were strangled by the FTA's shipping embargo.

Ronin took Hanjen with him. Miya and I stayed behind with

Joby, waiting. We didn't see either of them again, but Hanjen kept Miya informed mind-to-mind about every painful millimeter of progress that was made. And all the while Naoh haunted my thoughts like a bad dream. I wondered whether she was haunting his too.

I knew that Naoh was on Miya's mind, just like I was sure Miya was sharing with her everything we learned. But whatever Miya felt about her sister or her sister's threats, she wouldn't share it with me. There was a reason why a psion's DNA gave more protection against the Gift along with the ability to use it. . . . The idea that life had ever been simpler for Hydrans than it was for Humans was just one more dream of mine that hadn't survived the light of day.

It was a full month before the last square peg of compromise had been driven into a round hole of necessity: a general amnesty for members of the Satoh, freeing us to come out of hiding without being afraid that Tau's Corpses would murder us on sight for knowing too much.

Another FTA gunship came to escort us to the ceremony that marked the signing of Tau's revised charter and the treaty restricting their autonomy. The new agreements put them under the FTA's thumb for the indefinite future. I'd never expected to be happy to see Corporate Security come for me, but this once I didn't have any objections.

As we stood on the roof of Hanjen's house, waiting to get on board, Naoh suddenly appeared beside Miya. The Corpses around us swore and fumbled for their weapons.

She pressed empty hands together, with a deferential bow that didn't hide either her nerve or her unspoken tension. "I am here for the truce," she said in self-conscious Standard. "If there is justice now, I want to see it." She looked at her sister. I sensed an exchange going on between them that they shut me out of. Finally Miya held out a hand that wasn't quite steady. Naoh took it. They embraced with a painful joy that I could feel but couldn't share in.

The signing ceremony was taking place at the Aerie, the closest thing to neutral ground the negotiators had been able to agree on. It felt like closure, at least to me, to finish this where it had started.

As we entered the reception hall I felt a prickling sense of déjà vu, seeing Sand in his dress uniform standing there among the gathered vips in their combine colors. Perrymeade and Kissindre, Hanjen, and most of the Hydran Council members had already arrived, all of them going through the same motions of the diplomatic dance. There were no other Hydrans except the three of us, representing the Satoh.

There were no Tau vips at all, at least not yet. I felt my surprise reflected in Miya's mind as she hesitated beside me in the entrance with Joby in her arms. Joby looked around, wide-eyed as he took in all the people, the colors shifting like an oil film on water. "Daddy!" he called out as he spotted a CorpSec uniform across the room. But it wasn't Natasa, and my hope curdled as I took in the not-so-discreet scatter of armed guards around the hall. None of the uniforms was Natasa, and even the fact that they were wearing FTA colors didn't reassure me when I thought about why they were here.

Miya started forward again as Perrymeade and Hanjen spotted us and came toward us across the room. Naoh followed her like a shadow, staring at the details of the hall, its occupants—the wide windows with their view of the reefs, like the hungry eyes of a bird of prey gazing down on the Homeland, on the last fragment of Hydran culture and heritage. Her own eyes were slit-pupiled with unease, even though what we were doing here today should mean those things were safe after all; that in the future someone looking out at that view would see something different . . . something better.

I started after them, forcing myself to keep moving as my mind perversely turned my body into the center of a universe of stares. I told myself it was a good sign—that it was only happening because this time I could sense the crowd; my contact with the reefs, and Miya, had at least begun to heal me.

But too many eyes really were looking at me, at the Hydran clothes I wore because they were the only clothes I had left; at my cat-pupiled Hydran eyes in a Human face. . . . Suddenly I didn't feel like a Hydran, any more than I felt Human. I felt like a freak.

Sand went on staring at me even after the rest of the room had lost interest. I saw Lady Gyotis Binta behind him, the only other Draco vip I knew. "So," he said while Perrymeade and Hanjen greeted the others, "you seem to have taken our last conversation seriously."

I kept my face expressionless. "You can believe that, if it makes you feel better," I said.

He stiffened, and for a second an expression I didn't ever want to see again showed on his face. But then he smiled, an empty twist of his mouth, as Lady Gyotis stepped forward beside him. "I never imagined," she said evenly, "when we last met, that we would meet again under circumstances like these."

"No, ma'am," I murmured. "Neither did I."

"I feel sad, somehow. It's unfortunate that it all had to come to this."

"I guess that depends on your point of view," I said. "Ma'am."

Her control was good, but I saw her eyes flicker. Her hands made a series of quick gestures as she glanced at Sand. He answered her the same way, using a handtalk code I didn't know, one that belonged strictly to vips. A look and a peculiar smile passed between them. I couldn't even begin to guess what it meant; I only knew it wasn't meaningless this time.

Sand looked back at me again as Lady Gyotis drifted away. "I'm curious," he said. "Perhaps you'll humor me about this: Just exactly what is your relationship with Draco?"

"Draco—?" I blinked, expecting him to ask me anything but that. "I have no relationship with Draco. It's a null set."

"Then your coming here to Refuge was simply a coincidence—nothing more."

I glanced away, to where Miya was standing with Hanjen and Perrymeade. I watched her hand Joby into his uncle's arms and saw the smiles on all their faces. "No," I murmured. I looked back at him. "But if you mean, was I a croach for the Feds—no. Not until you forced it on me."

His mouth twisted again; he took a drink off a drifting tray and sipped it pointedly. The tray floated toward me. I took one too, and swallowed it down. "I see," he said. "Then would you tell me why you have Draco's logo tattooed on your . . . hip?" He glanced down, like he could see through my clothes.

I frowned, wondering whether his augmented eyes actually could. "How do you—?"

"Your contract labor records," he said.

"It's not Draco's logo." I shook my head, still frowning. "It's just a lizard."

"It's Draco's logo," he said flatly. "Do you really think I don't know what that looks like?"

I laughed. "I can't even remember how it got there," I said. "But thanks for letting me know. I'll think of you every time I sit down." I turned my back on him and moved away.

I crossed the room to the one small knot of people I felt safe with—the mixed cluster of Humans and Hydrans with Miya at its heart. She was talking to Kissindre; they looked up together as she sensed me. Kissindre smiled and moved away, touching my arm briefly as she made a place for me by Miya's side.

"We were talking about the reefs," she said, like she wanted me to be sure they hadn't been talking about me. "Ways the research team can learn more about the healing factor at the monastery, without disturbing it." The treaty we'd come here to witness made the last reef a Federal environmental preserve, off-limits to any combine's exploitation.

Tau had howled at that, just like they'd howled at the new laws forcing them to begin integrating Hydrans into their Human work-force. From what I'd seen Miya do—from what I'd done myself— I knew that even if those changes ate holes in the Human population's collective gut like acid, they weren't simply justice— they were right, and smart, and good for everyone. I hoped that one day Tau would look back and wonder what the hell had taken them so long to make it happen. The odds of that weren't good, but they were better than zero, which was all they'd been before.

". . . about the symbiosis between the cloud-whales and the Community, and interpreting the data," Kissindre was saying. It took me a minute to realize she was still talking about the reefs. She broke off. "You are going to work with us again, aren't you?"

I smiled. "Try and stop me."

"Why is this taking so long?" Naoh came up behind Miya, her hands picking at her sleeves like nervous animals. I remembered Miya's restless hands, when I'd first met her. "Where are the Tau people? Is this some trick—?"

"No, of course not—" Perrymeade said. He didn't finish it, as her stare set off his own doubt and concern.

"They will be here," Hanjen said, his voice even, his eyes willing his foster daughter to believe him.

"Where's Natasa?" I asked, looking up at Joby, who was riding contentedly on Perrymeade's shoulders. I glanced at Miya, feeling the part of her mind, the part of her strength, the part of her love, that would always stay with him, just like I could feel the part of it that would always be one with me. I imagined what a difference it could make to both Humans and Hydrans, if they could open themselves to the possibilities I saw every time I looked into her eyes and Joby's.

"He should be arriving with the others," Perrymeade said. "They've been talking about making him the new District Administrator here at Riverton, since Borosage is being transferred—"

"Transferred?" Naoh said sharply. I knew from the look she gave Miya that she was demanding an explanation, and that she didn't like the answer she got.

"He's going to prison. Right—?" I demanded. "He's not getting out of this. There's too much evidence of everything he's done—" I looked away from Perrymeade, searching for Ronin.

"Here's the Tau delegation now," Perrymeade murmured, and left my side abruptly.

Naoh watched him go, her expression darkening.

"Naoh—" Miya said. The word was both a question and a warning. She put a hand on her sister's arm, like she was trying to anchor her in reality.

Naoh slapped her hand away without touching her.

Miya backed off, but her eyes stayed on her sister's face.

I stopped watching them both as the new Tau Board entered the room, in the flesh this time, not virtual. All of them were strangers to me, which was good. They were as expressionless as a line of sticks.

Borosage was with them. He was still in uniform and heading a Security team wearing Tau colors.

Disbelief caught me by the throat. I jerked my stare away from him, telling myself it was just a formality, that there was no way in hell he could have survived the corporate massacre when the entire Tau Board had been deposed.

He looked toward us as they crossed the room, and his eyes were full of hate. The mind behind them was as unreadable to me as any of the Board members' were. "Miya—?" I murmured.

But then I saw that Natasa had come in with the Tau delegation. He broke away from the formation, and his rigid, unsmiling face came to life as he spotted Joby and started toward us. Miya didn't answer me as Joby's attention drew her own to his father.

"Daddies!" Joby cried, looking from me to Natasa, delighted. Natasa's smile widened; he held out his arms, and then Miya's concentration was entirely focused on making their reunion all it should be. I glanced at Naoh, went on watching her as she watched Borosage. She looked at him the way prey would watch a hunter . . . or a hunter would watch prey.

The Tau vips flowed into the waiting mass of Draco vips, FTA observers, and Hydran Council members, until they were all one indistinguishable mass of shifting colors and loyalties. They greeted each other with the hollow goodwill of the profoundly relieved. All of them were hoping their separate ordeals were finally over; all of them were trying to believe that even if this wasn't a position they'd ever wanted to find themselves in, it was better than the alternative.

A chime sounded, signaling that the ratification ceremony was beginning. The crowd began to move toward the wide doorway that led into the main hall, where the treaty waited at the center of a showy tech display, each segment glowing on a separate screen, hypertext ramifications and clarifications ringing them like haloes of enlightenment.

I leaned against a pillar, closing my eyes. The playback of a synthesized voice I recognized as Ronin's began to recite the terms of the agreement aloud, in case anyone here hadn't bothered to study it beforehand. I felt the terms of Tau's penance wash over me like cool water, leaving a pristine surface of possibility. Tau and Indy media hypers were everywhere in the crowd assembled here, recording every nuance as Humans and Hydrans laid the foundation for the future they were about to share, like it or not.

I checked off the terms of the treaty against the agenda in my head, my respect for Ronin climbing a notch with every need that was met: lifting of restrictions on technological exchange between Humans and Hydrans, amnesty for all imprisoned Hydrans, rehab and training programs, quotas for integrating Hydrans into the Human workforce, no more tampering with the magnetosphere to redirect the cloud-whales' journeys. And for the contract laborers, strict regulation of work safety conditions at all Tau installations, with FTA inspection teams on-site for the indefinite future.

Tau had argued that they couldn't survive restrictions like that; that their economy would collapse. The FTA's response had been, *Adapt and try, or die now*. Draco had had to back them up or lose more face—and face more trade restrictions on the rest of its hegemony. Caught between those pincers of power, even Tau couldn't squirm free.

I listened to the members of the new Tau Board mouth optimistic platitudes as one by one they touched the display, committing their approval to the permanent record. I wondered how surprised they'd be if it actually turned out to be better.

"I suppose you think this is all your doing,'breed?" a voice said behind me.

I turned around, suddenly face-to-face with Borosage. I barely controlled my urge to smash in his face—to wipe that smugness off it, to force him back behind the invisible line he'd crossed into my personal space. "Yeah," I said, forcing a smile instead. "Pretty much."

"I should have killed you when I had the chance," he muttered, his face barely changing expression. He glanced away. "Too bad you won't be staying on Refuge long enough to see what really happens to all your big ideas—"

"What makes you think I won't?" I folded my arms, leaning against the pillar again.

"You're being deported, genetrash."

I sucked in a breath, held it, while the words tried to paralyze my brain. "I think you got it backwards," I said finally. "You're not going to be around to see it all work out, because you're about to do some heavy time, you drug-dealing, sadistic piece of shit."

He shook his head, a smile spread over his face like a stain. "Not me, boy. Fahd's taking my fall . . . I'm still standing. I'm not stupid. I knew the Board and that cocksucker Sand would try to download the guilt onto me. I could see where it was all leading. They thought they'd take me down, but I got them first. I have my ways—" He tapped the metal half dome covering his head. "I have records of things you wouldn't believe; things they never even suspected I knew about them." I realized that he must have spent his drug profits hotwiring his brain with undetectable snoopware. "I know where all the bodies are buried—and who wanted them dead. Why do you think I'm still here, boy, when not a single member of the old Tau Board is?"

I glanced away at the last of the signers putting their seal on the official record, to applause that sounded as artificial as static. *It was done,* something in my head insisted. It was done, and there was nothing he could do to change that, nothing more he could do to hurt anyone I cared about, not even me. . . . I searched the crowd, trying to catch Perrymeade's eye, or Ronin's. I saw Naoh staring back at me, at Borosage beside me, as if we were magnetic north.

"I'm still in charge here," Borosage muttered. "And while I am, no freak will ever feel safe on this side of the river. And that includes you, boy. Especially you—" He raised his hand.

I backed up a step, my fists clenching, and hated myself for it.

(Borosage—)

It wasn't until I saw the sudden rage fill his face that I realized I'd only heard someone calling his name in my mind.

He turned around. Naoh was standing right there beside us, her eyes slit-pupiled. "I told you, never do that to me, you Hydran slut—"

Her face didn't change. "So you are still in charge, then? Everything else is a lie . . ." she said, out loud this time. "That is the Human Way—destroy your enemies before they can destroy you."

He smirked. "You know it, sweet thing. You know me . . . real well." He reached out, touched her cheek with a thick finger. I saw her barely stop herself from cringing away. "So now I'm safe, and you're forgiven. It'll go back to being the way it was, business as usual, between you and me, and your people. . . ."

A tremor cracked her control.

"Naoh . . ." I whispered. "Don't." I thought that she'd ignored me, except that suddenly I couldn't move.

"No," she said, her gaze still on Borosage. "I will never be forgiven. And you are not safe—" I felt the power shift focus inside her, felt it building as the pressure turned to pain inside my head . . . saw terror fill Borosage's face as she invaded his mind and took him over. A high, thin whine started in his throat; he began to drool.

(Miya—) I called, with blind desperation. *(Miya!)*

Naoh glanced at me distractedly, as if she'd heard me, and an odd smile played over her lips before she looked back at Borosage.

(Are you ready to die, monster?) she said, inside his mind and somehow inside mine. (Feel your brain . . . feel each cell in it begin to—)

"Naoh!" Suddenly Miya was there between us and inside our heads. Her hands closed on Naoh's shoulder like she was trying to physically drag Naoh out of her homicidal rage.

Naoh's fist shot out, caught Miya square in the face, dropping her like a stone with the unexpectedness of the attack. Naoh looked back at Borosage, whose face had turned a mottled purple. He was making a sound now like somebody being gutted.

I stood there, helpless to do anything but watch, the pain abcessing in my head. Miya struggled to her feet, blood running down her chin. She looked away toward the place where the crowd was still going through the motions of the Human ritual. Abruptly the empty doorway held a figure—Hanjen's.

(Help us—!) I couldn't tell if he even heard me. I saw his eyes widen, but before he could move Sand was standing beside him. Sand laid a heavy hand on his shoulder, murmuring something in his ear. I saw Hanjen's face slowly crushed by emotions I couldn't feel as he stood watching us, but doing nothing at all to stop what was happening.

Miya screamed with anguish and frustration, but only inside my head. She stood paralyzed by Naoh like I was now, helplessly watching her sister turn Borosage's brains to jelly in front of our eyes. I saw blood and something worse start to leak out of his nose. His eyes rolled up in his head; his body spasmed in the air like an epileptic puppet, when it should have been writhing on the floor.

Naoh's eyes flooded with tears; her face contorted as she embraced the agony I felt echoing through my soul. . . . Borosage screamed, and it was a death cry ripped from a living corpse. Naoh screamed with him as his death fed back through the circuit of insane rage that joined them like lovers. I felt my own heart stumble, suddenly realizing Miya and I were trapped with them inside the circuit—

My vision strobed, *black/white* . . . and then suddenly the horror in front of us was happening to someone else. Borosage pitched forward on his face, no longer a prisoner of Naoh's vengeance. When he finally hit the floor he was only a sack of meat, lying facedown in a spreading pool of blood and body fluids.

Naoh collapsed on top of him, her eyes wide and staring. Her pupils were pits of blackness; blood ran from her nose.

I swayed, barely staying on my feet as I suddenly got back full control of my body. Miya staggered forward. She collapsed in my arms, sobbing. The sound was hard and pitiless, and at the molten core of her mind the same white-hot sun of fury that had destroyed her sister was still burning.

"I love you," I mumbled, holding her close, trying desperately to reach her. (I love you, Miya! Please, please, don't leave me . . .)

She raised her head, her green eyes like an emerald desert, even though her voice still sobbed out grief. She took my face in her hands. And then her mind filled me with *tenderness/yearning/love* as pure and limitless as if the two of us existed only in our souls, looking down like the an lirr, untouched by anything earthbound, even the blood pooling around our feet.

(I can hear you. I can . . .) I thought, with incredulous joy. I realized then that in the split second before Naoh had died with Borosage, Miya had broken free, protecting us from the feedback of their deaths.

But she buried her face in my tunic, as if she could never shut it all out: the room, the horror, the truth.

A mob of guards and gaping strangers were already gathering around us. We held each other up, held each other together, held on to each other like drowners in a nightmare sea . . . like refugees.

"What the hell happened here?" Sand was standing in front of us now; his indignation was almost believable. Behind him a dozen Corpses were pointing their guns at us.

"Like you don't know," I said thickly. "Like you didn't let it happen." Sand glared a warning at me. "They're dead. She killed him . . . and it killed her."

" 'It'?" Sand snapped. " 'It' what?"

"The feedback," Miya muttered. "It's what happens when a psion kills. . . ."

"It's what happened to me," I said.

He went on looking at me; only the muscles in his jaw told me that he'd kept himself from saying something. He lifted his hand, brought it down; the guns disappeared, the ring of guards backed off, taking the crowd with them.

Sand stayed where he was, looking at us, looking down at the bodies of Naoh and Borosage. "I see," he murmured, at last. "There is a certain dreadful symmetry to this, I suppose. . . ." His mouth curved up in a cryptic smile like the one he'd shared with Lady Gyotis.

Miya lifted her head, glaring at him, like what lay behind the smile was perfectly clear to her.

As he met her eyes Sand's body tautened the way hers had, and I saw a totally unexpected emotion fill his face. It was one I actually recognized . . . fear. "No further questions," he murmured, and turned away. "Natasa!" he shouted.

Natasa pushed through the wall of stunned faces, carrying Joby. "Yes, sir?" He looked as grim and tense as we all probably did. He stopped short, like he was protecting Joby from what he saw, even though I could tell from Joby's face that he'd slipped into a fugue state when Miya lost control to Naoh. Perrymeade stood behind them like a worried shadow.

Natasa's face was expressionless as he moved forward far enough to glimpse the bodies, like so many conflicting emotions were filling him at once that they canceled each other out. I wondered where Hanjen had gone, whether he was breaking the news to the Hydran Council members or whether he couldn't bear the sight of this.

"Some bad news, and some good news," Sand said. "It appears District Administrator Borosage was the victim of a murder-suicide committed by the former leader of HARM. So it seems that you will become Riverton's new District Administrator, after all. Odd, isn't it, how justice is sometimes served by the strangest means." He glanced at the bodies, back at Natasa and Perrymeade. "Since you and Agent Perrymeade will be working together closely in the future, I suggest that you begin now, by dealing with these bodies. I will expect your report."

Natasa stood where he was, looking as vacant-eyed as his son. Perrymeade laid a hand on his shoulder; Natasa started. "Yes, sir," he murmured.

Miya freed herself from my arms. "I'll take Joby," she said softly, her voice almost steady. She was using Joby's need to pull herself together one more time, focusing on the one fixed thing left in all our lives. Joby blinked and shook his head as she gave him back control of his senses.

Natasa passed Joby to her, self-consciously but gratefully, under the gaze of every Human and Hydran who'd just seen their worst fears for the future acted out in their midst.

Joby wrapped his arms around her neck and kissed her cheek, beaming, oblivious. I wondered where in the nine billion names of God she found the strength, the control, to let him see and hear the world around him right now without seeing it through her mind's eye—a world bloodred with pain and ash black with loss. Maybe she found it in his smile.

The near silence of the crowd broke like a wave into murmuring voices, stunned, querulous, wondering.

Natasa smiled at her, at Joby, as if they were proof enough that what had been the past between their people didn't have to be the future—a smile not meant for the crowd, but one they couldn't help seeing anyway—one that said with every choice you made you lost something, but maybe you gained something too. He moved forward, with Perrymeade at his side, to face what had to be done.

The two bodies lay still in a blur of red, silent witness to the end product of all prejudice and hatred. I started as I saw Hanjen suddenly kneeling beside Naoh, gazing at her empty face and staring eyes. His body shook with soundless grief. He held her limp, lifeless hand like somehow she could still feel his presence, his anguish, a parent's love that no amount of bitterness or disillusionment or even death itself could destroy.

Miya came back to my side, and I heard her soft cry as she saw/felt Hanjen. Tears spilled down her cheeks at last.

Joby put his hands on her face. "Sad, Mommy—?" he whispered. His own eyes suddenly shone with tears. She nodded, biting her lip.

I touched Joby's shoulder, touched Miya's thoughts, proving to them that they weren't alone; proving the same thing to myself.

At Natasa's order half a dozen guards came back to carry the bodies away. But Hanjen waved them off as they would have touched Naoh. He picked her up in his arms, cradling her as effortlessly as a child, then turned to leave. Guards cleared a path for him and for Natasa and Perrymeade as they followed him out. More guards dragged away Borosage's dead weight. Servo drones moved in behind them to clean up the blood.

The crowd watched them go out of the room, and then they

began to close in on us like a murmuring sea, their words as unintelligible as the tangled wilderness of their thoughts.

Miya made a choked noise; I felt the grief that had frozen her to the spot beside me breaking down into panic. She looked toward the doorway that the others had disappeared through. I realized we'd both gone on mindlessly standing there, instead of following the others while we could.

"What the hell is going on? What the hell happened—?" Someone's hand fell on my shoulder. *Ronin.*

I turned to look at him, wondering how long he'd been there trying to get our attention. I shook my head, beyond words, while inside me I felt Miya's desperation begin to take on physical form— the tug, the pull, the beginning of a change that meant teleportation.

(Yes,) I thought, glancing at her. (Go. Go after them.) "We have to go . . ." I murmured, trying to keep my attention on Ronin.

"Not yet," Ronin said. His hand gripped my arm. "Not until you tell me what this means."

(Go,) I thought to Miya again. (Go on. I'll handle this.) She disappeared from beside me, taking Joby with her, leaving her gratitude behind in my thoughts.

Ronin and Sand both started as she disappeared, their reflexes getting the better of them—like they were both still afraid, deep down, of being sucked out of existence themselves. The voices around us crested in surprise.

Ronin took a deep breath. He looked at Sand as though he thought Draco's Chief of Security ought to be doing something more about what had just happened here than standing with his hands behind his back.

"It's being taken care of," Sand said, answering Ronin's unspoken question. "I can be of more use remaining here." I wasn't sure what he meant by that—protecting us, or protecting Draco's interests.

Ronin looked back at me, like he knew Sand wasn't going to give him an answer that meant anything. "What the hell happened?" he asked again, gesturing at the stains disappearing before our eyes as the cleanup crew of gleaming drones erased the last traces of blood.

"Nothing," I muttered. I glanced at Sand. "Nothing happened that wasn't supposed to."

"Dammit!" Ronin said. "That woman Naoh killed Borosage—or did he kill her?"

"It was a murder-suicide," Sand said tonelessly. "She killed him; she died. That's how it happens with the Hydrans. Obviously, she knew the consequences of her act."

"But, why?" Ronin shook his head. "For God's sake, we just signed a new treaty. The rights her people were fighting for are finally being given back to them. The members of HARM have been given amnesty."

"It wasn't enough," I said. "For her."

His expression then said he didn't know whether to pity her because she was crazy or resent her ingratitude. Finally the look on his face was just incomprehension of the alien.

"It's not so hard to understand," I said. "There were twelve treaties before this one . . . they were all just words."

"Words can be deeds."

"Words can be lies, too. You had to make compromises, didn't you?"

"Of course—"

"One was that Borosage stayed on as District Administrator?"

Ronin nodded. "The Draco Board insisted. . . ."

I shot a look at Sand. "I'll bet they did." I looked back at Ronin. "Borosage would have made sure nothing really changed in spite of the treaty. Like I said, that wasn't enough for Naoh."

"He was only a District Administrator—" Ronin protested.

"But he knew where all the bodies were buried," I said. "I guess now he'll be buried there too."

"Still . . . why would she do something like this, when she knew it would kill her?" Ronin waved his hand.

"Because . . ." I glanced at the crowd of vips beginning to drift apart, slowly heading back through the wide arch into the larger hall where the treaty table still shone like an altar. "Because she couldn't see any other Way."

His face said he still didn't understand. But then, I hadn't expected him to.

"It was unfortunate that this—incident had to happen in the midst of the treaty signing, of all places. But there was no real harm done," Sand said, "to anyone who didn't deserve it. We'll assign Natasa to Borosage's post, as you originally wanted us to.

The Hydrans hated Borosage; they can only be relieved by that change." He smiled faintly. "I expect we all can."

He looked away across the room, like he was trying to find even one person who'd be sorry Borosage was gone. "And now we're all free of an unstable Hydran troublemaker as well. As far as the purposes of this gathering, nothing really happened—just as Cat said." He looked down. The rug was spotless.

Ronin controlled a grimace. I watched him reabsorb his disgust until no more emotion was left on his face than on Sand's. The scars from his accident at the interface barely showed now, but I knew they must still be on his mind. He did this sort of thing for a living; I wondered how he stood it. "I see," he said, and he didn't say anything more.

"Well, then," Sand murmured. "If everything has been explained to your satisfaction, why don't we join the rest of the representatives in the banquet room and celebrate the good that has been accomplished here?" He gestured toward the doorway the rest of the crowd had disappeared through.

"Wait," I said. "What about my databand?" I held up my wrist. A strip of healing skin showed where the bond tag had been fused to my flesh. There was still no databand to cover it up. Ronin's was safely back on his wrist, but nobody had said anything about mine.

Ronin looked at my wrist. He glanced at Sand.

"It will be waiting for you on the ship that takes you off-world," Sand said.

"What—?"

"Tau has revoked your passport," Ronin said, not looking at me. "You're being deported."

I shook my head. "What are you talking about?" Suddenly I remembered what Borosage had said just before Naoh had attacked him. "That was Borosage's idea. He's dead. I—"

"It wasn't just Borosage's idea," Ronin said, making eye contact finally. "Cat"—his empty hands gestured at the air—"you almost single-handedly set in motion the events that led to this treaty agreement. That's an incredible accomplishment. But if you think that makes you a hero to the people of Refuge, think again."

"Do you mean the people? Or the Humans?" I said sourly. "Or

just the Tau Board and Draco? Who do you think they really hate more, you or me?"

He frowned, his mouth thinning. "No doubt they hate me, because I represent the power to actually make change happen. But that power also protects me. I can't guarantee you the same kind of safety."

"I'm not asking you to," I said. "I can take care of myself."

Sand made a soft noise of amusement as he glanced at my bare, scarred wrist. "All that aside," he said, "not only will neither Draco nor Tau take responsibility for your safety if you remain here—we have the legal right to deport you. Under corporate law, you are guilty of everything from using profanity in public to sedition. If you were to stay on Refuge, we would have to prosecute you on all charges." He shrugged. "Borosage got what he deserved," he murmured. "Consider yourself lucky."

"The agreement said amnesty for all HARM members—"

"But you're not Hydran. You're a registered citizen of the Federation. We didn't take your databand away from you, after all. You lost it."

"Tau's CorpSec tortured me! I was illegally detained as a contract laborer! You want to talk about crimes—"

He held up his hand. "Spare me . . . spare yourself. The decision has already been made. It will not be changed. Now, if you'll excuse me." He walked away and left us standing there.

I faced Ronin again. "They don't have the right. Tell him—"

Ronin's eyes were nothing but shadow. "I can't do anything. It's one of the points we had to grant them during the treaty negotiations. In order to get your record cleared of Tau's criminal charges, we had to agree that you would leave Refuge."

"You son of a bitch," I said. "You can't do this to me."

"You broke the laws of this world, dammit!" he said, his voice rising. "You saved my life, but you also broke the law! I got you everything you wanted for the Hydrans, to the best of my ability! But to do that, I had to make compromises. That's how it works."

"That's not good enough." My eyes blurred; I looked away. *Miya*—

"I'm sorry," he murmured. "I wish it was." And I knew from his voice that he was thinking just like I was of Miya, and Joby: he'd seen us together, he knew what they meant to me. He understood what this was going to do to us. . . . And he was sorry. But that didn't change anything.

"Goddamn. . . ." I turned away, my voice shaking, filled with a pain so deep and sudden that it made me want to cry out. I searched the building with my thoughts, searching for Miya. But she'd disappeared from my mind like she'd disappeared from the room, her own thoughts focused completely on Joby or on death.

Ronin was just as silent behind me, like he was waiting for me to get control of myself. Or maybe he just had no idea of what to do next, any more than I did.

I turned back, finally, because I couldn't stand here in this empty hall forever, with Ronin hovering at my back like a bug hypnotized by a light, turning my grief into some kind of freak show. ". . . got to find Miya," I said, managing to keep my voice steady as long as I didn't look at him. I headed for the doorway that Miya had gone through.

"Cat," Ronin called, behind me.

I stopped, my hands tightening into fists, but I didn't turn around. "What—?"

A holographic image of Natan Isplanasky appeared suddenly in the air in front of me: "I wanted to thank you," he said. His disembodied head looked me straight in the eyes, like he could actually see me. "And I wanted to ask whether you'd consider doing the kind of work Ronin does, for me, for the FTA—"

I let out a laugh of disbelief. I stood there, still laughing out loud, as I gouged out his phantom eyes with my trembling thumbs. "You *bastards*—!" I shouted as I turned back to Ronin. "You know what?" I wasn't laughing now. "The last time the FTA asked me to work for them, they'd just buttfucked me too."

He looked at me blankly.

"The telhassium mines, on Cinder: a combine conspiracy, a psion terrorist called Quicksilver. The FTA used some freaks— and I mean *used*—to bring him down. Maybe you remember."

He remembered. "That was you? You were one of them?"

"Tell Isplanasky he's mistaken me for somebody who gives a shit," I said, turning away again.

"He told me what you did for Lady Elnear taMing," Ronin called out. "I know what you did here. I don't think he's mistaken."

I stopped again, not turning back this time. "You've been

wrong before," I said thickly. I blew through Isplanasky's image like it was smoke and went on across the room.

"Think about it," Ronin called. "Just think about it—"

I forced my hands open at my sides. I made it to the doorway without breaking down, and went on through.

Three faces looked up at me together, from where three people crouched like one around Naoh's body. Natasa was gone, and he'd taken Joby with him. I realized from what showed on the faces of Hanjen and Perrymeade as they slowly got to their feet that they already knew what I'd just found out about my future, or lack of one. I choked on the wet ash of guilt and pity in their stares. Miya looked up at me, and I felt her incomprehension, dulled by grief. She caught my strengthless hand, pulling herself up, and her mind opened floodgates of *love/loss/pain/need/love*.

And then she made a small, strangled noise. "No . . ." she whispered, looking at Hanjen in disbelief, looking back at me as his nod confirmed the truth. "No, *no—!*" She lunged at him. Her fingers dug into his clothes, clawed at his flesh, like they were lies she could tear away.

Hanjen stood passively, grimacing with pain but not making a move to protect himself, until at last she clung to him, strengthless, hopeless. She didn't resist as I pulled her away from him, into my arms. We held each other for a long time.

Finally I felt someone's hands separate us, with gentle insistence.

Miya looked up at Hanjen, her eyes bleak. "Leave us alone," she said bitterly, out loud. "Why can't you—?"

"Miya . . ." he murmured. "The treaty is our last chance for survival as a people. The Way I have walked all my life was leading me to this—the Way that we both shared for so long. I know now that Bian was meant to walk it with us. If it had not been for him . . ." He looked at me. "I swear by the Allsoul . . . I did all I could to stop this." He looked down. "But I couldn't stop it. Not if it meant losing everything. . . ."

Miya's head jerked once, a nod, and I knew that she believed him, even though she didn't answer him, even if she'd never forgive him any more than I would.

"We must . . . take care of your sister," he murmured. "Before the Humans return and try to take her body away." I realized there was no sign of Borosage's body. The Corpses must have taken his body away already.

"What do you need to do now?" Perrymeade asked him awkwardly. "Is there anything I can do to help—?" He didn't make the same offer to Miya or to me. He didn't even meet our eyes. Maybe as far as he was concerned we were beyond help.

"We will take her back across the river, to rejoin the earth," Hanjen said, the formality of the words barely keeping them intelligible.

"I'll arrange for Wauno to take you back—"

"We have no need for that," Hanjen said gently. "But thank you, Janos." He bowed, a sign of honor and respect; one that wasn't meaningless this time. "You have become the advocate— and true friend—that you were meant to be."

"That I always should have been," Perrymeade murmured, glancing down. "That I always wanted to be, really." He looked up again, at us all.

I turned my back on him.

"I want to go with you," I said softly to Miya. "Let me come with you." I looked away from Miya and Hanjen, at Naoh's motionless body.

"Cat—" Perrymeade began, and looking at him I saw the fear in his eyes that I meant to go for good. That my grief and anger, or Miya's, might knock the scales out of precarious balance again, now that they had finally been set to weigh fairly between Hydrans and Humans.

"Shut up," I said, glaring at him. "I need a chance to say goodbye. You have to give me that much . . . that much time. I won't make trouble—" glancing at Hanjen, at Miya. "I'll do what you want. But all of you owe me that much. And none of you can say I don't keep *my* promises."

Perrymeade took a deep breath, and nodded.

Hanjen nodded too, with a solemn lack of expression that could have meant anything or nothing. Only Miya really looked at me, with her mouth quivering and her eyes full of unshed tears. Hanjen mindspoke with Miya for a long time, keeping it private even from me. Her gaze broke, finally; she stared at the floor, and her tears dripped onto the spotless carpet as she said aloud to Perrymeade, "We will return tomorrow."

Perrymeade watched silently as Hanjen and Miya gathered

themselves for the difficult jump. I felt Miya's grip close on my arm, on my mind. Perrymeade and the room did a fade to black.

Suddenly we were standing on the river shore, with the shadowed reefs rising up around us. I shook the echoes of the Aerie out of my head; looked at Miya, realizing that we'd returned to the shue we'd once gone to with Grandmother, seeking answers that already lay inside us. . . .

Miya and Hanjen kneeled down on the stones of the shore beside Naoh's body, gazing at it in perfect stillness, like they were praying; but the only sound I could hear was the sound of the river flowing.

I took the few hard Human steps to Miya's side, kneeled down, and touched her.

She didn't startle, didn't move, except to reach up and take my hand. The circuit of contact between us opened, and I felt the words flow into my head, filling my thoughts with a song of completion, of *sorrow/regret/longing,* and finally relief that one more journey on the spiral Way had ended, and a lost soul had returned to its starting point, to begin yet another journey. . . .

The talons of my own fresh loss closed on my heart, crushing my hope, my senses, my concentration . . . I let go of Miya's hand before the recoil of my thoughts poisoned her prayers. Alone in my mind, alone in the dark, there was nothing but the silence of broken promises.

I opened my eyes to the daylight and looked away along the shore. I wondered whether we were going to make the journey by boat into the hidden heart of the reefs . . . wondered how the Hydrans buried their dead. All I'd seen were artifacts inside the holy place—no trace of their owners. *No trace.*

I looked up at the reefs, down at Naoh's body, at Miya and Hanjen. I took Miya's hand again, and this time I let go of myself, let their prayers fill my head like the voiceless song of angels or of ancestors. This time I found the courage to listen, letting the prayer touch me, the mourning have its weight.

The dreamfall of Miya's memories fell silently, softly, inside me, until I didn't know anymore whether I was looking at her or looking at myself, until the death mask that I secretly saw whenever I looked in the mirror became the mirror, the shadows became light, and I saw my face in hers and hers in mine again, and knew there was a reason to go on living.

(Namaste,) Hanjen murmured. Miya echoed it, and I echoed it: (*We are one.*) The prayers for the dead were finished, and in the stillness that followed, my thoughts suddenly ignited with a burst of psi energy that blacked out my vision from the inside.

When my sight cleared, Miya and Hanjen were still kneeling on the stones, and the space between them was empty. Naoh was gone.

Before I could ask *where*—? the answer filled my eyes. *Into the reefs.* To join her ancestors' cast-off flesh and the cloud-whales' cast-off dreams; a tradition that must have had meaning for generations beyond remembering.

Miya looked up at last. Her eyes were clear again, rain-washed bright—until they met mine.

And as she went on looking at me, at what lay behind my own eyes, I suddenly realized that she could have stopped her sister. She'd protected herself, and me, from the recoil of Naoh's death wish. But she could have done more. She could have stopped it, as surely as she could have stopped her sister from stepping off a cliff.

But she hadn't.

I didn't ask her why. I knew, as surely as I knew that she'd had a choice and made it.

She touched my cheek, and her eyes filled with tears again. I raised my hand, surprised to feel wetness on my face, tracks of stinging heat in the cold wind. I wondered how long they'd been there.

(Namaste,) she thought, and her tears fell harder as I took her in my arms.

Hanjen stayed where he was, kneeling on the empty shore. He watched us just long enough to let me sense his guilt, his grief, his shame, his *anger/frustration* at fate—the emotions that wouldn't even grant me the satisfaction of hating him for what he'd done. He looked down again, tracing designs in the pebbles. I didn't know whether it was some final ritual act, or whether he was just trying to grant us a privacy his presence made impossible.

It didn't matter, any more than it mattered whether he understood what we were feeling. All that mattered now was that tomorrow I'd be gone from Refuge, more completely than Naoh, and right now I didn't know how I was going to bear it.

(Namaste,) I thought, but the tears went on running down my face, because it was nothing but a lie.

THIRTY-ONE

I LOOKED OUT the transport's wide window as we left Tau Riverton, watching the panorama of the reefs—the sheer-walled karst-form peaks, the shining thread of the river—as the view widened and fell away. I remembered seeing that same view as we'd arrived from Firstfall. My mind had been a blank slate then; it had been a striking view, nothing more. It seemed impossible to me now that I could have been so naive, so blind, only weeks ago.

(Cat—) Miya's presence stirred in my mind.

(Miya . . .) I thought, still holding her inside me the way I'd held her for the last time this morning in the open square by the waiting transport while they all watched: Hanjen and Perrymeade, Sand and Natasa. Kissindre held Wauno's arm in a death grip, anchoring herself, like she was afraid the same unseen force that was tearing me loose from Refuge might suddenly lay its hands on her.

Joby had been there too, in Miya's arms, in mine, and there'd been tears on his face as I kissed his forehead and told him good-bye. And he'd wanted to know *why?* and he'd wanted to know *when would I come back?* and I couldn't think of an answer to either of those things that he would have understood.

Instead I handed him the cloud-watcher's lenses that Wauno had given to me, and told him to watch the sky, because soon the an lirr would come back to Riverton, his home. And he'd asked me, *Then will you come back too—?* and I couldn't answer that, any more than I could ask Miya the only thing I'd wanted to ask her all through the sleepless hours of last night: *Come with me—?*

Because she wouldn't; because she couldn't. . . . Because no matter how much we needed each other—to heal, to make ourselves whole—Joby needed her more than I did, and we both knew it.

"You didn't ask her to come with you?" Wauno said finally, breaking the silence he'd kept ever since the transport had lifted from the square.

I shook my head. I realized that the thought must actually have reached his mind, and I didn't even care.

"Why not?" he asked softly, almost diffidently.

I looked over at him, surprised, because it wasn't like him to ask that kind of question. "Joby," I said, finally, and looked away again.

He grimaced, like he realized he should have known that without having to ask. After a while, he said, "What you did here— what you started—will be good for everybody. Someday even Tau will be able to see that."

"Hell will freeze over first," I said, frowning at the empty sky. "No good deed ever goes unpunished."

He shook his head. "The system will forget about you personally a long time before that. Most people have short memories. Wait a little, till things shake out here. Then you can come back—"

" 'The Net doesn't forget,' " I said. "Ever." I'd trip some flag in Tau's security programming if I ever tried to set foot on Refuge again; even I knew that much about the system.

(The system—) The thought echoed in my head.

Like a ghost in the machine. (Miya—?) I thought, remembering suddenly what she knew—what I'd taught her. If the restrictions on Hydrans using technology were lifted, like the treaty promised, someday she might find a way to make even a thinking machine forget. . . .

I breathed on an ember of hope, trying to keep it alive in the wasteland of my thoughts. My telepathic link with Miya was starting to fray as the distance between us grew; with every breath, I lost another shining filament of contact, until at last she disappeared into the static hissing of blood rushing through my arteries and veins: the sound of solitary confinement, the life sentence my body had given to my brain.

Wauno didn't say anything more, or if he did I didn't hear him. I watched the land below change and change again, sifting through the static in my head for any last trace of Miya, any stray thought, drinking the bittersweet dregs of longing.

By now the land below me looked totally unfamiliar. I could already have been on another world as I felt Miya's last straining fingertip of thought slip from mine and vanish into the trackless silence where all Humans lived forever.

I went on staring out at the day, at the surface of Refuge flowing past beneath us, still searching for some ray of the light no eye could see.

Wauno nudged me, finally, and I realized that he'd been trying to get my attention. I looked at him, feeling a kind of disbelief, like I'd actually forgotten he existed. He pressed cloud-spotting lenses into my hands and pointed. "Look. They're coming back."

I held the lenses up to my eyes, and saw the an lirr. They moved across the face of the sun, their formless bodies haloed with sundogs, colors bleeding through the spectrum across their ever-changing faces. I watched the surreal silver rain of their cast-off dreams.

I wondered then whether the truth the Creators had meant for us—both Hydrans and Humans—to understand, every time we looked up, had been the opposite of the message they'd left us in the Monument. The Monument was sterile, changeless perfection; a shrine to universal law. The cloud-whales' endless metamorphosis said that nothing was fixed in our individual lives, that every moment our fates changed, at any moment they could change again. . . .

That the things that made us what we were, that made our lives worth living, were always intangible and insubstantial, at least by Human standards . . . that if we didn't realize that, too often our lives wound up nothing but a refuse heap of half-glimpsed futures, half-formed relationships, broken hearts and dreams. That in the end, our lives were all dreamfall. The best we could hope for was that someday, somewhere, some random cast-off dream of ours might ease someone else's pain, or live on in someone else's memory. . . .

I held the lenses pressed against my eyes for a long time, long past the time when the cloud-whales had drifted beyond sight, long past the time when my eyes had stopped seeing. Long past the time when unshed tears left me too blind to watch the starport slowly expanding to fill my vision, as it swallowed the sky and the land that had once belonged to a different people . . . a world as green as the memory of her eyes.

The world was called Refuge, but I couldn't imagine why.

ABOUT THE AUTHOR

Joan D. Vinge has been described as "one of the reigning queens of science fiction" by *Publishers Weekly* and is renowned for creating lyrical human dramas in fascinatingly complex feature settings. She has won two Hugo awards, one for her novel *The Snow Queen*. Vinge is the author of *World's End, Tangled Up in Blue,* and *The Summer Queen*, sequels to *The Snow Queen*.

Also in her series about the character Cat are *Psion,* in which the character is introduced, and *Catspaw*. "Psiren," a novella about Cat, is one of her numerous shorter works. She also wrote the original bestselling *Return of the Jedi Storybook* plus other film adaptations, as well as *The Random House Book of Greek Myths*. Ms. Vinge is currently working on a major revision of *Psion,* and also on *Ladysmith,* a novel set during the Bronze Age in Western Europe. She lives in Madison, Wisconsin.